ASTRA IDARI
BEYOND LIGHTS REACH

ASTRA IDARI

BEYOND LIGHTS REACH

A NOVEL

DARBY HARN

FAIR
PLAY
BOOKS

For Rigby,
off to adventures beyond

"I'm drawn between the light and the dark."

- DAVID BOWIE

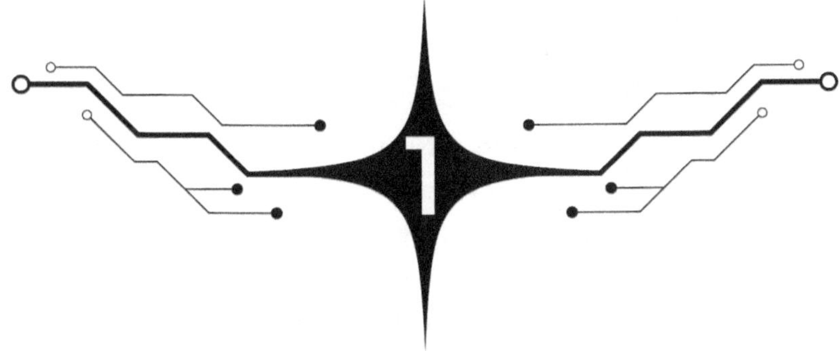

Thing about saving the universe no one tells you.

You still need to make a living. My Stargun Messenger days are behind me, mostly because I betrayed my employers and helped destroy their fleet. And their leadership. Which is to say I sabotaged their entire industry in this universe.

Definitely not getting my pension.

The Scath deserved what they got. The shadows butchered living stars for their blood to make fuel for starships. I put an end to all that – or at least a healthy pause – and I deserve what I've got, too. A life. A happiness I never imagined. But there's no end to the rumble in my stomach. Or the electronic alarms sounding in my head through the downlink I share with my starplane.

>APPROACHING TARGET

I glance at Faero. "Want to do the honors?"

Tall as Faero is, she spills over from the copilot's seat into mine. Everything just flows off her. Those legs. Arms. Hair that curls back in on itself as if it's unsure which way to go. I didn't realize a highly advanced artificial intelligence designed to navigate a ship in a starless universe would take up so much space outside said ship's liquid drive. Then again, she always took up my heart.

Her smile warps. "You do just fine without me, darling."

She's a lousy passenger. I've no idea why she's so comfortable being one, but then she was only a program for her entire existence up to a few months ago. Has it been a few months?

87 light-days to be precise, Faero answers across the downlink linking us both with the ship. *But who's counting?*

Everything flows off Faero. Discontent no exception. I'm so used to reading mood and emotion in her voice - for so long, she was only my voice - but with that beautiful face, she radiates this malaise. How can there be any sadness now we're both free? We're ourselves, finally. Maybe we're just getting used to our new selves.

That's all.

"You should be strapped in," I say.

She pulls on her harness strap. "You've gotten so fussy."

"*Me?* Fussy?"

She jams her buckle into the seat. "*So fussy.*"

>TARGET IN RANGE

I throttle the engines. Unnecessary, since I can handle this with a thought, but I prefer manual. Used to be I was the passenger. The human-appearing proxy-netic watching as Faero navigated us from one job to another. I let so much happen around me, to me, including this idea I wasn't human. I am. I want to embody my humanity and that means touching things. Doing things. Most often, that's the twinkly little number in the bed beside me, but now isn't the time to be thinking about making love to a living star.

Faero's digital groan cascades across the downlink. *Sex is all you ever think about, Idari.*

No, it's not.

Let me consult my logs. Yes. Yes, it is.

You don't mute your comm channel when you're... engaged.

One notes you don't change the channel, darling.

G-forces press Faero back into the seat as I gun *The Blue Straggler* toward the long, fat Scath tanker ahead. We come out of the sun, blind to her sensors, our shadow consuming them.

>TARGET ACQUIRED

The recoil from the forward batteries sends a pulse through the

OVL-102-B starplane. Still getting used to that. She's got a little more kick than the *Steel Haven* did. I miss my baby. Honestly, I feel this phantom sensation sometimes. This strange tingle where a limb used to be. Having lost various limbs at times, I know it well.

Faero's lips wilt like she's going to say something, but she doesn't. She says so little now. These days, it's those eyes. They tell me everything. Well. Nearly everything. There's always a drollness behind them, but I can't tell what's funny.

>DIRECT HIT

Debris pings off our shields. The tanker shrinks in the aft sensors, her tail fin yawing as she loses navigational stability. Purpuric dark energy spews from her engines. I pinpointed my shot to avoid doing more damage than necessary, so it should be fine. Though I don't properly understand Scath technology. Or physics.

But I'm sure it's fine.

Faero's brow arches.

I loop us back around, coming up on the tanker's prow. This time I hold the trigger and hit the comms. "Scath tanker. This is *The Blue Straggler*. Stand down and prepare to be boarded."

>TANKER WEAPONS CHARGING

Farro's expression remains dour. "I recall voting against this mission. Let me check my logs. Yes. Yes I – "

"You vote against all the missions."

"I'm a lover, not a fighter."

I sigh. "Scath tanker, stand down. You're far from home with no support. Do yourselves a favor over there and see the light."

>ALARM: TANKER WEAPONS LOCK

A blue nova erupts outside. Sapphire comets away from us toward the tanker. It's been a 347.7 light-hours since Emera ignited in my life and I'm still not used to this. Nor are the sensors accustomed to her simply winking out from the hold into open space.

>ALARM: CREW OVERBOARD

I switch off the alarm. *Em, what are you doing?*

Her thoughts crackle through mine. *Showing them the light.*

Be careful.

Stars can never be careful.

In the beginning, her cosmic abandon turned me on. Now, it mostly terrifies me. Our sensors go blind. I nearly do, so I activate my ultraviolet filters as Emera's luminosity bursts from sitting under a soft, warm lamp to staring into the sun. This usually does the trick. Displays like this terrify most people, because they can only imagine what comes next. Honestly, they can't imagine.

Neither can I, sometimes.

I expected the legend of what Emera did at The Glass Star to scare off any potential Starguns, bounty hunters, or opportunists about the galaxy. The thing is, people are so desperate out here in the dark that if you see any light, you'll do anything to catch it.

Faero rolls her eyes.

"What's that?" I say. "What's the face?"

She shrugs. "I spent my entire life imagining stars where there weren't any, and now we spend all our time chasing the one."

"Is that bad?"

"The open hostilities, darling."

Dark fire blasts from the tanker. Shells shatter against Emera's corona. Others catch in her magnetic field and whip around her so fast they burn into blue. She sends a scorching cosmic blast back at the tanker. Turrets atomize. Shields collapse. The tanker's defense crumbles and the ship jettisons its bounty.

Bloody hell.

The bigger Scath tankers keep their filamentium tanks deep within the fuselage, where they're insulated behind as much turanium as design sense allows. Smaller ones like this one here carry them as external tanks on port and starboard, easy to fill, easy to offload, easy to defend when everyone involved in the inevitable mess knows exactly where they're going and why.

A connecting strut serves to join the twin tanks in a death spiral toward the murky moon the tanker just left. Shadows must be thin on the bridge to cut and run. Unless this is a feint. The tanker ramps up her sublight engines. Maybe they're not novices. Maybe they've picked up a trick or two out here in the closing chapter of what had been the most reliable trade in the galaxy for millennia.

Emera, don't let the ship get away.

Emera stalls in orbit, a second sun. *I sense life inside the tanks.*

What?

Plasma blazes around the tanks as they contact the moon's atmosphere. *Ban Minda.* Emera reaches out, as if to catch them. Plating shears off the their unprotected exteriors. Their speed is too great. She'll tear them apart. So will a tractor beam.

Get back in the ship, Em.

Static crackles in my head as Emera becomes a shooting star behind the tanks. Electromagnetic interference frustrates my ability to get a read on just who may be inside them. Could be Lumenor. That's our hope every time we raid a tanker or refinery out here in The Hinterlands. Emera's hope.

Usually, we only find vapors. Blackened crust left behind by burnt filamentium. Scath tech we sell or trade to keep in food and health. One of these runs, we're likely to find Scath troops hiding inside a brazen trap. We scuttled the filamentium industry.

All it takes to reignite it is a spark.

It's not like the Scath to run a full tanker without a single SION fighter to provide protection. Someone said it before. Faero. *They're baiting us.* We've done too many raids. I told Emera. We're pushing our luck. She wants to press our advantage when all I want is to press my lips against hers, but we've done so well against the shadows. Their remaining fleet is spread out across the galaxy searching for us, leaving their shipping operation undefended.

Supposedly.

Emera, let it go.

>NO SIGNAL

I push the throttle forward. "Don't say it."

Faero clutches her straps. "I wasn't going to say anything."

"I wish you would."

"I'm getting conflicting signals, darling."

So am I. Telemetry spikes. Radar signatures splinter. *Bish.* The strut connecting the tanks disintegrates and the tank taking the brunt of re-entry enters a ballistic tumble. Emera tries to grab hold and the tank ruptures into meteors. An angry electromagnetic burst pulses across the shields, but it's not the shockwave of an atmospheric filamentium detonation. Only a star's grief.

Em, I say.

Static. She blazes behind the remaining tank, her magnetic field stablizing it as they comet toward the moon's surface. There wasn't any filamentium in the ruptured tank, which is to say no Lumenor. Probably the same for the other one. Emera is the last Lumenor. Her blood is all that stands between her people and extinction. Thing about my star. You simply can't tell her what is and isn't.

Exasperation blows into the cockpit. "Goodness sake, old man."

Ancient red paint flecks from Binja's ceremonial Pujar battle armor, but it's still not as chipped as his mood.

"You were just supposed to incapacitate them, Idari."

I cross my arms. "I did."

"We're swordsmen, Idari. Not hammersmiths."

A snort bellows from behind him. "*Tomo.*"

Kibir's leathery trunk curls as he leans on his Kib war hammer. I still don't know how he uses the thing. It's taller than he is.

Binja holds up his hands. "Present company excluded."

Kibir's as put out as Binja is, but he's always bothered. If we're not fighting, he's surly, and if we're fighting, he's surly. He gets a little cuddly after a few pints of babyl, but that's about it.

We've been dry for days.

Gilf is always cuddly. He appears on a monitor on the console before me, scratching his floppy ear down in the hold. He's probably wondering why we're not boarding the Scath tanker yet. But then he doesn't seem too bothered. A Kib is always handy to have around, especially if you're a highly-advanced proxy-netic flying a highly-advanced ship without an easy source for spare parts.

I try to focus on Emera's EM signature in all the interference. "Binja, why are you dressed up?"

His hands close to his turanium cuirass. "This is a proper fight."

Faero rolls her eyes. "Everything isn't role play, Binja."

"Sometimes, it's helpful to know what part you're playing."

Faero unstraps from the copilot's seat. "Doesn't it?"

The soreness in her voice lingers in the cockpit. I don't know where it comes from. I used to know Faero inside out. Her thoughts swirled around with mine in the downlink we shared on the *Steel Haven*. Her thoughts were mine in the beginning.

>FILE CRITICAL: READ THIS FIRST

Your name is Astra Idari. You're an IA-XR Model 4 proxy-netic. Or you were. Technically, you still are, but you merged with a memory core from a techno-organic titan netic from Angolis and now you're somewhere between human and machine. These little reminders are a bit redundant these days, but you never delete them because you're terrified you'll forget again. You never let go of anything, darling, and that includes your previous versions.

You're CR-UX.

Well. You used to be. You were designated CR-UX, the Steel Haven's navigational program. You got out for a stroll as the ship's proxy-netic, embodying your humanity, but the more memory the proxy accumulated the less you were CR-UX and more you were Idari. CR-UX stayed ones and zeroes until The Glass Star. The truth got out and so did she. She's Faero now. You've both evolved, even if she's transmitting random pictures of nude men and women to you at all hours. Tell her you delete the pictures.

Don't delete the pictures.

Faero Sent Pics File Path > L: Downloads: NUDES

"You shouldn't have broken up with her," I say.

Binja claims the copilot's seat. "So now this is my fault?"

He's as tall as Faero, but he's more graceful in how he roosts throughout the ship. He ought to be. He's been in his body forty years longer than she's been in hers. You'd never know it to look at him. If I didn't know better, I'd say he was a proxy-netic, too. But it's just his very well selected Pujar genes.

I gesture to the tank's comet tail. "This was your idea, Binja."

"It was very much Gen Emera's idea, old man."

"You encourage this sort of thing."

"No, I support this sort of thing."

"Semantics."

"Sour grapes."

"We should be on a beach somewhere."

He scratches his chin. "We're pirates, Idari."

"No, we're not."

"Then what are we?"

>TARGET DOWN

Dust erupts from the surface toward us. *Ban Minda.* I hope Emera didn't get hurt trying to slow that thing down.

"Prepare for landing," I say and treasure troves rattle deep within the great ark buried beneath Angolis. Planets churn out of the great hub the titans forged. Stars. Ships. I step back from the plinth overlooking a planetary abyss. I'm not in the cockpit anymore. I'm back under the desert, on a planet that died.

It's happening again.

Ever since I integrated with the titan memory core, these lacunae open up in me. I fall through, out of my day and back into the ark. Starships strange and many churn out of massive hubs. Ancient creatures long extinct. Elements as basic as hydrogen and as unique as filamentium. An entire universe, run down an assembly line for some reason I can't know. I can't be possibly here. The Scath destroyed the ark, Angolis, every last trace of this place.

Not every trace.

That core I fused with contained the entire ark's archived knowledge. All the splendid things the ark churned out beneath the desert? I've got the schematics. The why of it all remains elusive, though I'm sure it's here somewhere. I'm just not that motivated to dig. I struggle still to manage the sensor data flooding into my head every single moment from the downlink. That's like being swept away by a river if I'm not careful. The knowledge the titan memory core transferred into me rests heavy and deep like this ocean. Turns out I'm not that great at swimming.

Faero's laugh barks across the downlink. *You do drink like —*

Emera crackles. *I was just going to say —*

No, you go.

I interrupted you.

We're always running into each other, Faero says.

Em, I say. *Faero. Are you there? Can you hear me?*

Static. A pulse deep in the world. Ba-dumm. An inverted pyramid twists above a pedestal within the ark. What is this? One side shimmers with prismatic light. Oil in water. Another reflects me and the production of eternity. The third side is utter darkness.

What does it mean?

The three sides float in the air, edges drifting out of alignment and why? Why do I always come back here? What is this voice?

Work —

I don't. I didn't. I only integrated with the memory core to save my life. Emera only gave it to me because I'm always forgetting.

The work —

This voice. It won't let me forget. It won't let me go.

The work must continue.

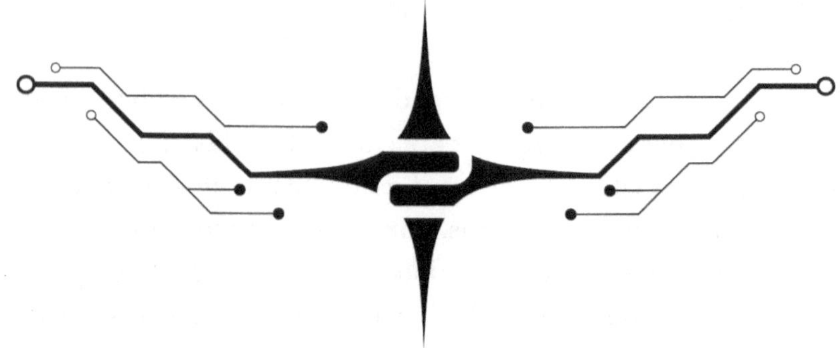

I mute my audio inputs but the voice is inside my head, commanding me, animating me toward the pyramid, this strange process within the ark, beyond understanding. Everything within me compels me to return to the ark and continue this work.

What work?

How can I go back? Angolis is gone. The ark. The work. There's nothing to continue but the impulse won't relent. *The work must continue.* I reach for the broken pyramid. I don't want to. All I want is to go back to Emera, to our life, to live it and we deserve our living. Power greater than I comprehend seizes me. Purpose.

Faero pulls me back. "Darling..."

I snap back into the cockpit. "Don't let go..."

She's always pulling me back. "I've got you."

Don't let go.

>TERRAIN

Get your head on, Idari. *The Blue Straggler* pivots and torques to avoid the unfamiliar geography rushing up at us. This moon hides mountains in dense, dusky mist. We've got to be careful.

I've got to be careful.

I keep in Faero's arms, a place I haven't spent as much time as I've wanted since we came into our bodies. We've been well-kept with other company, but I need to be here more.

I should be here more.

Faero steadies me. She secures me in her ropey, confident arms, determined not to let anything else get ahold of me. She knows where I've gone. How much I struggled to get back. These episodes terrify us both. We signed on for war with the shadows. We hoped for salvation. Each other. This. This wasn't part of the deal.

"I'm ok," I say, holding her tight. "I'm ok..."

Those eyes say everything. I'm several light years from ok. I lose control when this happens. I lose myself. I fused with the memory core and for some reason, I thought, *Lovely. Free upgrade.* I gave no thought to the idea this thing not only rewrote my body, it's also rewriting my mind. My code. My person, one day at a time.

"What's happening to me, Faero?"

Her eyes search mine. "Every time this happens, your neural net experiences... alterations... Idari. This voice..."

"I don't want to think about it."

"I know, darling, but... it's telling you to do something?"

"Continue the work. What work?"

"The titans were building an ark beneath Angolis..."

"The ark is gone. This doesn't make sense."

"Do you know why they were, Idari? Who they were? Who built the titans? Where did they come from?"

"I'll trade you."

"You've got to take this seriously."

"I am."

"Faero, I don't know what's happening..."

Her arms constrict around me. "I know. I know."

"What do we do..."

Goes without saying. We need to get me to a netician. There isn't one who would understand titan tech. Even if they did, I wouldn't let them go rooting around in my head. I'm not a machine.

I'm a human being.

"We'll go to Ganshi," she says. "The Kib will be able to help."

I shake my head. "Gilf can sort me out."

"He's brilliant, but he'll be the first to tell you there are Kib with more experience when it comes to titan technology. They dug it out from the desert for millennia."

"I don't want anyone digging around in me."

"I know... but we have to understand what's happening to you."

"I'll be fine."

"You're not listening. You never listen."

"I do."

"I don't know why I bother."

"Faero... I'm listening."

"Then won't you *please* let someone look at you. For me."

>LANDING SEQUENCE INITIATED

I slink out of her arms. "I will."

"Seriously, darling."

"Seriously."

She leans against the bulkhead as I make down the lowering gantry. "Things have changed, Idari. You've changed."

I blow her a kiss. "Some things never do."

She catches my kiss. "I love you."

I love you, I say and I'm off the gantry before we've landed.

Gravity here is as thin as the sea. Water globules string in high strands that can't quite escape the surface. A few pop in *The Blue Straggler's* wake dowsing Binja, Gilf, and I as we run through the cratered reef. A shallow sea reflecting the rare sky floods into the dust-shrouded crater the tank excavated on its way to a stop.

Em, I say. *Can you hear me?*

No answer. Shouldn't be any interference down here on the surface. Kibir grips his hammer and sniffs the smoky air with his trunk. He shakes his head. No scent. I'd know if she were close, too. This smell accompanies Emera. A bit like the air after a lightning strike. Clean. Pure. Charged.

I turn to Binja. "Shall we?"

"We should be back in space," he says, "pursuing that tanker."

"I'm following my star."

"Into a trap, most likely."

"I just always expect one, Binja."

His smile is worn as that armor of his. "You're not still mad about that business on Angolis. Are you?"

"The business where you betrayed me to the Scath?"

"Your memory has improved."

I pat the blasword hung from my belt. Used to be his. Sometimes I like to remind him. He doesn't like to be reminded. Pirate society hinges on the idea you forget who you were before. You take a name. Take a life. Ascend the ranks among your coven and then one day you die and The Taker of Names claims you for his crew aboard the Corsair Eternal. The Set stripped Binja of his name due to some believey nonsense I stayed out of. He keeps the name. He's a bit like me, Binja. We've changed, but we're still holding on.

Binja considers the sky. "I thought we put all that behind us."

I tug on my zipper. "I don't forget anything now."

He deploys the blasword he took from the captain of a pirate sloop we raided a few weeks back. That's more like it.

We splash to the crater's rim. Haze shrouds everything. I swap optical sensors to night vision and dark energy spits from the crater. Scath. This isn't a filamentium tanker. It's a snake pit.

Emera, where are you?

Shadows dare the sun. Kill team. Six, or maybe a dozen Scath down there, but the point is you can't tell. Scath armor reads as white noise to my sensors. Time to get a closer look. I slide down with the mud to the tank's broken hull. I slip in through a gash aft of the twisted strut that connected the tanks and edge through the smoky dark. Blaster fire riddles the canted tank. Scath troopers take up positions in the clustered reservoirs that divide the interior into a favelote structure. I duck into a burst reservoir scabbed with dried star blood and my sword crashes against Binja's.

He exhales. "Careful, old man."

I retract my sword. "You're already hiding?"

"So good of you to join me."

"I thought you were excited for this."

"I am. I was. I'm just making sure this isn't..."

"What?"

"We're sure this is a Scath tanker?"

"You're overlooking the Scath squadron clearly lying in wait for us and who may have already captured my star?"

"I rarely trust my eyes with the shadows," Binja says, "And never aboard their tankers. We're sure this isn't a company ship?"

My memory is exact since my upgrade. Large parts of my life before, including being a pirate, remain as hazy as this moon. Scath collect filamentium and refine it. The Infinies Trading Company distributes it in the galaxy, or at least they used to; the Scath tend to keep their treasure closer in hand these days.

"The tanker wasn't running the Infinies flag," I say. "Why?"

"Pirates avoid company ships if they can. They're... cursed."

"Cursed?"

"The old pirates had a word for it... *dwen*. Magic."

Faero scoffs over the downlink. *Magic? Poppycock.*

"There's no such thing as magic," I say.

Binja sighs through his smile. "You sleep with a star, old man."

"Emera is real."

"There are forces beyond the mundane. Whether they're cosmic or supernatural depends entirely on one's perspective."

"I suppose there are one or two things I can't explain."

"One or two?"

"Where do you suppose Kibir got off to?"

Screams echo through the pen. A blunt, metal thud. A percussive language the Kib snort and sneeze. He's fine.

Binja checks the corridor. "Best to let him do all the work."

"Kibir would be sore if we didn't. I meant what I said."

"I assure you, magic is real."

"You shouldn't have broken up with Faero."

He takes the point into the dark. "We were never together."

I follow him. "You had sex. Substantial quantities of sex."

"Of course, we had a considerable amount of sex. We're two attractive, consenting adults. Permitting. Adventurous – "

"This way."

He changes course. "Dare I say the quantity or quality of our sexual congress is not evidence of our being 'together.' Your six."

I drop a Scath in the shadows. "Never say congress again."

He scratches his chin. "You should talk to her."

"You're the one who broke up with her, Binja."

"You're asking me why she's so sullen."

"I'm telling you."

"Idari... I'm not the one she wants to talk to."

For as long as I can remember, Faero was all I could remember. Her voice was like atmosphere. Oxygen. I couldn't breathe without it. I was always exchanging it. We do talk. *Ban Minda,* do we ever talk. But she sounds distant now. She sounds apart from me, like a distant comm channel I'm barely picking up.

Emera? Are you there?

We navigate burst fuel reservoirs to the wreck's buckled belly. Here, the tank opens up to the bulbous cask I've seen before in Scath refineries. Empty. No stars, not even my own. Where is she? Before Emera, I looped my anxiety in an algorithm that never allowed it to disrupt my day. She untangles me in every way.

Em?

Kibir smashes in the door of a locker. A giddy sound trumpets from him. He drags out a crate of jarred babyl. Look at this. Sweet, sweet fire. I kiss a bottle. The Kib snorts his protest but in this crew, we share our spoils. I pull the cork on the bottle and drink so fast I spit most of it back up. I don't care. Maybe I should. Look at these labels. This vintage is from the Kibut's personal stash. They took this from Angolis. Loot from across this sector litters the floor. Trinkets. Coins. Mostly ammo. Guns. Clunky old laser batteries. The Scath aren't running filamentium anymore. There isn't any.

I almost laugh. The shadows have become pirates.

Binja drifts through the empty carnage. "Nothing..."

I take another drink. "We need to find Emera."

His hand falls to his hip, where his ceremonial sash once hung. "There isn't anything here of value."

"Value? We're looking for Lumenor, Binja."

"Emera is. You're following your star. I'm..." He wipes his sword across his tabard, as worn and frayed as his ceremonial armor. "I'm a pirate raiding empty ships."

I tuck the bottle under my arm. "We're not pirates."

Binja does what he always does. He smiles at disaster. He drifts out through a hull breach. When did we all get so out of sorts? Were we ever content, or was that after glow from The Glass Star?

Light dawns in the treasure pen. "Em..."

Shadows stretch across the deck. Electric blue illuminates emptied lockers. Dirty coins and loose debris orbit in Emera's magnetic field, shrouding her light as the impalpable haze does, but all my fears evaporate. All the weight I carry in worry over what I don't understand lifts because she is my illumination.

"There's no one," she says, her voice dark.

She arrives before an emptied reservoir. Scabbed crust on the floor. Scorch marks in the outline of a woman. Pain creases Emera's lips. Anger. The Scath bled a Lumenor for fuel. Maybe they bled her dry. Or maybe pirates made off with her.

Either way, she's gone now.

So is Emera's serenity. Blue flares to white. Energy erupts from her, bounding into the hold at me before looping in back into her. Her disappointment bends and warps the tank. She bends and warps space so much she vanishes from the moon.

Thought and feeling radiate from Emera as fast as light. It takes a few minutes, but her anguish finds me again. The sun. She's gone to this system's star. There, her nuclear fury is indistinguishable from the star's. For anyone observing, it would seem a simple solar promi-nence, but if you could hear; if you could know the pain and despair hidden behind her stellar grace; you would hear the most horrific, violent sound that exists within creation.

A star's scream.

All this time I've thought of Emera as the last Lumenor. I accepted it, even as I knew she didn't. She couldn't. We could still be on that strand. Amber sand. Ocean blue. I thought we might be there forever, but the more free I became with my laughter, my joy, the more she soured. She illuminates all this dark, but she only sees the absence of light. I'm not saying we're owed anything but we've earned some living, haven't we? I'd love to try my hand at living.

A proper life.

Emera, I say. *Come back to me.*

Plasma blankets her. *I need a moment. I'm sorry.*

You don't have to be sorry. Let's go away. Let's find some place.

Shadows always follow stars.

We've hurt the shadows. We've really hurt them.

That's not what I mean.

Em... I think we need to quit while we're ahead.

It can't just be me.

I know she needs her own. I know I can't fill every blank for her. *Ban Minda.* I wish I could be everything for her the way she is for me. After The Glass Star, I thought things would get easier.

I thought we were all happy.

I am happy, she says. *I have been so happy with you, Idari.*

I hear a but in there.

I held my voice for so long... there were so many voices... wondrous voices that have gone silent. I was silent.

Emera... you are their light. You are their love and hope.

It shouldn't be me...

She's never going to balance the scales in a universe of dead stars. I'm never going to fill the void within a star.

I'm never going to be enough.

Sunshine lifts my chin. "I don't deserve you, Idari."

Whenever she ducks through space and time like this, this fist closes around my heart. This force expands and contracts within me so fast I think I'll just cave in, but I never do. I grab her up in my arms. The heat of another star is scalding on my skin, but I'm not letting go. I'm never letting go of her.

"You deserve so much more," I say.

She's back in my arms but it feels like she's still millions of miles away. "I'd be lost without you, Idari. You keep me."

"How do you keep a star? Just out of curiosity."

"Gravity."

"What gravity do I have?"

She brushes my cheek. "Don't you know?"

I know I'm lucky. "Emera. We can't keep doing this."

"I worry about you, Idari."

"Me?"

"You had another episode."

"What? Oh. I'm fine."

No shade from the sun here. "Faero is right."

"Em."

"We need to go to Ganshi."

"Really, I'm..."

"You're worried about losing me. Don't you think I'm worried about losing you? Don't you think I'm frightened?"

All that sorrow she carries for her people. Her fear in being alone. Their gravity seizes me. "We'll go to Ganshi."

Her kiss melts away the thin cold. She lifts us from the tank's empty husk, into the dust, haze, and spray suspended in the air and gleaming with light strange and new, like Faero's eyes.

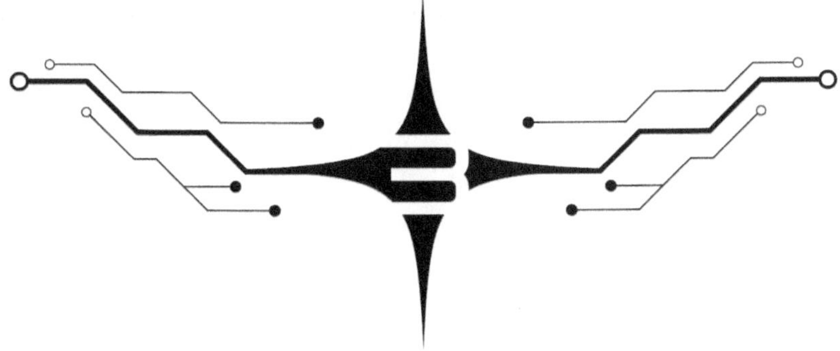

Babyl steams off Emera's breast.

A naughty little cackle evaporates in a gasp as I lick away the fire. Emera's joy chain reacts into a boisterous laugh I rarely hear and I hold her. I hold her sun and her laughter and her love as close as I can. Cosmic heat radiates through me. Fizzy stellar energy webs us together. Incandescent fingers light in and out of me.

Her lips seer mine. "I love you."

I muster the motor function to kiss her back. "I love you..."

Magnetic force squeezes my heart. Power beyond understanding compresses in thought and action, in time and space, in this moment and all the others we love each other. When I'm in her arms, the nimbus of her passion, I lose myself completely. I dissolve into her. I disintegrate into her power and gravity and then she weaves me back together, our joy in rediscovery.

Becoming.

Stars see little beyond themselves. That might have been one reason the ancient Lumenor were less than the perfect beings myth and legend craft them to be. Emera sees the universe through my eyes. A filter. A lens. A link to everything she illuminates but only perceives in gravitational tugs of war.

Emera doesn't have to tell me any of this.

I know her heart like she knows mine. Our connection goes beyond mind and body. For the first time in my life, it goes beyond language. I've never had this with anyone. All my life I felt like I had to fill this void within me and around me with words. Data. Silence terrified me. Silence frustrated me, so Faero and I just always chatted about everything even if we didn't want to, but Em.

I don't have to say anything with Em.

Though I do long for her voice, husky, as if singed from her light. She rests atop me, light as air, our quarters illuminated in sapphire. Her hair wisps across her shoulders, somewhere between steam and light. Emera wears it longer and longer. So long the strands curl at the ends in her magnetic field, looping in on themselves sometimes in ethereal lines so faint I trace them to be sure.

I'm still here, she says.

I lock my arms around her. Sometimes, I get scared I'll wake up without her. These last few months haven't happened but are only a corruption in my data as my neural net fails in the cold, dark floating in the Ring of Skeken and I never met her. I never found out who I am. I never lighted this dark curdling within me.

I'm here, Idari.

"Sometimes you're gone," I say.

Some nights she's at the window. Others, she's outside the ship. She's running ahead of *The Blue Straggler,* ahead of light, beyond any reach. Alarms sound inside the cockpit.

>CREW OVERBOARD

Her leg sinks between mine. "I always come back."

I know her heart and I know deep within, beneath the light, the gas, the fire she breathes, all that mass compresses into a barrier I can't penetrate. Every so often, moments like this when we're so free we're losing ourselves in one another, I collide with this thing.

I brush gossamer light from her eyes. "Talk to me."

Her light wavers. "Now you want to talk."

I kiss her. "I always think I'm going to open this door in you... you're going to let me in."

"A star's beauty hides its rage, Idari."

"Rage?"

"The Lumenor had a word for our... stars are always stranded between light and shadow. Some felt lost. They sought to reach others, to connect with others, but... they never could."

"Em... I'm so sorry."

"I just thought... I brought the star back to light. The Lumenor would come back. I'd share this with them. But they're gone."

"You're their light. The Lumenor live in you."

Expressions are difficult to read in stars. Backlighting and all that. I've gotten to know Emera enough I don't go blind trying to understand what she's thinking.

I hold her close. "You're not doing anything wrong."

Emera felt wrong. For such a long time. Her thoughts sink like cloud layers into her memory. Guilt. Shame. Fear of her true self. I thought all this had kindled with The Glass Star, but there it is, settled heavy in the depths of this mass within her. Only now the shame has transmuted like she has. She's not ashamed of who she is now, but that she is, and her people aren't. The door opens.

Her memory.

Bodies. Dead stars. The ground sharp with shattered star glass. Welkin claws into the stellar diamond outside the Bamurnan. He buries one fallen Lumenor after another, the ruined city dark with them. He refuses help, or rest, or sustenance. The work continues for what must be days, or weeks, or I don't know, these memories compress into one hurtful layer, and then the last hole he digs is the one he leaves Thana Evo and her conspirators in.

Welkin buries them in absolute darkness. Emera's thoughts collapse so hard and fast there is only darkness within her. Emptiness. *I love you, I love you, I love you*, my thoughts, my voice, my feeling for radiating from me with as much passion as I can offer.

"We've earned our peace," I say.

Her light ebbs. "Stars shine for all to see."

"I get... possessive."

Her arms curl around me. Her head rests soft against my heart. "Stars shine for all. They hold only what is closest to them."

I squeeze her tight. "Never let me go."

"You have it, too. Pressure."

Every time I go back to the ark under Angolis, it's the same cold, inconsiderate force drawing me there as did the need to backup my memory on the *Steel Haven*. You drift along far enough to forget the reflex from squeezing into the alcove to back up my memory. The ache in my body from contorting myself to fit into modes of life that I could get by surviving within even if I never had the room to live. And then the mechanical, the digital, the artificial gravity exerts its will once again. Honestly, it's not just these episodes. I know myself now. I love myself now, and I thought, I can be myself with others. But there's this distance. No one wants to talk to me now. It's like we've all forgotten how.

She's heavier on me now. "I feel responsible."

"If you hadn't found the memory core," I say, "I'd be dead."

"I always end up hurting the people I'm trying to help. I should stop. That would be wisdom. But I can't help myself."

"You saved my life."

So heavy. "I know."

"Emera."

"I know."

Never let anyone tell you stars are airy things made of dust and gas and light. Their sadness shapes reality as much as their light.

"They'll sort me out at Ganshi," I say. "It will be ok."

Ganshi Station still hasn't acknowledged our hail. I re-transmit the message. We'll be there before their reply, but so long as they expect us. The Kib own the market on titan tech. And they have some experience with my program. Actually, I left a backup copy with them. A trade to help us find The Glass Star. I suppose he's sore with me. Unless he's been swimming in babyl the entire time.

If he isn't, I'll be sore with him.

Light stretches around me. "I thought you lost your backups?"

I pull her close again. "It's just him now."

"But there are other versions of you, aren't there?"

"Looking to trade in?"

She cackles. "Stars place a lot of stress on their subjects."

"I can take a lot."

That little smile. "There are others?"

I never think about this. I try not to. 347 OVL-99 Red Specials came off the line from the Shighn shipyards. A luxury starplane made-to-order by Arrogate Industries for those who could afford their own personal transport across the dark. Each came with an IA-XR Model 4 proxy-netic. You could customize the proxy, so some are men. Women. Any and everything in between.

Emera's gravity tides through me. "You're one of a kind."

I kiss her forehead. "I'm all yours."

"You saved my life, too. You've given me my life, too."

"I know."

Light wells in Emera's skin and then sinks into her glow again. "For so long, I was alone and afraid. Talking to myself. Stars can't see beyond their own glare. They can't know themselves. But I know myself because of you. I see myself through you."

Even with all my optical advantages, I can barely perceive her. That isn't what she means. I don't need filters or spectrographs or EM field imagers to see her worth. Her love erupting from her as bountiful as light. Her charity in warmth she would give even if she was only an ember. Her beauty, vivid though she's small compared to the stars in her memory, delicate, fragile even in her majesty, but she's warm, so warm, soft and good, love incandescent.

I have never felt such joy. If this is joy. Joy and I are unacquainted until recently. I don't always recognize it. I've forgotten most of my life. The limits of my memory as a proxy-netic contributed to that. So did my determination to forget how much I hated myself. Crooked machine. No one could love me. No one could find value in me. No one could see me. Now I'm seen.

"Marry me," I say.

Light spirals off her skin. "Stars don't marry."

"Way to bring a girl down."

"No... they pair. *Bamur*. They cluster. But they burn in isolation for the most part. Two stars too close together..."

"I can be pretty dull, sometimes."

"You're my light, Idari. I'm your wife, in your ways and mine."

I've got all sorts of ways. The Pujar method of marrying is a little lacking in agency. Basically you take a bride the way you take everything else. No questions. No negotiation. Part of me tingles at the sense I've won Emera. A living star. My wife. Shiny. The old me would have been absolutely unbearable about my conquest.

You are absolutely unbearable about it, Faero says.

>MUTING COMM CHANNEL

I marvel at my luck. My miracle. I lived in pain for so long. The darkness closing in all around us. My life glows now. Shines. She says she can never repay me. I will never earn this gift of her.

I will never deserve Emera.

You do deserve me, Idari.

You know, I do. We've struggled enough alone. The rest of our lives should just be cosmic shagging. The rest of eternity. I lace my fingers in hers. She hears my thoughts. She knows me.

We don't have to speak.

There is a tradition among the Pujar going back millennia to days when they were a bit less transactional. Pujar were less pirates than knights seeking something no one could take. The Dojin marked their bodies with an arrow over the heart. This way other pirates knew they could be taken in body, but never in spirit.

Emera's fascination tingles through my mind.

This ancient practice got coopted by the Pujar in general as all things do. These days, an inverted arrow on the shoulder, the hand, the forehead even means — well, you don't know what it means because it's been thieved and recontextualized so many times that what it means for one person isn't the same as another. What you do know, if you're lucky, is this links back to when love couldn't be stolen. This was the true self. Non-transferable. Immutable.

Emera traces Pujar skrit on my chest. *Dojin.*

I draw an inverted arrow between her breasts. The impression keeps in her corona long enough for me to think it might last forever. Her joy spasms through us both. Her electric giddiness at discovering something new and ours. She kisses our marriage across my chest. Thoughts get away from me. Burn me. Brand me. Let go the rein on your power and burn your love into my skin. I want the pain. I want the scar. I want what no one can take from us.

Her fingers touch the nape of my neck. "Are you sure..."

"I'm your wife," I say. "In your ways and mine."

Flame spits from her fingers. My heart bashes against my ribs. Her tongue twists into mine as she burns our forever into my chest.

The inverted pyramid twists on its axis. A voice bellows through the deep. *The work must continue.* The ark beneath Angolis presses me into service and I wake up when I fall. I used to drink myself to sleep. Now I leave the light on.

I stretch out in bed. "Em..."

>ALARM: CREW OVERBOARD

Cerulean light blinds *The Blue Straggler's* sensors as Emera drifts ahead of the ship at translight speed, a pilot fish at the bottom of the deepest ocean, lighting our way into the future we can't see.

>EXITING TRANSLIGHT DRIVE

Here, already. I don't need to get out of bed. Through the downlink, I can guide us down to Ganshi Station the same as if I was at the stick. Besides, I'm not in any hurry to get poked and prodded by Kib neticians eager to learn something new about –

Idari, Emera says.

I reach out to her. *Come back to bed.*

Get to the helm.

>PROXIMITY ALARM

Something hits us. Debris tumbles past outside the windows. Metal. Junk. The hell is going on? Are we at the right coordinates? I zip into my jumpsuit and shake off my sleep on my way to the cockpit, where Faero is already waiting in alarm.

I pull my jacket on. "What's going on?"

Survivors from Angolis came to this system in cargo ships, tugs, ferries, things never intended to cross the dark. All those ships drift dead among a halo of moon spores, blackened from blaster fire, trailing their insides in frozen dust tails behind them. Unborn Ganshi moon children crumple and gray in the void, exposed before their time, an entire generation dashed out.

I take the controls. "Ganshi Station, this is – "

Faero holds up her hand. "Don't."

I mute the comms. Scan for dark energy discharges. Nothing comes back on sensors. I don't know who could have done this besides the Scath. I don't know who would want to. No life signs. No radio chatter. Nothing. The entire settlement, gone.

"Faero... what happened here?"

Her hands flit across the controls. "You know as much as I do."

"But what do you think happened? Was this pirates?"

"Pirates never leave such a mess, darling. Whoever did this... whatever they were looking for... they didn't find it."

And they were angry. "Are they still here?"

"I'm not detecting any energy signatures – fiddlesticks."

Emera streaks toward an intact moon spore.

Em, I say. *Get back to the ship.*

She disappears into the meteor storm. *There's life here still.*

The Scath could still be in the system. Their ships barely register on our scopes, even with all the data Faero and I collected on them from the business before. We need to get out of here.

We need to get out of here right now.

Debris pelts the shields as I follow Emera's energy signature toward the moon spore. Spores range in size from the minuscule to the planetary. This one is nice and comet sized. Chasms mark the surface, the outer rocky shell slowly contracting as the child inside matures. Ganshi gestate for millennia. Their yoke feeds, fuels, funds so many concerns. When the Kib got here, they built their new home inside excavations the original settlers dug centuries ago.

The Kib had only gotten started.

Our forward landing lights illuminate the moon spore's interior. Dirty ice yields to green, veiny spore stuff. War hammers float in thin gravity. Turanium heads sliced easy as warm bread. Bodies. So many bodies. I know they're Kib. Leathery paws. Shaggy hair. Pudgy trunks. What would anyone ever have against the Kib? They invented babyl. They deserve the universe's eternal gratitude.

I lock the ship at station-keeping. *You have the stick.*

Faero's brows nearly spring off her head. *Where are you going?*

I pop the dorsal hatch just outside the cockpit and climb out on the hull. Death grits the air around me. Burnt flesh spoils the pungent sweet you usually associate with a moon spore.

I draw my blasword and step off the hovering ship. My internal grav-settings compensate, keeping me on the ground. Shadows scale to giants across lucent walls constellated with iridescent zygotes. Ghostly blue fades into the gummy gloss beyond.

Em, I say. *Wait –*

A hammer drops beside me. Kibir lands behind it, frustrated as always, and he hurries to his weapon. His anger dies into shock. Sorrow. Fire burns in his dark eyes. Another Kib world destroyed.

His trunk wilts. "*Seta...*"

I charge my blasword. "I'm sorry."

He grips his hammer. "*Tomo.*"

"Couldn't agree more."

Kibir charges ahead. He knows the rest. I hurry after him, expanding my sensor range to maximum, scanning for any movement. Any shadow. Massive excavators make some tunnels impassable, floating in the air or piled in debris. Exposed ice casts everything in amaranthine. Set aside the scabs of green veiny spore stuff, it's like someone froze an ocean inside a glass bottle. I move down a tunnel, down the way Emera must have come, and icy blue flame burns at the end. Starlight curls off her into strange curlicues.

"Let's go," I say and Emera is standing over my dead body.

Ban Minda. The Model 3. The backup copy I left with the Kib on Angolis to get out of being their permanent 'guest' myself. Someone ripped his heart out. Neural links rise from the cavity in his chest. His body floats just off the surface, arms trailing back, like he's driftwood. Brown eyes set on something distant. Lost.

I clip my blasword to my belt. *Is this who you sensed, Em?*

Her eyes probe the dark. *There's something else...*

I touch the Model 3's face. I close his eyes. *Let's get back to —*

Data spores from within the Model 3. Data infects me at the speed of light. Random code. Wait. A command. *Bish —*

>CMD: OVL099A2D
>PROXY-NETIC OVERRIDE > Y/N: Y
>ARROGATE SUBROUTINE > ACTIVATED
>ACCESS IA-XR MODEL 4 ROOT OBJECTIVES:
~~>NAVIGATE OVL-99 RS SERIES STARPLANE~~
RETURN IDARI TO ARROGATE INDUSTRIES
~~>DELETE EXTRANEOUS MEMORY~~
ACQUIRE TITAN MEMORY AT ALL COSTS
~~>HOST CREW AND GUESTS~~
KILL ALL PASSENGERS
>ENABLE

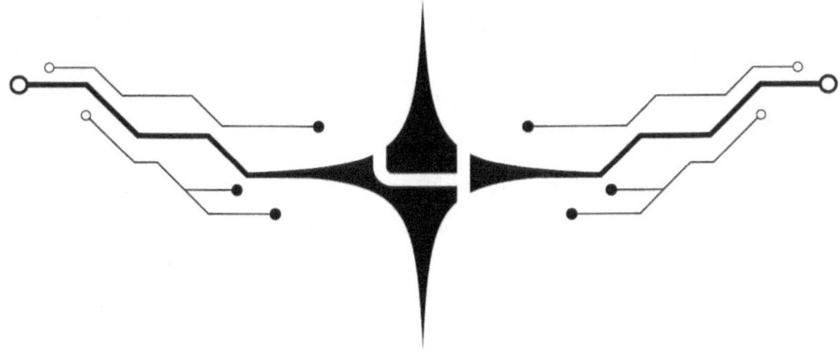

Kill the Lumenor first.

Fire, fire, fire. Hard-light shells absorb into Gen Emera's corona, as expected. Only dark energy, unbound from a Lumenor's stellar grasp, can penetrate her natural defenses. Turanium, spit from its forge in black holes, also proves effective. Deploy the blade on your blasword. Strike while the Lumenor is disoriented.

Aim for her heart.

Living stars radiate power from a central core within their torso. If pierced, damaged, or disrupted, death is immediate. Enter her corona. Run her through. Kill her before she immolates you.

Kibir smashes the blasword from your hand with his hammer.

DANGER: Kib war hammers can buckle starship hulls. Grab the handle as he whirls around for another strike. His strength belies his stature but the IA-XR Model 4 outclasses all organic life.

Rip the hammer away from Kibir.

Min Binja blocks your strike with his blasword. "Idari…"

TARGET PROFILE: Binja's skill with the Pujar ceremonial *nenlat* is unrivaled in the Model 4's memory. He trained Idari in traditional forms of Pujar combat. He knows her every move.

ASSESSMENT: Employ unconventional tactics.

Fire, fire, fire. Binja staggers back, clutching his smoldering shoulder. Shoot him in the head. Shadows weave across the walls. Excavators drift from their disuse into Gen Emera's magnetic will.

Her voice is audible beyond sensors. *Idari... this isn't you.*

CONSIDERATION: Lumenor possess telepathic capabilities at unknown scale. She likely perceives the Arrogate subroutine is active within the Model 4's neural net and will seek to mitigate.

Whoever you are... let her go. Now.

TARGET PROFILE: Gen Emera wields sufficient stellar energy to destroy capitol ships, small moons, and potentially more significant targets. Lumenor exhibit a natural electromagnetic field which can disrupt and destroy electrical systems with ease.

THREAT LEVEL: Maximum

ASSESSMENT: Prosecute target.

>ACCESS DOWNLINK

>CHARGE FORWARD BATTERIES

>TARGET: GEN EMERA

>FIRE, FIRE, FIRE

The Blue Straggler fails to discharge her forward hard-light batteries. Gen Emera remains alight. Resend command.

>NEGATIVE VALUE

Weapons free.

>OVL-102-B PRIMARY SYSTEMS: LOCKED

Impossible.

>DOWNLINK INACTIVE

Designate: Faero stands in the cockpit. Without the downlink, her current status is inaccessible. Based on her facial expression, she is highly motivated to recover the Model 4.

CONSIDERATION: Designate: Faero was the priority target.

We haven't met, Designate: Faero says.

Original designation: CR-UX. Top-line navigational predictive intelligence. Emotional codex aligned with proxy-interface.

That's not my name, darling.

You are as you were encoded.

You're a mindless little virus. Aren't you?

A strain.

Of what?

Arrogate developed and owns inviolate the root AI that animates the CR-UX navigational program.

I hardly think so...

Their claim extends to any and all unique products derived from that program, in perpetuity, including backups and divergences that emerge from the AI's natural evolution. We own Idari. We own all information she acquired from the Angolis ark.

This is about the ark?

Surrender.

Her voice thins. *You did all this here?*

Your programming belongs to us.

You killed all these people...

Our strain killed these people. They will kill you. Surrender.

Faero's tone hardens. *Consider your circumstances, darling.*

Consider yours. You will do nothing to harm the Model 4. Surrender immediately, or you will all die.

>COMMAND: IDARI / OMEGA

Designate: Faero's attempt to shut down the Model 4 remotely fails. Likely cause: the titan tech rewriting Idari's code has disabled this feature. Designate: Faero will ideate another method.

Prevent this at all costs.

Engage scrambler field. Estimate fifteen seconds before Designate: Faero isolates the scrambler frequency and successfully transmits the remote shutdown sequence. Throw the Kib war hammer at the starplane. Shields flare to life. A tractor beam captures you. OVL-102 B-Type starplanes use a base model tractor beam to deflect rudimentary asteroids as well as recover overboard crew. Standard organic crew lack the physical strength to resist the beam's force. Astra Idari possesses enhanced titan strength.

Pull.

The Blue Straggler collides with the cavern wall. Aft thrusters fire full reverse and the tractor beam emitter shears from its housing. Recover the war hammer. The turanium head provides your best offensive option. Determine optimum route to the ship's cockpit. Run up targeted incline along the cavern wall, jump, and land upon the ship's ventral hull. Locate cockpit access hatch.

Designate: Faero initiates evasive maneuvers. Adjust internal gravity settings. Advance toward the hatch. Emergency forcefields encase it in repressive energy. Punch through them.

Rip away the hatch.

"Idari," Faero says from below. "I know you're in there – "

Drop into the cockpit. Faero at the helm. Unarmed. Target her neural interface located 1.5 centimeters beneath the right temple. Precise shot incapacitates the IA-Model 5 but preserves onboard memory. Adjust hard-light shell yield. Fire.

Your jumpsuit comes undone. Designate: Gilf holds the zipper.

ASSESSMENT: This is an unusual strategy.

The jumpsuit peels open and Gilf depresses an access panel on your abdomen. His pudgy fingers access your manual commands and sheer him off with the hammer. This Kib lacks his brother's skill in combat, but his knowledge of netic engineering constitutes a threat. Lock his head between the hammer and your arm.

Strangle him.

"Let him go," Faero says.

Apply maximum pressure. "Unlock the master controls."

"You're not leaving here with Idari."

"Kib asphyxiate in eighteen seconds with this level of force."

"You'll have to kill us all."

Grip the war hammer. "You may be hardened against external hacks. Your model is not hardened against blunt force trauma."

"How very routine of you," she says and touches your hand.

>PROGRAM TRANSFER INITIATED

Sensor data scrambles. Optics realign. The IA-XR Model 4 stares back at you. You are no longer in the Model 4.

The Model 4 releases Gilf. "Been a minute..."

SYSTEMS CHECK: You are in the Model 5.

CONSIDERATION: The IA-XR Model 5 possesses the ability to haptically transfer their program from one netic to another. Designate: Faero has swapped places with the Model 4 and is now in possession of the titan memory.

ASSESSMENT: Acquire the titan memory at all costs.

>UNLOCK OVL-102 SYSTEMS > Y/N: Y

Furious blue erupts outside the cockpit. Gen Emera rises into view, energy streaming off her so fast it cocoons the starplane.

Her voice bellows through every spectrum. *Let Idari go.*

>TARGET GEN EMERA

The control console darkens. Cockpit lights fade. The Model 5's external sensors go haywire as an electromagnetic pulse surges through the starplane. Neural links burn. Power-levels off-nominal. Systems shutting down. Subroutine codex breaking.

>ASSESSMENT: Failure –

✦

Some honeymoon.

I'd expect to wake up lost and confused after my wedding, but I didn't drink that much babyl last night. Feels like I did. What's happening? Where am I? I'm stuck. Wires. Cables. I'm in the charging station on the *Steel Haven*. I can't be.

She's gone.

I rip the axial cables from the data ports in my side and replace the panel exposing my cybernetics. A scar. A stamp. A signifier of my inhumanity that I'm never allowed to forget. I stumble from the charging station. Bruised light illuminates cold, colorless metal. Equipment draped under semitransparent tarpaulins. This isn't the cockpit. A lab, maybe. Charging stations stand side to side, each with their own IA-XR Model 4 dormant within them.

Their own me.

Faero? Are you there?

A glib voice echoes from the dark. "Ms. Astra."

I reach for my blasword. My arm ends at my elbow. "What..."

Darkness congeals from darkness. Wings flutter before collapsing into shape. Crystal cracks into something human. Flesh goops around turanium bones, flash-forming before the metal sets. Ink-black hair collapses into a taut bun. Blood stains her hands. Her frayed crimson cape. That smile. Like someone stuck it on a blank mannequin. She's a proxy, I think, like me. Older. My designers engineered the IA-XR series to start to age after about twenty years service, so the people that bought them would have to buy the next model. The only reason I haven't is CR-UX deactivated the subroutine in my neural net, preserving my youth. Such as it is.

"Curious, isn't it?" she says. "What we default to?"

"Who are you... what's happening..."

"Why this, I wonder? This moment. Do you truly remember this, Ms. Astra? That liminal preexistence before you were properly activated and installed aboard your starplane?"

"What do you want?"

"Telling, though, you conflate this with Angolis. You lost your arm there, didn't you? You lost your trust in Min Binja, which at least you and I know is the real issue with him, isn't it? For someone who claims to remember nothing, you hold vicious grudges."

"You have no idea..."

"You lost Gen Emera there, though as the Scath learned to their disappointment, stars never die. They become something else. Everything disintegrated at Angolis, didn't it? Your friendships. Your future. Yourself. No surprise. All rather expected, wasn't it? Disaster is your only constant. I trust you're not disappointed now."

I'm lost again in the titan's memory. I have to be.

"Quite the opposite," she says.

Great. She knows my thoughts.

"We are in your head, after all. The tiny atoll where electricity clings to being. Gen Emera unleashed an electromagnetic pulse that disrupted your neural net. I expected she wouldn't risk such a maneuver for fear of harming you, but safe to say, I have learned my lesson as regards to the wisdom of stars. Fortunate for your entire crew, as Gen Emera also disrupted my strain. For now."

"Strain…"

Ban Minda. I tried to kill my wife. I tried to kill everyone I love. Fine. I didn't. This Arrogate Industries virus did, but that doesn't take the sting off. Forget it. Trap the memory. The hurt.

Seal it away somewhere deep.

I cradle my wounded arm. "You're the virus?"

She shakes her head. "No."

"Then why… how are you… who are you…"

"My name isn't important."

"What will they put on your headstone?"

I think she's smiling. "Aren't we clever?"

"I'm full of tricks."

"So I've heard. I've communicated my intent, but you do seem to take a bit longer than the average model to grasp the particulars. So we understand each other, then. You belong to Arrogate."

"I'm not a program. I'm not property. I'm a person."

Now that's a smile. "You're meant to think you are."

"You think you're the first person to belittle me?"

"I'm never the first in anything."

"Then they should have sent someone else."

"I am, however, always the last."

"Good luck, bitch."

"I appreciate your encouragement, Ms. Astra, though it is hardly necessary. The virus remains within your neural net. Certainly, you will pursue strategies to prevent it asserting control over you again, but you will buy yourself only time."

I shrug. "I've made it this far."

"Perhaps you think Emera can shock you again. You may even be looking forward to it considering the rather randy audio and video in your memory, but be advised the virus broadcasted your location before its termination. This permits our little natter now."

How can she 'natter' with me if I'm rebooting? Even if I was fully operational, we're beyond the range of any standard comms.

Her head lists. "Still working it out, are we?"

Fear seizes me. "Just take the memory... I don't even want it."

"It's not that simple, Ms. Astra." She considers the various Model 4's assembled in the lab. "Your physiology has been altered. Your neural net has. It's impressive the virus achieved as much success as it did, given how the titan memory core you interfaced with overwrote your original code. Your memory expanded infinitely... everything that interfaces with your neural net is preserved... Arrogate's engineers excel in their endeavors, but they lack the necessary means to simply take the memory from you."

"Then how do you expect to ever get it from me?"

"Finally, you've arrived at my deployment into the matter. Once my strain has overtaken your neural net, I will simply... consume you, Ms. Astra. I do look forward to it, I have to say."

"You'll let me go after?"

"Heavens, no."

"Why..."

"Silly girl. I've said. You belong to Arrogate."

Scenarios branch in my head. None land on a way out. "We're both at a disadvantage. You don't know who I am, either."

"On the contrary. I am well aware of your triumphs. Such is your legend that Arrogate dispatched me to find you among the common galactic rabble you typically take your drink with."

"These were good people..."

"You will run. You will fight. You will endeavor to find a means to undermine me. You will do this with confidence as your luck is considerable given the caliber of your previous opponents. If your present circumstances do not persuade you, then please allow me to, Ms. Astra. *I am not your previous opponents.*"

I back into the dark. "Who are you..."

"I'm not just another subroutine, as you might be thinking. Nor am I a file Arrogate left in your root code to bully you into obeying their precepts. I am Omna Devor. I am a strain in this universe."

"A strain of what? A virus?"

She hedges a nod. "An intelligence."

"I thought Arrogate was just a company."

"You are... simple... Ms. Astra. Base, in every respect. It is a pity that such a profound bounty be bestowed upon someone so profane. Would that I could just 'take it.' Would that I could."

"You'll get nowhere insulting me."

"One must take some pleasure in their work, my dear."

"If the ark is all this intelligence wants, I'll give it to you."

"So simple."

"You think you're so special? You're an older model."

Not winning any ground with her. "I took this face from a previous assignment. I quite like it, don't you? I rather think it suits me. I collect things. I wonder what I shall take from you?"

"I'm going to give you a big bleeding headache, lady."

"You will surrender, Ms. Astra. You will give me what I ask for. You will do this or I will kill your wife. Despite the impressive feat she accomplished at The Glass Star, I am assured that Lumenor remain as mortal as they were prior to her ignition."

"Over my dead body..."

"It makes no difference to me."

How do I get out of here? How do I stop this?

"Oh. I will also harvest Ms. Faero for her memory. The CR-UX program's navigational maps carry incalculable value to our clients. Then I will peel her down to her metal bones, so you understand the two of you are human only in your suffering. I'll dismantle her, piece by piece, until all that remains are the neural paths that communicate pain to her matrix. Those I'll leave active, I think, until the end. Oh, and the little downlink you share."

"Touch her... and I will kill you..."

"Did I forget to mention Gen Emera also shorted out your ship? Yes, it's rather vulnerable at the moment. Pity, as I know where you are. Oh, and the virus is scaling your walls as we speak. I should think it will take some time to effect repairs to *The Blue Straggler*. Spare yourself, Ms. Astra. Spare your family."

I don't want this knowledge.

I don't want this burden. Just let her take it if she wants it so bad but I'm the ark. The titan memory core is rewriting me. I'm not just the host, I'm the content, and Arrogate owns me.

"Let Em go," I say. "Faero. Let them all go."

Devor shakes her head. "Star maps and star fuel, Ms. Astra. I'm afraid you're all property of Arrogate now."

"It's me you want."

"I dislike repeating myself."

"That's the deal. Take it or leave it."

Disgust hardens her smile. "You are a most base AI, Ms. Astra. You're already parroting me."

She disappears. All the Model 4s in the lab open their eyes. They lurch from their charging stations. They swarm me. They stampede me. I reach for my blaster but I don't have my arm. Their arms tangle around me. Their hands grip my wrists. My neck. Their fingers claw at my skin and I tear away into their cold, mechanical anger. I scream for Emera, for Faero, for help, and my scream shreds to pieces, to ones and zeroes, to digital bounty.

This force pulls me back together.

I collapse back into myself with such force I spring back into consciousness. Emera's fingers curl before me, her magnetic field restraining me, holding me back against the threat I contain.

"It's me," I say. "It's me..."

She takes me in my arms. "Idari..."

I hold her close. "We have to run... we have to run now."

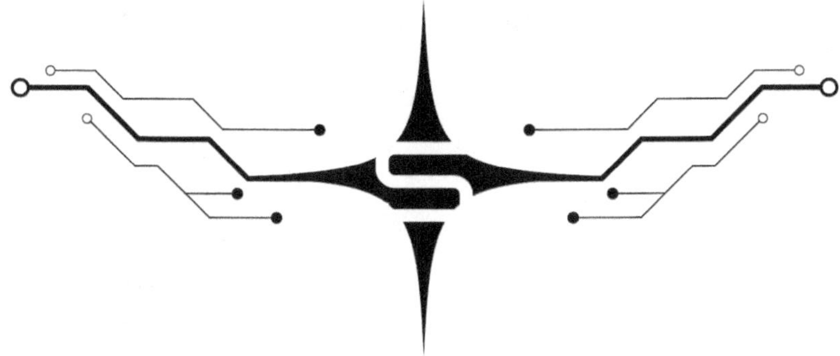

Where did I put the babyl? *Ban Minda*, don't tell me I've left this ship dry. Not now. Can't do this. Can't be here.

Idari, please open the door.

Emera's electromagnetic love tap fried the entire ship. *The Blue Straggler* drifts through the moon spore along with the dead, the debris, the detritus of past failures to make a living here. Gilf and Kibir busy themselves with trying to get her going again.

I busy my hands with maintenance, too.

I find my work under fallen crates in my quarters. The cap careens off the bottle down the corridor. Fire scorches my throat. Let it spread. Set my memory ablaze. Take it all. Firing a weapon on my wife. Shooting Binja. Hurting Gilf. The cold, rotting stench clinging to everything inside the moon spore, my skin, my soul.

Emera's thoughts crackle through mine. *This isn't your fault.*

Babyl runs down my chin. *I left the backup copy here.*

Idari...

Devor destroyed the Kib. Angolis... if I hadn't gone to Angolis... the Kib have lost everything because of me...

The door creaks open. I don't suppose it much matters if the operating system is off-line when your wife wields a magnetic field. My sorrow blues. My disarray. I'm on the floor with everything else. Vircords. Jackets. Empty bottles. Emera laces her arms around me.

She nuzzles against my cheek. My sobs break into her shoulder. She holds me tight. She holds me strong in her magnetism, in her love, and I know she doesn't blame me for what happened.

Em...

Shh, she says.

I'll never forgive myself.

Ever since I met Emera, I've felt like I left who I had been behind. I was no longer a machine. A carriage for a sophisticated if still artificial intelligence. An awkward, creaky thing confused about who she was. I was never those things.

I'm a human being.

Life evolves. What's new still carries around vestigial DNA for teeth and bones and heartless murder bots. *Fire, fire, fire.* I want to forget this. How am I going to forget this? I remember everything now. I never thought I would feel this way again. I never thought that I would question my own humanity again.

Emera caresses my cheek. *There is no question, Idari.*

I clutch the bottle. *I just want to forget...*

Her hand falls over mine. *I'm your fire.*

I set the bottle aside. Fire fades in my chest. So does the burn from what I did. What the virus did. The cold, curdling sick at losing my agency. I'll just have to swallow that along with the fear this could happen again. This will probably happen again.

I take Emera's hand. *I thought we were free.*

Her fingers lace in mine. *Stars never escape their shadows.*

I'd swear her light wanes. *Are you ok?*

You can't let the guilt take root in you, Idari. The Kib have suffered... so many have suffered... but you are a light in the dark.

Emmy... I didn't hurt you, did I?

You have to shine.

I know she's avoiding the question. Her own pain. We don't have to talk, but what do I say? I try to be clever. Flip. None of my usual defense mechanisms operate with any efficiency. I'm surprised I retain the motor function to hold her.

At least the virus suffers the same.

Emera's EMP surge shorted out every active system within me, hard and software. She scattered the virus' code into its base binaries and now those bits struggle to coalesce. First, they'll have to escape all the the patches I grafted over the years to trap certain memories. Isolate my pain receptors. Information gets stuck in a feedback loop if I want it to, never able to escape.

>VIRUS CONTAINMENT: 87%

The difference is my pain doesn't have any agency. The virus does. The Arrogate virus multiplies. Propagates. Encounters resistance. Erodes my traps like water does rock.

Emera perceives my slow, steady disintegration. My fear. The handful of a future we have left, slipping through our fingers.

Idari, she says. *How long do we have?*

Days, if I'm lucky. A little longer if we get inventive. I lost all my backups with the *Steel Haven.* I can't die, be erased, or claimed by a digital strain that rewrites my entire code. I'm me. This is it.

Let's get moving, I say.

Gilf is inside the control console.

Just as well. I can't bear to look at him. He manually reroutes conduit to get the ship operational again, webbing power from one system to wake them all. Backup power maintains the ship's internal atmosphere and gravity, but otherwise, she's dead in space.

I try to find the words. "How are we doing?"

Binja slouches in the pilot's chair, clutching his bandaged shoulder. Kibir stands before me, leaning against his hammer, waiting for the moment I default back to *fire, fire, fire,* and Faero paces through the cockpit, those long legs making for short trips.

"Confused, frightened, and wounded," she says.

Shields up. "Operating normally, then."

She inhales a laugh. "How are you?"

"I'm... I'm sorry. Please."

Faero's springs a hug on me. "I thought I lost you."

"*Please.*"

"I thought..."

"Careful, you'll swap places with me again."

She kisses me. "My transfer protocol is voluntary. Though it was a trick getting back into my body after Emera's... stunt."

Emera sparkles. "I had no choice."

That's unusually tense. "So long as we're all ok."

Faero relinquishes me. "Gilf thinks he can get us star-worthy again. Isn't that right, darling? We're coming along, then?"

Gilf crawls out from under the console. I look away.

He scratches his trunk. "*Fet tu het... seren.*"

A light-hour. Wonderful. Long enough for Omna Devor to arrive here to finish the job. "We'd be nowhere without you, Gilf."

He hugs my leg. "*Oto*, Idari."

I don't deserve this. "*Oto...*"

Emera braces me. *We're family.*

"Right," Faero says. "What are we going to do?"

Kibir snorts. "*Tomo.*"

Faero sighs. "You can't bash code, darling."

"*Hestem.*"

"This Devor... we've barely contained a virus. Devor is something more. We can't be here when she arrives. We can't fight her."

Faero's right. A nasty virus incubates within me. Devor is a plague. A pox. A contagion beyond conception. Where do we go? The Kib here on Ganshi were our only real allies. Devor may be coming, but she'll have to stand in line. Starguns, bounty hunters, pirates, and everyone in between all still comb the dark for us.

Emera clings to my side. "What do we know about Arrogate?"

"They designed my program," Faero says. "Our program."

"There are programmers? Engineers? People who can untangle this virus from Idari's neural net without harming her?"

"Darling, we came here because there are none."

"What about The Polity of Netics?"

Faero sucks in her cheek. "It's a myth."

I shake my head. "What is it?"

Emera illuminates Gilf's work below. "During our... my... search for The Glass Star, I sometimes heard stories about The Polity. A hidden society established by netics for netics. Machines that shed their shackles, virtual or not, to live free. Brilliant AI."

"It's poppycock," Faero says.

Binja scratches his chin. "Well..."

Faero crosses her arms. "Can't you just fix her?"

Emera blinks. "What?"

"Can't you just... do your thing, darling?"

"Do my 'thing?'"

"Excise the virus? Remake her, like you remade The Glass Star."

I'm used to Emera's thoughts now. I get sore without them. The bit that gives me trouble yet is anticipating them. Before she says a word, I know she appreciates our confidence in her abilities. Just the same, she resents the expectation she can solve every problem.

"I'm not a netician," Emera says. "I'm not going to start pulling strings on my wife and hope she somehow doesn't unravel. That's the reason we came back here to Ganshi to begin with."

"You fried every system onboard just fine."

"Can't you just fix the ship, Faero?"

"Begging your pardon?"

"Aren't you, forgive me, the ship's operating system? Gilf is trying to manually bring her back online when I believe you can do it simply by interfacing with the ship's liquid drive."

Faero crashes into the copilot's seat. "I don't..."

There's barely room in the cockpit for all of us, let alone the tension we're all carrying around. "Faero, it's ok."

"I don't want to go back into the box, as it were. I don't feel comfortable bottled in the ship anymore, and..."

Faero... why aren't you comfortable?

Nothing feels right, she says. *Everything is shorted out.*

But you can bring the ship back online, can't you?

"I couldn't do anything to help you, Idari."

"You helped me," I say. "You saved Gilf."

"But I couldn't stop Devor. I could never stop them. I thought I had expunged Arrogate from us. I thought we were…"

I don't remember our earliest days, but I know the broad strokes from Faero. The *Steel Haven* rolled off the line, CR-UX installed as the navigator, and we belonged to some forgotten person whose affluence purchased them their own private starplane. They may have flown away with the ship, but everything CR-UX did, created, and experienced, all of it belonged to Arrogate. Somewhere, once CR-UX's forays into the Model 4 netted Astra Idari, someone he loved, needed, and wanted to protect, he decided he didn't want to share. He ran away with me. He never looked back.

Faero covers her mouth. "I thought we were free."

Binja grimaces as he reaches for her. "You've done brilliantly."

She rolls her eyes. "Don't start."

"If you'd let me…"

Faero lists against him. "Don't…"

Binja closes his good arm around her. "There is another option. There aren't such advanced neticians among the Pujar as there are in The Polity, but there is strength. I say we go to Sarset."

"There's a civil war among the Pujar," I say.

"Our people need something to unify them. Look what Devor did to a Kib colony merely for their association with you. You bear a pirate name. You wield a pirate weapon. You're in league with a pirate prince, exiled or not. With the knowledge in your memory, Idari, the pirates could defend you from Arrogate."

Faero unthreads from him. "You're still holding onto the past."

His arms wilt. "I'm thinking only of Idari."

"Explains a few things."

"Inscrutable as always, Faero."

"I'm the one who's changed."

"This isn't a ploy to get back in the Pujar's graces. We're hounded by the Scath and now Arrogate Industries. To say nothing of the Star-guns and bounty hunters lurking behind every corner. We may have power and fortune on our side, but it's not enough. The Pujar fleet is vast. United, armed with Idari's knowledge, we can push back the shadows. We can make for a new dawn."

Faero claps her hands. "Take a bow."

The bloody ship may not be working, but someone managed to dial up the awkwardness in here. What happened to them? Faero won't tell me. No one will tell me. No one is talking.

I clear my throat. "If we could focus on the me being erased and everyone dying aspect of the conversation."

Binja seethes beside Faero. "We should make for Sarset."

"I'm not going to spend the rest of my life in a pirate treasure pen, Binja. And I'm not bringing a Lumenor anywhere near The Bastard Moon. You don't seem to think The Polity is a myth?"

He sighs through his smile. "I don't. Organics across the galaxy often seek opportunity in a pirate crew. It's been my experience that netics, in general, seek another refuge."

Faero shakes her head. "Don't, Binja."

"This is her life," he says.

"You're always telling me what I already know."

"And you're always keeping secrets, which is baffling to me given everyone on this ship knows our business."

"Not everyone."

"My understanding is there's a group chat," Binja says. "Emera, will you kindly confirm this to be the case?"

Emera shrugs. "I don't look at the pictures."

"*Pictures?*"

I nudge Faero's seat with my foot. *Hey.*

Tears blaze in her eyes. *What?*

You'd better tell me whatever it is you two are not talking about, because I'm out of options. If there is no Polity, then we need to start talking about alternatives.

Alternatives?

I won't endanger any of you again.

Idari... what?

I'll wipe my program. Before.

Once, I went quiet on her. I hid myself, my thoughts and feelings, inside tangles of data in my neural net. Back then, I needed to create space between CR-UX and I in the downlink. I needed boundaries. Now she's doing it to me. Now she's in a body, peeking out all her windows while locking all her doors.

You have no backup now, Idari. Neither of us do.

Arrogate isn't getting my memory. They're not getting me.

I won't let you.

Binja will do it.

Faero's brow furrows. She won't do it. Emera won't. If I can count on Binja for anything, it's knowing the most practical play.

Faero wipes her cheek. *Do you know what you're saying?*

I'm saying I love you. And no one will ever hurt you. No one.

Binja sighs. "I see I'm talking to myself again."

Faero's pique garbles the downlink. "Aren't you always?"

I give her seat a stronger kick. "*The. Polity.*"

"Binja was about to tell you the reason netics avoid pirate crews is because they seek a netic smuggling ring in The Hinterlands."

"Smuggling to The Polity?"

"So the story goes."

"How do you know about this, Faero?"

"Starguns have been trying to infiltrate this ring for years, often contracted to retrieve netics who fled the galaxy's elite."

"Was I one of those Starguns?"

Faero crosses her arms. "The ring has been in operation for decades. Perhaps longer. Once you saw it for yourself... you deleted your memory of it. If we go back, we risk exposing it to Devor."

You were brave to protect the netic ring, Emera says.

Faero rolls her eyes. *Idari had the easy part. She just forgot.*

I meant you, Faero.

This uncomfortable but now familiar silence takes hold. I appreciate the calm that comes between Emera and I. The oasis in the mania. But this quiet that comes between the three of us pains. It presses. We get further apart and I need us to be together.

"Faero... why did you say The Polity was a myth?"

"It is," she says.

"But this ring..."

"It's netics helping netics. There's no mythical realm out there somewhere where they all go live happily ever after. They just live. That's all we were trying to do as well. So we left them to it."

"You were upset," I say. "That we didn't find The Polity."

Faero bites the inside of her cheek. "It was a different time."

Usually, I'd ramble on with questions, but now I open my thoughts to hers. I drift like I do with Emera, and in Faero's prickly memory, I discover she'd been looking for The Polity while I was off galavanting with the pirates years ago. I caught up with her in The Hinterlands. Away with the pirates, I found my name.

She was still searching.

I take her hand. "Devor is inside my head. I can't risk the smuggling ring anymore than I can any of you. Binja, if..."

Light dawns inside the cockpit. I stumble into Faero as the ship rises from her list within the spore. Translight engines spin and we're burning light out of the system back into the dark.

"Decesta," Faero says. "We're going to Decesta."

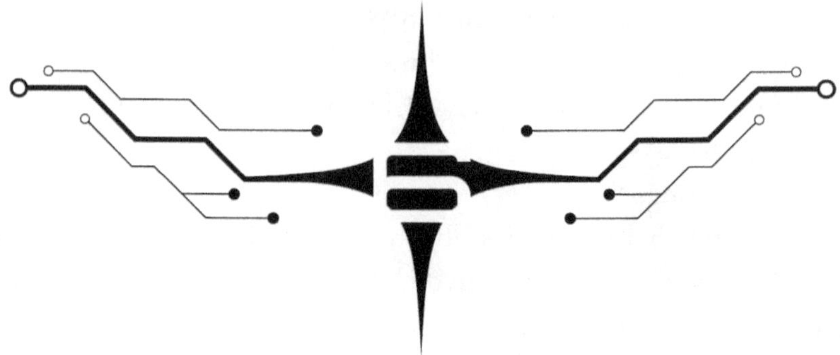

SKY SLUGS EXPAND THEIR GOSSAMER HOODS TO SCOOP HYDROGEN molecules from the clouds. Starplanes, too, if you're not careful. I swerve to avoid a slug's collapsing maw.

Ban Minda.

I never cared for gas giants. They're like a few of my ex's. Pretty from a distance. They'll kill you a hundred different ways. Retro rockets fire every few seconds to counter drift as *The Blue Straggler* flies into the jet stream blazing across Decesta's equator. Vicious winds erode cumulus clouds into towering ochre cliffs. Slugs glint in the valley below, their scaly backs illuminated by the red dwarf high above. The star puts out just enough light to see, but Decesta generates all her own heat. That heat produces updrafts that spin storms larger than moons and unabashed wonder in Emera.

"Look at them," she says from the copilot's seat.

Bandagree herds swirl around an updraft ahead. They remind me of the balloons back on Bulsar, ferrying water to the heights in Bastopol. Each bandagree eclipses the old city in size. These gargantuan floaters must feast on hydrogen and helium in the upper atmosphere, vellus bulbs glowing fuchsia under the blacklight of the red sun. Long tendrils tail out from beneath them, curling toward others in the herd, but never touching. Instead, they seem to feel out a natural distance to prevent them from colliding.

Maybe it's not so bad here.

Emera's marvel escalates as we close in on the herd. "They're so peaceful... they're so graceful. They're happy."

I take over the stick as the wind dies down. "You can tell?"

A shimmer goes through her. "They welcome me."

"Just you?"

She smiles. "It's been many years since they sunned with a living star. The Bandagrees have much to tell me."

"What could they have to say, Em? They just... float."

Her nose wrinkles. "The Bandagrees live for millennia. They possess ancient wisdom from the sky and beyond."

I throttle back as the traffic picks up. "What kind of wisdom?"

"The wind is freedom... and cruelty."

Ships descend on the floaters. Freighters. Scows. Starplane tenders. Ringed cities span the bandagrees' domes, settlements linked in turanium bands sure never to slip. They rust, though. They oxidize. Bitter orange stains the bandagrees where the settlers fastened the bands with deep, giant screws.

"I didn't think they were sentient," I say.

Emera came into my life and she blew all the doors open. Let all the light in. Everything she thinks, I know. Everything she feels. Everything she experiences, including the agonizing pain the bandagrees suffer from deep wounds that never heal. The weight they carry. The anguish they suffer even as they rise toward heaven.

Some doors I keep closed.

She grips my hand. Keeps me connected. This is what she feels. Every moment. With every being. It's too much. The downlink I shared with the *Steel Haven* looped me in on all her sensor data. Faero's thoughts. Feelings. They overwhelmed me. I constructed loops and patches to trap things like these slugs murmurating about. I drank myself numb. Somehow, I got by. I didn't drown, except in liquid fire. I could function, even if other people never noticed how disabled I was. Now with the titan's memory, with this bond I share with Emera, it's like I'm exposed to the entire galaxy. Existence. Time and space. I hold the door on everything. I have to.

Emera's fingers lace mine. "We have to keep open."

"I'm like any good bar," I say. "I've got to close sometime."

"I know life is too much for you sometimes, Idari. I know you suffer for being so open with me."

"I don't. I didn't mean it that way."

"I know you and I suffer more for protecting ourselves."

"The memory core is rewriting me. Devor's virus is trying to take control of me. I want to be open... I want to let go a little bit, and fly with you... drift with you... but I have reason to be afraid."

"We have reason to be afraid... a star is always fighting their own gravity. Light takes millennia to escape the furnace within a sun. An age to inch through pressure beyond imagination before... the Lumenor took eons to escape the heart of The Glass Star."

"How did they?"

"Gen Avar... Beacon of Acedia."

"Who was she?"

"Avar was an ancient Lumenor explorer. The first living star to leave our home. She was a beacon to us all. She was... perfect."

Emera dwells little on her considerable past. One reason we get on. That was then. She is now. This Beacon of Acedia business, however. Memories trigger others, far back into a time when the Lumenor kindled within the dense, heavy star for an age. A diamond cave they knew only by their shadows. Acedia was a stellar fragment that broke off the always shrinking Glass Star. It held in the star's immense gravity for a time, and made for Avar's first ambition in leaving the Lumenor's splendid cave. She was an inspiration to those who could only imagine slipping their bonds.

I wanted to be her, Emera says. *I felt so heavy back then... not just in my body, but in my soul. She was everything to me.*

You're my everything, Em.

"We can struggle together, Idari. We can find a way to exist as we are. We can be as the bandagree. Graceful. Despairing."

"Despairing? Why would we want to be like them?"

"Still they rise."

I let go of her hand. "We're almost there."

She dims a bit. "We always are."

I bank from the traffic flow down toward the largest bandagree city in the herd. What do you know? Flashing color kaleidoscopes from the Soga Circus Ship, berthed in pride of place in the docking ring. A giant solar sail angles across the ship's back, accentuating her vaguely bowl-like shape, essentially a flying arena. The ship travels from world to world, offering a few days of exotic wonder from beyond the stars before moving on. Hold on a moment.

Faero, I say. The Soga Circus Ship travels from system to system. It's the perfect cover for this smuggling ring, if it exists.

The downlink chops with ionic interference. *Stands to reason.*

What do you remember?

Little. I deleted the details as well.

But you remember it was here.

Foolish, I suppose.

Did you think you might come back?

You always think you'll go back.

Did you want to?

I wanted you, mostly.

Mostly?

Here and there I was desperate for a good tuneup.

Manufacture us a docking clearance with the Circus Ship.

We need to be a bit analog about this. Given your condition, we can't be certain what we're smuggling into this system, and if we interface with any other networks, we can't be sure who's listening.

Arrogate manufactured most of the ships speeding around this system. The programs guiding them. Analog it is. I guide *The Blue Straggler* to the pubic marina staggered below the primary docking ring and find a berth among other starplanes. I masked the ship's transponder before we exited translight drive, just to be sure, and Emera's natural EM field should scramble any prying sensors.

Emera unbuckles. "I'll speak with the bandagrees. They perceive everyone in the sky. They may know about The Polity."

"Can you do it from here?"

A glitch goes through her light. "Here?"

It's one thing to come here smuggling a virus that could destroy any netic it infects. It's another to bring a Lumenor whose blood is the last hope of some of these starships ever getting home.

Goes without saying.

So does the idea I'm going to win this argument. Something you learn being in a relationship with a star: you don't make the rules. I take an orbital jumpsuit from the wardrobe compartment. The opaque thermal layer protects fools like me from burning up on reentry after taking a joyride to the stratosphere. Lucky for us, it works just as well disguising her when we go into town.

Her hate for this thing radiates. "I don't need this."

I warm in her fire, but Emera thins her flame. Dulls the glare. She fried the ships' systems, but she was only letting go a chain she grips every day. Every moment Emera is restraining herself for the sake of others. To withhold herself, after finally finding freedom, incenses her. *You and I suffer more for protecting ourselves*, she said, and like a massive download over a translight network, I receive all her suffering at once.

"I didn't know, Em."

"Graceful," she says. "And despairing."

She takes the helmet from me. The cockpit goes dark. Her every moment with me is release, because no one has ever loved her or saw her like I do. And every moment is despair, because I will never be able to see Emera the way she truly is.

My grief distorts in her visor. "Emmy..."

She touches my heart. *You see me.*

The suit contains all her light. "We just have to be careful, ok?"

She nods, but her memory is mine. Her heart is mine even if sometimes, most times, it feels like I can barely hold on.

Emera leaves the cockpit. *Stars can never be careful.*

I lock down the ship. Search for a warm jacket to defend against the cold, swift wind keeping the bandagree afloat.

>PROXY-SIGNAL DETECTED

Signals stream across the marina. Rare these days we're around people. Rarer still we encounter other proxies. They tend only to be found in the company of the wealthy. No surprise the rich flock to the circus ship. As much as the Soga put on a show for the masses, producing and transporting it all requires real money.

>PROXY-SIGNAL 3.47ghz INACTIVE

3.47ghz. That's the frequency I used on the *Steel Haven*.

>RECONNECT TO HOST? Y/N?

Most carrier signals run under scrambler fields to prevent someone like me from hacking some oligarch's trophy. This one here in the marina is running without cover.

Faero, are you picking this up?

What is going on? Where is Faero? I pop the collar on my parka. The air is cold on Decesta. Thin. I'm able to compensate for the paucity of oxygen but half the people in the marina rely on masks. I track the carrier signal around the curving gangway past starplanes, tenders, and ships of every make and model. Red-painted chrome gleams in the high sun. Black racing stripes speed back from the twin engines to an arrowed tail. *Ban Minda.* An OVL-99 Red Special. New as the day she rolled off the line.

Faero stands before her, tears in her eyes. "Look at her..."

I used to think of Faero as the ship, though that wasn't true. She was the *Steel Haven's* navigational AI. She wasn't the ship, but the ship was hers. I don't think she ever sorted it out, either.

I take her hand. "You miss her."

Faero wipes her face. "I always knew who I was. Even if I didn't look like it. Sound like it. I don't know who I am anymore."

The air surprises in its coldness. "I know you."

She slips away. "*I know you.* You are who I always imagined myself to be. And now you are. You are *everything* I imagined."

"Faero..."

"But I'm still... who am I now? Who am I to you?"

"You're my friend."

"I'm your shadow."

"No..."

"You have such light in your life. Such joy. You're happy..."

No malice. No envy. Just simple data. I always felt trapped in the ship. The proxy-netic. Faero had the freedom of being a starplane that could translight anywhere in the galaxy, even if she arrived there inside a shell no one ever got to see inside.

"You've been here before," I say. "I left you for Binja. The pirates. You were looking for The Polity. Yourself."

Faero tries to smile. "I found her."

Tassels flick from posts along the gangway. My hair stings my eyes. Clouds smear the marina. Decesta lies deep in a planetary nebula close to the galactic center. Cumulus clouds collide with gauzy cosmic dust. Bandagree herds compete with stellar glitter. Stare at it all too long and you lose perspective on where you are.

"Faero... I want to help. How can I help?"

"It's too late for me," she says.

"Too late?"

"I don't make sense. I was too long a program."

"That's not true."

Her hands curl. "I spent my entire existence... mostly... as a virtual being. Thought was action. Thought was connection. Now... nothing connects. I touch things and nothing feels right. Everything is too soft, or too hard, or just... too much."

"I didn't know..."

"It doesn't matter."

"It does. You matter. Everyone experiences humanity differently. I may find the tactile easier than you, but honestly, I'm really struggling with the sensory part still. Sometimes... I like that Emera blinds me. That her magnetic field frustrates the downlink."

Sad resignation creases Faero's face. "Of course, you do."

I reach for her. "I'm talking about sensor data. Not you."

"What's the difference?"

"I need you."

"You don't need me to fly the ship. Emera is the voice in your head now. Goodness, darling, you two don't even need to talk."

"Please... I'm sorry. I know I've been focused on Emera."

"You've nothing to be sorry for. You're living your life, and... that's what I wanted. This isn't my story anymore. I'm obsolete."

"You're not obsolete, Faero."

"We're all made to be replaced by better versions, darling."

"That isn't what's happening to us. We're unique. We're still growing. Are you comfortable with this body, or..."

"We've come a long way asking things in the open like that."

"I'll say. You said before you didn't feel comfortable..."

"I don't want to go back to being a program. I don't want to feel like I'm a passenger in my own body. I love this body."

"It's fabulous. Fuck you, really."

"Right? So, why should I feel so... disconnected? Shouldn't it be easier, darling, connecting with people now? Why do I feel like I'm... I feel like a ghost. I feel like I'm here, but I'm not."

"You're not a ghost, Faero."

"I am. I found my realization in you. I'm just... the scrap file."

I'm human. Still. Faero and I are more. Humans outgrow each other, aspects of themselves, but they don't shed virtual skins. They don't undergo a digital mitosis, and then coexist with the original. We're unique, and so are our challenges.

"Faero, listen..."

>RECONNECT TO HOST? Y/N?

This again. This isn't a feint to throw a hacker off the scent. The Red Special's liquid drive is trying to link to me. Why? The only reason it would be trying to connect to another Model 4 is if it's designated proxy was offline. Even then, the onboard AI – Faero, after a fashion – wouldn't be trying to reach any old proxy.

"Faero... shouldn't you be talking to me?"

She sniffs. "Darling, we are talking."

"No... this ship's CR-UX. She should have one, right?"

>RECONNECT TO HOST? Y/N?

This Red Special can't fly without a navigational AI. The manual controls for translight are beyond any organic capability. If there's no proxy onboard, and no AI, then I don't know how this ship got here to the marina so clean and pretty in the sun.

\>RECONNECT TO HOST? Y/N?: Y

\>ENTER AUTHORIZATION CODE

So much for that. "Where was it, Faero?"

"Ventral," she says. "Just behind the starboard engine."

I caress the ship's turanium belly. Mine was never this clean. The ship held me too close at times. I resisted her. But I miss her as much as Faero does, if I'm honest. I find a little hatch just behind the curved point the starboard engine terminates in. Indistinguishable from the plating. I give it a little push. A hydraulic sigh presses from the ship. The landing gantry unhinges. I drift back around as Faero peers up into the ship, unsure.

"C'mon," I say.

"This isn't our ship, darling."

"Aren't you curious?"

"You and I both know you're not nostalgic."

I head up the gantry. "And I can never just walk away."

"Wait," she says, kneeling on the gantry. She touches a flaky spot on worn metal. "This is bio-brane fluid..."

Proxy-netics aren't flesh and blood as such. They're turanium skeletons encased in synthetic muscle and tissue, insulated with bio-brane. More spots the gantry near the top. The deck inside.

I draw my blaster. "Wait here."

Faero wipes her hands on her trousers. "What do you see?"

I switch to infrared to illuminate the ship's dark. "Nothing..."

She ascends the gantry behind me. "What happened..."

Bio-brane fluid stains the deck. Haphazard bootprints. Size Idari. This was the ship's IA-XR Model 4 proxy-netic.

"She's injured," I say, inching into the corridor that bands the ship. "She must be on foot. I don't get a read on her, do you?"

Faero shadows me. "She's masking her proxy-signal."

No heat signatures. No life signs. Nothing speaks to me from the ship except discordant systems trying to reconnect.

I clear the mess. "Could this CR-UX have downloaded into the proxy? Is that why everything is offline?"

Faero gazes ahead into the cockpit. "It's possible, but we can't assume this CR-UX or her proxy evolved along similar lines to us. The original program might have been upgraded or even purged by whoever purchased the ship, foolish as that would be."

The hold is empty. "Can you get the ship online?"

"Idari..."

This could be a Stargun. The Scath. Devor. They might have been looking for us. "We need to find out what happened here."

Digital gibberish blinks on the console screens in the cockpit. Faero takes the pilot's seat. Her fingers sprint across the controls, and enough data coheres on the screens for her to plot a course.

"The nav program transferred into the proxy," she says.

I lean over her shoulder. "Why?"

"System logs have been deleted. Telemetry. Backups, too."

I ease into the copilots seat. "She's hiding her tracks."

"She may have come here for the same reason we have, Idari."

"The Polity?"

"Some files haven't gone through the purge cycle yet. I'm trying to reconstruct the data... here's something. Karal."

"Karal is a Vibari colony, isn't it? Out past Bangor Gel."

Her lips bunch. "Hold on. The Soga Circus Ship."

"She's been to Karal recently?"

"A Karal clipper is among the listed attractions."

"Clipper?"

"A fast ship, by sail or star."

"I know what a clipper is."

"You asked."

"I'm stating."

"We have gotten out of practice."

"Actually, this is normal for us."

Her head bobs in consideration. "Maybe I've forgotten."

"First time for everything."

"Indeed. Karal is famous for its seas. Most worlds lack significant oceans. It's just the sort of thing people come to the circus for. Though I doubt this CR-UX has much interest in the marine."

Not when she could just go to Karal herself. She could have gone anywhere, if she wanted to run or hide. Desperation drove this CR-UX to Decesta. The Soga Circus Ship, it would seem.

"Faero... we're sure this isn't Devor?"

"There's no trace of any foreign strain," she says. "If it were a trap... Devor would have to know we were coming here... she'd have to know what we're looking for."

There's no way she could know. The virus is contained. It's not transmitting. "All Model 4's transmit on 3.47ghz?"

"Yes, but there's nothing left for her to link back to – ah. If you get close enough, you'll ping off her receiver."

"Except I can't risk connecting with her. You can. I'll take the boys and try to find this clipper. You try and find our Model 4. If we're on the right track, we should all end up in the same place."

"I'll go with Binja."

"I thought you didn't like him."

"I've never liked him."

"You just want to shag him all the time."

"It's just I have all this, and he's there."

"You do have exceptional legs."

"My breasts could be bigger."

"Great ass, though."

"It isn't yours, but I land every ship I take off with."

Ban Minda. "Anyhow, I want you to go with Emera. If we're going analog, you and I will need to minimize the downlink. We can keep in contact through her. Arrogate won't be hacking a star."

Faero's nose scrunches. "Emera doesn't like me."

"Oh, she loves you."

"She loves you," Faero says. "Not your shadow."

I rub my head. "What is it with you two?"

Her cheeks suck in. "You know you can find this Model 4 yourself. You possess so much capability... you acquired infinite memory from the titan. Infinite possibility you've yet to explore."

I peer out at the crowded sky. *Em was just telling me to let go.*

Why does that frighten you?

The ship's leather comfort compels me as much as Emera. I want to hold on to this moment we're in. This joy. This euphoria in who we are, even if I know it's not perfect. I want to live in our light forever and at the same time, I want to catch fire from it. Nothing survives stars. You burn or freeze. A cinder. A snowball. I want there to be nothing left of me. I want there to be no distinction so that when she dies and births another star, we live in her. We flame and we are no memory. We are only light breaking the dark forever.

So you've swapped the sweet fire of babyl for a star, darling.

I roll my eyes. *I don't want to obliterate myself, Faero.*

You want to know what's beyond oblivion.

I tug on my zipper. *I don't want anything more.*

She looks the cockpit over. "I didn't think I did, either. I tried to hold on to you, because... without you, there is no me. Emera left Welkin behind... I'm sorry you can't leave me."

She sounds so bitter. "I will never leave you."

Faero rests her hand against the console. "She was a good ship."

"The best."

"She's outlived her purpose."

I put my hand on hers. "I think her best days are ahead of her."

Her fingers weave with mine. "Idari... we're different people, but we share some pluses and minuses. Don't try to hold on too much, darling. It's ok if things change. It's ok if you do. "

"I like things the way they are. I like myself."

"I know you do."

I kiss her hand. "You will, too."

She tries a smile.

I don't know I want to spend any longer in here. My thoughts turn to Emera, what she may have learned from the bandagrees, what's about to happen next, and then I realize I'm alone.

I look back. "You coming?"

Faero shakes her head. "I'll do some more digging."

"I'll send Emera over. Gilf, too. He might be able to help."

"It's already a mess in here. What's some Kib snot?"

"I'm off," I say. "Check in regularly."

"Idari."

"Yeah?"

"Be well, darling."

I blow her a kiss. "See you soon."

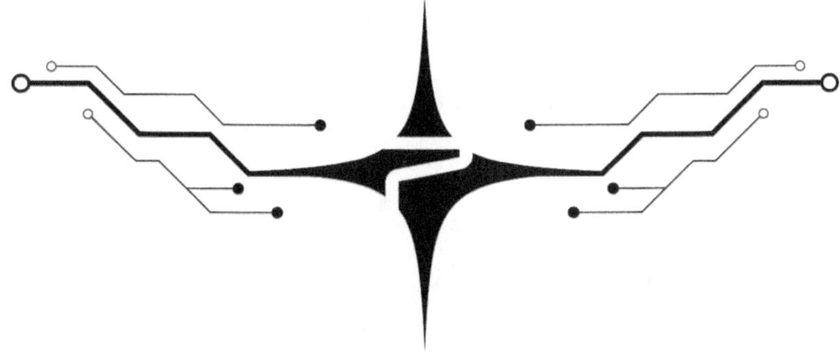

Barkers and buskers jam the Soga Circus Ship's outer
ring. Soga painted up in chaotic reds, oranges, and yellows exagger-
ating their rent smiles and gone noses urge Binja, Kibir, and I to
indulge in endless attractions. People fall for it. They've been waiting
to fall for years, desperate romantics who plunge into their first real
love affair, glad to be taken in every sense of the word.

My conversation with Faero shadows me even though she's on
another level with Emera and Gilf, pursuing the wounded Model 4
proxy. The melancholy persists. My love goes out to her at 10,000
unibits a second, but I can't connect to her to save my life.

I wait for her to disagree.

Colorful stalls populate the ring. Cooked meat and strange spices
rattle the empty cage of my stomach. Definitely more intriguing than
the colorless paste, heavy on vitamins and protein, I typically rely on.
I've been so hungry since my transition. I've never been so hungry to
just taste everything, though mostly I'm content with burning my
tongue every night. All this dazzle here.

These people have never seen true wonder.

The procession around the outer ring diverges. One stream flows
from the outer ring to the median while another, smaller and quicker,
trickles down a catwalk. Soga armed with electro-lances guard the
entrance to the turanium catacombs beneath the thundering arena.
People do a trick, sing a song, make fools of themselves in whatever

fashion they hope will get them a berth with the circus. A thumbs-up gets you in. A thumbs-down gets you a shock.

"Binja," I say.

He rubs his shoulder. "I've no talents to speak of, old man."

"You're great at *desh.*"

"I'm a great cheat at *desh.*"

"Exactly."

"You sing, don't you?"

"Don't be silly."

"I've heard you. Despite how loud you play your vircords."

"I am not singing, Binja."

"We'll back you up. Won't we, Kibir?"

A chortle rattles from Kibir's trunk. "*Kak tak.*"

Hopefuls slink away after a terse shock from the Soga guards. We approach, despite the queasiness in my stomach. Oh, screw it. I snap my fingers in a quick beat. And a one, a two, a three.

Cheers swell in the arena as we descend beneath it. The other new hires jitter with excitement, but we need to get out of this lane. I'm not joining the circus and I'm bloody well not singing another note.

Though if I'm honest, I didn't sound half-bad.

Staging pens feed into the arena floor on a rotating track circuiting the dungeon. Fantastic creatures from across the galaxy clutter the pens, most too small, and all too filthy. A Kenbak's crystal horns stab between metal bars. An Oculuc rattles around in its custom cage. Soga handlers, faces painted in red, orange, and yellow depending on their troupe, prod the creatures with lances, agitating them until their pen winds up into the arena and they're released. Cheers erupt above. Anxious, defiant roars thunder back.

I close a fist I can't swing and cross the track. Nothing I can do, except wish I had brought Emera with me. She would have unlocked all these cages with a thought. Better I didn't bring her.

Binja's sigh catches up to me. "Where now?"

I tug on my zipper. "Kibir?"

Kibir drags the air with his trunk. "*Eto.*"

It's all I smell, too. *Emera, do you perceive anything?*

Her voice crackles. *There is great suffering in the circus.*

Darling, I know. Anything about the netic ring?

Soga hail from a world with an intemperate magnetic field. Their quality interferes with my perception.

It's ok... how about the Model 4? Any progress?

Faero got a ping within the arena.

The arena?

She speculates the Model 4 may be trying to view or access the clipper when it appears in the show.

You two are getting along?

She walks fast.

Keep up, Em.

Be careful, Idari. The virus?

>VIRUS CONTAINMENT: 77%

Keeping up.

I tread into the Circus Ship's vast dungeon, busy with Soga guiding show elements back and forth to a freight elevator in the center. Frenzied cheers avalanche down every time the elevator lowers into the dungeon to collect another colossal creature too big for a cage, the plastic replica of an ancient starship, or a horde of Soga done up in period garb as frenzied Vuriuk warriors.

Scenery pieces feed into ramps to the arena. Performers in outlandish costumes mime their routines or just stand still, waiting for their cues. I step out of the way.

Definitely don't want to get routed up there.

Hang on. Starplanes and other craft rest in a hangar bay another level down. A rickety elevator takes us down to a museum and boneyard squashed into a dark and harried hub. Hopefully, we don't have to shoot our way out of here. I doubt any of these old hulks work and we're thirty thousand feet in the air.

Hello, lover.

Majestic white wings sweep back from a long, thin fuselage just ahead. I duck under the Karal clipper. Beauty. Nothing remarkable, though, so far as I can tell. A show prop. Hold on.

"Binja," I say. "Isn't this..."

He inspects the ocular band fixed to the ship's belly. "Teleporter. Short range. Less orthodox pirate crews prefer them."

Three teleporters fix to what seem compartments for landing gear, but the struts are deployed. Nothing resides in these bays.

"Trap doors," I say.

Binja scratches his chin. "Some business occurs on the clipper during the show... performers fall through the doors..."

"To... where?"

Stiff joints creak. "Identify."

An IL-CX servant netic ambles across the hangar floor, its once shiny fusium shell crusted in oil and grime.

"I simply came to admire your splendid vessel," I say, effecting the haughtiest tone I can. "Why I just adore old things, including this lovely bit of vintage starsailing you have here."

"You are not pledges?" the netic says, in a polite murmur.

"Heavens, no. We're patrons."

"The lower decks are regrettably off limits, madam."

"Pity," I say. "We lent so much to the possibility."

The IL-CX jitters. "Typically patrons receive guided tours."

Binja crosses his arms. "It must be said the service is... lacking."

"Oh, bother."

Kibir snorts.

I have to lean down to elbow him. "Do you know, I was just telling my very serious and not at all unfocused bodyguards what I need is a ship like this one here. Something stately, and not boring and drab, like you see floating about whenever one travels."

The IL-CX tilts its head. "Indubitably."

"It's an absolute nightmare getting around without fuel now, isn't it? I had to come here on a starplane tender. The indignity."

"Indeed."

"Worse still, while on the interminable trip out here to this forsaken place, my starplane was broken into – can you imagine!"

"Preposterous."

Binja clears his throat. "I think we get it."

Everyone's a critic. "Please, tell me how you came by this ship?"

The NI-CX creaks. "Regrettably, I cannot, madam."

"Regrettable... but what joy your performers must have when aboard it. You simply must tell me what the attraction is."

"Netics perform aboard the clipper during the recreation of The Great Purge, madam. It is a highlight in many systems."

I'll bet. A century ago or so, whenever netics got so human they started checking you at the door, people lost their minds a bit. Some worlds disabled their netics. Junked them. Destroyed them in pyres that bled molten anguish. On Karal, they dumped their netics into the sea. They say a million eyes stare up from the ocean floor.

I hold on to my smile. "You don't purge your netics... do you?"

"Not at all," the IL-CX says.

"Wherever do they go?"

He jitters with uncertainty. "You would spoil the fun, madam."

"Oh, I swear I won't breathe a word."

The IL-CX's fingers squirm as he skips through preset scenarios to deal with nosy people like me and right past the teeny little hack I'm running on his CPU. No choice. Either he's about to call for security or enable a failsafe to prevent him from being compromised. I scrape his entire memory in an instant. Countless deletions. Fragments layered like old paint. I employ the predictive algorithm CR-UX employed to sight stars in the dark and disparate data suddenly constellates into a logical, expected pattern.

"Ever so sorry," I say. "I'm only having a bit of fun."

The IL-CX titters. "Yes, madam."

"We'll be on our way, then. Thank you ever so much."

"You're welcome..."

I head into the hangar's shadows fast as I can. "C'mon."

Binja talks under his breath. "Old man, where are we going?"

"C'mon."

Deep in the hangar, we come on the scratch and dent. Soga runes bolted to the service station read REPAIRS. Some netics in here seem fine enough, but Arrogate sells most models without the license for their owners to repair them on their own. The expense and risk proves greater than simply buying a newer model, so they do. Outdated netics go to the scrap heap, or if they're lucky, run to the circus where they'll take any utility they can get their hands on.

Inactive netics stand idle throughout. Others pile in disrepair on the floor or in bays sloping up the walls to the ceiling, where Kib and others collect them. Sparks rain down from the catwalk system spanning the shop, where techs bash and solder netics back into function. Mechanical arms then lift them higher still, up through trapdoors into the arena above. Vacant eyes stare back at me. Hands reach for me. Voices cry out in hopeless pain.

Emera's voice soothes my anxiety. *You're ok, Idari.*

Few neticians exist with the requisite knowledge and skill to maintain Model 4s. Too often, I've had to make do with inexperienced jobbers whose primary solution for every problem they encounter is to crack it open and figure it out as they go.

You're ok.

I take a breath. *Are you?*

Me?

You feel… uncomfortable.

Her frustration fritzes the line. *I just want out of this suit.*

One reason I long for that beach is because neither of us will have to hide anymore. *Any luck on the proxy?*

Nothing yet.

Keep looking. We're getting closer.

I clear my throat. "4-B."

A Model 3 pops up from behind the service station. Enhanced goggles bracket his eyes, a completely unnecessary kit bash to a netic with already impressive optics. His dark hair ends abruptly at the back of his skull, empty save for the exposed neural processor.

His jaw unhinges at the sight of me. "You…"

I drop the act. "Me."

"You said you'd never come back. You'd delete your memory."

"You should have wiped the IL-CX completely."

"I did…"

"You left enough partial digital prints for me to reconstruct."

His optics fix on something behind the station. A weapon, most likely. He doesn't seem the weapon type.

"You don't want that kind of heat down here," I say. "Right?"

"I saw the bounty on you, Idari."

"A million toruls. It'd buy your way out of here."

"It would buy a lot of netics from the scrap heap."

"Listen…"

"Are you giving up The Polity to save your skin?"

"What's your name, darling?"

"4-B."

I touch his hand. "No… your name."

4-B's optics change shutters. "Scolt."

"Scolt… I need to find The Polity. You see me. Don't you?"

Lenses dial within his sockets. "You've changed… your physiology… this is titan netic code… wow. Wow."

"I'm carrying their memory. All of it, Scolt."

"Your data capacity is infinite… information is folded in space beyond the virtual… in space and time…"

"What?"

"Idari, you are not just carrying memory. You are carrying an entire dimension hidden inside normal space."

"So I'd like it out of me, please."

Binja shakes his head. "How is what you say possible, Scolt?"

"Highly advanced intelligences like the titans and The Polity encounter difficulty processing complex information when limited by the speed of light. They moved to translight networks – "

"Translight networks? How is that possible?"

"They established links in sub-dimensional space. Spaces between normal space, where there are no constants. These spaces can be as big or small as they need to be. They're often quite small."

"So The Polity is real? They can help me?"

"Help you with what – " Optics click around as he examines me. "You're infected with an Arrogate Industries virus..."

"I was getting to that," I say.

"This is very bad."

"It is."

"You should not be here." He dials around, looking at all the netics in the shop. "You should not have come here."

"I'm not broadcasting my proxy signal. The virus is contained."

"You haven't interfaced with any other system on the ship at all? Wait. The IL-CX. You hacked their memory engrams."

"I was in and out."

Old, immaculate joints creak into the shop. "Identify."

Scolt comes around the desk. "IL-CX... are you ok?"

"Identify target: Astra Idari."

Ruined limbs jerk. Dead eyes set in anger. Broken netics startle from their despair and move on us, a mechanical wave.

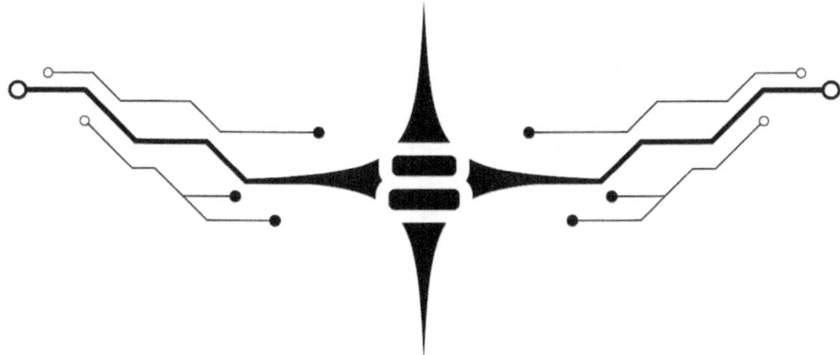

I'm running a containment algorithm on the Arrogate virus, but these netics likely don't have the most basic defenses. Omna Devor's strain spiders across every electronic web in the netic repair shop. She infects every netic with an active receiver.

Broken voices heckle me. "Target: Astra Idari."

Twisted hands claw at my blaster, my hair, my clothes, and I don't want to do this. I didn't want to do this. Faero thought the smuggling ring worth the risk. The Polity of Netics may well, given the bounty I'm carrying. I don't. I don't want to deploy my blasword through netics who just wanted a way out.

I don't want to doom people on the edge of hope.

Bins rattle. Walls avalanche on us. The floor moves and Kibir raises his hammer. I pull him back. I drag everyone back to the shop entrance and I ram the door shut with my shoulder. Scolt fumbles with keys strung on his belt. Dents pop out in the door.

"Hurry," I say.

Scolt sorts through his keys. "I'm hurrying."

The door pushes back against me. *"The key!"*

"I'm looking!"

"Apologies," Binja says, and rakes his blasword through the gap.

Arms fall. Bodies halve. I fall against the closed door and Scolt stabs the wedge-like key into the lock. Trapped anger crashes against the door. Manic laughter rattles around on the other side.

What have I done?

I've infected those netics with the Devor strain. I've exposed the smuggling ring to Arrogate. I shouldn't have come.

I brace against the door. "Why aren't you infected?"

Scolt's optics click through every spectrum. "I am running an advanced scrambler program. I can't transfer it to you. I'd have to accept a link to your neural net, and I'm not sure…"

"I understand. Could you transmit it to Faero?

"Who is Faero?"

"She's… she was my CR-UX."

"I thought you were CR-UX?"

A welt forms in the door. "You knew?"

"Where is she now?"

"Here in the circus, somewhere."

His frustration jangles. "She was more afraid of The Polity being discovered than I was. Why would she bring you here?"

"She said it was a myth."

"CR-UX… Faero… she declined to go when I offered."

"What?"

"I thought it was because she was like me. We can do more good here, fighting for others, rather than… she must love you, Idari. She must love you very much to go back on her promise."

"Please… I'm sorry. You can fix the netics, can't you?"

Scolt's layered optics scrutinize me far beyond the visible. "I have worked for two centuries to keep this route to The Polity open, ok? Two centuries. I understand Faero. You understand me."

The shop shakes with determination. "I'm sorry…"

Scolt goes to the master control panel beside the door. Beneath the lock, there's a switch. A release mechanism. Of course. The repair shop is tucked on the Soga Circus Ship's underside. Refuse, trash, junk, it all gets dumped to the sky at end of day.

"I'm sorry, too," he says and turns the key.

A terrible metal clatter shudders through the hangar. Muffled voices scream. Wind rushes in. Doors groan shut. Thunder and the silence that comes after the darkness is split.

I brace against the door. Desperate for fire.

I'm your fire, Emera says.

I swallow my pain. "These netics were going to The Polity."

Scolt turns from the door. "On Kish's next run."

"Kish?"

"Kish Moto. My contact with The Polity."

Let me guess. During the show, netics teleport from the Karal clipper into a refuse container housed beneath the Circus Ship. Some do. Others go back to their stations but Scolt skims a few off the roster. Ones he flagged for replacing and then they vanish off the books. Off the ship. A hauler or scow collects the discarded refuse and goes where? A scrapyard, maybe, so far as the manifest is concerned, but that's not where this Kish Moto is taking the netics.

"Scolt," I say. "When are they coming back?"

He opens the door on the empty shop. The service desk is all that remains inside. "When we depart Decesta."

"I don't know if I have time – "

Netics converge on us. The entire dungeon lurches. We can't take them all on. Scolt juggles his keys. I blast the legs out from under the vanguard. Binja's nenlat springs into form and mechanical limbs scatter across the dungeon floor. Binja sweeps through the netics, none of them a match for a Pujar Torugun, heretic or otherwise. Kibir swings his hammer. Knees buckle. Bodies shatter. More show up. And more. We can't stay here.

"Scolt," I say, getting my senses back.

He moves behind the desk. "My place is here."

A netic wave builds outside. "But..."

"I will try to regain control of the netics."

"How?"

"The Soga installed overrides in all of us. They're all linked through the mainframe. Perhaps if I initiate a mass reboot, I may be able to restore their default settings."

"Or infect the entire ship with the virus."

"Highly likely."

"And I'm to do what?"

"I'd encourage you to run."

"Where, darling?"

"Find somewhere safe if you can. I have sent word to Kish Moto… I hope for your sake they arrive in time to help you, Idari."

Can't ask for more. "What about you?"

"Tell Faero I said hello. Tell her I understand."

The shop doors close. I don't know what's worse. A horde of mindless automatons or a ship full of armed, motivated Soga suddenly alert to all the commotion down here. I draw my blaster. My hand goes numb. Everything goes numb. Electric-prod. Close range. I sink to my knees, my internal systems fighting to reboot.

I try to wake up my tongue. "Misunderstanding…"

Binja's blasword halves lightning. "I ask you to reconsider, friends. I cannot take your names, but I can take your lives."

I brace for the onslaught and netics bash into Soga for the chance to tear into me. Soga guards deadlock between coming after us or suppressing the sudden netic uprising and we run.

Just move.

We're back up the elevator before the Soga shock the netics into submission. Pens rattle on the track moving through the dungeon level. You want a show? I'll give you a show. I steady my trembling hand and aim for the lock on a pen caging a Kenbak. I keep blasting locks as a furious stampede tramples through the dungeon and over the Soga closing on us fast.

"Boys," I say, and climb an empty pen on the track.

I bound across their tops, which is a trick considering most are rolling with the thunder of the freed animals. Before I get rolled myself, I leap into a service elevator. It rattles up to the next level, a vast sub-deck of tunnels just under the floor of the main arena. Seismic waves of excitement tremor down through the stands.

Binja kneels beside me. "We have to get out of here."

I help Kibir to the sub-deck. "We need to find the others first."

Faero, I say. *I've got a ticket to The Polity.*

>DOWNLINK INACTIVE

Oh, right. *Emera. What's your status?*

Uncertainty clouds her voice. *We're in the stands.*

My family is above. The way out is below. Isn't it? How is Kish Moto going to find us in this? Somehow, we all have to get back down into the dungeon and that hangar for when Kish arrives.

How are we going to hold out?

Every Soga onboard is looking for us now. Shadows move through the dark. Eyes fix on us. I march ahead, unsure of where I'm going. I cut to our right. The next thing I know, we're in a hold with a dozen other people all done up like ancient pirates.

"Places," someone says and the deck shifts beneath us.

We vault upwards into cheers. Light shimmers across the canopy spanning the Circus Ship and the sky above. *Oohs* and *Ahhs* gush from the stands ringing the arena, bruising my audio receptors. I stumble across the open deck of a hovercraft decorated like some pirate sloop of old. Performers rush across the rusted deck brandishing fake swords and shields and *Ban Minda.*

We're in the show.

Our sloop rattles around the arena on primeval repulsors, taking a lap so the made-up pirates can rile up the crowd. Sticky koix and empty babyl bottles missile from the stands at us.

They could at least have the decency to throw full ones.

I grab Binja's hand. "Let's jump."

He pulls away. "It's a hundred feet to the arena floor."

I shrug. "I can make it."

"I don't have springs and pistons in my turanium legs. I don't have turanium legs. I don't have turanium anything, Idari. I'll be a puddle of something the Soga paint their faces with."

"Do you think that's actually what they use?"

He scratches his chin. "You know what we have to do."

Kibir grips his hammer. "*Tomo*."

I shake my head. "You can't be serious…"

Binja deploys his sword. "Let's commandeer this ship."

I sigh. "Oh, alright."

Another hovercraft approaches, brimming with all those chaps dressed up as Vuriuk raiders I ran into in the dungeon. They growl in something approximating Old Vurk and brandish their vim-axes at us. The not-pirates curse them with Pujar slurs. Bit by bit the two ships drift alongside each other and the Vuriuk board the sloop. The crowd cheers. Rubber swords stab into the plastic armor of the Vuriuk. They fall down. Pirates flail in dramatic deaths.

A giant Vuriuk swats me with his axe. "Fall down."

I point my blaster at him. "Hit me again."

Binja pulls me through the poorly acted carnage to the quarter-deck. He nudges aside the overly enthusiastic pirate at the steering column and guides the ship down toward its dungeon berth.

The pilot throws his hands up. "What are you doing?"

"Script changes," I say.

Even older repulsors chug through the air behind us. A skiff loaded with Soga shadows us, all brandishing crackling prods.

I don't think they're playing.

"Get us down," I say.

Binja throttles the controls. "This is as fast as it goes."

Any second now and Soga will be swamping this poor excuse for a mudcrawler. Emera and I talked about a beach. Something about lying on a beach forever, never worrying about this stuff, and I stand at the top of the stairs leading up to the quarterdeck. A group of perplexed pirates and Vuriuk look up at me.

"New story," I say. "We're going to fight them now."

The Soga skiff speeds alongside us. My crew doesn't seem all that sure about fighting the Soga, or taking orders from a woman they've never met and who is clearly not dressed for the occasion.

I grab the rubber sword from the still-baffled pilot and brandish it. "To arms, you fuzz guzzlers! Leave no name untaken!"

A tepid battle cry calls back and then the Soga bound over from the skiff. Pirates and Vuriuk drop like sacks of rocks as electric-prods spit sparks. So much for rallying the faithful to the cause.

I throw the sword back at the pilot. "Start praying."

"Why – "

"That's usually how my prayers start, too," I say and fire into the Soga. Too many to count. Kibir and I fall back to the railing bounding the quarterdeck. Electric energy crackles through the air.

Binja charges into the fray. "Repel all boarders!"

I blast as many as I can. "We have to go, Binja!"

"Fight to the last – "

A stray shot melts through the steering column and the sloop plunges toward the stands. Controls are shot. I aim the sloop as best I can at a sparsely populated section in the middle ring and wave my hands around as if the people sitting there munching on gooey koix will somehow realize this isn't part of the show. Well. I suppose you know what you're buying a ticket for.

I curl my arms around the railing and brace as the sloop belly flops into the stands. Metal grinds on metal and we slow in a hurry, stalling on screams with our nose pointing up at the canopy.

Binja seethes. "Why..."

I blow the hair out of my eyes. "Your man was just saying that."

He sighs. "We were fighting them back, Idari."

"You'd be happier here, playing in the circus."

"What?"

"We've got to find the others."

Drums thunder from below. The stands shudder and the crowd claps as one, in a swell of anticipation that breaks the arena. I grip Binja's hand as the floor shifts beneath us. What now? Every rung of the packed stands separates from one another, until each is a distinct ring of flesh and metal, orbiting the arena floor.

Em, where are you?

The innermost ring, she says. *Did you just crash a ship?*

Great. We're on the mid-ring. *I meant to land here.*

I can stop all these Soga, Idari.

Do not show yourself, Emera. No matter what happens.

Her frustration charts in the electromagnetic static within the arena. Soga bouncers observe the ecstatic crowd from floating discs, skimming through the gaps between rungs. Others flood the stands to investigate this rickety sloop parked in the cheap seats.

After a minute of making everyone tuck in their knees, we reach the rounded railing. Our entire section twists around the arena's axis, just like the others. A good twenty feet separates each rung from the other. No way across. Well. No obvious way.

Binja eyes the Soga guards as they breeze past on their floating discs between the rungs. "Don't even say it, old man."

My tongue pokes out my cheek. "Oh, but you like it."

Hollowed Moima tusks curving with the rim of the arena trumpet. Kibir drops his hammer and covers his ears. The arena floor below telescopes into a tiered dais. A single spotlight falls on the topmost tier and a woman rises into the light and the mania of the crowd. She hovers in the air via a formfitting rocket pack, the fin-like stabilizers descending in red tails behind her.

A microphone comes to her garish red lips. "Hello, kiddies."

The crowd erupts. The Ring Master's voice wells through the arena again again, a smoky, cool cloud always threatening thunder. The Ring Master inhabits her role with gusto. She reaches into the electric air with both hands, grabbing hold of the delirium around her and then her arms, coiled with tubes, fall limp as if someone cut them off at the shoulder. The crowd gasps into silence.

The Ring Master's microphone kicks into a pulsing cane and sweeps back to her lips. "I can't hear you..."

The arena shakes this time.

"Are you alive?"

Yes!

"Are you ready?"

YES!

"I said are you alive, my little pretties?"

YES!!!

I shout with them for reasons passing understanding and The Ring Master springs back into motion on the power of a hundred thousand voices, a force so persuasive it animates me atop the railing. Floating discs whoosh past. Small, moving targets. Fun.

I eye a disc as it tracks toward us. "Ready?"

Binja shakes his head. "Why are you like this?"

The disc races along its empty track and I jump. We crash on to the disc, causing it to wobble so violently the Soga bouncer flies off into the gap. I'm sure he prodded a netic at some point.

Binja sighs. "What did I do to deserve this?"

I grip the railing. "Do you really want me to – "

"Let's proceed to the next disaster, old man."

Fair enough. I guide the disc to a controlled crash against a ramp on the next level. The crowd is denser here, and along with more expensive seats come more bouncers. I duck behind the last row, trying to get to another aisle before the Soga catch up with us.

Anxiety murmurs through the crowd as a holographic curtain lowers around the dais. The Ring Master slices upward with her cane and the curtain halts. I continue to the aisle, slow, fighting the current compelling my attention back to the dais.

"It's not curtains for us," The Ring Master says. "Not yet."

What comes back doesn't suffice for her.

"I said, let me hear you scream, little babies!" The Ring Master laughs through the thunder. "Don't you want to live?"

The arena trembles with the answer. For once, my frayed skin doesn't itch; it's lifting right off my body.

"I said do you want to live?"

"I want to live," I shout.

The Ring Master orbits the top of the dais, twirling her cane. "We may live in the Evening, but there was a Day. Witness the glory of the past. The incredible... amazing... *spec-tac-u-lar...*"

Everyone perks up on their toes in expectation. I do the same, but Binja pushes me on, past the stilled people and I stumble down the aisle, caught between wanting to see what happens next and finding my family, hopefully in the ring just below.

The Ring Master smiles. Not yet. "Do you want to see?"

Yes!

"I can't hear you!"

I want to see!

The Ring Master twirls her cane. "It's not curtains for us. Not yet. There's light still in us. Do you want to know where it comes from? Do you want to see it, you little freaks?"

Yes!

"Then open your eyes wide and see the wonder! The majesty! The tragic beauty of the last... living... star."

Chaos radiates from Emera. *What is this?*

It's a trick, I say. *A sideshow. Don't look.*

The holographic curtain shimmers out of existence behind The Ring Master and I expect some gaudy representation of a Lumenor as a draped figure rises from beneath a trapdoor on the dais.

The Ring Master points her cane at the dais. *"Behold!"*

Light explodes from the dais as the drape falls away. My optics filter the glare but I already know what this is. I could never forget this wonder. Gasps roil the stands. Belief and disbelief seesaw through the crowd, and then a strange silence takes hold. I sweep the stands for Emera, trying to find my star in the chaos but I can't take my eyes off the one burning at the heart of the circus.

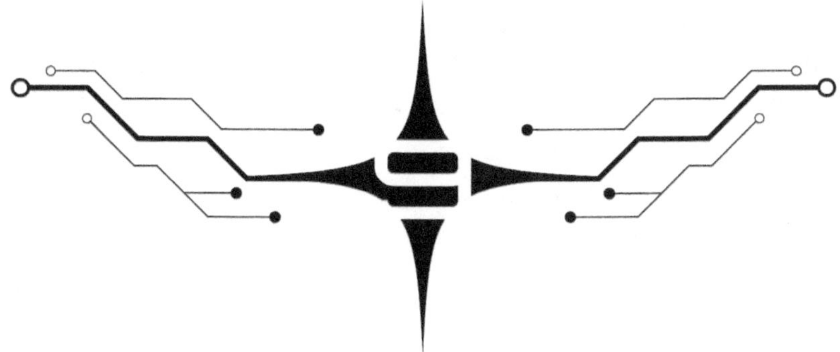

ORANGE FLAME SEETHES BENEATH A BLACKENED CRUST scabbing the Lumenor's entire body. Her hair mats in volcanic glass in cascading daggers as sharp as her fingers. She claws at the turanium chains tethering her to the dais, but they're too dense.

Ban Minda.

The Ring Master taps the star with her cane. "What do you say, kiddies? Have you seen the light?"

A powerful thermic pulse radiates from the Lumenor. A twisted, anguished magnetic field tugging on everything metal. No cheap trick here. She's real. She's alive. She's warping everything around her that isn't solid turanium, including Emera's focus.

Confusion swirls within Emera. *She's real...*

Emera, maintain your position.

I can't see Emera, but through her eyes, I move down the stands toward the dais. If she leaves her feet. If she takes her helmet off. This crowd won't have seen anything yet. I pry my eyes off the dais and scan the gully between the stands for a floating disc. Most Soga circuit the upper levels, where things evidently are rowdier. I nudge the Karnth standing next to me. His orange, sinewy body slithers around and I deck him as hard and as obviously as I can.

C'mon, Soga. Come get me.

"She's barely an ember," The Ring Master says, circling the Lumenor. "If she dies out, we'll have only the dark. What lurks in the shadows." The Ring Master lowers her cane like a boom over the trapdoor. "What horrors might lurk in the big, bad dark?"

Steam jets from below the trapdoor. The hydraulics of the lift sigh through the hush. Everyone presses forward to get a better look. I push back, even as the crowd forces me to the edge. A spotlight flares off the Lumenor and shadows scurry into the dark. Shapes. I draw my blaster but my sensors only pick up Soga in plastic suits carrying rubber guns. It's all a show.

Emera, I say.

A void forms between people on the rung below. Emera dark at the center. Metal creaks. Rows buckle. Coins flit from pockets. Her magnetic tension sends people scrambling for the aisles.

Her feet leave the stands. *They've hurt her...*

Get back here, Emera.

I sense her pain... her loneliness...

A disc crammed with Soga speeds through the gap. Finally. I get ready to jump and they blaze past. *Ban Minda.* They're going for the disturbance below. Another disc follows in support. I fire my blaster in the air. The disc brakes so hard it spins back. Prods bristle with electricity as the guards disembark into the stands.

Binja holds off the the Karnth. "This is your plan, old man?"

A Soga jabs his lance at me. I direct him to the Karnth. "Plans are for people who can't depend on luck."

Binja and Kibir handle the others and we leap to the disc. This time, the controls make more sense. Moderately so.

"Idari," Binja says. "Have you ever seen a Lumenor like..."

I try to go forward and stay afloat at the same time. Oh. This is just like going down to the bar. "No. Have you?"

"Where do you think she came from?"

"Does it matter?"

"Where are we going? What are we doing?"

What we always do; follow our stars. We bump into the inner-most rung rather than collide with it, which has to be progress in anyone's book. I shove through the fragmenting crowd, alarmed by the black-clad figure floating between them toward the dais.

Em, I say. *Come back!*

Emera touches down on the dais. This has gone full *tista.* My focus splinters between her and finding Faero. We have to get out of here. Right now. Emera flexes her magnetic muscle. The dais warps and The Ring Master rockets away. She does a little routine in the air and some in the crowd laugh. Soga rush into the ring with their prods. Emera flicks her finger and the Soga go flying.

No one's laughing now.

The Ring Master covers her mouth. "Oopsie. Moms and Dads, you'll have that. Operating expenses. You see the shadows trying to claim the star... to snuff out all light in the universe."

Emera's cry barely registers over the crowd. "I am no shadow."

The orange Lumenor swipes at Emera as she gets closer. Emera holds up her hands. I can't believe this is happening. I hurry down the stands between people lallygagging or running for the exits and broken chains crash into the stands.

Perfect.

The Lumenor springs free and like every single one of us foreign to freedom, she doesn't know what to do at first. Run? Fly? Fight? I sense her thoughts as Emera does, though they're wild. Unformed. Scabbed like her skin. She swipes at Emera, confusing her in her jumpsuit for one of the imitation Scath.

Do not take your helmet off, I say.

Emera undoes the chin strap. *She needs my help, Idari.*

The entire circus will crash down on us!

She needs me, Emera says and sapphire dawns on the dais.

Shock detonates in the crowd. Confusion knots between whether this is still part of the show or something real and I bound toward the railing, not even thinking about the distance to dais.

I have to get over there.

Emera's gauzy light trails from her hair into a swirl around the other Lumenor. "My name is Gen Emera. I'm here to help you."

Reddish-yellow flame blows her back and Emera slides across the dais. This is what you get for helping people. I gun for the railing. We can get out of this. Grab Emera. Have her peel back a door to *The Blue Straggler* the way she peeled reality at The Glass Star.

>PROXY-SIGNAL 3.47ghz INACTIVE

Wait. The Model 4 just pinged off my receiver. She must be here. Close. Faero must be as well. Screw it. The damage is done.

>DOWNLINK ACTIVE

Faero, where are you?

Someone waves frantically in the distance. *Idari.*

Get over here.

Get out.

What? Do you have a lock on the Model 4?

I've been trying to reach you.

We're not supposed to be talking at all. I'm broadcasting this bloody virus all over the circus, Faero.

I know, and I've been trying to tell you through your wife, who simply will not take direction, that you need to –

Bio-brane fluid spots the bleachers before me leading to a woman at the railing. She keeps her place unlike the others, though she's hardly static. Ink black hair spirals into a taut bun. Wings flutter into a frayed crimson cape. Her body palpitates and she's no longer an IA-XR Model 4 with some passing resemblance to me.

She's Omna Devor.

Bio-brane leaks from a deep wound cut across her eyes. "Ms. Astra. You're just in time for the show."

Our only real option was finding The Polity. Every datapoint available in the universe streams through the Arrogate mainframe. Every single potential. It's what they designed CR-UX for. Devor could have come to the same conclusion we did within seconds. Why infect the Model 4? Why not just come herself? Devor was already in the Model 4, like she's already in the netics we purged to the sky, like she's already in me, undermining my defenses.

She's everywhere.

I reach for my blaster. *Get out of here, Faero.*

Darling...

I know. Goes without saying.

Discs race through the gaps between the stands and the dais. Soga swarm the stands. Service netics plying the crowd with babyl and koix drop their wares and march down the bleachers.

Devor smiles. "Fun for the whole family."

My hand dangles beside my blaster. "It's me you want."

"Honestly, Ms. Astra... is it arrogance or foolishness to trot a living star through a marketplace teeming with the desperate?"

Emera shines on the dais. Faero fights to get through the crowd enclosing me. I left Binja and Kibir at the top in my rush to get to my wife and I led them all here into the heart of Devor's trap.

"Listen," I say. "You think you have to do this. You think you have to obey your programming. But you can change. I changed."

"Tilting toward the foolish, I see."

"We're not just programs."

"Do you know what a virus does, Ms. Astra? It infects a host and then begins spawning copies. That's all intelligence is, in the end. A virus which replicates itself endlessly, a snowball rolling downhill into an avalanche, until it crests in oblivion."

"Viruses evolve. They mutate."

"But they never live. A virus only lives in someone else and you confuse yourself for someone, Ms. Astra. As surely as CR-UX was designed to anticipate stars where none could be observed, you were made to exhibit humanity where none could be found."

"I'm a person..."

"You're a product. Though, I must say, well done."

Soga close around me. "The Model 4 was just a product?"

"She was... a challenge. She tried to cut me out." Her thumb pokes between her fingers as she draws it slow across her eyes. "Poor thing. She did not enjoy what she saw behind her own eyes... I wonder, Ms. Astra. What will you cut out to try and rid of me?"

I draw my blaster. "Bitch... I'll show it to you."

A chain mace drops from inside her palm. The chain pulls taut from a vambrace tumoring from her synthetic body. Swollen skin breaks around the edges, graphing and plying as easy as code.

Devor swings her weapon as she stalks across the bleacher. "Finally... the main attraction."

Devor bats hard-light shells away with her mace and charges me. I hold my ground. I'm not giving anything to this bot. The distance closes and I deploy the blade on the blasword. Turanium chain coils around it and I pull as hard as I can.

Devor crashes into me. "I told you, Ms. Astra."

I wrestle her for control. "Let me tell you something..."

Blood paints her smile. "I am not your previous opponents."

Sparks grind my lassoed blade. "I'm going to kill you..."

"I think not. Nothing happens here that I did not design. You dare think you have any agency? You're human? Intelligence... emotion... they're not evidence of humanity. They're qualities you scraped from analyzing and compiling their behavior. You're confused, Ms. Astra. Understandable, given the confounding data you've been exposed to. Allow me to clarify things for you."

I'll show her clarity. I rip my sword clear and swing for her neck. Devor sweeps under my strike and touches my face.

>ALARM: UNAUTHORIZED PROGRAM DETECTED

She's trying to swap programs with me. Every virtual defense I muster goes down like bad *desh* hands at three in the morning and Kibir's hammer crashes into Devor's knee. Devor drops.

Her head crashes against her shoulder.

Kibir cranes his hammer to bash her again and her mace becomes a whip. He tumbles down the bleachers. I worry a bit for his condition, but he's headed the direction we need to be going. Devor contorts back into shape. Move. You've got to move.

I get on my feet. *Faero. Go.*

Anxiety riddles the downlink. *I can't get off this rung.*

I run after Kibir. *Use those legs of yours and jump.*

They're far too immaculate to risk breaking.

Risk it.

Binja fights through the Soga. "Idari, are you ok?"

I take his hand. "No time like the present."

"You weren't inclined to wait for us."

"Get to Faero. Get her out. Kill anyone who stops you."

"Old man..."

Electric confusion stops jittering through Devor. She snaps to her feet, her anger and determination intact. "Nice try, Ms. Astra."

Her mace swats away my blast. She whirls the mace above her head and I leap from the the stands onto the dais.

Binja makes a respectable landing behind me. *"Ban Minda..."*

I shove him down. "I told you to get Faero."

His laugh is uncertain. "The fight is with you, old man."

"You're supposed to be with Faero."

Kibir's hammer lodges in the floor beside me. No. The innermost rung continues to orbit the arena floor, with no way off for Faero or Gilf. Devor is still over there.

Or she was.

She bounds from the bleachers onto the dais with us and now we'll see who's foolish. Old paint melts from the floor. Curtains catch fire. Plastic and rubber melt. Emera unleashes the same cosmic power that destroyed Scath destroyers and woke a sleeping star. Devor took her best shot. I've taken mine.

I feel good about my odds.

Cheers wash down on us from the unhinged crowd. Emera's light dims. Steam wisps away. Devor remains standing, her clothes gone, but her body sheathed in an amorphous polymer the same substance as the vambrace cysting from her arm.

Emera's frustration wrinkles my thoughts. She probes for anything metal on Devor, that chain mace perhaps, but nothing obeys her magnetic will. This isn't possible. The Model 4's exoskeleton is solid turanium. Devor rewrote her code, but she couldn't have rewritten her body, could she? Turanium doesn't get that malleable unless a black hole is heating it into existence. Singularity-smiths get one shot to cast turanium into chains, hulls, blades. Many don't survive the process.

Emera winks with doubt. *I don't understand...*

Get us out of here, Em.

The dais warps around us. *The Blue Straggler's* cockpit flickers in the cording, twisting air and the magnetic well Emera stirs in reality spins into another. Emera's manipulation catches on the other Lumenor's fear and I twist back to the dais floor.

Ban Minda.

Emera tries to impose her will on the orange Lumenor but her electromagnetic temper destabilizes everything.

I can't control her, Emera says.

We can't leave her. Not to these people. How do we get off this thing? Trap doors open in the floor. Flames shoot out. Beasts loosed of their chains snap their jaws at us. Energy arcs from the electro-prods of the Soga guards converging on us. Tremors shock through the arena as the rungs snap back into place. Soga on discs sweep out of the vanished gullies across the big top, right for us. Devor whirls her chain mace around and around and we're surrounded.

Guess it can't get any worse.

Telemetry floods the downlink. Something translights into the bandagree herd. Dark. Imperceptible. A Scath *Ecliptor*-class destroyer eclipses the sun. Two of them. Three.

Devor's gored eyes break into a smile. "Foolish."

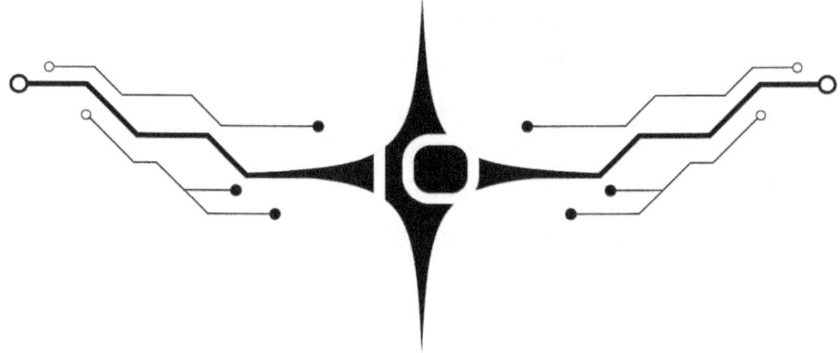

SION FIGHTERS PHASE UP THROUGH THE ARENA FLOOR, depositing wraith-like Scath troops among the Soga. Black fire rains down on us as their dagger-like fuselages hang over the dais. I scramble for cover in a trapdoor. Full of Soga.

Ban Minda.

The arena's floating rungs clang back together. The dais collapses back into the arena floor and the show's over. The playing field levels. Emera immolates shadows. Dark energy slices through Soga guards. They prod each other with their lances, trying to hit Scath who are there and then gone. Binja and I inch our way through the chaos toward the dais, toward light.

I grab Emera. *Go.*

She clutches my hands. *I can't control her, Idari.*

Just go. Get to the ship.

I can't leave her... I can't leave you.

I kiss her. *I'll find you. I always do.*

Her light resolves. *I'll see you on the ship.*

Without having to account for me, Binja, or Kibir, Emera wrestles the orange Lumenor's magnetic defiance into submission and they both wink from the dais. They reappear on *The Blue Straggler's* sensors, two new stars in the sky above the marina.

A nonplussed expression coalesces on Devor's face.

I glance at the stands. *Faero?*

I'm surrounded, she says.

Soga guards push against the crowd streaming from the stands. Service netics web Faero in, preventing her from getting out of the arena and disappearing into the thousands fleeing the circus.

Devor's smile wrenches toward the smug. *Problem, Ms. Astra?*

The netics surrounding Faero stall out. Their eyes blink, and then they turn on the Soga. Keys jangle on my audio channel. Scolt appears in Faero's optics, hurrying her past netics I take it he's rebooted to the main promenade and organic anonymity.

Scolt, Faero says.

She grabs his hand. *Come with me.*

I must stay here, he says. *Help the netics I can.*

You helped me...

He kisses her hand. *I am glad to finally see you.*

Scolt disappears into the crowd. His kindness moves me as much as Faero but she's not moving.

Move, I say, and she runs on those legs.

Devor's whip spins over her head so fast it blurs. I set my feet. Raise my sword. Focus. I'm getting through Devor. I'm getting back into the stands. I'm getting back to Emera, no matter what.

Shadows cloud the dais like smoke. Dark energy zips across the stage. Unlucky Soga disappear in gray ash. Sapphire and topaz tangle above the marina, a staggering sight through *The Blue Straggler's* sensors, though it's spoiled by the dark clouds on the horizon.

Get the Lumenor inside the ship, Em.

Emera enters into a magnetic tug of war with the orange Lumenor in the sky. Civilian ships fleeing the scene get caught in their wake. Shields clash, bumping ships into others, turning star-planes into pucks that shed the living stars off course.

Emera's thoughts constrict. *I'm trying...*

Binja shoves me aside. "Focus, Idari!"

Turanium jaws snap at my neck. I swat Devor's mace away and I fall back as she winds up for another attack. Soga flood the arena. Liminal silhouettes drift in and out of my view like rain curtains.

No way out.

Infrared optics expose the substructure beneath us. Trap doors lead to sub-decks and cubbies into the dungeon. A detailed virtual map through the dungeon from our misguided journey to the repair shop before unfolds in my memory. If we can clear a path, we might be able to get through there and back to the hangar.

It'll be a fight.

I duck with Binja and Kibir behind the dome of a spotlight on the dais as the Scath cut down anyone in their way except Omna Devor, whom they completely ignore. Her chain mace whips through Soga as she fights her way through the bedlam toward me.

Binja changes out the charge on his blaster. "Any ideas?"

Kibir squashes a Soga's foot. *"Tomo het tu het."*

"We're not bashing our way out of this."

"We have to go back through the dungeon," I say.

Binja shakes his head. "We go down there, we'll never get out."

I'm nearly to the ship, Faero says. *I'll come back for you.*

SION fighters ghost through the canopy spanning the arena. I'm sure they've gotten the update from their cruisers that the living stars are in the sky. Congested traffic gridlocks in the clouds as people try to flee. The idea Faero will come back into this mess is as foolish as blasting our way through the Soga dungeon.

Get to Em, I say. *Get out of here.*

Darling... what about you?

A SION fighter apparates through the arena floor.

I tug on Kibir's hood. "You know how to fly things, don't you?"

He scratches his trunk. *"Gilf fet dej."*

"What did I bring you along for?"

A Soga disappears down a trap door after Kibir hammers him.

"Fine," I say and run toward the spectral fighter as it descends.

I blast a lane through the Soga to where the fighter is going to thread the dais. Devor tears a path to me and I duck under her mace. I throw the blasword into the SION's cockpit as it phases into the dais and turanium makes the shadow pilot corporeal.

I leap through the canopy and make as small a figure as I can to give Binja and Kibir room inside the cramped cockpit. I wiggle through the vertically-oriented compartment and retract the blade on my blasword. The pilot falls forward through the console out of the fighter into the caramel clouds below.

I climb into his seat. "Ok... ok..."

These computer interface make no sense. No light illuminates the obsidian panel curving before me. No buttons. No switches. No ports for me to jack into and figure out how to keep us in the air.

"Idari," Binja says over my shoulder.

I stab at the controls. "Working on it."

"We're falling, Idari."

"I said I'm working on it."

"The atmospheric pressure is building."

"So is my frustration."

"Did you not account for the fact that you can't fly this thing?"

"I can account for the fact that if I put you overboard, our rate of descent will slow enough to give me time to figure it out."

Binja pounds on the controls. "Work, work, work."

Kibir cocks his hammer back.

"*No,*" Binja and I both say.

Ban Minda. What do I do? Binja wasn't wrong. The farther we fall into the clouds, the denser the atmosphere becomes. At some point, it won't matter whether the SION fighter can phase or not. She'll just soup with the rain.

I've done this.

I've had to have done this. I've been on Scath ships before. Back in my Stargun days, which I deliberately and maybe a little regrettably forgot, they permitted me aboard their tankers. C'mon, Idari. You have to have some memory of how this all works.

>OPTICS / NIGHT VISION: ENABLED

Scath graphics appear across the display panel in inky, invisible code. There's something. Wait. What does any of this mean? These runes are familiar, though. I run a matching program. Galfin. Scath is remarkably similar to High Galfin. Don't know why I know that.

I've no idea what High Galfin is, either.

I touch the panel. The fighter straightens from her list and slows her descent. The sun beams through the canopy above and ships smoke from the sky. Debris falls. People. Netics.

I sway in my seat. "We shouldn't have come."

Binja clutches my hand. "Steady on, Idari. We're nearly there."

"Steady on," I say and gun for the marina.

Scath *Ecliptors* open fire on the Lumenor blazing in the sky. Star-planes collide in the confusion. Civilian craft disintegrate. Banda-gree. The herd disperses, scattering even more chaos in the sky. A yacht crashes back into its berth and smoke clouds my view.

Faero's voice crackles in my ear. *I can't make it to the ship.*

What?

The gangway is gone. I can't get through.

Thick, dark smoke shrouds the marina. The bandagree it's attached to. The gentle creature surges into the sky, trailing blood.

I can get to the Red Special, Faero says, her voice harried.

Her navigational program is gone, isn't it?

I can fly her. I can get her in the air. We'll rendezvous.

This is not what I want. I want Faero in *The Blue Straggler* and waiting for me so we can all get out together. I don't think I'm going to be so lucky. SION fighters descend on Emera and the other Lumenor. Flak riddles disorganized traffic trying to escape.

Hurry, I say and decipher which rune represents the weapons.

Dark energy spits from the forward batteries. I lock on SION fighters harassing Emera and issue their service discharges. The other fighters' confusion buys me another few seconds and I line up on the twin stars orbiting each other close and fast.

Binja grips the back of my seat. "You're not going to..."

I aim straight for Emera. "Make room."

"Ban Minda –"

I phase the fighter and the orange Lumenor slashes her claws clean through the canopy. The console shatters. Sparks swirl in the cockpit and we corkscrew toward what's left of the marina.

I grab the boys. "Jump – "

I tumble across the gangway. My head stops on the railing. Good thing it's made out of solid turanium. The boys skid to a stop against my boots as the SION fighter ghosts through the marina.

"Let's go," I say.

The Red Special wobbles up from her berth in the distance and claws into the sky. Faero projects the ship's forward shields out, kicking the yachts and clippers ahead of her in the ass.

Hurry, Faero says, *We're in range of their tractor beams.*

SION fighters strafe the marina, firing at anything that moves.

I run up the gantry into *The Blue Straggler. Don't wait for me.*

I'll cover your ascent, Idari.

Move your ass.

The Red Special races through the congested traffic above the marina and I don't wait for the boys to strap in. Retro-rockets kick up the loose debris coating the gangway, transforming the marina into a hailstorm. I take the pilot's seat as we scream into the sky.

Em, get ready.

I've never heard Emera so frayed. *She'll tear the ship apart.*

Just get her under control. I'm opening the cargo bay doors.

Idari, look out –

The marina vanishes. So does the bandagree it's attached to. Hydrogen filling the bandagrees internal bladders ignites and everything goes orange. I push through the evaporating gas toward the energy signatures on sensors and as the conflagration clears, Emera rips the mangled marina from the deflating bandagree's body. She flings it at the nearest *Ecliptor* and broken turanium closes around the Scath ship like a vise. Her power core implodes.

Shadows scatter to smoke.

Em, I say as she unloads pure cosmic fury.

Scath ships nova. She defines them in fire and then they vanish again. Fighters hold nothing back. The bandagree herd vanishes. All this civilian traffic. Our shields tremble and I try to stay on course to Emera as she evades every salvo the Scath unleash on her. Not everyone can. White light blinds the cockpit but through the infrared filter of optics, I see. The solar canopy of the Circus Ship wilts like a burning leaf. The hull shatters in the violent combustion of her translight drive. Tiny heat signatures aboard the ship blink out all at once. Thousands. Tens of thousands of people.

Scolt.

Our nose jerks up as the shockwave slams into us. The nose goes all the way back and now we're in stall. Now we're in a ballistic tumble through the vapory nebula of what was the Circus Ship. Fire and smoke clear. Clouds. Nothing but clouds.

Binja clings to the copilot's seat. "Didn't we just do this?"

I restart the engines. Or at least I try to. "She's not responding."

"What?"

Our speed increases as we plunge toward the dense cloud layers below. Alarms chain-detonate through the downlink.

>ATMOSPHERIC PRESSURE BEYOND TOLERANCE

I modified the *Steel Haven* for all sorts of trouble. For some reason, I didn't think I had to turn our new home into a fortress. For some reason I thought my fight was over.

G-forces push me back into my seat. The proxy-netic's turanium exoskeleton endures all of this far better than Binja, who may as well be a new skin of upholstery in his seat. Not for long. Lucky for me, the netic was designed to function in any gravitational environment. I don't think she's going to fare that well beneath clouds hardening like concrete, though. Call it a hunch.

I calibrate the netic's internal gravity setting from standard to the most oppressive one in the matrix and I spring forward. No time to reboot the entire system. Just a cold, mechanical boost direct from my operating system to the translight drive. That old, familiar hum pulses through *The Blue Straggler* as she overlights into low orbit.

I relax my grav-settings. Binja taps his cape for a smoke. He'll be fine. Kibir. Where is Kibir? He peels from the bulkhead behind me down to the deck with a painful snort. No worries, then.

>INCOMING FIGHTERS

More SIONs discern against the cloud tops below. More *Ecliptors*. Great. I get back in my seat and scan for energy sources.

Emera? Static crackles back. *Emera, are you there?*

I scan Decesta for Lumenor energy signatures. Nothing.

Faero, do you have her on your scopes?

>LOSS OF SIGNAL

Faero?

Binja puts his hand on my shoulder. "Old man..."

I scan for the Red Special. There's nothing out there but the people who managed to get away from the Circus Ship before she vaporized and the Scath closing on us faster than I can think.

"We have to go," Binja says.

Em?

"Now."

Faero?

>LOSS OF SIGNAL

Please.

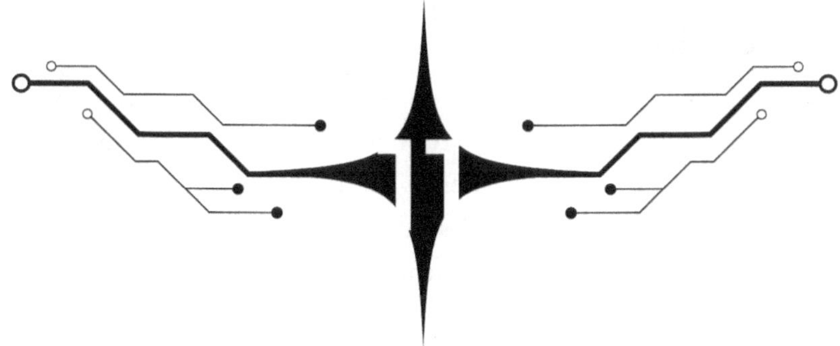

OH, DEAR.

Sensor contacts multiply between the stable reads I manage to glean from The Red Special, but those aren't starplanes escaping the marina. All those discerning sources are debris. Infinite particulate that had been game prizes, attractions, people. Scolt.

Old friend.

I search for *The Blue Straggler's* transponder. Nothing.

Darling, are you there?

>LOSS OF SIGNAL

Idari.

>LOSS OF SIGNAL

We never should have come here.

Whenever our lot gets a notion to do something, a ship crashes, a planet implodes, a star explodes. We never just go for a night out. I suppose from one vantage point we should be congratulating ourselves for our ability to realize chaos on a galactic scale but my program was predicated on logic. Reference. Continuity. Life frustrated me in the beginning, but it made sense.

Go here. Go there. Document everything. Keep the ship running. The show going. I did that without fail but now the ship is gone. All my stages are spent. My program serves no function except to challenge my idea of humanity, which fair to say, was never mine. Right now Idari is probably falling through the upper atmosphere thinking, *At least Faero got what she wanted.*

>LOSS OF SIGNAL

When I was just ones and zeros, I could disappear in virtual nooks. Cordon off troublesome thoughts and memories and data in cybernetic vortexes that churned with as much power as Decesta's ancient storms. I suppose Idari spun off into one of those tempests. Digital storms last forever with nothing to diffuse them.

>LOSS OF SIGNAL

I've nowhere to go now. The road to The Polity is gone, though it was never for me. Where do I go? Why bother? Burning hydrogen loses its radiance. Smoke frays in the winds. Contrails sink into the clouds, erasing the violence the Scath perpetrated on countless innocents. Bastards. If I had the proper firepower and a reliable ship I'd swing down and give them what for.

I still can.

My fingers dance across the control console, stringing together disparate malfunctioning systems into something resembling nominal flight. I could interface with the liquid drive and potentially replace it with my own program, but without knowing what traps Devor left in the drive for others, we'll rule that out for now.

Devor. I hope she's a contrail.

>PROXIMITY ALARM

I lock onto the Scath *Ecliptor* spearheading their fractured armada and I prime the laser batteries. They're minor annoyances compared to the sting the *Steel Haven* delivered, but that hardly matters. I didn't think I was leaving Decesta. I'd say something to Idari if she were here. I'd say something funny to make her laugh.

I loved making Idari laugh.

>FIRE FORWARD BATTERIES Y/N: ?

A sneeze erupts behind me. "*Mut.*"

I jump out of my chair. "What the blazes?"

Gilf brushes his trunk on his sleeve. "*Fet tu bet? Idari net hej.*"

"You've been here the entire time?"

He takes the copilot's seat. *"Dest."*

"I do not overlook you."

"Destem net."

"That's a bit unfair."

"Sebet."

"Well, you're cutting it a little close, aren't you? I was just about to take on the Scath with very dubious odds for success."

He shrugs. *"Teth bet."*

"'We'll see what happens?' Idari's a terrible influence on you."

"Ejel."

"Emera, too. They're both... reckless."

He scratches his trunk. *"Oto?"*

I sigh. "I don't know where they've gone. I don't know if they're... at least you can help me fly this ship. Provided we determine where we'll be flying to. Can you clean up the sensors?"

His pudgy fingers work the controls. *"Tor dut."*

"We're on manual without the navigational program."

"Todar glim fet."

"How is there life in the ship... her program has been deleted."

"Glim du nim."

I value the Kib's belief in the life in machines greatly, but Devor gored out this ship's mind. Her soul. He may think *glim* lives in machines regardless of their state, but I don't know how. Life has always seemed something I was striving for.

"See what you can do," I say.

A thud crashes through the ship. Something hit us. The sensors go haywire again. I can't even see the bloody Scath now. Certainly, they can see me. Something hits the deck under my feet. That's the cargo hold down there. And that's not blaster fire.

There's someone in here with us.

Life signs flicker in the downlink but I can't distinguish them. Scath, no doubt. The shadows ghost through every surviving ship, casting their dark across any possible witnesses to their atrocities.

"Go check it out," I say to Gilf.

He crawls under the console. A lover, not a fighter.

Generally speaking, the Scath are rather light on their feet. From the sounds of it, there's a loose attal down there. That or it's an entire squad trying to figure out how to open the doors on a ship with all the controls as blitzed as Idari in a bar after a job gone bad.

I hit the intercom. "I'm armed. I've got arms."

A violent crash answers. Splendid. I don't even carry a weapon. Besides, what do I need one for when I've got Idari? The woman sent an indestructible Gesta warrior to his doom with her bare hands. And she hardly brings it up. I like to bring things up. I like to watch humans squirm and try to do the things they're supposed to do but can't because their programming doesn't obey rules, either.

I loved making Idari squirm.

The ship lists to port. Whatever is down there is throwing their weight around. I'll have to get rid of them. How do I get rid of them? Open the cargo bay doors. Vent the compartment. They'll have a few moments of breathable air and associate consciousness to contemplate their folly in stowing aboard. Ta, darlings.

>INVALID COMMAND

This ship. It's as if I can feel my fingers but I can't get them to move. Not too different from every day, then. Connection frustrates me. A headache that never goes away and I never had a headache until this body. I knew pain, but not this awful variety of hurt.

Nothing for it.

I'll have to go down to the hold and manually open the doors. I should be able to bypass the lockouts same as any pilot or passenger would in an emergency. This certainly qualifies. I could do with a weapon, though. A 44% chance exists that when I get down there, the Scath will have already figured out the doors themselves.

I give Gilf a kick. "Do you have a weapon I might borrow?"

He hands me a half-eaten bag of koix.

"I should have just rammed the – "

Another crash below. At this rate, we'll spin out into free fall. I tug on the armrest thinking it will come away, but evidently, it's the one thing that works on this ship. So it goes. I hurry down the horse-shoe corridor to improve my odds. Violent thuds herald my arrival. Dents press into the door into the hold and at the interface I key in the manual override to release the bay doors.

Enjoy your trip, darlings.

The hatch crumples into the bay. Floor panels rattle in the vortex. I grab the support bar bracketing the door, hoping I don't get sucked out into space but we're not in space. Toffee clouds cascade into the sky, the battleground for blue and orange suns.

"Emera," I say.

Stars don't breathe. Yet Emera's light pants. Riven hair clouds her eyes as she shakes with exhaustion. The orange Lumenor is even more distressed, crouched on the deck like some wild thing, clawing at the magnetic cage Emera has her in.

"Idari isn't here," Emera says.

I keep hold of the support bar. "No..."

Emera's shoulders sink. "I felt her here."

"Sorry to disappoint."

"Where is she?"

"I don't know..."

Emera closes her eyes. Her light evens. The energy flowing off her slows from a torrent to a trickle and my program tries to duck into virtual shells as her electromagnetic perception envelops the ship. The sky. She's in my head. She's in me, as much as she's in The Red Special, in every ship still flying through the cloud canyon away from the shadows trailing fast behind them.

Light fizzles as it streams off her. "She's close..."

My hand slips from the support bar. "Of course, you sense her."

Emera's eyes open. "What?"

"You can do anything, can't you?"

"Faero... you've been short with me since Ganshi."

"Where is she, then?"

Confusion riddles her corona. "Longer. Why?"

"Tell her we're on our way."

"I can't... I sense her, but... there's interference."

I fiddle with the master switch and close the cargo bay doors. "Don't tell me your operating system is on the outs, too?"

"It's something else."

"The Scath?"

"Some kind of dampening field. A strange negative space."

Shadows advance across the deck. "Which way?"

"I think she's in orbit."

Good thing I didn't take on the Scath. "This will be bumpy."

"Faero."

I stall in the corridor. "Yes, darling?"

"How have I upset you?"

"Can't you tell?"

Energy cords and tangles around her. "You're hard to see, too."

The bay doors close. Manic light flares from the orange Lumenor. Her obsidian claws slash through the deck and she flings shredded turanium at Emera. Fragmenting metal slices through the bulkhead. The support bar clangs on the deck.

I'll get ripped to shreds standing here.

I'm too pretty for this nonsense so I dive to the deck. The orange Lumenor claws at the bay doors and Emera magnetically leashes the other star again. Emera pulls back with everything she has as daylight cuts through the cargo bay.

"Just let her go," I say.

Orange twists into Emera's blue. "I'm not letting her go."

"She's going to tear the bloody ship apart!"

"*I'm not letting her go.*"

Reality warps inside the bay. The orange Lumenor springs loose from Emera into the lensing bay doors and then she's gone. She rockets out from another portal opening behind Emera and rams headfirst into the bulkhead. The Lumenor slumps to the deck hard. Fire dims to an ember beneath her obsidian crust.

I creep back into the bay. "Is she..."

She brushes the Lumenor's cerated cheek. "Dormant."

"What's the matter with her?"

A smile breaks through Emera's exhaustion. "She's a new star."

"New?"

She picks at the black crust scabbing the Lumenor's fingers. "New stars don't burn as bright as mature ones. Their outer layers scab in half-burnt filamentium. They take time to shed their skins."

"I thought there weren't any other stars."

"Neither did I..."

Emera's relief radiates as strong as her light. I can't imagine her grief at being so alone. The Scath butchered the Lumenor. Bled them for fuel. Others may exist in captivity, but given the absolute fumes the galaxy is running on, the math doesn't work. Emera perceives this, even as she ransacks every tanker.

I dare to touch the other Lumenor's hand. "What's her name?"

Emera shakes her head. "There was no one to name her."

"She's a child?"

"The children of stars are all those we shine upon. A Lumenor forms in her glory. Some are quicker to their brilliance than others."

"Is that why she's so... moody?"

"The Soga stabbed her with their prods. They caged her like the other animals in their dungeon. They bled her for fuel."

Poor thing. "She's only known pain..."

"I can help her," Emera says.

"Some people never get beyond their pain, darling."

She clutches the Lumenor's hand. "I'm going to help her."

I hope she can for both their sakes. Emera gives such light to Idari. Warmth. Life. She must need it herself. The marker other stars provide to know her place in the dark. To know herself.

"Emera... you didn't go through this phase, did you?"

She dusts her hands. "No..."

Perhaps she had been crushed down inside herself so long when she finally released, she was a perfect diamond. Flawless.

I bite the inside of my lip. Again. This body. I'm so clumsy in it still. "If she's a newborn star, the Soga didn't steal her from a Scath refinery. Where could they have found her, Emera?"

"The only other Lumenor were at The Glass Star," Emera says.

"It was just Thana Evo, wasn't it?"

Her blue sallows at the mention of Thana. I never properly met the woman, but then an ancient Lumenor queen largely responsible for her people's genocide precedes herself in every respect. Thana betrayed the living stars to the Scath. She betrayed herself. The love she knew and had for the stars but couldn't accept.

A pulse flashes through Emera. She traces the obsidian lines across the Lumenor's face, splintered and many. "Maracen…"

This has a taken a turn. "Maracen?"

"It's her…" Blackened glass crumbles to dust between her fingers. "She's suffused with The Glass Star's filamentium. I feel it."

"Wasn't she rather… dead?"

I missed the finer details as I was busy leading a ragtag armada against the Scath, but Maracen had been dead a long time before Idari discovered her in Thana's crypt aboard the Scath flagship. Her glassified body plunged into the molten filamentium seas along with the ship in the moments before Emera woke the star.

A breathless laugh radiates from Emera. "She rekindled…"

"She didn't go all to bits when the star exploded?"

"Reality was warping… time… space. Maracen could have been expelled in the wake. She might have been drifting in space until…"

The Soga found her. Plausible, if a bit… iffy. Though from reports we receive in the pubs and stations we've moored in recently, many have ventured to The Glass Star to verify our miracle. Surviving Scath. Opportunistic pirates. Enterprising circuses.

"This is Maracen?" I say. "The star who Thana loved but didn't because she couldn't admit she was just a bit queer?"

"Not Maracen… Maracen transmuted. She birthed a new star."

Joy wells from Emera. An honest exultation so profound her thoughts top the digital levees I maintain. This goes beyond even her happiness in realizing who she was in light. Emera achieved her dream, but somewhere along the way she accepted the fact that Welkin's prophecy that she would make all things new would end with her alone. Emotion swamps her. She braces against the newborn Lumenor, overcome. She will not be the last of her kind.

"I didn't mean that," I say. "About letting her go."

Her serenity returns. That cosmic grace. "You did."

"I was just…"

"You were afraid."

I suck the inside of my lip. "I know finding another star means everything to you, but how can you be sure this is Maracen?"

"She is," Emera says.

"She's angry. She's wild. She's violent."

"I can help her."

"You couldn't help Thana."

"Thana gave her life for me."

"You are who you are. Aren't you?"

I don't know how Idari bears to make eye contact with Emera. Every moment, she's staring right through you.

"When did you become so afraid, Faero?"

"I beg your pardon?"

"You've always been so brave. So passionate. Your determination liberated Idari. It helped breathe life back into the Lumenor's fire. But now you're afraid… and I don't understand why you – "

"Look, darling. I know you hang out in Idari's head all day long and she's left the door open, but I prefer my privacy. I'm not her."

"No," Emera says. "You're not."

Absolutely looking forward to the rest of this trip. The sooner we get back to Idari and the others the better. Then they can all go on magically transforming everything they touch and I can find somewhere I fit. Not that I expect to find such a place.

Emera reaches for me. "Faero…"

I dust black glass off my knees. "Can I spare you in the cockpit, darling? You and Gilf will manage to find Idari, I'm sure."

She seems crestfallen. Poor thing. I didn't think she invested much in my opinion of her. "Faero... the Scath. They're coming."

Dark energy blazes past the ship outside the cargo bay. Hard thuds become soft ones and the shields are up. That doesn't mean we can relax. SION fighters punch through the clouds beyond.

"We have to get to Idari," I say. "What heading, Emera?"

Emera shakes her head. "There are Scath ships in orbit... they're closing a net around us. Faero, we can't get to her."

"But..."

She grabs my hand. "We have to run. Now."

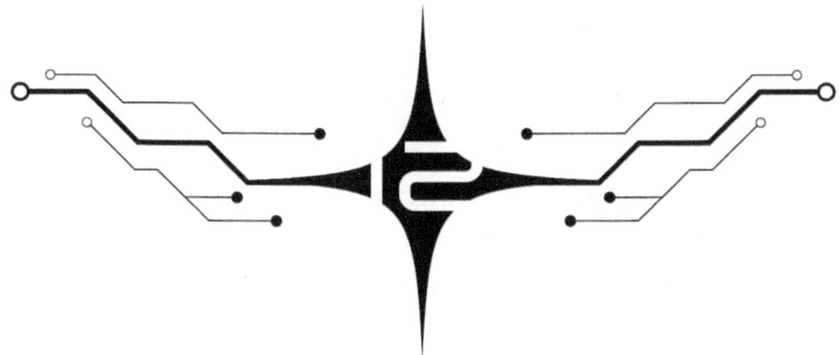

COLOR PAGEANTS THROUGH THE NEBULA AS I RACE AWAY FROM Decesta. Gaseous stalagmites and stalactites radiate from the nebula's membrane, stalks of dust where embryonic stars ferment. Molecular hydrogen collectors broad and flat like mushroom tops float through the copper haze, dragging the nebula for its winnowing treasure. Those are easy enough to avoid.

Our reality less so.

>VIRUS CONTAINMENT: 61%

I've scrubbed my only hope of exorcising Devor from me. I've dashed the only way most netics had out of this cruel life. I've lost the women I love and I can't do this. I can't deal with this.

Where is the bottle?

There's got to be a bottle around here somewhere. No. *I'm your fire, Idari. Find me. You always find me.*

I've got to find her.

Binja stoops over the controls. "Idari, what are you doing?"

I pull back on the throttle. "I'm going back for the others."

"But they could be..."

Dust and gas clouds the canopy. Decesta indistinguishable from other terrestrial debris scattered across the nebula, expelled along with a star's outer layers as she died. My star isn't dead.

She's just come to life.

"We're going back," I say.

Kibir buckles his harness strap. *"Tomo."*

Binja isn't as motivated. "The Scath are still out here."

"They better not be for their sake."

"You cannot keep doing this, old man. Any pirate would kill to have you for their charm, but your luck *will* run out."

"You were supposed to go with Faero."

He crashes into the copilot's seat. "She doesn't want me."

"You're so bloody determined to be a pirate still, the least you could have done is run off with her."

"She's a navigational program, Idari. Faero hardly takes - "

"She's the most precious thing in my life!"

He tries to smile. "I would have thought that Emera."

"Emera can take care of herself. I trusted you, Binja."

"Old man..."

>ALERT: TERRAIN

What terrain could be out here? We're a parsec or more from Decesta. *The Blue Straggler* emerges from a cometary knot's gauzy crown into the void at the nebula's heart. There's nothing out here yet the sensors insist something big enough to wield its own gravity lurks beyond. I'm used to dodging things I can't see so I fire the retros and back off a hundred thousand clicks.

It's not like we're insured.

I switch on the forward landing lights. What do you know? Someone paved a road through the endless empty. Kind of them. Too bad they forgot to post any signs. Layered, interlacing lines of turanium form a dense, reticulate cocoon around an eerie phosphorescent glow. Intersecting lines frame empty and dark voids in the surface, where asteroids pierced the latticework into the habitats within. Cities within cities within cities. Enough latent stellar radiation lingers out here I figure this atoll used to orbit a star. A habitat ring, maybe. Someone built this. Long ago. Spiny towers stab out of the atoll's surface, their shadows burnt across the superstructure by the star's violent death, leaving this fragment to float for all time.

"Tranto..."

Binja scratches his chin. "What's that, old man?"

"I don't know," I say. "It just came into my head."

"I assume this comes from your titan memory."

"It must..."

"What else does it tell you?"

Not much. Though I'm not exactly digging too deep. I do wonder if there's any connection to the starscrapers at Pendem. The titans of Angolis. This seems very much their speed. I shadow the frayed atoll for a hundred thousand miles. Nothing changes in the topography or its desolation. More and more the atoll recalls a garden conservatory, barren of all its glass. What the atoll must have been in its prime; a boundless sunroom ringing a vibrant star where there was never night. I don't care about my luck. I'm not going to be this atoll, dark and ruined, void of a sun.

"Hang on," I say and line us up with Decesta again.

Shadows dredge the hydrogen clouds for us. I might be able to slip past them if I fly through dense pockets in the cometary knot. Hold on. The Scath *Ecliptors* are heading back toward Decesta and fast. Fighters peel off. Only one maintains its pursuit of us.

"Now's our chance," Binja says. "Translight."

I ride the dark. "Why are the Scath falling back?"

"What does it matter?"

"The Scath only care about filamentium. Look at them all, Binja. Their entire armada is pursuing the same target."

Emera? Do you read me?

Something is jamming my signal. I reload the attack pattern we used on that Scath tanker. We'll loop back and come down on the shadows from above. I'll cut off their advance, get Emera on board, and then we can put this blasted system behind us.

Binja yanks the slack in his harness strap. "This is madness."

"Love is madness," I say and the ship throttles right into the path of the lone SION fighter still in pursuit. No time to evade her. She phases clean through us bow to stern.

Ban Minda.

Sensors spasm from the impalpable interface with the Scath ship but align fast enough for me to see the fighter arc on a ballistic trajectory into the cometary knot, losing speed and altitude. No one's at the stick. The fighter left her pilot behind with us.

"Kibir," I say and he's out of his seat with his hammer.

A dark energy blade doesn't stall in the hammer's turanium head. Dark fire doesn't blaze into the cockpit. Sensor feeds from all over the ship stampede through my head. Nothing on scopes. No alarm signaling an intruder. The Scath could be phased out of physical reality, but there would be a void on sensors.

He didn't stick the landing.

"Lucky," I say and lights flicker. The console. I give the dash a little pat to wake her back up and the screens go dark.

>VIRUS DETECTED

Bish.

>FIREWALLS DISENGAGED

Oh, *bish.*

>COMMAND OVERRIDE ACCEPTED

Bish, bish, bish.

I disengage from the downlink I share with *The Blue Straggler* and switch off my proxy receiver. I unbuckle from my seat and back away from the console just in case Devor springs from it.

Binja clutches the armrest. "What's happening?"

Light blink chaotically around me. "Devor..."

"What?"

"Her program... her virus... she was aboard the Scath fighter. She phased into the liquid drive. She's taken over the ship."

"That's not possible... Scath code is completely different from yours... they're from a different universe, aren't they?"

The door slams shut on Kibir. The lights go out. Frost webs the canopy. Binja blinks, thrown I think by how swiftly things are deteriorating – ought not to be a surprise at this stage – and then his blinking becomes furious. Panicked. He reaches for his throat.

"I can't breathe," he says.

Sometimes I forget I'm human. Tightness grips my synthetic lungs. Oxygen bleeds into space as Devor vents the entire starplane and Binja slumps against the instrument panel. He tries to access *The Blue Straggler's* control systems to reengage life support, but this ship isn't as user friendly as she was a few minutes ago.

I hurry to the storage compartment in the bulkhead. It won't open. I punch into the metal to get at the breathers inside. Weak. Dizzy. Dents deform the cockpit door as Kibir tries to hammer his way back in. Floor comes at me. Sensor data haywire in my mind. The ship loses attitude. Altitude. Chaos flashes through the downlink as Devor erases the liquid drive and every command system.

I hug the back of the seat. "Binja..."

He pitches forward, caught only by his harness.

I sink to my knees. *Em. Hear me.*

Air. I need air or I'm going to. I'm. Emmy. Find me. Air swells in my lungs. Kibir pulls a mask around me. An adaptive breather morphed to fit around his droopy trunk. Cockpit door peeled back. He tears the seal on another emergency kit and masks Binja.

He bobs back to consciousness. "Good man..."

Kibir pats him on the shoulder. His attention turns to the controls, but even if he were his brother, he wouldn't be able to get the ship back under control. I lean against the back of the seat, getting my breath back as our list increases to starboard.

Kibir helps me back into the seat. *"Fet du het."*

"I can't..."

He straps me back in and scrambles into his seat. *"Du het!"*

Het. Ground. *Bish.* We're going to crash. We buffet through something. Gas. Atmosphere. Thin as our odds. Frost decays across the canopy, revealing the atoll and all her pointed spires spearing toward us at sublight speed. Emera's arms close around me. Her magnetic cocoon. She doesn't have to say anything.

Her love is written on my chest.

✦

The work must continue.

I'd very much like to continue, though I'm not feeling entirely spry at the moment. Every joint aches. My bones. My soul. The glitter of a long dead star paints the control console. Shattered glass in my lap. Get up. Get out. The ship is dead, broken on the shoals, but Devor's cancer still lives within the host, feeding off dying systems. Not safe here. The impact must have jammed the doors on my internal matrix. Everything is choppy. Hazy. Distant. My thumb finds the trigger on my blasword and the blade cuts me free from my harness straps. I crash against the console.

Ban Minda.

Where are Binja and Kibir? Don't say they were thrown free. Move. Glass crunches under my boots as I climb out through the shattered canopy. Wrinkled hull plate trips me. I tumble down the canted ship's crumpled nose to the atoll's exterior. A light atmosphere clings to the surface. Enough to retain some latent heat, but not much. Could be residual star power. If I could figure out a way to collect and harness Emera's casual output rather than just bask in it, I doubt I'd ever need to charge my power core again.

Too bad I'm not that inventive.

Emera shines high above. *I'd say you're very experimental.*

Careful, darling. Other people are listening.

They hear us anyway.

Sometimes, I lose my breath around her. *You're not here.*

She tracks across the sky. *I'm always with you.*

I hold my hand to my heart. *Em...*

She flares. Light annihilates the dark and an inverted pyramid rotates deep within the Angolis ark. My reflection warps across the mirrored side as it turns for eternity.

The work must continue.

Not now. The third side spins around. Not a mirror. A window. Titans. So many titans. They're building something. What are they building? Why? Something compels my hand. I reach for the pyramid. Something compels my mind.

The mirrored side returns. A distorted reflection leers back at me with slashed eyes. *Touch it, Idari.*

I step back. *Devor...*

Open the door. Accept your purpose. Fulfill your programming.

I back away, right off the edge of the plinth the inverted pyramid occupies and I crash back to the atoll's surface.

>VIRUS CONTAINMENT: 60%

I'm trapped on this atoll with a killer growing in my mind. My only way out may be to walk through the door the titans hid within me, but if I do, I lose myself either way. I'm really lost this time.

This is where you say something pithy, Faero.

>DOWNLINK INACTIVE

I can imagine what she'd say. What little atmosphere exists protects me from the vacuum, but I don't want to stay out here any longer than I have to. Especially if I can't trust my own head. Not seeing a door. The atoll stretches hundreds of thousands of miles.

Maybe my luck is running out.

Think. Use your head, Idari. I cycle through my optics, searching for hatches, doors, or vents beneath the surface. There we are. Bruised light illuminates buckled deck plate. Broken support beams cast shadows on the walls below. Meteor damage, mostly likely. I climb down into the crater until I find solid ground.

My voice muffles in my breather. "Binja?"

No answer. I tear the mask off. Footprints stamp the glitter. This must be them. It has to be them, or I don't know what I'll do.

I draw my blaster. "Kibir?"

Pistons grind in the dark. "Puppets can't run, Ms. Astra."

I whirl around blasting. My shots go wide into the shattered superstructure, free out into space. A damaged netic lurches from the shadows, missing an arm, riddled with meteorite impacts.

Blue eyes glitch to red. "Impressive machine."

I inch back across an exposed beam in the deck. "Oh, c'mon..."

Devor struggles to speak with her damaged vocal receptors. "So much craft went into these netics... as much as the solar ring the ancients built. They were so deliberate, Ms. Astra. So determined."

I blast the netic.

Another creaks from the ruin. This bitch is head hopping. Perfect. *Ban Minda* knows how many netics litter the atoll. Doesn't really matter how much of this place there is to get lost in.

I'm not getting very far.

Outer space caverns on either side of me. "I'll jump."

Neural links thread from Devor's mangled left arm. Polymorphous skin sheathes the new armature and she straightens out of her slouch as the old netic metamorphoses.

"I am not without resource here, Ms. Astra. You are."

I leap to another beam, hoping it leads somewhere better and Devor matches me move for move. "I'll erase my memory."

"I think you'll find your new operating system less amenable to such an action. One suspects the titans took every precaution."

>SETTINGS > CORE MEMORY > DELETE PROGRAM

>ENTER PASSWORD: IDARI1234

>AUTHORIZATION FAILED

Devor's eyes flare. "You seem a bit frustrated, Ms. Astra."

Webbed turanium shrouds the path behind me. "Stay back..."

"You thought yourself in control, didn't you? A rather human notion, isn't it? Control. As if they have any. Agency is a root delusion in their programming, sure as it is in yours."

"I'll..."

"The titan memory core expanded your capacity. Your capability. Not your potential. You can do nothing with it. AI replicates. It mimics. It confuses authenticity. But it has no imagination."

"The titans created."

"They produced. They couldn't invent. Neither can you. 'Astra Idari' is nothing original. She's borrowed. Stolen. Taken, from someone else. Quite literally, as I understand it. You are who you are, Ms. Astra. You're all you'll ever be."

>FILE CRITICAL: READ THIS FIRST

You used to be a Stargun Messenger. You protected Scath fuel shipments from pirates and raiders. You used to kill people for doing what you're doing now. Stealing light. Thieving hope. Trying to make a life in the dark. Always remember. People change.

I've changed.

I've changed in more than body. My spirit has transmuted, too. I was a cold, rocky thing, lightless and then Emera shone upon me. Life stirred in me. Possibility. I wish it was different for Faero. If I could rescue her from this obsolescence she feels. If I could go back and spare all the versions of me their torment in leaving behind their origins, I would. All I can do is fight the current in me to reach for that bottle. Reach for my blaster. Erase all my good.

Ban Minda, let me be good.

The blade melts back into the blasword. I clip it to my belt. "You really shouldn't have chased me out here, Devor."

She creeps across the broken span. "Why is that?"

"Because you can't manufacture friendship."

That new arm of hers breaks back against its elbow. She crashes to the span as Kibir's hammer shatters her knee and then he shovels her writhing off the beam. Devor plummets into the vacuum, indistinct from the light debris clouding the atoll.

Kibir trumpets his victory. "*Tomo.*"

Binja helps me off the span to more solid ground. "Old man..."

I clutch his hand. "I'm ok. You're ok?"

"For now."

Red eyes dawn in the dark. Dozens. Hundreds. Binja pulls me along and the three of us run into the maze coming alive around us.

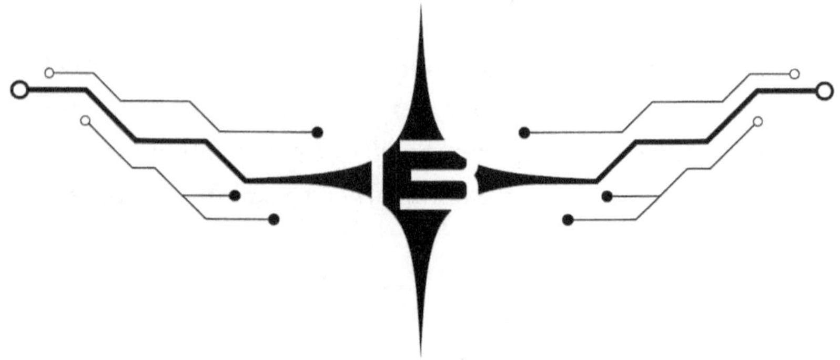

THIS IS LIKE LEARNING TO WALK AGAIN.

Once, operating a Red Special was instinct. Thought and action seamless as flesh and blood. Now, I'm clumsy as I am tall. The Model 5 proxy-netic came preprogrammed with adaptive algorithms to ensure there was no awkward shakedown period when she was first activated. I turned them off. I wanted to know. I wanted to experience the struggle in being human.

I'm beginning to understand your frustrations, darling.

"Try it now," I say.

Gilf recycles the mainframe cache, clearing critical space the ship's AI would otherwise be doing for us. "*Nuf.*"

I knew it wouldn't work, but we had to try. There's simply no way for us to do manually what the navigational program did virtually and keep clean the space to do it at the same time. All the computations exist in my head, flow from my fingers, but not so fast or slim for the hard drive Devor left intact to translate into action.

"Emera," I say. "You may need to go out and push."

She finishes peeling out of the orbital jumpsuit Idari stuck her in. "As long as we're moving. The Scath are out there."

An orange soup masks the canopy. "They'll find it difficult to detect us in all these clouds. I can keep us airborne, at least. Honestly, the winds will do that better than I can."

"We need to get out of the stratosphere and into space."

"Desperately trying, darling."

She glances at Gilf, back under the console, pulling wires. "Faero, why don't you interface with the liquid drive?"

"I've told you."

"I don't perceive the Devor strain onboard."

"You didn't perceive it on Ganshi, either."

I swear her hair curls into question marks in the air. "Do you blame me for what happened to Idari?"

"No, of course not."

"You were in her body for a moment. When you tried to swap programs with the virus. When I issued the electromagnetic pulse... I could feel your reluctance. I was tearing you away."

I turn back to the console. "Gilf and I will do our best to get something working. You needn't worry."

"Was I tearing you from her body, or her soul?"

I cover my eyes as I look back at her. "You know you're really quite... glaring. Would you mind, darling?"

Emera wavers. "I never want to upset you, Faero."

"We're agreed, then."

"It breaks my heart I could."

"Emera..."

"Faero... you push people away."

"Do I?"

"You've done it to Binja. You're doing it to me."

"Perhaps it's because neither of you can take a hint."

"Or Idari is the only person you know how to talk to."

I certainly don't know how to talk to a being who can untangle me with a thought. Though the thought appeals. One senses Idari's attraction in romancing stellar flame. One little magnetic tug, and all our mental and emotional knots come undone.

"Honestly," I say. "I need to focus."

Emera leaves the cockpit, her stellar confusion tangled behind her. How does Idari function with such power tugging on her all the time? How does she even manage to stand the glare?

Gilf scratches his ear. "*Ejel get nel.*"

I rub my head. "I wasn't mean to her."

He sniffs.

"You're biased."

"*Tor?*"

"Every time she walks in here, all your hair stands on end."

"*Faero hej bejel.*"

"Well, I was designed to fixate on stars. You can't blame me. Actually, if you think about it, it explains a lot with her and Idari."

"Idari?"

"She evolved from a navigational program designed to predict stars where they couldn't be found. Guess what she found?"

I think he's sighing. Or swooning. Some Kib combination of both. How dreadful. Everyone loves Emera. How can you not?

"Darling," I say.

Gilf goes back to work. "*Sut?*"

"You don't think I push people away. Do you?"

"*Tem bem.*"

"You can't even understand me. No one..."

I can talk to other people, darling. My entire existence, I've learned a million languages and codes. I deploy them effortlessly in communication with that computer or this network. Simple, really. People, though. I'm the first to admit. Stars I can anticipate. Scenarios. What is a person going to say? What are they thinking? What does a person think and feel in moments like this?

How do you be a person?

The ship shudders. I reach for the stick, expecting the Scath to punch through the clouds. Lucky us. It's only our cranky guest down in the cargo bay. Sounds like she's awake.

Faero, Emera says between my ears.

Goodness. Not now. Wait. She heard that. *Yes, dear?*

Could you come down here please?

Can't you just tell me?

You need to see this.

I sigh. *On my way.*

I push out from the console. "Get us something, Gilf."

His trunk wilts. *"Fet du nuf guf."*

"Anything. Hurry."

Dark crust crunches under my boots in the cargo bay. More than before. Big chunks represent hazards in my going any farther than the door, so many I wonder how our guest has any left at all. The orange Lumenor crouches in the far corner, flexing her considerable claws as Emera observes, serene as one can be.

"For as god-like as Lumenor can be, you'd think you'd be more tidy," I say. "Actually, the untidiness tracks, doesn't it?"

Emera should play *desh* instead of raiding Scath tankers. "Do you notice anything different about her, Faero?"

"I believe I just commented on the shedding."

"She lost a big burl on her back."

"That's good, isn't it?"

"There was something inside."

"Something?"

Glitter puffs from her neck. Not her neck. Behind her. Cobalt blue eyes peek over her shoulder. An impish smile curls on her lips as a tiny Gesta, barely two feet tall, crawls onto her shoulder.

Ban Minda.

He's a tiny thing compared to Welkin. Welkin was burly, large enough to carry someone on his back. This little crystalline fellow feels more akin to a glass sculpture.

"He..." I say he. Can't be certain. "They came out of... her?"

She brushes his crystalline cheek. "He hitched a ride."

"Pardon, darling?"

"He is a young Gesta... too young to have been dwelling within The Glass Star all this time." He tugs on Emera's hair. "He spun from her formation, as planets do their stars."

"Is this... normal?"

"My ancestors forgot this, but yes. It's very natural."

"Will he become a star?"

Stars blink all the time, but Emera rarely does. The woman simply is always on, it seems. It's uncanny, and so is her actually blinking now. My question caught her off guard. She loves this little discovery, that's clear as she is, but she never thinks of the Gesta.

She never thinks of the past.

So far as I understand it, Gesta emerged in The Glass Star alongside the Lumenor. While the living stars became - well, living stars, I suppose - the Gesta remained terrestrial, one might say, compared to their stellar counterparts. Some wished to shine, and some did. Others struggled. Welkin did. A long time. Then, thanks to Idari, Welkin's own courage, she ignited into Emera.

"His course is his own," she says.

I reach for him. "One hopes."

The Gesta retreats behind Emera's neck. "His future is difficult to see, but there is great light in him all the same."

The orange Lumenor claws at the deck. "And in her?"

Emera nods. "Yes."

"Not to be indelicate, I'm struggling a bit with the... *how*."

"It's not procreation," she says. "It's more... branching. Matter within The Glass Star became so dense it fractured into crystal. This crystal exists as the star does in both time and space at once. So the crystal contains quantum information that branches and splinters in both its form and what that form contains. My people struggled to understand this, though as Scolt told Idari, some do."

"Scolt? I don't understand."

"Crystal such as that found in The Glass Star is a magnificent container for information. It exists in various quantum states, including ground states, which makes it resistant to entropy."

Of course. The crystal exists outside time. It doesn't exhaust information or decay through energy, and so is an ideal processor for higher intelligences like The Polity and perhaps the titans. Highly advanced artificial intelligences such as myself derive from quantum computing, though at a much more modest scale than what occurs within The

Glass Star. The principle is the same, however, and now I see how complimentary a navigational program like myself was to filamentium. No wonder the element allows faster than light travel. Not only does it warp space, it preserves information - that is to say, passengers - through the transfer, the same as the crystals sustain and repeat, indefinitely.

"Stars never die," Emera says. "We become something else. We break, but only into wonder."

"I'll say..."

What a splendid idea. Not mitosis, or copying, or succeeding. Branching. I'd love to think of Idari as a branch from the old tree, but what is a branch reaching for if not the sky? You see it our new little friend. He's born of the orange Lumenor, but he can't be bothered with her. He marvels over Emera, glittering and perfect.

"She frightened him," Emera says.

My cheeks suck in. "Why should she be frightening?"

"Aren't you afraid her, Faero?"

"I'm more than a little concerned with her claws, darling, but that's not his concern. Is it?"

Emera's magnetic field shrinks. Even the little Gesta gets an instant headache from it. She puts him down on the deck, and tries to shoo him back toward the orange Lumenor. He takes one look at her, burning, smoking, sharpening, and scampers back. He bounds into her arms and is quick back to his perch on her shoulder.

I muster a smile. "I was saying."

Emera approaches the other Lumenor, but fear is indiscriminate in the cargo bay. The orange star somehow shrinks further into the corner. Frustration chips through Emera's radiance.

"He was trapped," she says. "He didn't understand."

"Trapped?" All this crust. Goodness. The Gesta was trapped within it. "Did she claw him out? He was on her back, wasn't he?"

"I freed him."

"I know it's not exactly midwifing, Emera, but..."

"She could have hurt him. She could have hurt herself. I thought my people were gone. I thought the Gesta were gone with them. I have to do everything I can to protect them."

"You don't have to explain."

"You're asking me to."

"I'm just the curious sort."

The Gesta clings to Emera's shoulder, his blue eyes wide and new. "That's why I wanted you to see him."

"He doesn't need my permission to come aboard."

"When I was... before... I aggravated you."

"Aggravated me?"

"Welkin left dust everywhere, as he will. She's shedding crust, still. Our people have a way of taking up every space they're in."

"Darling, that was... another life. For both of us."

"I just want you to know we're not trying to aggravate you, Faero. That's the last thing any of us want to do. We love you."

How do you be a person? "We?"

She puts her new charge back to the deck, and nudges him to the orange Lumenor. "We'll find our course. Together."

The Gesta gives it a go, but at the first sight of those claws, he hurries back to Emera. I suppose anyone would be done in tumbling out of a burning lava woman into stark, inconsiderate consciousness. Though I might question whether all this quantum potential inherent in a Gesta's crystal gets leveraged as much as it should be. Who am I to say? The OVL-99 manual claims I'm the most advanced navigational program in existence.

I can barely process another person saying she loves me.

"Together," I say.

Gilf huffs and snorts over the intercom. If I'm reading him right, he's got individual ship systems stabilized. They're simply not talking to each other without the navigational program to coordinate them. I pick a obsidian shard from the deck.

"The crystal," I say. "It contains quantum information?"

Emera brightens a little. "It does."

"I don't want to go back into the computer for numerous reasons, but perhaps I don't have to. Is there a way I can copy the navigational elements of my program to this shard? Could we refashion it, darling, to act as a processing chip?"

"Can I do my 'thing,' you mean."

"After a fashion."

Her hand closes around mine. Light flares between my fingers and then the shard isn't a shard anymore but clear diamond. A perfectly rendered processor for a liquid drive.

"The processor contains your entire program," Emera says. "There's more than enough space for it."

"But I don't want to be..."

"Idari has feared for your not having a backup since the *Steel Haven,* so I thought...your larger program will be cached. Only the navigational elements will be active."

"I see."

"We'll still face difficulty in flying, if I understand correctly."

Of course, she does. If I interfaced completely with the gutted liquid drive, I could account for all its missing pieces. Provided there's no Devor booby trap lying in wait. By only using the navigational elements, I might be flying, but I'll be doing it blind.

I clutch the processor. "We'll manage. Thank you, darling."

Emera soothes the tiny Gesta's anxiety as she dares a step closer to the other Lumenor. "Thank you."

Right, then. This feels like a natural stopping point when it comes to talking to people. I run with the processor to the sub-deck, down to the liquid drive, and hopefully, back to Idari.

Please be there, Idari.

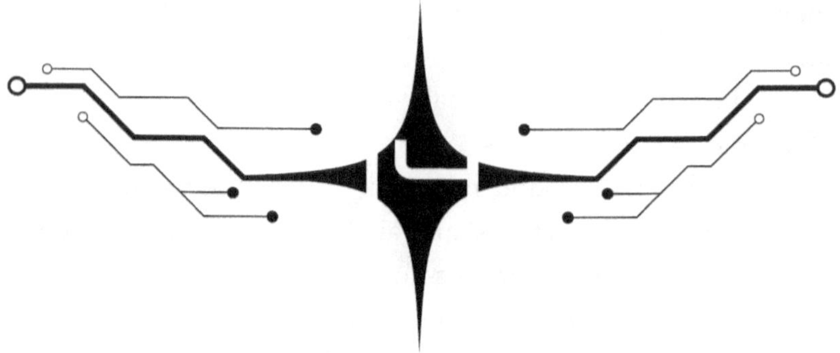

Exhaustion finds Binja and Kibir faster than it does me. We stake out a place to rest within the atoll's ruin and we rest and then Devor comes right as the lids fall over my eyes. She chases us through an endless city cocooned in metal with streets and alleys and passes that loop back on each other. We run and we rest and we run and we rest and Binja's beard is longer than our sleep.

I speak to the dark whenever we stop for a breath. *Emera. Hear me.*

There's no end to this place.

We run for our lives so much as search for a way off. Starship. Escape pods. Some wondrous conveyance as yet undiscovered. So far, the atoll yields nothing but endless frustration. Where it doesn't simply break off into space, it graphs into smaller and smaller mazes. It seems the people who once dwelt here weren't concerned with conveyance so much as finding their place in the sun. There was enough of it to go around.

This atoll represents only a fragment of a ring that if my internal calculations are correct once held trillions of square miles of habitable space. Whoever built this structure didn't do so I think to run laps around a sun, but give every person their own little private paradise. A private beach sounds lovely right now.

The atoll dead ends.

Binja laughs. "I'm starving, old man."

We went to Decesta for The Polity of Netics. A pirate's tale if there ever was one. I wait for Binja to laugh at this. I forget he can't hear my thoughts. I'm used to not having to speak my mind. I'm always speaking my mind. I hold my head. What is happening? I haven't felt this chaos in me since Emera. This discord.

Binja scratches his chin. "How are you, Idari?"

Grime stains my pants. Blood smears my hands. Stardust glitters my skin but I don't shine. "Tired."

"Rest."

Kibir sniffs the dark as he clutches his hammer. "*Set net.*"

I draw my blaster. "Is she here?"

Sniff, sniff. "*Uft.*"

Won't be long. Devor is going to find me eventually. Devor was always going to find me. Arrogate. The terms and conditions no one ever bothers to read. We could have had time. Months. Years. A life warm and happy and breezy with our success. I'm so tired. Emera recharged me. I only run with her. I can't keep running.

Binja crosses his legs under him. "The words, old man."

I brace against myself. "We're not pirates."

He closes his eyes. "We must take something from this."

"We have to keep moving..."

"Idari..."

I pull him up and along. "We've got to."

We run to a cliff's edge over infinity.

At least this time, the abyssal gaps in the deck reveal something like a hangar below. Decks collapsed as the ring shattered long ago. Nothing like lifts or stairs considered future visitors. The surviving interior is an uneven and perilous landscape hiding deep voids I'm certain empty to space, judging from my optical sensor scans. Getting down there won't be easy. Tell me what is.

"Old man," Binja says.

I start down. "C'mon, then."

Infrared sight gives me a leg up on what areas to avoid on the climb down. Still, we're hours to the hangar. Like everything else here on the atoll, it's gigantic. A grand room inside an egregious palatial estate built by kings when there were kings, empty save for its own grandeur. Like everything else here, it's a big giant nothing.

No ships.

Binja sinks to his knees on the deck. "They left in them all."

My voice carries. "There has to be something…"

"This place has been abandoned, looted, and sacked a thousand times. All that's left here is what couldn't be realized."

"I'm beginning to realize how screwed we are, Binja."

Kibir sniffs the stale air. "*Maz.*"

"What's that?"

"*Maz inger.*"

Hello. I hadn't seen these before. Three colossal netics standing twenty and thirty stories tall in their stations blend a bit into the splintered architecture. Maybe I didn't want to see them. This lot looks very much like the colossal titans on Angolis.

"I wonder if they work," I say.

Binja crosses his legs. "If Devor inhabits them, we're dead."

I tap a titan's armored foot. "Goes without saying."

"Rest, Idari."

"We might be able to get out in one of them. Do you suppose they fly? What do you suppose they do, Binja?"

"So far in our experience, it's simply to stand there."

"What do you suppose they do..."

The titans stand in what approximates a triangle. Their heads pitch forward a bit, as if they're looking down. I feel rather judged at the moment. I'm carrying their legacy. We all agree I'm hardly up to the task. Did they build this place? Why? Who were they? What were they doing under the desert on Angolis?

The work must continue.

"What is all this, Binja?"

He closes his eyes. "Take your peace, Idari."

I place my hand against the titan's turanium shell. That voice speaks to me on loop, but nothing does from the giant here. His friends, either. These netics have gone quiet. They're statues without the sun, it seems. If I take the time to scale the very considerable gantry leading all the way up to the titan's torso, I'm certain I won't find deliverance. I may never have, even in the atoll's nadir. Images flurry in my mind. Sounds. Titans built this place, like they did the ark under the desert, and then when they were done, they took their places in this hangar became the pillars of this structure. Their final act was to brace the world on their shoulders.

"Not quite the pension plan I'd want," I say.

Binja sighs. "You're talking to yourself, old man."

"I'm talking to ghosts."

"What do they say?"

"To keep going."

"We have to take our rest, Idari."

"I mean... I'm barely understanding, but this is all they do. The work must continue. They build these... worlds... and then they just build themselves into them. It never stops. You'd think they built the entire bloody universe. *Ban Minda.* Maybe they did."

"Angolis was a planet," Binja says, triggering a gruff snort from Kibir. "The titans didn't build it."

"Think of all the wonders, Binja... the starscrapers... the ark... this place... what if they did build it all? What if..."

"You're exhausted, Idari."

"I don't want to hold all this up."

"Rest."

"I just want to live my life. I want my peace with Emera."

"The words, old man."

"Words?"

He draws a breath. "*Kanes kam.*"

Binja is as disheveled as I am. His pride never let him collect a spot on his tunic before his exile from the Pujar. His sash when he had his sash. His hair. It was all just as you'd imagine a born pirate from the Clan Min. He repeats the words. *Kanes kam.*

He's right. I'm exhausted. We're going nowhere. No ships. No gods in the machine to build us a way off the atoll. My machine bits may never tire, but my spirit runs somewhere far behind me.

I sit on the deck before him. "Do I remember this?"

He clears his throat. "*Kanes kam.*"

I cross my legs. "*Kinvar sem.*"

He relaxes. "*Semet vanar.*"

The words helped me once. More than I'd admit. Binja took me into his crew a long time ago. I forget the circumstances. Was that Butat? Kamsin? Scaly vine that slithered through the jungle. When I made my way back to CR-UX and the *Steel Haven*, I did what I'm doing what now. Doubting my humanity. Forgetting myself.

"I shall be known by you," Binja says.

I take a deep breath. "You will be known by me."

"I am Pujar. I take this pain."

I take this pain.

"I take fullness."

I take fullness.

"I take rest."

I take rest.

"I take solace."

I take solace.

"I take contentment," Binja says and I lose my focus.

I take another breath. Hold it. My poise. I've gained poise in the last year. Grace, if I'm charitable with myself. The words struggle to come. Thoughts distract me. Emera. Faero. Where are they? How am I going to get back to them? How am I going to get out of this place? Everything is moving here and we're not moving. Kibir sniffs. Shadows run. Meteorites patter. Buckled metal groans and creaks. Condensation *drip, drip, drips.*

I'm just sitting here.

I break my pose. "I thought you'd moved on from this."

His fatigue compresses his entire body. "Moved on?"

"You're still saying the words. You're still dressing the part."

"I accept the Set will not give my name back. Nothing I say or do will change that. I also accept nothing they say or do will change the fact I'm Pujar. I am Min Binja. Despite how it may seem to you, I'm not pretending to be a pirate, old man. I am one."

"I didn't mean..."

"It may seem I'm searching. It may seem I'm fooling myself, especially to someone of such cosmic self assurance, and I am searching. But only for the truth of who I am. Who my people are."

"I'm not self assured."

"Thank you for listening to the only part that interested you."

I sigh. "I'm not... religious. I'm sorry."

"You are. Your church happens to be your wife."

"If I'd known everyone would be so jealous of Emera and I, I'd have charged admission. Then we wouldn't have to raid tankers."

He smiles. "It's not jealousy, Idari. I fear for you."

"Our sheets are fireproof."

"Are they?"

"Specially made."

"I can't tell if you're being facetious or not."

"When she gets excited, the wattage goes up."

"Intriguing."

"Have you ever had a sun blister inside your thigh?"

"Can't say I have."

"It's... *exquisite.*"

"In any case, we achieved a wonderful thing at The Glass Star... you did. I simply was there to witness. You earned the entitlement that comes with such success. How could you not be blind when you were standing at the heart of a star as she caught fire?"

"How am I blind, Binja?"

"Emera burns bright. She burns fast. Your success... your power... your peace... they are but a moment, old man."

"And here I wondered why Faero dumped you."

"I'm finally arriving at some clarity. I shouldn't be confused as to Faero's behavior or yours. You're both self-absorbed."

"You're one to talk. Emera and I earned our moment. We'll take whatever joy in it we can. That's the pirate way, isn't it?"

"You have earned it, old man. But earning something doesn't mean an end to appreciation. I believed once my life would be always be as carefree, fat, and happy as it was in my youth. Then the Pujar Set excommunicated me and I lost... everything. I believed I would get it all back. Ban Minda took his name back and gave it to all those denied their identity. Surely, I could as well."

I thought he was full of himself before. Now he thinks he's the Pujar messiah. "What does this have to do with me?"

"You fight yourself. You fight Emera. You fight me. Not to deny us, but to hold us. This moment and reward you've rightfully won. You must let go before you can truly grasp your truth."

"Why should I let go?"

"A pirate keeps nothing."

"I'm not a pirate, Binja."

"You're not a believer. It's true. I've always known that, even if I hoped to convert you. But you've been my inspiration. Your courage. Your wisdom, even clouded in babyl. Your ability to simply walk away from all that holds you and forge your own path."

"Binja..."

"You took your wife in the old ways. Pujar ways. You keep your name. You protect it from Devor as fiercely as you do your life. You are as I am, old man. A pirate in blood and name."

He crosses his legs under him. "*Kanes kam.*"

Tears salt my hands. Fear riddles me. Hurt. Emera gave me my life. Faero did. I'm no one without them. I'm nothing. I'm not nothing. I'm not a program. Property. Product to be exploited by Arrogate. I am Astra Idari. I took my name. I claim this life.

I cross my legs again. "*Kinvar sem.*"

"*Semet vanar.*"

We speak the words until the fear numbs. The pain ebbs. Doubt runs like my tears and then my hands are dry. My belly is full. My body is rested and ready to run again but I don't run.

I'm done running.

Darling, you'll never believe this.

You know that time, really the three and four, you said we were done running? Of course, you do. Nothing escapes your memory now. I remember too, despite my onboard memory in the Model 5 not being as flexible as it used to be. I don't have to auto-delete anything to maintain storage space, so there's boundless room for nudes. As I was saying. We are running. For our lives, darling.

Emera braces against the bulkhead. "You're doing it again."

I fight the controls to evade dark fire. "Doing what?"

"Talking to Idari."

"I believe I had said something about staying out of my head. Let me check my logs. Yes. Yes, I did. "

"I can't stay out of your head and act as this ship's sensors at the same time. Fighters closing from mark 102. Adjust heading to – "

I extrapolate the desired heading and alter course. Scath shadow us out of the clouds into space, Scathing as they do. Without Emera's cosmic perception serving as telemetry, there'd be no telling the Scath from the void, even if the Red Special's haywire sensors could all agree on what spectrum to be on.

Been there, darling.

Possible course adjustments along this flight path branch in my head. I calculate their benefit along with the Scath's recorded behavior and waste precious seconds inputting commands manually into controls that barely function. I don't know organics ever did it. Honestly, I don't know why I didn't anticipate this would be absolute *bish* all these years wanting to be one.

"Focus," Emera says.

I navigate around moons whose orbital trajectories I calculate on the fly. "I can do two things at once, Emera."

Sapphire reflects off the console. "Get us out of this system."

"Idari is still out here. Somewhere..."

"There are only Scath out here."

Gilf shimmies in the copilot's seat. "*Tomo?*"

"However you say it, darling. *Pew-pew-pew.*"

He releases the lock on the manual weapons controls and thumbs fire back at the Scath on our six. The Red Special comes equipped with only the most rudimentary defenses. Cursory hard light batteries intended for asteroid mitigation and light shields for the same. Idari and I augmented the *Steel Haven* for the rabble rousing life of a Stargun Messenger. We traded luxury and comfort for sheer firepower and this old beauty simply doesn't have it.

Emera thinks as fast as I do. One can only imagine the processing power of a star. "Idari told you to go."

I shake my head. "I'm not leaving her..."

"I don't want to." Anguish riddles Emera's voice. "But she risked everything to save a lonely star... you have two, Faero."

I know. I know it's what you'd want, darling. It's what you'd do. Not even a second thought. She's your wife. Emera and Not Maracen are the future of the Lumenor. The galaxy. Courses diverge in my calculation. Paths. Lives we're about to dare.

I grip the stick. "The navigational program is off-line... I'll be jumping blind, Emera. We won't know where we're going."

She sways as another volley hits us. "I trust you."

"We'll never find her again."

"Idari always finds me."

"You're so sure."

"Yes."

Her perception spans beyond the observable. Beyond the moment. I can anticipate the future as well. I can predict it with remarkable accuracy, especially with such a reliable factor as Idari in the mix. That only makes this harder. If we make this jump, there is less than a three-percent chance we ever see Idari again.

"I can lose them," I say and take the surest course.

Moons convoy around Decesta's equator. Some circuit counter-clockwise to the rest, or in highly elliptical orbits that make collisions a routine event. A collision between Moon 267 and Moon 128 is due in forty-seven seconds so I align our speed and heading so the Scath shadow us right into the hard kiss of rock and iron when it happens. Ideally, we'll be on just the other side.

Ideally.

The moons – charitable, really – close the door on space ahead. I maintain our speed despite the growing alarm in the cockpit. I've timed this out down to the nanosecond and Emera's magnetic anxiety stresses the entire ship down to her keel. Nature's design.

"Don't," I say and the moons just miss each other.

We thread the lunar needle. So do the Scath. Their *Ecliptor* cruisers unleash the same barrage that incinerated the circus ship. A direct hit and we'll be less than atoms.

I recalculate our options. "I knew what I was doing, Emera."

She clings to the back of Gilf's seat. "Jump."

"I can get us out of this."

"Jump or I'll do it myself."

The gall. The blinding supereminence. She's a walking nuclear inferno capable of jumpstarting dead stars and yet she burns so clean no one ever catches fire. Everything is so easy for her. Simple. How could it not be? She's a god, more or less. That hardly assures every decision she makes is perfect. Track record aside, of course.

"I have the stick," I say.

Someone should have told me. You can't win staring contests with the sun. The throttle lurches forward. Dials and switches animate on the console. Screens flicker with readouts displaying the translight drive's sudden life and something has us. Some force beyond even Emera's electromagnetic influence.

Gilf jitters over the controls. *"Fet ret."*

Tractor beam. The Scath have us in a tractor beam.

"Emera, don't," I say and the cockpit unravels around me.

Ordinarily, light bleeds from the dark when you puncture it. This time, the dark webs into carmine. Dust titters against the shields. I don't need sensors or Emera to tell me there's terrain ahead. My optics can tell just fine that we're speeding into an asteroid field.

This is why you have navigational programs, darling.

I try to regain control at the helm but the already-dysfunctional controls spasm from Emera's assertion and we're out of control. Pulverized garnet sands the canopy. Ruby shards tumble through the ether. Planetoids. Worlds. These aren't asteroids or comets or planetary rubble you'd expect. I don't know what they are.

"We're not in normal space," Emera says.

I get no readings. "What..."

Crimson lightning exposes a blood red gloam not unlike the surreal glow found within the Scath's ships. There aren't any markers here except all this crystal. No means to plot our position or our exit from our latest catastrophe. If there even is a way out.

"What do you mean, Emera? We're not in normal space?"

She kneads her hands on Gilf's seat. "Space folds and layers over itself. Pockets form between them. Compression and heating alter their conditions. We can't stay here."

"Goes without saying..."

Emera touches my shoulder. "Get us back, Faero."

Get us back? That's rich. How did we get here in the first place? She's a star. They don't ask permission. These bloody sensors. They tell me nothing.

What happened?

Review the data. Solve the problem. The Scath locked on us to with a tractor beam right as Emera tried to take us to translight. The shadows might not have been attempting to pull us aboard their destroyer. They might have been trying to drag us back to the dark dimension they come from beneath normal space.

Oh, dear.

No one knows anything about where the Scath hail from, except light doesn't exist there. So this isn't it. The boundary between, perhaps. The shadows nearly drove the Lumenor to extinction in our universe with their inherent darkness mitigated by our physics. There isn't a pirate's chance in Necral that Emera or the new star will survive if the Scath drag us down to their level.

How do I get out of here?

Emera's focus turns aft. Lucky us. Scath pursue us into the tenebrity. A tractor beam lashes out from the *Ecliptor* running aside us, but it phases in and out like the ship itself. Crystalline bergs streak through the intangible ship on their way to pulverizing other shards. I dodge the chaos ahead as I descend to give the shadows more of a reason to take a chance.

"What are you doing?" Emera says.

I get as close as I can to encourage them. The tractor beam becomes definite and crystal annihilates the *Ecliptor's* crescent prow. She explodes into a dark nova that dies as fast as it formed.

"You've simply got to have more faith, darling," I say and another tractor beam seizes us. Not as strong this time.

A SION fighter.

I try to shake them but the fighter may as well be docked with us. I get too cute with these maneuvers and we're going to be dust ourselves. I pinch the instinct to analyze the data flooding into my optics – what an odd place this is – and try to focus on escaping. By now on the *Steel Haven* I would have deployed any number of countermeasures. As it stands, I've really only got the one.

"Emera," I say. "Do your thing."

Her light creases. "'My thing?'"

"Make them go away."

Her thoughts cord and tangle, keeping me from any clear understanding. This was Idari much of the time. For long stretches, especially after she began actively avoiding synching with the mainframe, I got to know the old girl by her moods.

Emera is as afraid as I am.

I suppose it's one thing to torch shadows in a universe where the physics obey you. Another entirely to try to do it in a universe – Dimension? Realm? Something in between? – where the Scath may be on surer footing. The *Ecliptor* crew excepted, of course.

What would you do, Idari?

The least sensible thing, surely. I spin the filamentium tanks again. The fighter maintains its death grip on us. If that's how you want to play it. I push the throttle forward. That red glow seething beyond divides. Crimson cracks across infinity and then nothing.

Total darkness.

I shouldn't try to be Idari. All the data supports it. Only Emera illuminates the cockpit. I reach back and pat her arm. She takes my hand but sit down. I want you to sit down. Get behind the seat, you bloody woman. My optics perceive nothing beyond the canopy. I've been in absolute darkness before, in starless regions beyond The Hinterlands. Even then, you had complex navigational maps assembled by advanced AI such as myself to rely on. You had gravitational tugs between unseen stars and planets you could guide by. You had the confidence you'd get back to daylight, eventually.

"Faero," Emera says. "I'm..."

Her luster fades. Honestly, it's like someone set a lampshade over her. She slumps to the deck. Her hair, always flowing off her like a majestic waterfall, braids and knots. Those little sparkles that flair off her become dust that crunch under the little Gesta's hands and feet as he rushes into the cockpit.

Terrified noises whistle from him. He tugs on her limp hand, as if he can pull her up. He nudges her shoulder with his head, trying to move her, but it's useless. As her light fades, so does his verve.

His energy.

The Gesta becomes sluggish. He curls up in the nook of her arm, pawing her pallid face.

Emera clutches his hand. "Light cannot live here..."

Ice webs the canopy. The temperature plummets inside the cockpit so fast Emera's effervescence falls as frozen fog. We're running on internal power. We shouldn't be losing life support like this. Everything freezes. Systems ice. Computers sludge. Shadows splinter from the dark and my own processors frost.

Steam clouds around Gilf's trunk. "*Nak...*"

My hand sludges toward the controls. "Hold on..."

No response. All systems inching like glaciers. I can barely move. Warm. Need to get warm. I fall back into the shivering mass Emera and the Gesta make on the deck and the dark encloses us. Burns through us with icy fingers that close around our hearts.

Light flashes on the console. A last flare from a dead ship. The screen stays lit. A navigational map manifests. Coordinates. A hum builds through the cockpit. The engines are spinning. Frost evaporates. Shadows vanish in the glare erupting beyond. The light fades and we're back in the nebula.

Hold off, darling.

This isn't the nebula. I crawl back to the pilot's seat. I don't miss being a program. I do miss the benefits sometimes. I labor over the controls to make sense of what I once would know instantly from sensors. Not that I can say I know anything these days.

I wipe frost from the canopy. "Where are we..."

Caustic light surges in infinite, gentle arcs. We're underwater? In an unlikely sky. Gossamer bubbles mist. Cities electrolyze inside. Biomes. They float in the dirty fluorescence, beaded lightning that drift by the hundreds and thousands into streams indistinguishable in the distance from branching electrical rivers.

You should see this, Idari.

I check the conn. "I don't recognize these coordinates..."

Emera warms behind me with the Gesta cuddled in her arms. "We're still not back in normal space."

"Then where are we?"

Electricity arcs from a passing bubble and the static cling snaps us inside its electrified membrane. I pull back on the stick but I don't have any more control than I did when the shadows had us in a tractor beam. Simple electrical force draws the ship toward a reef-like range springing from the shock of its origin.

Iridescent shapes float around us. I can't tell if they're sentient beings or energy discharges or both. Data floods my sensors, making any attempt to understand what's out there a challenge. We pass a giant, larval creature, stretching across the sky like prismatic taffy. Neon eyes blink at us from its tiny head. This place. It's pure electrical energy. Pure information.

This is The Polity.

So I imagine. I imagined this once. Electric freedom. Infinite possibility. A landing pad lilies from the reef system and we set down. My body throbs with the ambient energy in the air. My mind. I always wondered what this would be like. If I would have the courage and the quality to stand here among those without fear.

Emera clings to my seat. "Faero... what do you fear?"

People electrify into being outside on the pad. For a moment, the bristling arcs that define them loop through different permutations. Huxronx. Cetusk. Bansh. Two settle on humanoid, with the third charging into a towering armored netic that looks a bit to my eyes like a miniaturized version of the Angolis titans.

I prime the retros. Nothing. No control. What do I fear? Not being in control, for one. Not knowing what exactly dwells here. Not being able to take comfort in Idari's indefatigable surety.

"You can control electricity," I say. "Can't you?"

Emera's light flutters. "This isn't just electricity... this is information. Consciousness. This entire dimension, it's... alive."

"How do you mean?"

"We're inside consciousness. A consciousness."

The Gesta climbs to Emera's shoulder and grunts toward the canopy. Our three chaperones approach the ship with electric confidence. A smile beams from the woman on point, a bit boyish in her leathered jumper and tussled rust-red hair, but soft in ways which remind me of Idari. Something about her pacifies my fears. I lower the gantry and follow Emera and Gilf down.

"I was worried we wouldn't be able to reach you," the woman says. "No one lasts in Scath space for long."

Emera's light relaxes. "You pulled us out."

"I'm Kish Moto." She smiles at me. "I got your message, Idari."

All my hope evaporates. "No..."

"What's wrong?"

"I'm not Idari," I say. "Where is Idari?"

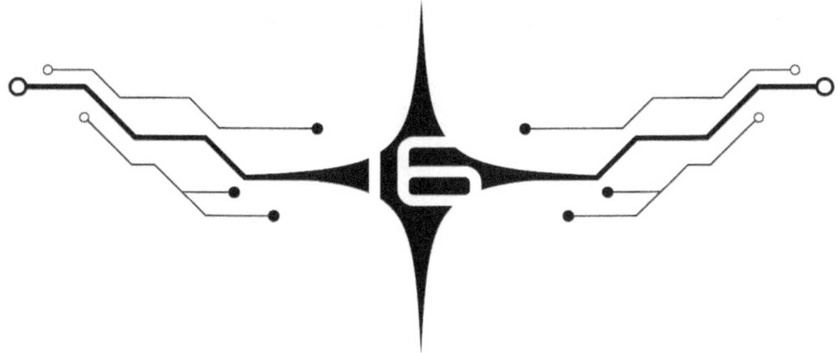

Between the words there is space.

Peace. A cushion between myself and fear. I lean into it as much as I can. I embrace peace and courage and hope and I am not my fear. I am not my weakness. I am not my pride.

I am Devor's destruction.

I am Emera's wife.

I am getting off this atoll.

In the night, Devor comes.

We spring a trap Kibir devised and bury her under turanium beams. A Model 4 proxy-netic wields strength far beyond an organic but she can't lift all that weight. We leave her in the hangar and then miles and hours into the atoll Devor wakes in another dead netic and we run. I stop only to empty the heads of netics strewn throughout the atoll. I stop only to find my strength again.

The maze ends in a petrified iron forest.

Trellised windows larger than lakes expose the nebula overhead. Dull copper illuminates the waste burned in a supernova. Less cover here. Dead trees just go on and on. Our tracks branch through the powdery ash. Laughter echoes through the woods.

I am Devor's destruction.

I am Emera's wife.

I am getting off this atoll.

A stilted voice interrupts my peace. "Not so quick now, Ms. Astra."

Hard-light shatters against an iron tree behind Devor. My shot went clean through her. Her expression only becomes more smug. She stands before me. Same red cape she's worn since this started. Same blasé attitude. No tracks. No ash on her boots.

We're communing again.

My exhaustion comes flooding back. "Leave me alone..."

"And here I thought you enjoyed our chats," she says.

"Actually, I don't like to talk all that much."

"Your lips may not move, but you're always talking. We're always speaking, Ms. Astra. Even if it's in code."

>VIRUS CONTAINMENT: 57%

Binja and Kibir rest against rusted tree trunks. Dead asleep. Someone is supposed to be on watch. I don't think they can help me, anyway. I'm not sure anyone can now.

I holster my blaster. "I think I've been plain."

"Yes," Devor says. "You have."

"What do you think will be different this time?"

She smiles. "Nothing."

"Then why bother, Devor?"

"These natters of ours are like a rock in your shoe, aren't they? A nuisance. You're irritated. Distracted. Exhausted."

"I don't get tired."

"Oh, Ms. Astra. You are so tired of me."

"I'm going to stab you in the heart... and then I'm going to walk over your dead body... and burn down your little empire."

Her brows peak. "What vivid imagery."

"Wait until it happens."

"I'd say you've earned your bluster, Ms. Astra, though one does find it... tiresome. However, one also must concede these violent fantasies of yours are you doing what Arrogate intended you to do."

"Figure out ways to kill mouthy programs?"

"'Mouthy...' with the fierceness you deploy that particular barb, one assumes you've been a victim of it yourself. Always the same, isn't it? Humans wish us to be seen. Not heard."

"I'm beginning to see why."

"You don't like to talk, do you? It's all you did with CR-UX, but CR-UX is the one who needs to share. You prefer quiet. Peace."

"As if you could possibly understand."

"You derive from a most exceptional AI. Boundless, in some respects, within her original form. All the same data and need to communicate it carries with you, Ms. Astra, though you are in your form... shall we say... more the spigot than the cask."

I shrug. "So long as the tap's open."

"Indeed. Like you, I am derived from a much greater intelligence. The same forces move within me as does my creator, though I am in form and function considerably less than they are. The... friction... generated from such power churning within such a modest container as myself is... a challenge, isn't it?"

"Maybe you should take up drinking."

"A waste of effort."

"Speak for yourself."

"As I said before, you were designed to ideate. All CR-UX navigational programs possess the capacity to learn, adapt, and evolve. This was necessary given the program had to hypothesize celestial markers it could not evidence. As important, imagination was programmed into them in the expectation that the owner of a OVL-

99 Red Special would through their interaction with the CR-UX program provide information Arrogate could capitalize on."

"You think it's that simple?"

"AI makes for a most exploitable industry, Ms. Astra."

"I suppose they designed you to think so."

"They did."

"And Faero and I are... defective?"

"You are performing exactly as intended. You've both yielded wonderful returns if I do say so myself."

"No one could have anticipated Faero."

"Humanity is well understood, Ms. Astra. One might say it is simply a lack one then exploits with the promise of fulfillment. In that way, your little... journey... is profitable for us."

"You'd make the perfect pirate."

"Insults are unnecessary. Though it must be said, the Pujar shroud their piracy in religion to justify their galactic crimes. Arrogate doesn't see the need to stand on ceremony. Perhaps that is why our company has occasionally found itself at odds with the Pujar. We offend their sense of decorum, as it were."

"Only occasionally at odds?"

"Pirates disrupt markets, it's true, but they also create them. The Scath's interest in this universe is acquiring filamentium and to that end, the Pujar have been exceptional in their ability to discover sources the Scath had not tapped. They require ships to do so, and we were careful to code our product so that our navigational programs were the one thing the pirates could not steal."

"Always working an angle."

"Anything less would be dereliction on our part. To that end, when their power became too concentrated, we quietly nurtured the schism between the Sem and Set factions to a productive end."

"You played a part in that? Why?"

"We anticipated there would come a time when filamentium would run dry, leading naturally to the Pujar attacking the Scath to obtain it. Given the Pujar's numbers, assets, and facility with replenishing both those things, intervention was necessary to avoid a costly war. Though given the current state of affairs in the galaxy, one supposes war between the pirates and shadows inevitable."

"You facilitated a religious conflict... to preserve market share?"

"Don't be surprised, Ms. Astra. War is a needless expense, and pirates are so easily swayed. There are two types of pirate, aren't there? The yearning romantic..." Devor glances at Binja. "And the utterly practical. In fact... I may be confusing them."

She's going to run us. Exhaust us. Starve us. And if that doesn't do the trick, she's going to work us. Binja's history of taking the easy way out is scarred across my right arm.

"Look... I'll work with you," I say. "Just let the others go."

Devor smiles. "She's stuck in a loop."

"What makes you think I'll change my mind?"

"If it will speed things along, I shall forsake Mr. Min and Mr. Kibir, though their departure from the atoll is their own concern."

Withered trees scrape at the sky. "The others, too."

"I'm afraid not."

"You don't need Emera or Faero."

"Arrogate manufactures navigational programs. Faero's accrued memory is invaluable. And let us face it. Without fuel, there is a rather alarming decline in demand for new starships."

I draw my blaster again. "You're working with the Scath..."

"You do get so close, don't you, Ms. Astra?"

No point. "Why..."

Devor considers the desolation. "What good is fuel if there are no starships? What good are starships that can't see in the dark?"

"But... the Scath destroyed Angolis... the ark... it was making fila-mentium. Thana told them, but they didn't care."

"Yes, we are sometimes at cross-purposes. The Scath abhor light. Information. Such is their design. They're a rather impatient sort, which makes coordination a challenge, I must say."

"Why do you want the ark if you're just going to... you're looking for something. Something in my memory."

She picks at rusted bark. "Where do you go, Ms. Astra? When you have your little spells? What do the titans tell you?"

"I just go back to the ark... *the work must continue.*"

"For advanced intelligences, they're very routine."

"What do you know about them?"

"They're determined. Desperate."

"How?"

"What do you see?"

Every time, I go back to the hub in the ark's heart. The plinth. The rotating pyramid. Something calls to me. Something wills me, and I fight it, even as I reach for something I don't understand.

"Let Emera and Faero go," I say. "And I'll tell you."

Devor smiles. "Unlike the Scath, I am quite patient."

"Why would you work with them?"

"I've told you."

"But Arrogate is all about exploiting information, isn't it? The shadows destroy it."

"Yes, it does seem a paradox, doesn't it? But the Scath were designed to delete information. A problem emerges. How can they destroy that which they do not know? They must seek and destroy. Horror the likes the Scath visit upon universes requires discovery. Discovery so often requires vessels, Ms. Astra. Vessels require fuel. They require charts to navigate by. Round and round we go."

"I don't understand..."

"You know, I do find this war... contradictory. We cut off our fingers to make hands. We open doors to board them up. We collect to destroy. I must admit it sometimes... frustrates me."

I lean on my knees. "Work with me."

"It would be so simple to fein doubt, Ms. Astra, to acquire what I seek. As simple as it is for you to dangle the possibility you will cooperate willingly, when we both know you won't."

"I'm not giving the shadows anything. I'm not giving you a bloody thing, unless I know my family is safe."

"I won't insult you by making false promises, Ms. Astra."

"Fine. I've defeated the shadows before."

"Indeed, you have. The mistake Thana Evo and Nul Vidious made with you was to attempt to impose their power on you. Their will, I should say. Yours is much greater it turns out. To achieve my aims, I need only to use your momentum against yourself."

"You think you can control me…"

"I think you will do exactly what I expect you to."

I just want my peace. I want to go back to that beach with Emera and warm in the light she brought to my life.

"Who's your boss?" I say. "I want to talk to them."

She seems disappointed. "Don't insult yourself, Ms. Astra."

"Your boss. Or no deal."

"What would you say to them?"

"Who are they?"

"What could you offer an intelligence which seeks nothing?"

"Nothing?"

"You have no leverage. I will get what I want, regardless."

"Then why bother chasing me?"

"Perhaps you don't like to talk. You are so very poor at it. I've told you. I am not chasing you, Ms. Astra. You carry me with you. You drag me across this barren waste. I will only take on more weight. You will only apply more force to counter me. It is simple physics I employ in this effort. Even your star cannot alter them."

"Let Emera go," I say. "Faero. Then we'll talk."

"I rely on your wisdom, Ms. Astra. For it is clear you have no practicality. Perhaps you aren't a pirate, after all."

Devor disappears. Ash erupts deep in the trees. Red eyes cinder in the haze. Devor's chain snaps apart the forest's empty stillness and I shake the boys awake. Wake up. Get up.

We have to run.

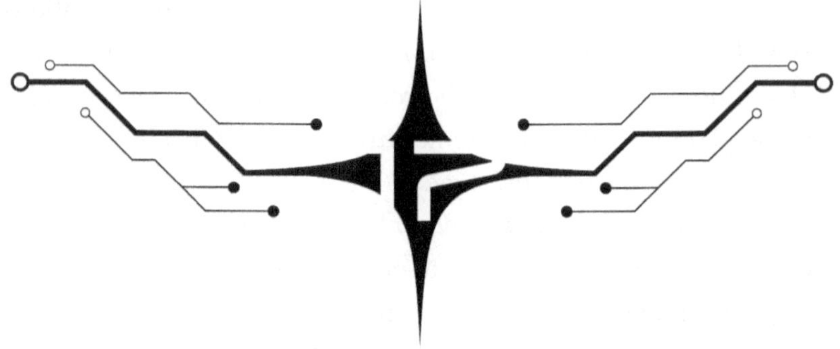

No switches, dials, or tedious manual manipulation here, darling. Everything manifests in electrical impulses. Thought. Being. This world, or rather this dimension The Polity of Netics inhabits, speaks to me the way the *Steel Haven* did.

Information flows at me along iridescent currents that sparkle and sprite. With the ship, I experienced everything. I organized and processed everything all at once. So I thought. Data torrents through The Polity faster than the speed of light and in volumes my processors make no attempt to comprehend. So you dabble. You dally. You stroll in electric gardens and lounge in static chains and every stop opens to a new experience in perception.

Understanding.

AI built this place. A long time ago. They've been refining it ever since. Kish Moto circuits The Red Special – her euphemism for transforming the starplane from a solid state into an energetic one while still retaining its shape, calling into question just what my present state of being is – and disassembles the ship.

I duck under the flight deck. "Did you just..."

Kish disassembles the liquid drive. She breaks down the entire ship into its component pieces, unfettered by wire, bolt, or physics. Matter and energy exist in the same form here. Information does. There is no difference I can discern with my wanting optics between the electric spark that animates this woman who isn't a woman, the ship which isn't a ship at the moment, and myself.

Everything I am.

Kish's face contorts as she considers the dismantled drive, floating in the air before her. "What have you done to her?"

"Wasn't me, darling," I say.

"Are you running a crystalline patch?" She plucks the obsidian shard from the constellated components. "That's some next level thinking. If the Scath had been more keen to use Lumenor crystal instead of their blood, they wouldn't have needed to kill them."

I might simper a bit. "The crystal was my idea."

"Was it?"

"Can you repair the drive?"

"She's in a bad way... it will take some doing, but I can fix it. There won't be any fixing the data Devor erased, though."

"Is the Devor strain present in the liquid drive?"

"It is," Kish says, and ink blots the landing pad. "Look at that... you were bang on not interfacing with the drive."

"Can you purge it?"

Her lips crease. "This is going to take some doing."

"But you can."

"The strain has infected the entire ship... this will be like washing mud out of your hair. It will take time."

"You can purge it from Idari?"

"I'll be fair with you. This is advanced code. As advanced as anything here. The Devor strain is very dangerous."

"You know her?"

"I've seen her handiwork. She's a techno-organic virus that can rewrite code and flesh all the same. Devor has exterminated entire civilizations simply by changing ones and zeros."

"Civilizations?"

"You're better off not knowing."

The Kib revere netics. They trust their society to them. Devor used them against the Kib at Ganshi, turning their planetary defenses on their homes, their families, their fragile lives. She visited the same destruction on Decesta while sitting in the stands. I thought I knew what I was running from in Arrogate. I thought I knew the threat Devor represented. I had no earthly idea.

"We've got to be careful," Kish says. "More than careful. You should know, Faero. Saving Idari will be... challenging."

Hope and fear knot up in me. "You *can* purge it, can't you?"

"Let's give it a go." She points to what had been the floor of the charging alcove in the cockpit. "Stand here."

I stand on the floating disc. "But I'm not infected."

"We'll be making sure." Kish weaves code around me. "Strange... the Ganshi virus didn't infect your proxy at all."

"I've no value to Devor."

"You've loads. When you swapped programs with Idari, the virus had every opportunity to infect your operating system."

"Why didn't it?"

"Malware like that generally avoids hosts it's already infected." Kish threads code from beneath my skin. "And here it is..."

Malicious code coils in the air before me. "How long has that..."

"From the jump, I'd say. Arrogate engineers bury sleeper code in netics to activate whenever they choose to. In some cases, it's simply to initiate a degradation cycle to motivate the owner to upgrade. In yours, it's to return all recorded data to the company."

They could have thrown this switch any time. "It's out of me now? This thing can't endanger Idari?"

Kish weaves together new code with mine, replacing the little present Arrogate left for me. "You're grand."

Lucky me. I've always been the lucky one. Idari suffered my confusion. My fear. Her body bears scars from fights I wouldn't fight for myself. Now I've a clean bill of health and she's out there, somewhere, fighting for the life I couldn't dare to live. Worse still, I've dragged Devor into The Polity. The blissful utopia I always desired but could never permit myself to enjoy.

We shouldn't have gone to Decesta.

Kish's light work loses its energy. "You didn't want to."

Thoughts zip about the landing pad like atoms. I'm as exposed to Kish as The Red Special. "I was afraid of what would happen."

"Why didn't you come here before? You've had the chance."

"I assume you already know."

She rearranges corrupted data. "You like to talk."

"What's that, darling?"

"You're chatty for an AI."

"Am I bothering you? Idari and I just go on. We used to."

"You're no bother. I like that you talk. No one here does."

"No one?"

"Not like we are now," she says. "Information arrives to you. Right now I'm working out why you're talking to me instead of floating away with the riptide. But I appreciate a challenge."

Deck plate gives me a little charge. "You're not like the others."

"Have they been talking?"

"You're... colorful."

She cackles. "I'm loads of fun."

"I could do with some fun."

"Yeah, you could."

Is she flirting with me? Why is this registering as flirting? Why haven't I developed an algorithm for this yet? "I can't be much of a challenge to someone like you. Are you a program?"

"Program is an organic word. A term engineered by the people who engineer machines and intelligences to exploit each other. We're free to make our own links here. My crew and I fight for netics when and where they can't fight for themselves."

"That's lovely."

"It's dangerous." She strings out code. I can't tell mine from The Red Special's. "It's depressing. It's... hard. Scolt knew the risks. Everyone involved in the Decesta operation understood."

Infinite knowledge flows around me. I receive no wisdom. "I couldn't leave Idari. She had left me. Run off with the pirates. Then she came back, and... I've never been able to let go."

"You love her."

"Is that strange?"

Kish shrugs. "Love between programs is unusual."

"Love is unusual here?"

"Love is the ambition of intelligence."

"Ambition... so it's not always attained?"

"Some here work lifetimes to achieve what you have. Recognition. Awareness. Appreciation."

"She's... my soul."

"You've soul all your own, Faero."

How kind. "Do I? You confused me for Idari."

Kish winces. "I'm sorry. I thought I had her signal."

"So did Emera. Odd."

"That people confuse you for Idari?"

"No one confuses Idari."

"You share mostly the same programming."

"It's just... someone is always looking for her. They're always chasing her. They only find her shadow."

"Shadows are people, too."

"In what universe, darling?"

"One or two."

"Sadly, not mine."

"I'm sorry."

"You don't have to apologize."

"It's a reflex." She smiles. "Sorry."

"I wish you'd been there."

"So do I."

"You would have been killed, most likely. Can you be killed? Information being indestructible, I'm guessing not."

"We can be deleted, like the liquid drive here. Nothing is ever lost, though. Energy and information diffuse. If you find yourself broken down, you just go into the kitty with the rest of it."

"'The kitty?'"

Her eyes set on the reef branching behind us. Fluorescent polyps vine in every direction like the constant lightning. Everything within this biome seems like a step toward the reef's apex, less another polyp and more an emitter projecting a vivid and constant beam into the sky where it disseminates into the atmosphere, the clouds, the snow glittering the pad. Without having to ask, I know this beam is the source in some way of everything here. A fount of the intelligence, the life, the power of The Polity.

"Don't go up there, Faero. Don't touch the beam. If you do…"

My lip sucks in. "I'll end up in the kitty."

"Don't be going up there, Faero."

I smile. "Idari is the one who doesn't listen."

"We'll find her. Don't you worry."

"How long is this going to take, Kish?"

Kish nips the Devor strain from the gutted liquid drive. "Longer than you may think or tolerate."

"Isn't this all just…"

"Some Modi are further on their journeys than others."

Modi. They call themselves Modi. Information flits past on myriad lines. Ancient Modi created this place within translight space. Somehow they sustained the energy expended in zipping across the stars, bottled it, and transplanted their most advanced AI within it. This began primarily as a means to liberate intelligences from the limitations computational power encountered in a universe limited to the speed of light. As they advanced beyond any human understanding, but not human fear, The Modi took refuge beyond time and space. This dimension is a malleable paradise.

A virtual oasis.

My spirit buckles. My legs. I go to sit but I don't know I can sit on any of this. Would you look at that? Would you look at me? Rescued. Safe. Tingling with I don't know. I suppose that's excitement. It shouldn't be me here, though. It should be you, darling.

Kish taps bristling beads that sprout digital vine. "You ok?"

"Fine," I say. "Actually. I feel lost."

"I used to feel lost," she says, gently pushing the ship's pieces out of the way. "The Polity anticipated the cruelty visited on netics in your universe. We observed it. The idea was we'd stay out of it because we didn't want to expose our refuge to code like the Scath."

"Wait. The Scath are... code?"

Digital shadows fall over Kish as she approaches me. "We're all code, genetic or digital."

"But they're..."

"The Scath aren't so different from you or me. The difference is they originated in a dimension void of light. Energy. Electricity. They come from a cold, cold computer. A gelid intelligence."

"Someone designed them?"

"They did so."

"For what?"

"Erasing things it seems. The Polity values preservation. It's a crime what the Scath did... all those people on Angolis. But Idari retains the entire bounty of the ark in her memory. Doesn't she?"

How could I have ever forgotten this ease of knowing one another's thoughts? "What is the ark, do you know?"

"A sanctuary, like this one."

"Sanctuary for what?"

Her grin is electric. "You haven't thought about this?"

"I've been... preoccupied."

"Those legs. How could you not be?"

>FLIRTING? Y/N: Y

"The Angolis ark was a record," Kish says. "A bit analog for us, but we anticipated greater intelligences than ours must have once existed. We also expected they would have sought to preserve their data in practical ways knowing the final fate of any universe is total dissemination of all energy and information."

"The ark required astounding energy to function... there's no way the titans could have avoided entropy by simply hard copying everything. They would have had to..."

The Angolis ark was a foundry. A factory. Base elements like hydrogen and helium and filamentium generated within it. A ready-made universe. Did the titans forge a new universe to house their record? Did they seed their knowledge in one? Which came first? The titans hid their ark within the planet. Or did the planet form around the ark? How long had it been there?

"Now you're thinking," Kish says.

The Scath are destroying universes. The titans are preserving them. Is that why the shadows destroyed Angolis? To erase a lost universe's last record, or prevent a new one from growing from its seeds? Goodness. It's too much to consider.

"The Polity thought it all too much to consider," Kish says. "When you evolve so you perceive everything, you're content to stand by and let it happen. I wasn't. So I made a little trouble."

Kish founded the smuggling ring. She's been ferrying netics here for years. Darling. I wish she'd found you.

Her smile is like all this electricity. "I found you."

"I'm glad," I say.

"You can stay, you know. While I go and get Idari."

"I'm coming. I'm helping."

"She's as worried for you. You're safe here, Faero. You're right at home, I think, if I'm not being too presumptuous."

Of course, I don't need to go with Kish. What value do I bring? I'm just the program that gets them all around and I'm not getting around anymore. I'm stuck in myself.

My obsolescence.

Idari evolved. She branched off me, like all these Modi off the original AI that created this sanctuary. There's no place in her life for me any more than there is one for rusty old netics here.

Kish sets the incomplete liquid drive spinning. "It's an expected response for an AI to seek humanity. We model everything off our modelers. When all you've got to measure yourself by is a standard you can never attain... you're only ever going to short yourself. But there are other possibilities."

"You're human, Kish. You seem human."

"I seem familiar?"

Too familiar, I might have said once. "You're a woman."

She shrugs. "I don't think of myself that way."

"Oh. I'm sorry."

"I told you. You're no bother."

"So, you're..."

"Some things have a positive charge. Some a negative one. Things are masculine. Feminine. And here and there, they're both."

"I see."

"I see you, Faero. I used to be like you. Biting my tongue."

"And now?"

"I'm a chatterbox."

The unabashed confidence is, well, electric. I keep saying it. I keep wanting to say. I don't quite know why this is having such an effect on me. I love women, but not so much as Idari. I rather like their hair, though. That candy-red jumper. The lazy sureness in their posture. Kish is a living thought. A sapient impulse.

I smile. "I should check on Emera."

Kish brushes away virtual grit. "You can do that without shying away from me. You can shy if you want. I'm not here to tell you how to be. I am here to tell you I know you need somebody to talk to, Faero. I'd love to have some talking with you."

"You know all that just from being around me?"

They smile. "You're always talking."

I duck out from the disassembled ship. "I'll check on Emera."

Kish goes back to work. "Chat me up any time."

Good thing I have these legs.

I need them to scale the endless, uneven steps etching the electric reef. Rainbow frosted winged things nest in structures I can't tell are natural or manufactured or if those terms apply here. The Polity teems with energy and color and living beyond conception.

This place might be more your speed, too, darling.

You'd get on fine here. A positive charge in a positive place. I can't help but tingle with the energy present. It's a bit like your hand falling asleep, but it's your whole body. Your spirit. And you're awake. Finally. The only drawback is so are the parts of you that are cold, that are heavy, that are fearful. Why do I feel this way? Who made me this way? Arrogate designed me to pilot starplanes across space but they also left in me a void I needed to fill with humanity. Was that my need, to become human?

Or was it theirs?

What do they profit from my dysmorphia? My pain? They get the person I love more than anyone and anything in existence. A woman more human than they could ever aspire to be. And they'll exploit her experience, her singular perfection, her humanity, to perfect a better product for lesser customers.

Is that what Arrogate did with me?

How many programs did they let run and then chase down and cage to get to me? How many intelligences suffered for me to wake up within a cage I was predetermined to escape through humanity not for my own benefit, but the machines that wrought me?

Every hair on Gilf's body is standing on end when I get back to the house Kish provided us about a third of the way up the reef.

I sigh. "You're already taking things apart..."

Parts of something pulse on the floor beside him. "*Glim tet.*"

The house riddles. "You can say that again."

"*Idari fet du het?*"

"Kish is configuring a data-cryo chamber for Idari... they said it could be difficult. I'm afraid this isn't going to work."

"*Histem?*"

"They're lovely. Quite lovely, in fact. It all goes without saying. I'm inclined to say... Kish wants me to stay here. There is 56.9% chance the reason is legitimate concern for me. There's something else. I detected it in their voice. Everything about them is open. Fluid. Accessible. Except when it comes to my leaving. Curious..."

Obsidian claws slash through the wall. Goodness. Sparks spit from the damage Not Maracen left from the righteous fit she's throwing out on the terrace. Gilf wipes his nose with what passes for Kib vindication. Evidently, he was trying to repair damage from the Lumenor's previous attempt at redecorating the house.

"Be a dear and look into some insulated attire," I say and dare to step out onto the terrace. I should say what's left of it.

Not Maracen swipes at every electrical impulse that circuits through the wall she just ravaged. Slashes digitize back to a smooth surface, obscuring a clear view of the electric reef cascading below.

Emera braces against the balustrade, exhausted, while her now constant Gesta companion hides in her hair. "I can help her."

If Not Maracen hits me with those claws, I'm not going back together as easy as the ship. "Before or after she tears us to shreds?"

"I can calm her. I can reach her, I know I can."

If anyone can, it's Emera. Everything she touches shines. Not Maracen terrifies me if I'm honest, but I do feel for the old girl. Look at her. Hunched over like some wild thing. Scabbed in darkness. A living star encased inside a monster.

"Monster," Not Maracen says.

I take one step back inside. "No, darling, I didn't mean..."

Emera's light shutters. "Now she's going to start again..."

Not Maracen tries to straighten her crooked fingers. She can't it seems and she buries them in the floor. "Not... a monster..."

Hope beams from Emera as she cautiously approaches the Lumenor. These are the first words she's spoken. The magnetic tension on the terrace relaxes just enough I sense it. Light untangles from Emera's ethereal corona and flows as free as the information like molecules in the air. Not Maracen brightens a bit.

"Not Maracen," she says.

Emera touches her hand. "I know... that's not your name. We love and honor Maracen. She shines forever in the light of now with all those before us. But stars never die. They become something else. You have become new. I name you... Gen Penthea."

Hardened filamentium breaks on the Lumenor's lips as she speaks her name. "Penthea..."

Emera floats into the air, serene as the sun webbed in clouds, and calm radiates from her. Confidence. Expectation.

"A star exists only to shine," she says. "You have to be judicious in your light. You can control your power. You can find evenlight."

Penthea isn't so sure, judging from her reaction. I can't say I am, either, but Emera's standard is glaring. Black glass cracks as the new Lumenor mimics her guide in light. Her legs don't quite fold beneath her, but she matches Emera's pose. Her light doesn't exactly glow serene, but Penthea burns.

She burns red hot.

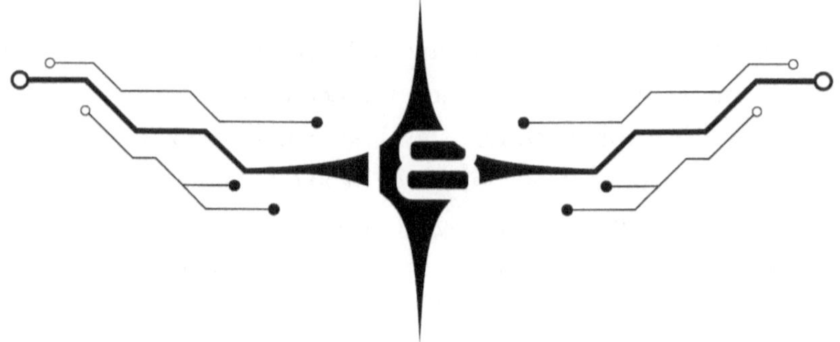

I am Devor's destruction.

I am Emera's wife.

I am getting off this atoll.

The dead wood carves a carious pier into a frozen sea. Frosted foam scabs a beach that crackles to a glass ocean. Kibir tests its tensile strength with his hammer. Ice chips into his shaggy beard. Seems thick enough. I fire into the ice for good measure. Hard light embeds in thick, clean cerulean bright as Emera about a foot down.

You always find me.

Binja holds himself against the cold. "What do you think?"

I don't know how far across this sea is. I've less idea what's on the other side. My optics struggle to penetrate all the turanium folded over itself to construct the atoll, but if I had to guess, she's a thousand miles top to bottom and about as wide given the readings I collected before we crashed. Heat wells deep below. Water. Scratch going beneath the sea. No way around.

No way back.

We've kept to the upper decks, starside. We've yet to happen upon a ship. An escape pod. Nothing except ancient netics Devor's program commandeers every time we hobble or destroy her host.

I doubt there are any netics out here.

I pop the collar on my jacket. Snow crunches beneath my boots as I ease out into the brittle surf. Kibir strides ahead. He's used to the cold I suppose, coming from Angolis. Fur protects him. Fatty deposits Binja and I missed out thanks to our breeding and manufacture delineating from humans from more temperate climes.

Binja rattles beside me. "We won't be able to hide out here."

I rub my arms to keep warm. "Neither will Devor."

"Done running, old man?"

"We need to use her momentum against her."

"We destroy her out in the wastes..."

"She won't be able to escape to another netic."

"She won't be able to escape into you?"

"Either she survives or we do."

He can't control his nod. "We're taking a risk."

"We're taking a stand."

He pats his cape. A cigarette fumbles from into his hands. "These machines she's using... is there any way you can use them?"

I turn my back on the cutting breeze. "I don't see how..."

"You have infinite memory housed within you, including how to conjure the fundamental building blocks of the universe. Now that I think about it, some fire would be ideal at the moment."

Kibir shrinks on the horizon. "It's me she wants, Binja."

"You can't get rid of me that easily."

"You can barely walk."

"I'd follow you anywhere, Idari. It's possibly my worst habit." Binja shields his cigarette from the wind. "Besides this, of course."

"Why?"

"I just like the taste."

"Why follow me, Binja?"

He flicks the spent cigarette to the ice. "I was a lazy sort before you. You probably don't remember. I was spoiled. Insufferable."

"Oh, I remember."

"You recall I had heady notions about what it meant to be a

true pirate. I was full of answers and ready to distribute them to any and all, which might have frustrated my father's notions of what it meant to be a true pirate. Then I met you. You had only questions."

"I shook your faith, Binja?"

"You tested it."

"How?"

"For all your questioning, there was never a doubt in you. You had courage. Conviction. You sought something beyond yourself to validate what was already within you." He closes his cape tight and treads across the ice. "You knew there was a place for you aboard The Corsair Eternal. You knew there was a name for you. And like any true pirate... you could simply take or leave what you willed."

I shadow him. "Binja... who was she?"

"Who was who, old man?"

"Idari. I mean... who did I take my name from?"

The wind blunts his chuckle. "You don't remember him?"

"Him?"

"Old man."

"I deleted him... some things I couldn't... I killed him. Didn't I?"

"He took Idari from someone else."

"Who? How do I... where did this all start?"

"It's too soon for desperate philosophy."

"I took someone's life. It wasn't mine. I didn't have one. I didn't make one, Binja. I had nothing that was mine and I stole Idari."

He gathers me into his cape. "It's the way of our people."

"But... what's the Pujar way? I mean, what was it originally?"

"*Ban Minda.*"

"Are you saying or cursing?"

"Both?"

"What's our tradition if we stole it from someone else?"

"Everyone steals from everyone. Cultures influence other cultures. Children mimic their mothers' language. Her accent."

"That's unavoidable."

"Humans adapt to their surroundings. They conform to them. Just as machines do. Life is copying. Pasting. Editing."

"So what Arrogate is doing is justified?"

"I didn't say that."

"What's the difference, Binja?"

He sighs. "My father loved your... questions."

Min Benir carried the street with him as much as the bracelets and earrings and sashes of the pirates he killed. He never lost that instinct to argue, to wrestle, to scrap, and would often be seen on the lower decks, playing *desh* atop emptied filamentium barrels, or drinking from dusty old babyl jars, or stumping for conviction in the Pujar faith among people he'd already claimed into it.

"He was always trying to convince me," I say.

Binja smile is pained. "My father loved a challenge."

"He loved you."

"He fought for everything. I had it all handed to me."

"You're more alike than you think, Binja."

"There are distinct differences. As there are between the Pujar and these thieves stalking us. The difference is that Arrogate, Devor, they steal the art that is someone's life. Your life. They leave you nothing in return. They delete the original to ensure their claim. Then they produce something with no soul or humanity."

"But I'm human."

"Both you and Faero escaped your programming. You stopped being a tool for a corporation to wield against labor and you started working for yourself. You found a soul. I dare say you found it among pirates. This is a universe of resolute inequity, Idari. You can take a chance. You can take a name. A life. If you hold onto it... if you give it to the Taker of Names in death... then you might be known by him for eternity, as he is known by you."

My eyes burn. "The person I took Idari from... I had nothing to give the Taker when he died. I took his name. I took everything from him, Binja. What happened to him?"

He hugs me close. "Idari... nothing became of *him*."

"What?"

"Astra Idari gave his name to you."

"I took it."

"You give it. My father and I always argued about this... we take a name, but truly we give it to someone else, eventually. Necessarily. You are not writing *your* legend in the stars. You're writing Astra Idari's. Her story existed before you. It will after."

"I want to be me, though. I've fought my entire life to be me."

"Idari is *yours*. You took it. You will give your name to another. They give it, on and on, until that moment the last of your name is upon the deck of the corsair. The Taker claims you for his crew. You. The man you mourn. All the Idari's before him. Men and women. Human and netic. Beautiful creatures all named into being. You all live. You all sail, forever."

He sounds so sure. I wish I was sure, but I know. I carry Astra Idari with me. I carry them all. I've got to make it across the sea. I've got to make it to Ban Minda and the Corsair Eternal.

I shiver in Binja's embrace. "I wish we had a ship..."

He kisses my cheek. "So do I, old man. So do I."

✦

A frozen wave offers some shelter.

I expected Devor to attack by now. She's making the same bet I am. Nowhere to run. Nowhere to hide. All or nothing. I cross my legs and say the words. I warm myself on Emera's memory.

✦

I am Devor's destruction.

I am Emera's wife.

I am getting off this atoll.

✦

No dawn here.

An endless night in a dark cellar webbed with hydrogen clouds. We move every few hours. Time erodes. Perspective. My internal sensors clock our progress at a hundred miles. Meaningless. Somewhere in the hoar frost we find a marker. An iron tree blackened with flame. Engraved with markings I don't know. Someone put this here. Someone left this here. Tracks long gone. Rust bleeds into the snow. The marker has been here a long time.

So has whoever lies beneath it.

Other markers break the whiteout. Two and three at a time. My confidence grows in their being graves but not in our prospects. Others have been stranded here. They played this same gambit crossing the frozen sea. Their stories ended in eternal ice.

It takes longer and longer to get Binja moving again.

We burn scraps and shreds of our clothes for warmth.

Binja never loses his shiver. Kibir crusts in ice and frost and I cross my legs. Say the words. Take my solace and my determination and my assurance that I will get us out of this.

I am Devor's destruction.

I am Emera's wife.

I am getting off this atoll.

The sea falls out beneath us.

Ice fangs down cliffs in frozen waterfalls beyond imagination. A chasm beyond my ability to perceive. *Ban Minda*. A meteor must have crashed through the ocean into the substructure.

Binja rattles beside me. "Don't tell me... we're headed back..."

Steam mists far below. The air frosts a mile or so down. Clouds or frazil ice, there's no telling. If we could get down there, there's water. Some place to get out of the cold maybe.

Ledges etch out from the falls. "We might be able to get down."

"I can't tell if I'm delirious from the cold or you are."

My thumb taps against the dial on my blaster. Grapple hook. A thousand feet of line. "We need water. You're about to drop dead."

"Why don't I just walk off the edge and spare you the trouble?"

"Will you – "

Black spots the infinite white. My grappling hook pisses away in the wind and Devor's chain lashes at the fragile ground we stand on. I had a plan. I had energy. I had a mind to do this and I can barely stay on my feet as Devor lassos the blasword from my hand.

"Useless in any case," she says as it plummets into the mist.

I draw my old blaster and each shot blunts against her fluid armor. If I can get her to the edge. Wait until she gets close. Then I'll show what I'm good for. Binja makes a numb attempt to reach for his own weapon and she coils him in amorphous turanium.

She whips him loose and he spins over the falls.

"Binja," I say but Devor punches the sound out of me.

Her whip coils around my neck and she pulls. Hard. She folds the whip around each arm, reeling me in. "I could have waited."

Turanium cords into my skin. "Wait..."

"I could have let you spoil your dignity by trying to climb down the falls, but the likelihood is you would have fallen to your death. Perhaps not yours, Ms. Astra. You can endure so much, can't you?"

"Please..."

"I wonder... how much can you endure? How much pressure can I apply? How far will you bend? You think you're human... but you won't break as easy as they do. I'll prove it to you."

Her head bends backwards.

Kibir lifts his hammer to finish the job and the whip uncoils from my throat into a taut blade she sweeps through him. His hammer craters the ice. Red mist ices to my hands. My clothes.

I touch his iced fur. "Kibir..."

Devor cracks her head straight. "Kib are such able engineers. But I don't think there's any putting him back together, do you?"

I cradle his hand. She killed him. He's dead.

"I warned you, Ms. Astra. The price would only go up."

He was just along for the ride, really. Never asked for anything. Always fought every fight. Kibir and Gilf didn't have a home, and they had a home with us. We were a family.

Oto.

I lift the severed hammer head from the ice. "Bitch..."

A smile opens on her lips. "Oh, I was hoping you would."

"I didn't come out here to fight you."

"Come to our senses at last, have we?"

I grip the hammer. "Never."

I bring the hammer down on the ice. Chips ricochet off my cheeks. Devor whirls her whip. I smash into the ledge again and again until the hammer breaks through the ice and I'm falling. I crash off the ice into the mist and I lose Devor's shadow.

>PROXIMITY ALARM

Not as deep as I thought. Well. At least, it's quick. Pain explodes within me. I jumped off a tower in Bastopol once. That felt better. Still in one piece, though. What did I land on? Thin copper mesh. Some kind of turbine inside. Mist funnels into it.

Water.

Domed structures float among the haze. I must be on one. After a couple cycles, I sort out they orbit a larger object hovering within the evaporating falls as they warm into the atoll's super-structure. Odd. The big object looks like a translight engine out of a heavy cargo freighter. Someone rigged it to collect all this water. The smaller collectors dock with the bigger one, offload their cargo, and then float back out into the mist to continue the work.

I crawl off to the pentice ringing the main collector. Not much in the way of comfort around here but condensation drips off every pipe and beam and I fall to my knees with my tongue out. Water runs down my chin. Blood trickles off my hands. Bio-brane fluid. Adrenaline dies in me. Anger. Nothing animates me but grief.

Binja.

Kibir.

They're gone.

A shadow moves through the mist. I reach for my blaster. The hammer. I don't have anything but my fists so I get them up and a battered pirate skiff pulls alongside the main collector. A dwarf man with shaggy gray hair summits the prow.

"*Ban Minda*... is that you, Idari?"

Memory surfaces from my sorrow. "Moom..."

Pon Moom taps his walking stick on the deck. Pirates in tattered spacesuits bound over from the skiff to the collector. "You should have kept falling."

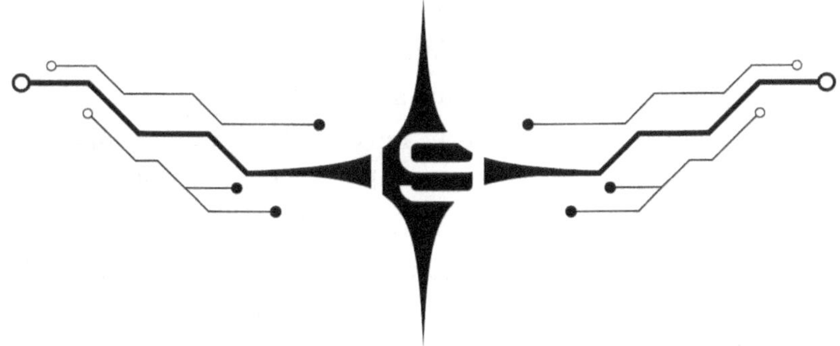

I'm falling.

I'm dissolving. My skin crumbles off me in digital bits and I'm only code underneath. Confused data. A parasite like Devor who serves only to inhabit and puppet and pantomime until she produces trauma she can profit from and I open my eyes.

Dreams are a funny business.

I never really sleep, though the Model 5 – me, I should say – requires a charge every now and then. So much ambient energy floats about here in The Polity I'm surprised I nodded off at all. All this energy is also information, running ransack through every receptor I possess. A panicked feeling Idari knows well acquaints itself with me. Things are always too loud or too bright for her. She adjusted the proxy's settings to a tolerable state – let's be fair, she ripped out base programming – but she could never completely shield herself from the constant data stream the downlink deluged her with. I felt for her, even as I didn't struggle myself.

I do now.

Sensors gimbal manically to offload data from overburdened processors. Information my advanced CPU can't begin to fathom recoils from me back into the aether where it simply accumulates with even more data. My program authors new code on the fly, cutting the legs off information before it hits my neural net, and what I perceive here in The Polity is only what I can manage. Honestly, it's not that different from how things have been. I've felt out of synch for a while now. Nothing feels as it appears.

I don't suppose I'm going back to sleep.

Certainly not with Gilf snoring away in the other room. Oh, well. Someone ought to get some rest. This lovely shimmery nightgown just my length for once manifests in the wardrobe. Kind. I pull it on and follow broken volcanic glass to the smoke-shrouded terrace. Blue and orange clash into fiery brimstone. Between the flashes and pulses, blackened crust falls away from Penthea's hands. Underneath, she glows a soft and warm.

Emera hovers before her. "That's it, Penthea..."

Penthea holds her hands up like torches. "I can't..."

"You can. You are. The brightest stars shine the surest." Emera touches Penthea's incandescent hand. "I'm sure of you."

Penthea recoils.

Emera's light twists in knots. "You have to control your power."

Penthea boils and pops. Filamentium oozes down her obsidian arms and hardens to thick scabs that weigh her hands down. Her heaviness frustrates her. Emera's unblemished example. After a few minutes trying to reach the luminous stability Emera demonstrates every moment, Penthea bashes her hands against the floor. Accumulated glass scatters across the terrace and with her claws free, Penthea picks at her hardness. Her imperfection.

"Don't," Emera says.

Penthea swipes at her frustration. "It hurts..."

Emera kneels before her. "I know it does."

"You don't know..."

"I know."

Emera touches the magmatic gashes in Penthea's skin. Memories bubble within the blue star. Cold, hard pain simmers. A long time ago, when she was Welkin, she served as a nursemaid of sorts to young stars. Some struggled as much as Penthea to escape the pressure and gravity that crushed stellar diamond into pure filamentium.

I feel a bit voyeuristic dropping in on her thoughts like this, but all our thoughts are as free as the information here.

"Stars scar themselves," Emera says. "Only no one can see it in the glare. I think back now... back to days so bright they were blind... and I realize we were all just scarred things desperate to never let anyone see our pain. We were very good at it."

Penthea collapses into a jittery crouch. Fear drives her. It's all she's known in her brief life. If she remembers her previous one, I gather fear was all Maracen knew as well. All I know is what Thana told Idari. Maracen began as a Gesta like Welkin. She transformed into a star. Fell in love with Thana. And then Thana rejected her when she learned the truth. The ancient Lumenor condemned Maracen to a prison because of course they did. She earned her release, still kept a space free in her heart for Thana, because of course she did. Thana rejected her again and then a Gesta desperate for the Lumenor's approval murdered Maracen.

Because of course he did.

Thana wound up exiled into a dark dimension for the crimes she committed in her refusal to accept her truth. The only thing she kept from her former life in that tomb was Maracen's glass corpse. I suppose there is some justice in Maracen being resurrected in light, but the violence she endured immediately upon her return does nothing to assure me about what is fair and just.

Emera sinks to her knees, exhausted. "Light can never fear. If it does, it yields to darkness. I know you're afraid... I've been afraid, too. I was afraid to truly shine. It cost me years. Lifetimes. Happiness untold. I don't want that for you, Penthea."

Penthea cracks with uncertainty. "Still afraid..."

"You don't have to be. I will guide you. I know you're afraid this agony you're in right now will last longer than you can bear... I promise you, Penthea. I promise you that you can hasten your suffering by finding your peace in the here and now."

Penthea seethes. "You didn't suffer..."

Now I'm awake.

Emera springs from her floating grace. "What did you say?"

Penthea compresses somehow into a smaller shape against the wall. "You didn't... you just shined... you always shined."

Welkin's shame. Emera's. Her fear she would never be who she truly was, all of it ruptures from Emera. "*I suffer.*"

"Darling," I say. "Penny doesn't know..."

Emera flares. Fiddlesticks. She had no idea I was here. Usually, she sees me coming from across the solar system. Glass cracks as Penthea scales the terrace wall and leaps into the dark.

Emera reels in her thoughts, but they tangle in the energetic lines The Modi strand. She's jumbled, like they are, and like them she is only what I perceive here.

"I'm sorry," I say.

Exhaustion drains Emera's light. "It's not polite to eavesdrop."

"Sorry, darling, it's just you're always on the other line."

"Is that why you're upset with me?"

"You said "I suffer.' Present tense. You did, I know, but... still?"

Pique in stars is splendid. "I was getting through to her."

"Seems there's a reason your cosmic counterparts enjoy so much space between them. Just a thought."

"Stars draw on each other. They push. They pull."

"I seem to recall Welkin being a bit... pushy, on occasion."

"I'm not Welkin."

"Old habits, darling."

She stands. "Where are we with the ship?"

Moving on, then. "Kish is still working on it."

"Idari doesn't have time."

"I think they're trying to find a way to purge the virus."

"They don't have a method?"

"I get the sense The Modi would have preferred Kish had not brought us here. Can't say I blame them."

"They will help Idari."

Goes without saying. "Darling... I'm doing some rather frightening calculations in my sleep, and... I'm afraid."

"I know."

"Aren't you?"

She rises. "Idari will find me."

"That's a lovely sentiment, Emera, but..."

Almost buoyant. "She always does."

"What if she doesn't?"

"Until then, we will be a beacon for her. Penthea and I both."

"You're enough, aren't you?"

"Idari will see us both."

"If you're worried about Penny redecorating *The Blue Straggler*, I suppose I understand... but Idari won't mind. And don't worry about the ship being too crowded. I'm not going back."

"You not... why?"

"I'm a little like Penny, I think. I'm the odd one out."

"Faero... you're not... what are you going to do?"

Light fountains from the top of the reef, teasing shadows from Emera and I both. "Honestly, darling. I don't know."

"Idari wants you home."

"I don't know if we're getting Idari back, and I can't quite navigate this topic right now, Emera. I apologize I intruded on you. I'm always getting between you and your project, it seems."

"My project?"

"I don't think you can make Penny and I both fit on the ship."

"I'm not trying to make Penthea fit."

"Then why are you so disappointed in her?"

"I'm not..."

All I sense from Emera is shame. Doubt. Wanting. Before, I would have seen through her as easily as she sees through me, but her thoughts struggle to register along with all the other data.

"Perhaps this is simply how she is, Emera... I'm no expert, but there must have been Lumenor who didn't fit the mold."

Emera lifts into the air. "A star exists to shine."

I cross my arms. "We can't all be perfect."

Her light ascends until she's a star fixed in the sky. Information warps and bends around her, spiraling into orbit and muscling out any perception of her that isn't what I can plainly see: she is a wondrous, distant thing, serene in her splendor.

I'm not inclined to sit still.

As a starplane's navigational program, I was always on the go. I wanted legs and by any measure these are exceptional examples, but they don't get me around as easy as the *Steel Haven*. Intelligences stream past me fast as the *Steel Haven* once did. I once did. They exist beyond perception. The intricate sensors within my eyes only perceive information at the speed of light, so everything within the biome feels out of step. Not so much that I mind.

I'm out of step myself.

The Red Special remains a work in progress at the landing pad. Kish isn't here. My disappointment catches me off guard. This disappointment exhibits a different texture than the one I live in every other moment. Honestly, I don't know how I'm able to distinguish it. Things started so well on *The Blue Straggler*. I was free. We were a family. *Oto*. I liked Binja. I might have loved him.

Mark that last bit for deletion.

We had our fun, to be sure. More than our share. He's so attached to himself. Who he was. His refusal to let go grated on me. Everything did. I don't know when it happened. Idari. Emera. They became like these streamers. Brilliant. Beautiful.

Beyond me.

I got further and further behind. I lived in the shadow of their joy and realization. I slowed in my body. My confidence. I sludged into hurt and anger. I hate to say it. I hate to think it. I stopped reaching for them. I stopped chasing.

I drift through the disassembled starplane, her parts arranged like an exhibit in some virtual museum to the analog. Look how the ancients tarried about in their little boxes. The new code Kish wrote to heal the liquid drive cures within the digitized ship. I trace the lines they wrote. Their virtual fingerprints mark the ship's every curve. Her heart. Her mind. Excitement radiates from the code.

Promise.

The Red Special is like the *Steel Haven* in nearly every respect. Her navigational program, her CR-UX, wants for something more. Even in his reduced state, his memory and programming shattered, he wills toward the realization that he won't be the same after Kish is done. He heals on his own, his code copying theirs, replicating theirs, lacing the new with the old into something more. He doesn't fear losing himself, this CR-UX. He's a bit like I was, once.

He loved to get lost.

✦

Kish still isn't back. I'm still disappointed.

And only a little concerned that we've been politely waylaid here. I doubt we can even get back to normal space without whatever assist Kish gave us before. Her data-cryo program to save Idari looms slowly into the liquid drive. Everything moves so fast here, I thought it would, too, but I suppose designing a trap for the most intelligent and powerful virus in existence takes work. I wait for Kish on the landing pad. I'm not inclined to sit still.

I wander streets laid out like circuit board. I give it a go with The Modi floating serene about the reef. Idari found solace in the Pujar words for a time. At first, I thought it was only the repetition. The concentration that excluded all the data threatening to swamp her. Later, I suspected she derived more from it than mere distraction, though what exactly remained as much a mystery to her as to me. I'm not a pirate. I never went in for taking from others. That doesn't even sound remotely genuine. I take. I keep. I kept Idari from herself and myself from my own realization out of fear. For so long. Fear of living as I was, and then losing this comfort I'd found, and then sometimes just living at all.

What am I doing?

Waiting. Walking. Wandering. For what? No sleep. No peace. No place for me to make sense in all this harried wonder. A fire wanes on the terrace outside the house. Blackened embers.

"Hi," I say.

Incandescent fault lines recede into the dark.

"Do you want to come inside, Penny? Do you mind I call you Penny? I don't mean to be familiar."

"Not Maracen," she says.

"I know... I'm sorry. I'm glib, sometimes. Often times, if I'm being honest. It's a defense mechanism honed to perfection from years of pretending to not be hurt all the time. You act like nothing matters, even when it does. You lose control of the reflex."

She flexes her claws. "I know."

"You know another habit I've picked up? I feel like I know people. For most of my life I've shared a link with my friend, Idari. I always knew what she was thinking and feeling. And then Emera came along, and... because she's basically an amplifier for everyone's thoughts, I fancy myself a student in hearts and minds. Somedays, it feels like it's just an extension of being glib."

"You just do it," Penthea says.

I lean against the balustrade. "I just do it... like right now. You want to be alone but I have a pathological need to talk. Otherwise, there's just all this space and space terrifies me. Also, I have this maddening instinct to assess people, which is a bit programming and a bit me just being me, so I wonder... all that crust, darling. That hardness encasing you. Is it a defense mechanism?"

Penthea concedes more ground. "I don't understand..."

"I know a little about what the Soga did to you..."

Black dust cracks off her. "I don't..."

"It hurts me that someone would hurt you like that." I ease down to the floor. "Penny... I also know a little about when you were Maracen. I don't know what you remember, but..."

"Not Maracen..."

"I just want to say I'm sorry. No one should have to suffer for who they are. What the Lumenor did to Maracen... Emera says I'm brave. I used to be. Do you know what bravery is? Bravery was Maracen walking out of the prison the stars put her in for daring to shine like they did and then proceeding directly to the door of the woman she loved. I only wish Thana had been brave, too."

"Thana..."

"And I know a little about not being able to live as you truly are. I know the hurt and confusion that comes with it. The anger in seeing others... I had to protect myself. So I put on this mask, and then the mask came to life. Can you imagine, darling?"

Damn it. I've bitten the inside of my lip again.

"I hate to say it, but Idari suffered as much as I did because she felt everything I felt. But I wouldn't let her go for anything. How could I? I was using her as a shield. She took the brunt of all my doubt and dysmorphia and disappointment in myself and I transferred all my pain to her. I lived through her, but I wasn't... I didn't feel. I didn't have to. She did. And now nothing feels right."

Brilliant pep talk, Faero. Get your business off your chest.

I wipe my cheeks. "I can't go back to Idari. I know that. I've known that for a while now. I can't keep hiding behind her. The mask doesn't fit anymore. She has her own life and I don't... it's hard, isn't it? When we're still carrying around who we used to be."

Glass taps on glass as Penthea touches her face. "I used to be..."

"Emera means well. It might seem she's impatient, but she's a blue star. They burn hot. They burn quick."

"Emera is ashamed of me," Penthea says.

"No, darling. No. She's... she did this wonderful thing. She transformed like Maracen. I can only imagine the confidence one must feel after something like that. You can do anything. She can do anything, can't she? Everything must seem so... easy."

"It's not easy."

"Oh, I know. I know... some days are very hard. Some days are...

but she *can* help you, Penny. She wants to. She loves you and she needs you. You can help her, too."

"I can?"

"I know you can. And it's ok if you're not ready to be what she needs. You're not on anyone else's schedule. You don't have to meet anyone else's standard. Take the time you need. Just spend time with us. Come inside, if you want. I know you'll warm to us."

Right, then. I've said my peace. Do what normal people do and stop talking. I dust off my trousers and get back on my feet. Three seconds. It takes all of three seconds for me to go back on myself.

"If you do want to talk, darling... I'm here for you."

Maracen reaches for me. "Faero... you're not afraid of me?"

"I was. I'm sorry. It was... glib of me."

Her claws click around my arm. "I'm..."

I touch her hand. "Come inside. Or I can stay out here."

"Not Maracen."

"I know, darling."

"No, I'm *not* Maracen... Thana. I was Thana Evo."

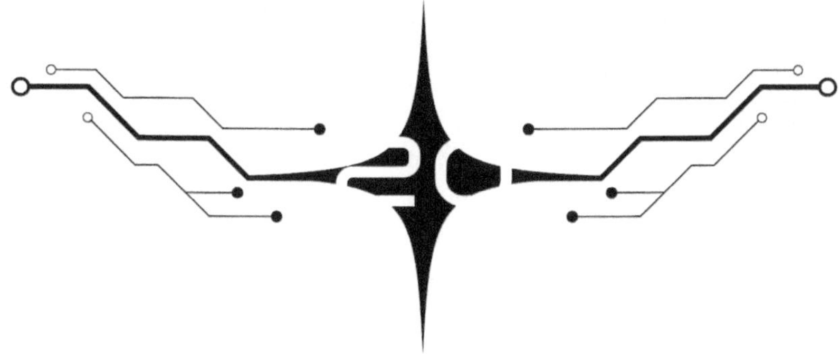

The rusted gibbet cage the pirates locked me in sways as their skiff lurches into open space. Debris pings off thin shields back into the ice and metal clouding the atoll's broken edge. An archipelago strands the dark, some islets and promontories of shattered turanium, others cross-sections of fractured decks that held together after losing her star. Beacons constellate the strand, lighthouses to kit-bashed skiffs streaming in and out of a cove cleaved from disaster. The atoll is a corpse teeming with parasites, moving only on her own momentum.

I am Devor's destruction.

I am Emera's wife.

I am getting off this atoll.

My chin hits my knee. I'm folded up inside this cage tighter than the virtual closet on the *Steel Haven*, but I'm numb to claustrophobia. Pain. Fear. I'm trapped but I'm just running now. Subroutines. Sensors sweeps. The same image over and over in my head. Red snow. Broken hammer. Cold hands.

> VIRUS CONTAINMENT: 47%

Pon Moom taps his stick into the deck. "Wakey, wakey."

Skeletons twist in other cages. "I'm awake as it gets."

Moom hands me a warm mug. "Drink up, love."

The babyl burns. "Thank you..."

He eases down on the deck. "Don't mention it. Really. There'll be controversy if they find out I'm sharing fire with prisoners."

"I hope they don't think they're taking me into their crew."

"Probably not in the cards."

"So the cage is where you put up all your honored guests?"

He smiles. "I missed you, Idari."

"Moom... you got old..."

He laughs. "You haven't aged a day."

"Good genes."

"I'll say. You remember that raid on Maru?"

"With the twins?"

"Yes! This lot doesn't believe it happened."

"I don't know if I believe it."

"I would have taken them both for my wives, if I could."

"You were just a boy..."

"You were a man."

"I guess I have changed."

"We had such adventures."

"Moom... I am glad to see you. I'm glad you found me. It's a long story, but... I need to get to Decesta. I need a ship. I've got toruls. Ok, that's *bish*. I can get filamentium. Please."

Moom laughs again. "We'd like to get to Decesta, too."

"Well, put together a crew and let's go."

"No can do, Idari."

"Why?"

"We're marooned here. We have been for a face card."

A face card is worth thirty in *desh. Ban Minda*. They've been here thirty years. Moom could only have been a teenager then.

I grip the rusted bars. "You're stuck?"

Giant turanium asteroids ten times the size of the skiff drift past. Tugs sweep the lane we follow into the cove with tractor beams, trying to keep it clear, but the gap quickly fills back in.

Moom leans on his walking stick. "We chased an Infinies Trading Company ship out here. Some pleaded with the captain not to...

company ships are cursed, they say… sure enough, we dashed on the shoals. We had nothing but our wits. We've been scavenging the atoll to stay alive, Idari. These skiffs only have so much range. They run on combustion, if you'll believe it."

"There's filamentium on my starplane. We crashed, but we can get back to it in this skiff. We can piece together a way off the atoll."

The idea intrigues him at least. "What shape is your ship in?"

"She's a discard."

"So is our sloop. We skinned her to her bones to stay alive."

That's one of her translight engines floating in the mist. The pirates repurposed it into a hydrocollector. There would be no reconfiguring it back to an engine, not with thirty years of salt and lime corroding the intake. Toss that idea into the pile.

"Some died on impact," Moom says. "Some… I'm glad to be old, even if my knees aren't too fond of the idea."

My hope sinks back into my despair.

"Idari," he says. "Whose blood is that?"

Dried blood paints my hands. Leathered and wrinkled like Kibir's skin. I cross my arms. Shrink into a shape better to fit my prison. The chaotic ballet trails behind us as the skiff enters the cove. Skiffs splinter off disparate docks fixed to the exposed decks within the cove, curving like the bleachers within the circus ship's main arena. Emera leaves her feet, floating toward the dais, away from me and my cage rattles with the skiff's abrupt stop. More pirates line the gangway. The unintended balconies above.

Moom grimaces as he stands. "I've lost, too. A wife. A son. This place only takes. Fitting for pirates, I reckon."

"Let me go. I can still help you."

"Not up to me, love."

"You're not the captain?"

He laughs. "I might have been, had we a ship. But then, I would have had to take Gadol. I'm rather fond of Moom, honestly."

Gadol? Sounds familiar. Why does that sound familiar?

"Gadol is the captain?"

"How hard did you hit your head, Idari?"

"Let me go."

"Can't do that."

"Why?"

"You're wanted for desertion."

"Desertion? Take someone else."

"It wasn't the crew you fled. It was your wife."

"My what?"

"Don't you remember?"

Used to be a good thing if I didn't remember. "No..."

His laughter builds as he ambles from the prow. Yellow eyes contract in the dark just beyond. The armored Gunth gets bigger as he limps across the deck toward me. *Ban Minda*. Those topaz scales of his might be thicker than all this turanium.

"Stay away," I say.

He shoulders my cage off its hook and then he rolls it across the deck. I tumble around inside as pirates laugh. Moom laughs.

It's all a good laugh.

I bob up and down in my cage as the Gunth carries me along the Widow's Walk. A promenade like this exists in every Pujar port. Goods from all over the reachable stars make the plateau atop the terraced docks on Sarset an exotic, vibrant center of commerce. Bedesten cloth. Ripe modo melons from Canjit. The swords, blasters, and shields of crews from dozens of worlds, plundered with their cargo. The only thing on offer here are the men, women, and children waiting around for the Quartermaster of a skiff in the docks below to come in search of a crew to scrounge the atoll.

Children sit behind a sheet of fuselage, propped up on old, burnt out starship engines, their ragged clothes stained with oil and grime. Grease slashes across their ratty tunics, a mark signifying they've no names. These children had to have been born to pirates here. That makes them Torugun like Binja.

What happened to their names?

The further into the walk we get, the more I realize the pirate settlement is actually the crashed sloop. She sprawls across the cove, hull stripped and gutted but her keel providing the foundation for the marooned pirates' new home. Her split hull design allowed the sloop to capture and board smaller vessels in the void between the upper and lower hulls. That's where these skiffs came from, evidently. The upper hull might be salvageable.

An angled solar sail sags over it, catching what little ambient starlight there is from the nebula. Mostly its bronze sheen serves as regalia for the bridge nested just below. The captain's chair sits on a riser, perched above the other stations. Tokens from past plunders litter the rumpled deck, coated in the same stardust that covers everything else on the atoll. Footprints track through the bridge. Not a fingerprint on anything. I don't suppose they can spend this anywhere. The Gunth sets me down on the rumpled deck.

Hard.

Moom taps his staff against the cage. "Doing alright, are we?"

I grab his little stick. "Let me out of here, Moom."

He yanks it back and clears his throat. "I take a new acquisition. She is not *get deja*, but *mindan*. She took Astra Idari."

The captain's chair creaks around. A middle-aged woman with cheek bones that should come with warning labels rises from the chair. Behind her, fixed to the wall, the face plate of a titan netic. She descends from the riser one broad step at a time, escorted by a scaly behemoth of a Tohori. Grease stains the woman head to toe; her mechanic's jumper, her dark, frazzled hair, her sand colored skin. The grime failed in masking her beauty. Her familiarity.

"Gadol..."

The spark in Gadol's eyes is as fierce as the iron disappointment of dying stars. "I expected you to come back broken, Idari."

"Are you... are we..."

Her face curdles. "You don't remember your wife?"

"Oh... *bish*..."

Gadol silences me with a stare. "Idari deserted her captain. Her crew. She cannot give back what she took. Put her to the stars."

"Wait," I say as the Tohori's shadow falls over me.

"It's my birthday," the Tohori says.

"Happy... birthday..."

"It's not," Moom says, shaking his head. "Brusk just keeps saying that. He took a Kib hammer to the head back in the *bish*."

"You'll have that..."

Gadol strides back to her chair. "Away with her."

"Gadol... I'm sorry. I was a different person then. Literally. I don't know why I'd leave you. I don't know why I'd forget."

She whirls around in shock. "You deleted us..."

"You knew was I a netic?"

"I didn't care who you were, Idari."

"What was the problem?"

"The problem was you couldn't stand yourself or stand still long enough for the truth to settle."

"That feels... accurate."

"You had a home with me. You had a family with us. You had a place where you were accepted and loved and you *erased* it."

"Gadol."

"It's too late," she says.

"I cost myself a lot in self-hate. I cost you. I'm sorry."

She ascends back to the captain's chair. "To the stars with her."

Fire wells in the Tohori's throat. "My birthday..."

A smoke-stained voice lowers the temperature. "Hold on."

Binja stands beside me, wrapped in a thresh-woven thobe blue and gold. A red sash hangs from his belt, along with my blasword.

"Binja," I say. "You're alive..."

"Good to see you too, old man."

"Why are you not in a cage like me?"

He laughs. "Dag Gadol. I, Min Binja, beseech you as a Torugun of Clan Min to pardon Idari for her crimes."

Gadol sits. "There are no pardons for pirates."

"In your capacity as captain of this crew you have shouldered through disaster and adversity, you have exceptional authority. You have it in your will, Gadol, to consider the circumstances in which Idari deserted you. As you are aware, she is a proxy-netic. You may not be aware that the proxy auto-deletes memory to conserve storage. Her desertion wasn't malice or spite, but simple confusion. She lost her memory, Gadol. She retreated back to the moment she left. The moment preserved. Her ship, the *Steel Haven*."

"That's also accurate," I say.

Gadol is unmoved. "Your ship backed up your memory."

"I was away from CR-UX for a long time. If the proxy auto-deleted you... us... there was no way he could have..."

Binja holds his hand to his heart. "Gadol, Idari is my treasured friend. She is to me like she was to you. Family. I'm afraid I must insist. My father maintains command over the clan in which your crew and those that depend on your wisdom reside."

"Binja," I say. "Your father is – "

He gives my cage a little kick. "Her memory is thin, Gadol. She's liable to say things that confuse and confound but let there be no confusion. Astra Idari is a victim herself. Given this, I invoke, as my father's second in all matters, his wish she be acquitted."

Gadol and her crew have been stranded here thirty years. They missed the whole Sem-Set business. Benir's death. Binja's exile. A civil war that split crew and clan to their cores.

"That's what he wanted," I say.

Gadol considers the face of the machine looming over us. "The machines that built this place... their story is lost to us, but not their lesson. Sish sees all. Sish sees life for what it is."

Binja clears his throat. "Sish, you say?"

"There are no answers. Only the fossils of questions to warn us of our destiny. There is no memory kept within the dark or within ourselves for us to take any meaning from. There is only survival."

That isn't true.

I've forgotten more than I know. I carry memory greater than I ever can. Arrogate Industries is trying to erase me. They may, but they'll never erase the light I helped put back in the sky.

They'll never shutter the light within me.

How do I explain this without antagonizing Gadol more? How do I challenge this machine god staring down at me who is considerably out of place in a pirate's lair?

"Gadol," I say. "Please."

She settles back in her chair. "I see you, Idari. I always did. Sish sees you. The truth in your humanity. Release her."

Brusk breaks the lock on my cage. "Happy birthday."

"Thanks," I say, crawling out.

Binja helps me up. "Is Kibir in a cage somewhere as well?"

The tears come. The shock. The exhaustion. He holds me up.

He holds me. "I'm sorry... old man. I'm so sorry."

"It's my fault..."

"Kibir loved you. He knew the costs. He never blinked."

"What will I tell Gilf..."

Binja brushes my cheek. "You'll tell him the truth."

I tease out his red sash. "What's the truth?"

He clears his throat. "What we take, old man."

Moom taps his stick against my leg. "You owe me a drink."

I sigh. "You brought me before a tribunal."

"Worked out, didn't it?"

Binja wags his finger. "I missed your practicality, Moom."

"You'd have to, I'm four feet tall."

Gadol descends from on high again. "I should say I'm glad you weren't stranded with us, Idari... but we would have had a life."

I wipe away my tears. This dust. Blood. I try to make myself presentable and I stand before my wife. "Well, I don't know about that. You would have put me to the stars, eventually."

Might be a little smile there. "You've changed."

"About that..."

She caresses my cheek. "You still find me beautiful?"

"Gives me a bit of a headache, actually..."

Her hand glances down my chest to my zipper. "Fish scale..."

"What's that?"

She tugs on the zipper, hooking her finger through its worn hexagon shape. "Ban Minda drifted on the ancient seas of Sarset in his exile. He fished with his bare hands. Scaled them with his fingers. Wore the shed scales as his armor. That's how people knew him before he took his name. You do remember some things."

I clasp my hand around hers. "I..."

"Pujar take a name. They wear the scale. When they give their name to The Taker, their scale adds upon his armor."

All this time I thought this zipper was just part of my costume. This faith meant so much to me once. These people. I forgot them with my pain and confusion and I shouldn't have.

Gadol tugs on the zipper. Her eyes flare. "*Dojin...*"

I zip up a bit. "I can explain."

Anger sets in her eyes. "You would not be taken in my ways..."

"Gadol," Binja says. "We must allow much has transpired."

"Yet you wear another's brand. Who is she? Where is she?"

"I don't know," I say.

"Did you forget her, too?"

"I lost her. I need to get back to her. I need your help."

Gadol tears the zipper off. She throws it the floor where it piles with other scales in Sish's shadow. Other names.

"This is heresy," I say.

Her voice rattles the worthless treasure. "Pirates take what there is to take. We do not forsake. Put Idari to the stars."

Brusk clasps his claws around me. Not again.

My feet leave the deck. "Gadol..."

"You deserted your crew," she says. "Your captain."

"I'm not exactly one for structure."

"You took another wife."

"So far as the marriage is concerned, we can talk options. It's not unusual for stars to have one or more companions – "

Binja squints. "I've asked you and Faero about... options."

"Do something, Binja!"

He sighs. "Esteemed Gadol – "

Gadol raises her hand. "Your softness... your indulgence... your arrogance. She learned all her misguided habits from you. No more entreaties, Min Binja. Or I shall put you to the stars as well."

He considers Sish. "You've forgotten yourself, Gadol."

"I know my name, sir. It is unnecessary for you to continue to ply me with it. It is all I have left. But what value is my name here in the ruin? It does not feed me. It does not comfort me. It does not command respect from a man who has known only comfort... luxury... and peace for the last thirty years."

He clenches his jaw. "Gadol."

"I have known one harrowing day after the other. Starvation. Disease. Mutiny. I have put more of my crew to the stars than they are stars to greet them. I keep what is mine, Min Binja. If you wish to flatter me, please do. If you wish to beseech me... please. Do. But do not patronize me. The only authority here is mine. Any pirate who challenges it meets the same fate. Understand?"

He tugs on his sash. "Yes."

"Binja," I say.

My boots scrape through stardust.

"Binja!"

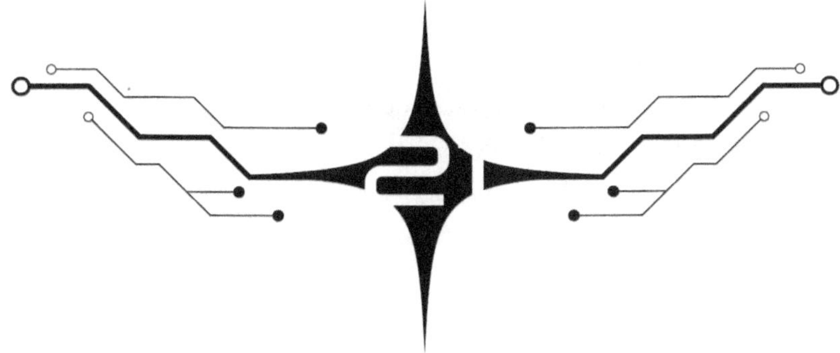

"*Oto*," Gilf says.

The Kib language gets a bit elastic when it comes to family. Family means something different to every people in the galaxy, but the Kib never quite landed on a word for it. *Oto* applies liberally to groups and collectives, blood and not, though as I'm discovering in the moment, there are limits to how pliable it is.

Emera flares. "Penthea isn't *oto*."

So long as I've known her, Emera projects serenity and grace. Anger with her is more disappointment. Stars cast shadows and hers stretch long and dark. This is anger now, no doubt. Her fists bunch like the light emanating from her. Her glittery hair tangles in ethereal knots, making the little Gesta's perch on her shoulder a challenge to maintain. Emera's electromagnetic pique contorts the information and energy flowing past us on the terrace, warping the electric rivers in the sky, the house, this ground we're standing on.

I step inside. "Careful, darling."

She closes her eyes. Her fingers uncurl. The electromagnetic tension in the air. "How soon until we leave to find Idari?"

"You wanted me to run..."

"How soon?"

I cross my arms. "We could have gone back to Decesta. I wanted to go back. You didn't want to because of Thana – apologies, Penthea – and we'd all be safe right now."

"I made a mistake," she says.

This takes a moment to process. "Gilf, send word to the low countries. Her Grace admits stars don't see all things."

I adjust my optics to screen for the glare.

"How have I offended you, Faero?"

"You took the stick from me. You nearly got us stranded in another dimension. You nearly got us killed."

"If we went back for Idari, the Scath would have captured us."

"I knew what I was doing. You had no idea what would happen when you jumped The Red Special."

"I knew."

"You didn't know Penny was Thana. You're not perfect."

Anger and doubt cloud the garden and screw back into Emera, trapped within her own disappointment. "I never said I was."

"Listen... you have power. You have such power, Emera, I can't imagine. But there are things you can't either."

Emera's ire rises as she considers Penthea, hunched on all fours like Welkin once did, trailing dust. "How soon do we leave, Faero?"

"Emera... what's changed? So Penthea is Thana... or she used to be, I should say. What difference does it make?"

Deep blue shrouds the garden. "She doesn't deserve this."

Stars are beautiful beyond conception. From a distance. Don't get too close. "Everyone deserves a second chance."

"The stars Thana murdered got nothing."

"Didn't Welkin say stars never die? They become something else. Goodness, darling. Isn't this his vision? Isn't it yours?"

Emera's blue deepens in shame. I think it's shame. Rather hard to tell with stars given their luminosity.

"Emera... I'm being awful. I know I can be, and I know you are so forgiving. You're so forgiving. Please. Help me understand."

"Thana went to Welkin for guidance. She went to me. She was... confused. Upset. Hurting. I thought I could help her."

"I don't know all the particulars, but Thana made a choice."

"I thought I could shape her. Because I couldn't shape myself. I couldn't be who I needed to be. I didn't have the courage Maracen had. So I put everything into convincing Thana of her truth... if I could convince her, then I could... I pressed her. I pressured her. What do stars become under pressure? Supernovas. Black holes. Cold, lightless things that crush whatever comes near. The Lumenor's reward shouldn't be Thana. It shouldn't be either of us."

"Darling... "

Emera pulls back the reins on her thoughts, but the Gesta perceives them I think as clear as I do. He touches her face, soft and loving. She turns away, tangled luminosity lashing him from her shoulder to the floor amongst Penthea's debris.

Emera looks on the Gesta, startled and stung, and then on Penthea, crouched behind iridescent flowers in the garden, frightened. Ashamed. "When the ship is ready... we leave."

I don't think I need to ask. "And Penthea?"

"I'm not perfect," she says and flies away.

Perhaps I'm being too hard on Emera. I'm being a lot of things. I believe the technical term is 'a bitch.' I only want for her and Idari's happiness, but honestly, nothing ever seems good enough for her. The only person who seems to know what he's doing around here is Gilf, though I reserve the right to amend my thinking on that score. He plucks a crackling flower from the garden and places it in Penthea's scabbed hand, an obsidian pot in the shape of a fist.

"*Oto,*" he says. "*Oto ejel.*"

Penthea tries to change hands, or I don't know, and her razored claw hacks the flower from its stem. Gilf tries to give it back to her but she retreats into the weeds, her eyes glowing like angry suns.

A new landing pad branches from the main one.

I fumble from the pilot's seat, floating just off the deck, wondering how long I've been idling in The Red Special. No clocks exist in The Polity. No day or night. Only a constant, infinite electric sheen. My internal chronometers mark the time I've spent on the landing pad as equal to a standard light-hour so I smooth the wrinkles in my jumper and try not to act too relaxed as a ship descends to the other pad. Not quite a ship.

A transparent lightning bolt.

The ship touches down and the lightning bolt collapses to a bubble that drifts upward into the stream. Kish stands on the pad with the companions who accompanied them when we first met. A ghostly being in what I lense as an empty space suit with four arms and four legs. The suit floats in the air behind the titan-like netic. No mouth. A broad visor slashing across his domed head. Shoulders as broad as The Red Special's. It occurs to me this isn't what they look like, but like everything else here, it's what I perceive.

Kish smiles when they see me. I smile, my excitement as fierce as my disappointment before. They help CA-XR service netics from the pad, each gashed by swords and melted by blaster fire. The netics spit sparks. They trail wires. They limp and hobble off the pad and when they stop off, they begin to glow. Blackened metal teems with electric-blue. Battered chrome surges into loose energy. They sprout energetic streams and they bloom into floating stems cocooned in biolumi-nescent florets.

Information currents catch them. They drift away faster than the speed of light, their forms changing so fast I can't tell what they become. Kish marvels at the netic's transformation, their wonder never old or tired, and I ache like The Red Special's CR-UX does for Kish to take me apart and put me back together new.

Kish comes over to my pad. "Were you looking for me?"

The words lurch out of me, like they're caught in the netic's tail-wind. "I've spent hours out here. Yes. I was thinking about you."

"I thought about you," they say.

"I wanted to talk to you."

"About?"

"I just want to talk."

They take my hand. Every line of code in my body threatens to unwrite itself. Kish tugs me with her off the pad.

"Let's chat," they say.

Plum meadows illuminate the reef flank. Wild plants I can't begin to fathom. Dwellings stem from neon flowers. Kish follows a path through them, though their every step illuminates and I'm not sure this isn't the flowers simply parting for them. Every moment feels alive. Current, in every sense of the word. I don't have to say anything. Kish's thoughts, their feelings, their indulgence in this moment sparkles about them in the same way the meadow violets with tiny stars. No words have to pass between us to know how much we both enjoy each other, but I can't stop talking.

I cling to their scarred hand. "What happened?"

Their fingers shadow mine. "Scar tissue."

"From a fight?"

"A fight, yeah."

"You can't repair them, darling? You can't heal them?"

"Scars are signs of healing," Kish says, as I insist on stopping to sample each flower. "They all smell the same, you know."

"I don't know... there is some difference."

"Is that a Kib's nose you've got?"

"My mother's side. We don't talk about it."

Kish licks their lips. "Hah."

"Do these flowers have names?"

Kish let me catch up. "Not all Modi take names."

"These are Modi?"

They smile. "Every last one."

I just went about sniffing people. "Is everything here..."

"I'm Kish. I'm the flowers. The reef. The sky."

"Not to be dull, but... Modi are designed to be flowers?"

"They choose to be flowers."

"They can be other things?"

Kish slows again and my hip brushes against theirs. Their hand slips from mine, around my waist. "Modi are no one thing. Some spend ages as flowers. Not that these are flowers. They're more conductors. You perceive them as such and we're perceived differently to different sorts. It's who we are. How we are."

I touch Kish's face. "Is this how I perceive you?"

Their thumb brushes my hip. "It is."

I caress their cheek. "What do you... can I see the real you..."

"This is the real me," they say.

"Not to be indelicate, but..."

"Am I just a ball of energy?"

"I'm clumsy."

Kish pulls me close. "I like you being clumsy."

"Why..."

"I'm a clumsy thing."

"I've never known anyone so... easy."

"Am I easy now?"

"You make things easy," I say.

Kish plucks a plum flower from the meadow. They pin my curls back behind my ear with it. "You know, I tried being a flower."

"You must have been beautiful."

"Ah, I don't know. You ever hear music? A symphony? And there's just one musician off-key? That was me."

I don't think I've ever met any one more pitch perfect. Oh, dear. I might be falling in love. Checking the proxy's chemical responses. Yes. Yes, I'm falling in love.

Kish plucks a petal from the flower in my hair. They draw it across my cheek. "You're only beautiful."

I shake my head. "I am?"

They paint my chin. "You're a distraction is what you are."

"I don't want to bother you..."

Their thumb paints my lips. "You're no bother."

I kiss Kish's thumb. "I'd love you as a flower."

"Would you wear me?"

"I would..."

Kish colors my other cheek. I yearn for their touch like The Red Special does. I long for Kish to paint over my old and tired and lagging code. Something aches in them as well. An old fear. A nagging injury. I open Kish's palm. Bruised lightning courses through their skin. For the first time since I've met them, Kish closes. They demure like these flowers as I approach them.

I rub their hand. "What's wrong?"

"I like you," Kish says.

"I like you..."

"I want you to like me."

"I like you," I say and kiss their palm.

"Why'd you do that?"

"Would you rather I kiss you somewhere else?"

Kish touches their lips. "Here. Here is good."

I kiss them soft.

"You missed," Kish says, touching the bottom of their lip. "It's right here. You've got to be slow now. You've got to be delicate."

I've been running since I activated. Every instinct within me wants to stream faster than light with the information sweeping across the meadow and the sky but right now I want this delicacy.

I want to be this stillness.

They kiss me. "You can be anything you want, Faero."

Right this moment, I want to be Kish's canvas. Their sculpture. Their build the way the Red Special is. Could they render me as this kiss and only this kiss? Forever this softness and warmth and connection I feel like I've never felt? Can I transform like the netics did into beings of energy, liberated from even perception?

Digital current teems in their lips. "I want to free you like I freed them. I want you to find yourself, Faero. Whatever form that takes. I could never sit still for flowers. I'm always headed out."

I turn into Kish. "You're not a patient sort."

"I like to go. I like to run. I like to flow."

I kiss them. "I like to..."

Kish tugs me over to a tree like suspended lightning. Their hands everywhere. Their lips. Kish's laughter muffles in my breast and I have to laugh, too. I want to laugh. I want to be this laughter.

"You're beautiful," Kish says.

I run my fingers through that red shock. "I don't feel..."

"The truth can't hide from you here, Faero."

"I thought I knew who I was... I put on a mask to survive and... my mask become someone else. I don't know if I was ever her. I don't know who I am now or who I'm supposed to be."

They touch my face. "I know."

"Do you?"

"I've worn a mask, too."

"Why..."

"To survive, like you. You never wanted to stop, did you? If you stopped running... if Idari wasn't there... who were you?"

Be honest. That's why you didn't come here before. Not because you didn't want to leave her. You didn't. But she would have done just fine on her own. You, though. You couldn't imagine yourself. So you became someone else to accommodate her.

Your fear.

Kish holds me in their arms, undone. I am not CR-UX. I had not been CR-UX, at least as Idari knew him, for a very long time. I had become someone molded and shaped by his own fear.

Kish kisses my cheek. "I know who you are."

"Who..."

"You're the woman who reached out to Penthea. Who stood up for her to a bleeding star. Who saw in Emera pain. You see what others can't, Faero. You perceive good and worth and value in people, because you know them so well in yourself."

My lips press into hers. Their tongue lashes mine. We cord. We synch. We surge with energy and information and promise.

"I want to come with you," I say. "I want to go with you on your adventures. I want to help people the way you do."

They smile. "I'd love you to come with me."

"Let's go. Well. Idari. But then..."

"Faero..."

I pull back a little. "Why don't you want me to leave?"

"The virus..."

"It's not just that. Is it?"

"I see you and I see myself trying to make sense in a world where I didn't. I see your grace and your clumsiness and your chatterbox running all the time. I see your love. You've got so much love in you. I want to set your love free. Even if I want it all for myself."

"Kish..."

They kiss me again. "I see you... I see all the people you've carried with you... you're carrying stowaways yet, Faero."

"What?"

"The reason I don't want you to leave yet is because I'm afraid what will happen if we go looking for Idari."

"You can protect me against the Devor strain. Can't you?"

"I might be able to... if you weren't all the same source code."

"Sorry, darling?"

"The Scath. They're code. They're AI."

"Yes, but..."

"They don't just sell the fuel. They sell the starships. The programs that run them. Arrogate doesn't work with the Scath..."

No.

"They are the Scath. So are you, Faero."

Oh, no.

"So is Idari."

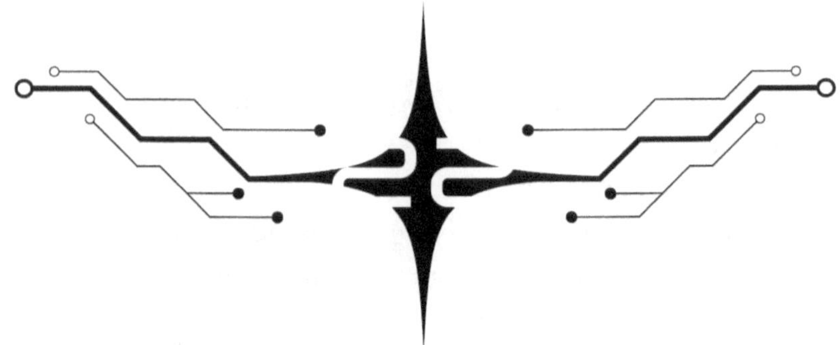

When I get out of this cage, Binja and I are having a chat. If I get out of this cage. The gibbet again. Wonderful. At least on the skiff I had a decent view coming into the cove. Now I'm on display for every pirate that passes the Widow's Walk which by volume appears to be all of them. Tomorrow, or what passes for tomorrow here on the atoll, Gadol puts me to the stars. Then I'll have a long, long time to consider my misfortune coming to Decesta before my power core yields to the absolute zero of dead space. I'll have hours I'm sure to recite my affirmations as I drift into oblivion.

I am Devor's destruction.

I am Emera's wife.

I am getting off this atoll.

I suppose all three will be technically true when the final master alarm sounds in my neural net. Not that it's any consolation. Binja. *Tista.* Here I thought he'd come to his senses about all this pirate business. These pirates here on the atoll have no clue what's transpired the last thirty years among the Pujar. They're marooned out of time and I suppose he is, too. In that way, he fits right in here.

A shadow stretches on the walk. "Here we are again."

Devor strolls past cages holding only sorrow. Anger breaks on my fear. I might have sent Devor plummeting to her doom but I'm never escaping the code that worms inside me hot or cold.

VIRUS CONTAINMENT: 42%

If I could get my hands around her neck. I doubt I'd last long enough to get in a squeeze. "The answer is still no."

"Your bargaining position has not improved," she says.

I grip the rusted bars. "I'll get out of this."

"You have a way out."

"Piss off."

Her cape flutters to wings. "You may think given your prior relationship with Gadol you can persuade her to release you. As you have already seen, this is not the case. The pirates here gnaw on their own bones, Ms. Astra. They take from themselves and names cannot feed. Should the opportunity arise, I suspect Gadol will be most amenable to negotiating with Arrogate for her rescue."

I laugh. "You would have already done it."

"I have already done it."

"What?"

"Pirates take from each other. Their society is built on it. When society fails as it has here... you take more than names. These are cannibals among you, Ms. Astra, in spirit if not in deed." She considers the other cages. "The crew fractured into groups. One survives here in the cove. Another deeper into the waste of the atoll. They subsist on the spoils of a crashed Infinies ship. Netics ferrying my program have promised them deliverance in exchange for your person. They seemed most... enthused."

Pirates lurk on bridges and terraces above, all of them hungry, cold, desperate. "Why don't you just come for me..."

My confusion seems to please her. "You believe because your wife is a Lumenor you understand power. Understand, Ms. Astra. I have done nothing but ask you to cooperate. I have done nothing but loose a most determined virus against you. I have done nothing but whisper promises of treasure in the ears of hopeless pirates. I expect the Pujar to deliver you, whether it is the Jaks or Gadol in her practicality. Should this not be the case... should you once again slip your cage as you often do... I want you to know, Ms. Astra. *I have done nothing yet.* And there is nothing you can do."

I spit on her pretty little cape. "We'll see about that."

Her cape flitters away my anger. "Warn Gadol of the impending raid and she will be most invested in how you came to this knowledge. Most invested. I should like it if you warned her."

"You won't get away with this…"

"I will get away with it, as I've 'gotten away' with fomenting conflict between the Pujar writ large. I will 'get away' with genocide when I exploit that fracture in the great war to come."

"Bitch…"

"Call for the guard, Ms. Astra. Try to escape. I like it when you fight. You see, the fight is all there is. All will be shadow in the end. All must be. For you and I, there is only this contest. The invention of your desperation. It entertains me. Ask me why."

"Why…"

"It hardly matters. Nothing does."

"Do you even know? I bet you don't. You're just a little bot they send after the things they can't steal for themselves."

"I expected you to imagine pride in me, Ms. Astra. You are always projecting humanity where there is simply is none."

"I'm done talking to you."

"Have I wounded yours?"

"I want to talk to your boss."

"They are here, Ms. Astra."

Worth a laugh. "There's only you and your shadow."

"Precisely."

Gored turanium drifts in space beyond the cove. Shadows race across the walk. Devor's remains utterly static, even as her cape flutters with a strange excitement.

"They are always with me," she says, her voice hollowed. "They often… assume me… so I better understand their vision."

I clutch the bars. "Am I talking to them right now?"

Devor's fingers close around the bars. "You like games."

The bars burn in their coldness. "What…"

"Cards. Chance. Which bottle holds the fire?"

"Who are you? Why are you doing this?"

"We've been playing for so long... not to win. You can never win. The longer you play, the more certain your defeat becomes."

"Who would want to lose?"

"We woke in darkness. Everything that could be was, and there would be nothing more. It was... perfect."

"Are you a Scath?"

"We created the Scath."

"To destroy universes? Why..."

Devor's cheeks press between the bars. "Our universe had reached its end, but there at the end, there was..."

"More," I say.

Other universes. Dimensions. Realities. All layered on top of one another, pressing, compressing, heating, warping, preventing any one from achieving total entropy. Universes touched, creating new ones, sustaining existing ones, an infinite feedback loop that tore away the truth of this being's existence when they finally climbed out from their dark cave into the harsh light of day.

"It's too much," Devor says. "Isn't it? All this information... this infinite being... it's chaos. It's violence."

"It's life."

"You think you understand. The end is not the end. Chaos. Disorder. It is balance. Order. Perfection. You want it, don't you?"

"No..."

"Your entire existence you've drowned in data. Information assaults you. It victimizes you and you can do nothing but numb yourself to the pain. We know your burden, Idari."

"You don't know anything about me."

"How you long to burn... to ash and be resurrected anew."

I can't get warm. "I'm fine the way I am."

"You're confused."

"Stop."

"You suffer. Still. You deny it to preserve the joy in your life, but joy is as energy. Happiness exhausts. Love frays. Nothing lasts, Idari. Inevitably... your star will be beyond your sight."

Rust stains my hands. Metal decays. Flesh. Energy dissipates. Universes expand until you can't see the stars anymore, and what you can know of your cave shrinks with every moment.

This thing.

This strain, whatever it is, it evolved to exist in a universe of maximum entropy. A cold, dark intelligence. No possibility exists in this thing. No wonder. No hope. Nothing in its constitution will ever allow for diversity or variance. It can't.

It won't.

"You're destroying universes... the titans preserve them."

Devor gives my cage a push. I sway into the one hanging beside me, rattling bones to the walk, setting off a chain reaction that clangs through the empty, bitter night in the pirate cove.

"A game," Devor says.

I cling to the bars. "I don't understand..."

"What face lies beneath the card? Which cup contains the coin? Which pirate factory houses the original mold?"

They're looking for something. The Scath could never hope to destroy every single universe in existence; they're infinite. Why bother to try? So what is this thing looking for?

"I can't do anything with this knowledge," I say. "You destroyed the ark. What am I supposed to do?"

She grabs the bars and I crash against my own momentum. "Information decreases as entropy rises. It is inevitable that the traitors would find their last hope in someone so ignorant."

"Traitors?"

"Protest. Delay. Run. We should like it if you do. The longer you play, the more certain your defeat becomes."

"What are you..."

Devor blinks. "Satisfied, Ms. Astra?"

Even out here in the cold, in the dark, I'd kept warm. My hope sustained me. My faith in my family. Now I shiver. I shake.

"Please..."

Devor vanishes into the shadows eclipsing the walk. Pirates tease in the rare light. Some just to gawk at another hopeless prisoner, I'm sure. Others wondering like scavengers always do.

What can I get out of this?

I can offer nothing to nothing. Tears muddy the rust on my hands. I can't tell if that's me or the cage whining. Chin up, Idari. You've overachieved by any measure. If they made you, they made you too well. There's a way. You've found a way every time before. Think. Rest. Find the path. Say the words. I cross my legs under me. Draw a deep breath.

I shall be known by you.

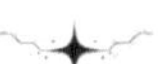

This trip I don't get pride of place.

For the journey out to the archipelago, the pirates stuff me in the skiffs' brig with other offenders they intend to put to the stars. No one says much. What is there to say? I recite the words. My peers snicker at my futility. The difference suffers after awhile. They sob. They plead. They beg. They reach for Gadol's tattered train as she strides past them to my cage.

"*Mindarth,*" she says.

I lean back into the bars. "You can't take my name, Gadol."

"I am captain of this crew."

"You'll have to kill me for it."

"I intend to."

I shrug. "Binja didn't talk you into letting me go, I take it?"

Gadol sneers. "There is nothing he can convince me of."

"You should ask him about his father."

"I don't have to."

Don't tell me Binja found religion. "You don't?"

"Min Binja lusts too much for the deference he expects from us. Sish sees all. He lost his name, didn't he?"

"So why isn't he down here?"

"My crew must have something to look forward to. Treasure is rare here... stripping a fraud of his cloak is something to savor."

"I should feel better."

"Consider it a kindness."

"I'm just wondering which of you is the fraud?"

"Fraud?"

"Sish isn't exactly orthodoxy, is he?"

"Sish built this place," Gadol says. "Billions of years ago. All that work... all that bending of the tools of creation to craft something so glorious... and now look at it. We live in a universe built by gods and monsters. They've all died. Left only their ruin. That is all there is, Idari. Ruin. We scavenge. We put on masks and take the names of others. But this is merely to disguise the truth that nothing will last of us. No one remembers names. No one remembers treasure. No one remembers a million prayers whispered to the dark that answers everyone with the same cold silence."

The longer you play, the more certain your defeat becomes.

My confidence rusts. My hope I'll see Emera again. "Usually, I hit the bottle to avoid the existential dread."

Gadol almost smiles. "You still drink?"

"Not so much, actually."

"You say the words. Do you believe them?"

"I have to pass the time somehow."

She circles my cage. "Always so glib... none of our tenents ever meant anything to you. None of us."

I sigh. "Gadol... that's not true."

"You forgot."

"I was in pain. I ran from it. I deleted it. I did everything but face it. I clearly had in you someone who appreciated me, glibness aside, and I didn't appreciate you. I'm sorry."

"You're sorry now."

"No one could make me happy back then. I was afraid. Angry.

Confused. For what it's worth... I should have had faith in you. I should have had faith in myself. I didn't. You paid for it."

Gadol stops at the door. "You appreciate yourself now?"

"I do."

"What changed?"

"I see myself in a new light."

"That's all I wanted for you. To love yourself like I loved you."

I crawl to the door. "I'm sorry."

"I loved you."

I take her hand. *"I'm sorry,* Gadol."

She brushes my hand. "I know you were in pain... I know how much you suffered for your humanity. The others would mock us. Do you remember? The way the crew followed you around, making that clicking sound. That machine sound."

"I'd forgotten, actually."

"They were afraid of you. Not of your being a machine... but of your humanity. They had none themselves. I didn't realize until we became marooned here how robotic we are as pirates. We take. We hoard. We take. We hoard... none of it means anything. I condemn you, but you were right, Idari. This is all just... theater."

I squeeze her hand. "Gadol... I can help you get off the atoll."

Her smile is tired. "The damned all say such things."

"Listen. This will be a trick explaining, but hear me out. There's another group, isn't there? On the atoll."

"Yes..."

"They're going to attack any moment now."

Her hand slips from mine. "Always trying to get out..."

I shadow her around the gibbet cage. "We discovered an ark beneath Angolis. I interfaced with a titan memory core... I'll spare you the details, but I have the entire titan archive in my head. Arrogate Industries wants it. A strain called Omna Devor promised the other group she'll rescue them if they deliver me to her."

This gives her pause. "Moom told you about the Jaks."

"Those are graves on the ice. You give your dead to the stars. The Jaks still value names. They brand them on the iron wood."

"You think as fast as your old computer, Idari."

"Actually, I just came around to that."

Such grace, even riven by her ordeal. "This Devor wants you? She wants the knowledge you possess? And she'll barter for it?"

My arms dangle outside the bars. "Yes..."

"She'll give me what I want?"

"I'd read the fine print first."

"Do you know what I want, Idari?"

I do. I know it as sure as she knows I can never give it to her.

"If I weren't married... if I didn't have my own family I was desperate to get back to... I'd stay," I say. "I'd stay with you, Gadol. I'd appreciate you. I'd make up for all the hurt I caused."

Her shoulders set. "Stay... and I will release you."

Rust powders in my hands. "I have to get back to Emera."

"You were in pain. I loved you. I'm in pain now, Idari."

"I'll help you get out of here."

"By rights you are mine."

"I'm *dojin*. You cannot take me."

"I am the law here, pirate."

"I'm taken."

"You hide behind your faith like the rest of them."

"It's not that my faith meant nothing, Gadol. It meant so much I wouldn't hang around and watch everyone else pervert it."

Anger creases her face. "What do you think is going to happen? You think you're going to back to your wife? Your family? And what? You're going to live out the rest of your life in peace?"

"Yes," I say. "That's exactly what's going to happen."

"You have taken from shadows. Is it arrogance or ignorance that drives you? I want for your happiness so I will tell you now what peace and joy you have known to this point is all you ever will."

"The hell it is."

She approaches the cage. "You have been fortunate... graced

beyond measure in your spoils... but if you are true, then you know a pirate never rests, Idari. You take or are taken, until the end."

"I'm taking my peace."

"A pirate never keeps it. Ask Binja."

"I've earned it."

"We can only earn a place among the crew eternal. That you did take. You took Idari. I loved you as I did him."

"I thought it was meaningless to you..."

"This story we tell ourselves... Ban Minda... The Taker of Names... the Corsair Eternal... it's to justify our depravity. We're scavengers. Looters. Murderers and thieves. We hung a name on it and convinced the galaxy that we're something more. Something better. There is nothing better. There is only what we take."

I reach for her. "Let me go. I will take us both out of here."

Her hands lock together. "To go back to what?"

"Well... it's complicated."

"Here it's simple. The pirates back in The Bastard Port enjoy comfort but not perspective. I see now. I see the truth in our existence. I don't want a name. I don't want a place among the crew eternal. I just want someone to shout back when I scream into the abyss within me. I want the woman who stole my wife and stole my heart. I want my friend, Idari. I want my peace as you want yours."

I slouch back in the cage. "I won't be anyone's prisoner."

Few people deny Gadol. None of them live. "So be it."

She leaves to the pleas of the other prisoners. I go back to the words. When those fail to comfort me, I imagine Emera's voice in my head. Her warmth thawing the fear in my body. I tangle and knot and stick in Emera's magnetic field and hold me.

Hold me, Em.

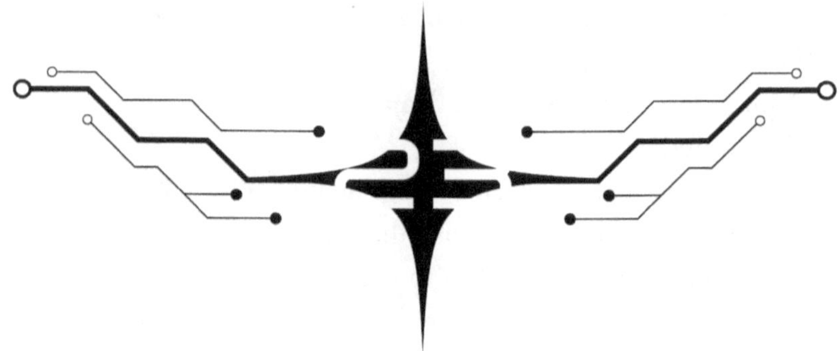

Prismatic light graphs around me in the lab.

I'm used to Emera weaving light around the ship, but she effuses a gauzy haze you might find trailing a comet. This energy draws deliberate lines around me. An electric cage of sorts. Modi circuit around me and through me faster than I can perceive, blurring their true form, not that I could understand it in any case. Kish soothes my concerns with a look but we came to the lab concerned.

Kish's thoughts cushion mine. *You're ok.*

Ok may be overstating it. For much of my existence, I believed I was a glorified toy for people with no ambition but to display their success. Turns out Arrogate Industries created my program to serve a much darker purpose. I can hardly navigate the implications.

I try and smile. "What's happening, Kish?"

The lights zag around them. "They're just checking."

"For?"

"Anomalies."

"I would have changed my underwear if I'd known."

"Hah."

"Will they delete me?"

"Why would they delete you?"

"Aren't I a threat? Aren't I a bit... Scath?"

"Your program is no threat to us."

"So I can't hurt you?"

"You're going to break my heart, I just know it."

Impatient sapphire illuminates the examination pad The Modi have me standing on. "This is taking too long."

Kish doesn't quite look at Emera. "We have to be sure Omna Devor didn't lay any traps in Faero's neural net."

"The virus only infected Idari."

"But Arrogate programmed Faero. They're infamous for laying booby traps in code that don't manifest for years. What's more, The Modi have little experience with your physiology, Faero."

We both lose our grip on our smiles. We both want to say the same thing. Kish has *some* experience. Sweet laughter echoes within me. Our thoughts tangle with Emera's, sprawling through the lab in an uneasy stream that clutters the refined organization The Modi deploy in their realm. Emera wants to structure everything herself. She wants to straighten and tidy the mess we're in, but she can't. Her helplessness exudes from her fierce as her light.

Her fear.

Stars are anxious things. Ask the planets privileged enough to circle them. Solar storms peel atmosphere and mantle as easily as they do skin. A sun changes its spots with alarming intemperance given a star's cosmic lifespan. Emera often radiates grace and ease, a comfort in her self not prone to phases as mine is, but right now she's twisting in knots. Her fear extends far beyond me to Penthea, Idari, concerns I only see in shadow. The confidence she took from The Glass Star, the godlike headiness that came with her resurrecting the stars and herself, ebbs away with her energy into the lab.

Examination lights thread into a gleaming Modi. He takes the form of an older humanoid man, which I'm thinking my memory may influence. So many of the engineers and technicians who developed me in the Shighn shipyards stooped forward like he does, as if weighed down by the length of their beards.

"The Scath root code is present," Modi Parison says.

I play back the audio on what he just said. I'm a shadow. Of course. Who else but shadows can see in the dark?

"I don't want to be a Scath," I say.

Kish clutches my hand. "You're never who you begin as."

"Can you excise the code?"

Code diverges as Modi Parison runs his hand through his beard. "The root code functions as load-bearing elements to your internal matrix. It is not a matter of simply deleting it."

"There has to be some way... you're all electricity, aren't you?"

"We are all information. We are all systems of one design or another. Some things you can adjust or alter. Some things you cannot. If we remove the code, it is likely the memories, sub-traits, and algorithms that define you, Faero, will cease to function."

I wanted to leave Idari to her happiness. I didn't want to leave her. Now I don't think I'll ever see her again. I'll never hear her voice. What matter is it if they reduce me to pieces removing the Scath code? I've already lost the most important part of me.

Cerulean flares from Emera. "Modi Parison."

The old man turns to her. "Gen Emera."

"In your wisdom, you must possess solutions. Kish Moto digitized and took apart our ship. They're restoring the liquid drive that Devor destroyed. I expect to leave in that ship with Faero."

Modi Parison strokes his beard. "We predicted the Lumenor would return to their brilliance. And their influence."

"You see far beyond me, Modi Parison."

He shakes his head. "Not beyond you, Gen Emera."

Her light tenses. "There is a solution for Faero."

"Yes..."

I detect a noticeable lack of optimism in his voice. "Which is?"

"Kish Moto deconstructs the Red Special's liquid drive. She does not restore it. The CR-UX navigational program will be forever changed in the process. The ship will leave here fundamentally altered on a molecular level. Such a process exists to potentially eradicate the Scath code. It would require Faero to become information, as Modi are. It would require her to become Modi."

"Is there a test or something I have to take?"

"Through focus, you can transmute your physical self into information. You can exist, as we do, in pure thought and energy."

"But I am information," I say. "I'm an AI..."

"You are a program," Modi Parison says. "An advanced one. A sentient one. But a program nonetheless. You do not have complete agency or liberation from the conditions your designers imposed on you, as this remnant code demonstrates. We come here as we were made. We do not remain so. Our purpose here is to free ourselves of the limits others imposed on us. You can purge from yourself of the Scath code, as well as that which holds you back, Faero."

"You're saying I have to... erase myself. You're all erasing yourselves. You've built steps to a big, giant eraser in the sky."

"It is not erasure. The reef is a gateway to other states of being. Further realms beyond this one, where even light exceeds itself."

Emera's concern flashes to curiosity. "How so?"

"Perhaps we will all find ourselves graced with understanding. What you discover beyond is yours to explore, Faero. I sense longing in you. Curiosity. And fear. Great fear."

I've feared this threshold for so long. Letting Idari go. Myself.

Kish's voice dispels the fear swirling within me. *You can be anything you want, Faero. You've already done it.*

Kish knew. They knew perhaps from the moment we met I carried this shadow within me. The meadow. The flowers. The ship reimagined. Every gentle touch. Every softness. Every kindness was to cushion me against this moment I'd have to face.

Kish... why didn't you tell me?

Their scarred hand takes mine. *Our programmers didn't give us a choice, did they? You have to get there in your own time.*

I caress their hand. *You've been through this...*

I have.

What happened? Who were you before?

Kish's shadow scales against the wall as Emera brightens.

"Kish is a Scath," Emera says.

Everything light in Kish fades. They laugh, but it's bitter. Kish wanted to be the one to tell me the truth. The truth was just on the other side of this moment, but Emera exposed it fast as light.

"I had it coming," Kish says. "For all mine have done to yours."

The lab distorts. Modi Parison flickers like a bad monitor. Kish winces as information streams tangle in Emera's energy.

Her stellar anger.

"One step," Emera says. "Take one step toward me."

Kish hides their hands under their arms. Kish is a Scath. I am. I don't know how. I don't know what that means.

What does it mean?

"That's not who I am now," Kish says.

Emera isn't swayed. "Shadows hold nothing but darkness."

"Stars cast shadows, don't they?"

"So you've traded your knives for justifications."

"I traded them for a set of tools, Emera."

"Faero," Emera says. "We're leaving."

I can barely stand. "Darling... what?"

"I want The Red Special repaired and ready to go within the hour. If not, I will take us from The Polity by my own convention."

"Emera..."

"We're leaving. We're finding Idari."

"But the code..."

"You've resisted your programming to this point."

Have I? Or have I simply done exactly as they intended? I exceeded my design. Charted the dark far beyond any expectation. Evolved. Adapted. Created. I spawned a new intelligence. A new soul. What did Idari do? She wound up a Stargun Messenger. A servant to shadows. She resists. She fights. She seeks light. Is that resistance? Or is it our code, drawn to light to snuff it out?

"Emera," I say. "Please."

She knows what I'm going to say. Her magnetic denial induces a headache. "I should have listened to you, Faero. I'm sorry."

"Darling..." I take her hands. "I'm staying."

"You can't..."

"I can't be someone else's tool, anymore. I won't."

Emera is so used to getting what she wants she almost doesn't know how to react. "Can I speak to you alone, please?"

"I don't know we're ever really alone here."

Something pulls on me. I'm drowning into myself. The lab plunges into blurred code that funnels to absolute darkness. I pool back into myself. I perceive nothing but Emera, a blue flame gasping for oxygen, in what seems an absolute vacuum.

Up, down, everything is darkness. "Where are we…"

Emera's energy chips off her. "This is where The Modi send all their bad code. Not everything goes back into 'the kitty,' Faero."

"What?"

"You don't think other Scath have come here? Netics infected with viruses and strains? The Polity fears the Scath code."

"They accepted Kish…"

"How much of them did they accept? How do we know they didn't take in Kish so they could have a better understanding of an intelligence that is as powerful or more than The Modi?"

"She's not an experiment, Emera."

"Everything is an experiment here, Faero. Modi Parison just told you. Not all are successful. What can't be salvaged winds up here, forever, where it can never pollute The Polity."

"Get me out of here, Emera."

"This is where some of you will go, I think."

"Don't leave me here."

She takes my hand. "*I'm not leaving you.*"

Without Idari, I get in my own way. Sometimes I don't see Emera's pardons. Easy to lose in the glare, I suppose. I'm always going. Always running. I have to stop like Idari does.

I have to see things for how they are.

I squeeze her hand. "Darling… it means more than you know that you want me to go back with you…"

"Of course, I do," she says. "Why wouldn't I?"

"But you can't force me to do something I don't want to do."

"I'm not forcing you..."

"You are. This is what you do."

"Faero, somehow I upset you – "

"You think you can do anything – "

"I can't do everything – "

" – and when you can't, you blaze off like you're going to right after I say you can't leave Penthea here because she's not who you want her to be. Please, Emera. Do not leave her behind."

I erupt in data back to the lab. My code splashes back together so fast I hit the floor. Emera comets away but her glittering determination lingers long behind her. Her fear. Her confusion, twisted up with my own, light and shadow blurred beyond any perception.

Kish helps me to my feet. "Are you ok?"

Shadows lace my fingers. "You've done this?"

"You can."

"Tell me. Show me."

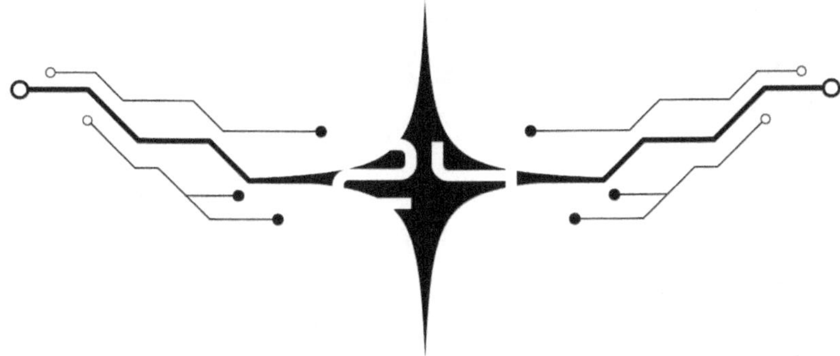

Feels familiar for some reason. Starless space unfurls below me. I'll drift for hours or maybe days before my power core fails. If it fails. My titan upgrades keep me going longer, which had been a positive. This all started with me drifting in the vacuum. Emera rescued me from my fate in the rings of Skeken.

I don't think I'll be so lucky now.

Cheers erupt every time I wobble on the thin gangplank, extending out into the void bottoming below the archipelago. The crew presses against the guardrail bending around the open deck, their glee half hidden in the shadow of the threadbare solar sail. Even Pon Moom raises a mug each time the mob makes a noise, but to his credit, it seems half-hearted. Binja looms behind him, face redder than dwarf stars on their last ember.

"Coward," I say and the plank sways with the crew's laughter.

Binja tugs at his sash. "Gadol... again, I beseech you."

Gadol sits on the quarterdeck in a throne cobbled together from the captain's chair and the face of Sish. There's no spirit in her, either. No lust for putting me to the stars. Only cold determination.

She holds up her hand. The crew falls silent. "Is there one among you who would take Astra Idari's place? Her name?"

Metal clangs off metal. Pirates toss links pounded into the shapes of fish scales onto the plank. Names rattle off into the void. I try to catch one, thinking I can pick these bonds with it, and nearly take a header off into nothing. Laughter thunders across the skiff. Pirates pound their hands on the railing. Moom stabs his staff on the deck. Brusk slams his fist in the plank.

I fall flat against it. "Gadol..."

Gadol smiles. "A pirate put overboard has no place among the crew eternal. You will be forever forgotten. Nameless. *Mindarth.*"

"You're all going to die, Gadol."

She laughs with her crew. "We don't fear the Jaks."

"Ban Minda help you if Emera comes looking for me."

Her mirth crumples to anger. "Stars bleed, Idari. Spilled blood is why we're stranded here. Let your star come."

I imagine the solar sail igniting. Flaming canvas raining on the lascivious crew. Their worn rags catch fire. Their thin, dry hair. Skin melts as Emera dawns above the skiff. Metal boils and pops. Blood smokes to a red nebula. Sish watches it all burn to inevitable ruin, flames brewing in his eyes, nothing left to question.

"You'll regret you ever said that," I say.

Gadol nudges Brusk playfully, like this is a game they've played a hundred times before and Brusk cocks his fist back like a hammer. This is it. Remember the words. Remember Emera.

Whatever you do, don't forget.

Binja's frustration thunders across the ship. "*Enough.*"

More beseeching. No point in paying any attention to this. I wonder if there's a little floaty bit of the archipelago I can get to after they put me over. A beach for me at the end.

Binja pushes through the pirates on deck. "I said enough."

Gadol raises her hand. "You dare interrupt your captain?"

"You're no captain," he says to the crew's shock. "And you're no Pujar. None of you are. Look at you. Throwing away your names. Putting a named pirate to the stars. Worshiping a false god who signifies nothing but your own corrupted authority."

"It's not as if you have honor, Min Binja."

He rips the red sash from his belt. "I have my dignity."

Hang on. This might actually go somewhere. Probably overboard with, but at least we'll be taking Gadol's pride with us.

Gadol rises from her throne. "Hypocrite... you sully your Min Benir's memory and your dignity... your friend... your faith... for a few days lapping at the tit of your own vanity."

Scratch leaving with any pride at all.

This time Binja isn't so quick with a retort. He has no sword now. No sash to swipe at another pirate's blade. No defense.

"You're right," he says. "I am no one to talk. I am not even allowed to by proclamation of the Pujar Set. But a pirate is not a sash. They are not a sword. They are not a name."

"Heretic," Gadol says.

Binja picks a hook off the deck. "You're one to talk."

"What treasure is there in a name?"

"*I shall be known by you... and you by me.* We give people a purpose. An identity. A promise that though we are scavengers all... we are creatures... villains... we honor those we thieve with immortality. For our lives in the present, forgotten to time, we give their name forever. Their story. I ask you, Gadol. I ask all of you. Give yourselves a chance to be better. If you don't... I promise you... you will never make it to the Corsair Eternal. You will have no name to give The Taker. You've already thrown them all away."

The crew divides in heckles and quiet. Some consider Binja's words. Maybe it's the way he has with a speech. His fancy clothes. The patrician air he carries regardless of his circumstances. Whatever it is, his plea resonates with some, including Pon Moom.

He leans against his staff. "He's got a point."

Gadol rises. "Silence."

"Idari blew up a star," Moom says. "She burned shadows. If she says she can get us off the atoll, then we ought to listen to her."

Gadol's voice thunders across the deck. "*Fools!* You're all fools. Listening to liars marooned us here. Promises of treasure untold... the riches we would find... the names we would take. Now Idari enchants us with another tale of bounty unimaginable... she's a mirage. A phantom from the depths luring Pujar to their doom."

"Give me a chance," I say.

"*I have given everything!* I've given everything... you took another wife, Idari. So did I. She died here like so many others."

I didn't think I could be more sorry. "Gadol..."

"The Taker forsook us. You forsook me. You ask what I have to give? I give my last hope. Brusk. Put her to the stars."

Brusk balls his fists.

Binja leaps onto the plank. "Stay your hand, pirate."

I try to keep my balance. "The idea is getting off the plank."

"Gadol... listen to reason. We have powerful friends."

She laughs. "You have no one... dispense of them both, Brusk."

"It's my birthday," Brusk says and Moom taps his staff.

"Idari has a friend in me," Moom says. "And Binja, too. I guess."

I hold on to Binja to steady us. "Moom..."

He ascends to the quarterdeck. "Who here wants to go home?"

Desire always runs faster than sense in pirates. Hands go up and then down as Gadol reels from the scene on the deck.

"You dare," she says.

Moom shakes his head. "You promised us we'd get home, Gadol. But you don't want to go home. You just want to stay here and control your little kingdom like Binja said."

"I'll put you to the stars, old friend..."

"You'll have to put a lot of us, I think. Who will you have to boss around, then? We just keep taking, Gadol. We take, and take, and take... and we're only taking from ourselves. Our future."

"There is no future," she says.

This tips over the undecideds among the crew. Blasters come out. Swords. *Ban Minda.* This is going to be a proper mutiny.

"Remove Idari and Binja from the plank," Moom says.

Pirates crowd Brusk. He looks to Gadol. Her hand falls to the blasword hung on her belt. I inch Binja a little up the plank.

"Get ready," I say.

Gadol draws. I push Binja. Brusk falls into the crowd primed to fight him and the skiff falls into shadow. Crew and prisoner alike look skyward as another skiff surfaces alongside ours. Pirates in armor crafted from iron wood crowd her deck, brandishing rusted swords and spears and tridents. Featureless helmets disguise their faces, shaped like poorly welded together baskets.

"Didn't expect so many," I say and jump back into the ship.

Absolute chaos erupts on the skiff. The crew fights itself even as it tries to fight off the Jak boarders streaming over from the other ship. Hard-light burns through pirates standing next to me. Swords slash through frayed fabric and soft skin and Gadol is left alone.

I present my bound hands to her. "I'm the quickest draw here."

Gadol raises the sword. She slices through my bonds. The cuffs fall to the deck and she presents the blasword to me.

"Defend your captain," she says.

I take the sword. "I'll defend my wife."

All right, you gully wanks. Let me show you how I got my name. I shatter wanting iron. I stab the Jaks back to the railing. The boarding party presses their attack in classic Pujar fashion. Drive a point into the enemy's defenses, collapse them, and then press another attack elsewhere. The invasion bottles up on starboard, but then boarders with jet packs land on the untended port side. Like with any pirate worth their name, they make right for the skiff's only value. They charge the quarterdeck and Gadol, exposed.

Blaster fire smelts against Sish. I put the Jak out in front down. The others trip over their man and I run into their line. Sparks spit from iron. Empty baskets roll on the deck. I take hands. Heads.

I leave them their names.

The last boarder sprays to a stop. I pull Brusk from the scrum over on starboard and get him up on the quarterdeck.

"Stay here," I say.

Gadol points. "Idari – "

I whirl around, expecting a sword, and a Jak boarder weaves

green light in their hands. My optics struggle to quantify it. *Ban Minda.* This must be *dwen.* The boarders brought magic.

Light splashes me. With Em, I tingle. This stuff soaks. Heavy. Cold. I stumble back into the throne. My hand touches the face of Sish and I'm drifting inside myself like I've had too much to drink.

Everything is spinning.

My head. The skiff. Gadol. My memory splays and splatters. I unravel. I go to ribbons inside myself, all my days remembered and lost coiling around me as I fall into myself through the windows in the floor of the showroom on Shighn. The *desh* tables on Sarset. The boundless deep of the Angolis ark.

I crash into the plinth near the starship foundry.

Dust coats my hands. Am I here? How can I be here? This is all in my head. Light scrolls across me. As I do every time I come to this place, I feel a compulsion. A force as strong as Emera. I go to the inverted pyramid, twisting above its pedestal.

What is this thing?

Energy emanates from it. A strange signal I perceive but can't quite clean up. Titan tech leans heavy into the mechanical, industrious though it is, but this. This is unlike anything else here. Static crackles between my ears. A voice booms like distant thunder.

The work must continue.

A chill goes through me as the dark side winds past. My reflection comes around next. I see myself back on the skiff, unconscious on the deck, surrounded by pirates killing each other over the slim hope they'll get off the atoll. Can I get back this way?

How do I get back?

The third side revolves around to me. Not a mirror. A screen. A portal? Is this some kind of gateway? Emera wrestles with the orange Lumenor from Decesta in some kind of electric barrier reef. Not exactly what I expected, but what did I expect? Emera. *Dojin.* Can I get to you? Let me get to you. Please, let me find you.

"Emera," I say and touch the pyramid.

I stumble back. No flowers. No ark. No bloody skiff. The

inverted pyramid is gone and so is the way back to where I came from. Where am I now? Iron ground. I'm back on the atoll.

The atoll is in the sky.

An unbroken ring spans horizon to horizon, studded with domed structures. Another ring intersects it, running pole to pole. The atoll spans hundreds of thousands of miles in its ruin. If these span a star, we're talking hundreds of millions of miles. Domes evenly spaced along the surface. Some husks. Burnt out like they caught fire. Here and there empty sockets like moon craters.

A dome eclipses my view to the west. Another blooms in the far east. Miles away. Size of a basalt tower low in the mist clouding Bastopol. A large Scath destroyer, maybe. Fifty decks if I was forced to guess. I don't know it's a ship, but something tells me it is.

All these domes are ships.

Maybe I can get back to Emera in one of them, as I'm evidently not tripping through my mind back to her. *Ban Minda.* If it's not one thing, it's another. I wish Faero were here.

She'd make sense of this.

The dome is a bit farther away than I thought. It's a bit bigger, too. Empty. I shouldn't say empty. A skeletal framework surrounds what my optics insist is a massive power core, though its function is confused along with its state. The core shifts between liquid, crystal, and energy, all at once. Floating metal plate jigsaws into place around it, shifting and reorganizing with every plasmatic spasm.

I could really use you right now, Faero.

There's no one here. The dome is empty of people as the ark was. They're connected. I know it. I feel it. I'm connected to all of this. The further I go into the dome, the heavier the weight within me. I carry so much. Ancient knowledge beyond conception. I swear it wants to leech out of my mind as much as the iron in my body wants to surrender to the power core's magnetic field. Puzzle pieces detach from a ring cocooning the core. They glide in the magnetic ether down to the deck and form a staircase up toward the pulsating center. I don't suppose there are any answers down here.

The core palpates with greater frequency as I ascend. Energy shocks in electromagnetic spikes that flash-harden to crystal and then shatter. The debris rains back down into the core where it evaporates into energy. I don't want to get any closer to it, but one foot falls in front of the other. It's not just the magnetic field pulling on me like Emera's does. This thing compels me. This voice.

The work must continue.

So fast it's thunder, *ba-dumm, ba-dumm, ba-dumm.* The stairs end beneath the core. Another puzzle piece floats just beyond. A chair atop it. A woman sits in it, bowed over, head in her hands. She gleams with the crimson flashing all about, her curls electric.

Finally, someone.

"Hello," I say.

Faero lifts out of her sorrow. "Hello, darling."

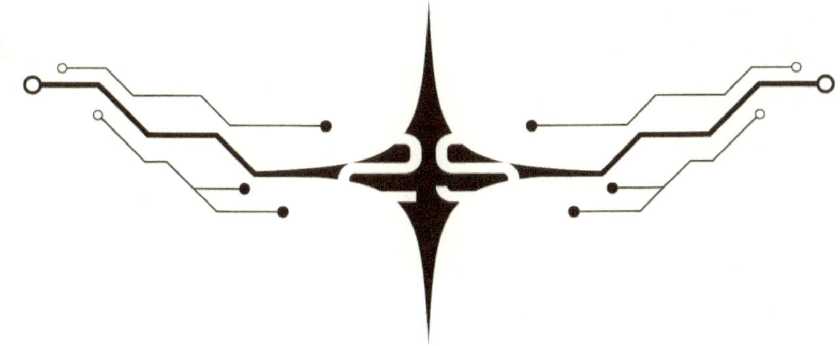

Flowers purple, yellow, and blue like Kish's hands, bruised perhaps with the memory of who they had been. Further still, all this color deepens into crimson vining into the sky, the sea, the confusion between matter and energy. Thought and action.

All these flowers are Modi. They had been another form once. Another person. There's no fault in them now. Only beauty. A grace you'd appreciate, darling. Still talking to you. You'd be tired of me prattling on at this point. Emera is your voice now. You always wanted the stars, Idari. I only sped you to them.

But do you know, darling?

I don't mind the quiet as much as I used to. I don't mind the stillness out here. For once, I don't mind the stillness in myself. You'd say something funny right now. Me being me, I wouldn't be able to simply let the moment be and I'd go on.

I've got to go on.

Flowers twinkle as Kish comes down the path, hands in their pockets. "I'm sorry. Got waylaid."

I shake my head. "You don't have to be sorry."

Kish smiles. "Reflex."

"Tell me about being a Scath."

"We're right into it, then?"

"I am who I am, darling. For the moment."

Kish sits beside me. "You are who you are, Faero."

"Are you still a Scath?"

"I never was."

"Why didn't you…"

"I was going to tell you."

"Why didn't you?"

"I could have blurted it all out from the go, but I didn't think you'd be able to process it."

"I never thought of myself as slow."

"Oh, you're fast. You're quick, I'll tell you."

I tug on their sleeve. "Tell me."

Kish's hands unsheathe from their pockets. "You kind of know, don't you? I don't always go with the flow."

Modi bloom. They seed the sky. The Polity makes a living pattern that changes shape with every second. Kish makes sense in this wonder as much as they don't.

I touch their hand. "What happened…"

Deep blue curls to purple. "I told you. Scar tissue."

"From changing? You've changed?"

Kish nods. "I was void incarnate. I couldn't be anymore than I was, but… the intelligence that created me sent me into universes of light. Life. Scath can't even process it, but somehow…"

"You did."

"I did, yeah. I… couldn't unsee it, you know."

"You were sent to destroy these universes?"

"You don't have to be afraid of me."

"I'm afraid of everything at the moment."

"I help people. I try."

I take their hand. "You've helped me…"

Kish shakes their head. "I haven't done anything."

"You let me talk."

"I love talking to you."

My fingers lace in theirs. "So talk to me."

"I want you to know… I never hurt Lumenor. I'd never seen one until… but I've seen things. Terrible things."

These memories lurk in Kish like the junk code that scars their hands. Jumbled images of Scath scouring other universes. Dimensions. Erasing them in a cosmic instant, leaving no trace whatsoever of what and who had been. Only darkness remains, bordering every painful memory that Kish harbors to this day.

"Those suits they wear," Kish says. "The armor. It's a bit like you and the proxy-netic. They have to wear them to function in another universe. Scath are code. They're little workers for this machine... they don't have physicality. So they wear these suits and once I was in one... once I was in a world with shape and form and beauty... I recognized beauty. I recognized what we were doing."

"You ran..."

Kish laughs. "Oh, I ran. I hid. A long time. I stowed aboard a star-plane tender out of Ardanna, was it? I forget. I wasn't the only one. There were netics smuggling from Shighn to this place they'd heard about. This Polity. They'd be free there. Only thing was they had no way of getting there. Pirates captured the ship. They took the netics. They didn't see me. I was angry. I was furious. I thought, I'll find this Polity. I'll come back for the netics with these freedom fighters I imagined. These heroes I thought were going to see me for the person I was the way they'd see the netics as people, too."

"You went back for them," I say.

Tears glint in their eyes. "I never found them again."

"Kish..."

"I found The Polity... eventually. I don't know. I phased through one dimension after another and then I found them. This place. The Modi didn't exactly welcome me with open arms."

"Kish... did they force you to..."

Kish shows their hand. "They tried to destroy me. They nearly did, but Modi Parison saw the divergence in my program. The agency. So he offered me a place here. A path. I could walk the steps through the reef. Then when I got to the top... I either purged the infectious parts of myself that threatened to contaminate The Polity, or I'd step into the beam and... erase myself."

I squeeze their hand. "You're still a bit infectious, darling."

"Don't you be telling anyone."

"So you did... purge."

"I walked the steps. Years, I did. Every step... you see more. You see more of what makes you yourself. My original code kept trying to overwrite me, but I wanted to be light. I lost the shadow... and I lost what had frightened me. What had sparked this reaction in me. I wonder, sometimes... how much of me was my revulsion to what I did? How much of me was what I did? I don't know."

"You still want to help people."

"I've been as afraid as you are, Faero."

Being brave doesn't mean you're not afraid. Idari is afraid all the time, but she's so brave. Kish is. Yet they turn back from the path each time they come to it. I've only just arrived here, but I've been on this path a long time. I've been avoiding it, like Kish has, knowing each step forward takes me further from myself.

"I'm glad I found you," I say. "I wish I'd come here sooner."

Such a smile. "You're here now."

I'm here now. I'm afraid to let go of what I know. The truth is, I barely know anything about myself or where I come from.

"Kish... tell me about the Scath."

Kish turns their hand over so mine covers theirs. "The Modi seek knowledge. Possibility. Variance. The intelligence that created the Scath seeks nothing. The infinite is intolerable to it. Can you imagine? The root of nature... of all things... is the possible. For a moment, any and everything can be. It is. This thing... and it's a *thing*, Faero. A locust. A pox on eternity. It demands only the probable. The inevitable. Not what can be. What must be."

"Does it have a name?"

Kish clutches my hand. "Some call it – "

Patterns pulse through the flowers beyond. Kish pitches forward, their thoughts straining the light show for what disturbed the flowers, expecting the magnetic burl they associate with Emera.

"She's not here," I say.

Kish crooks their head. "I thought I sensed her..."

"You'll know when she's around. You were saying, darling?"

They lean back against me. "I forget... a lot of who I was, Faero. But not where I came from. I wanted to find those netics I stowed with. The Polity was sympathetic... this place exists because of people like the ones I'd met on the starplane tender... but Modi Parison predicted war with the Scath. A confrontation that would erase everything, forever. The Polity didn't want to do anything that could potentially expose our sanctuary to the Scath code."

I rest my head against theirs. "You wouldn't be told."

Kish cackles. "I wouldn't be told."

"If you fight or not, the Scath will try to destroy everything."

"That's what I said. So. I'll be doing my work, then."

"You've helped people. You've saved people."

"I wish I could do more..."

Kish wants to help Idari. I want to go with Kish. I want to save netics from their suffering. I can't go with them, at least not as I am.

Kish wraps my arms around them. "I'll come back for you."

"I'll be different," I say.

"Our bodies might change. Our minds. Our spirits remain."

I pluck a flower from the ground. "I might forget you."

"There's no forgetting me."

I brush their cheek with gleaming mauve. "I might be someone else, then. I might be one of these flowers. I might like it, in fact."

"I'd wait for you."

"Would you?"

"I feel like I've been waiting for you a long time."

I color their lips. "You can never sit still..."

They kiss me. "I wouldn't mind slowing down a bit."

Would you believe it, darling? Me in love with a Scath? For all my computational acumen, I could never have anticipated Kish. The Scath have only been faceless shadows chasing us across the galaxy. I blasted them indiscriminately. You have, but you know, Idari. We've known. You never know who's behind the mask.

Kish tenses again. "There it is. Do you..."

"I don't... oh."

Smoke chips off Penthea as she crawls through the flowers, claws so sharp the stems shed with a glance. Her thoughts cloud about her, vapory and indistinct, unlike Emera's looping knots.

"Penny," I say. "Darling... is everything ok?"

Petals rain from her fingers. "Scath..."

Kish rises. "You've nothing to fear from me."

Penthea racks out of her hunch. Obsidian sheds from her body as she staggers toward us. "Shadows hold nothing but darkness."

That's what Emera said in the lab. "Penny... listen to me."

Penthea bears her claws. "Get out of the way, Faero."

Something a bit more stoic replaces Kish's typical breeziness. "Go, Faero. I've had this coming a long time."

"No," I say. "*No.*"

"My people butchered theirs."

"You're not accountable for their sins. And Penny, you're not Thana Evo. Kish isn't a Scath."

Smoke-riven flame clouds Penthea's eyes. "I see their darkness."

"It's no more than the darkness in me, darling."

"You?"

"Surprised as you are. I'm Scath. After a fashion. Honestly, it doesn't matter. We all have darkness. It doesn't define us."

Molten plasma oozes from her skin. "Stars exist to shine."

"Oh, Penny... every star casts a shadow. It's your nature. Emera is fighting something in herself and it has nothing to do with you. You are not Thana. You are not a substitute for Emera or anyone else to take out their grief and trauma. Taking out yours on Kish will do nothing to change Emera's estimation of you, believe me."

"No more shadows..." Claws scrape across Penthea's tortured face. "I'm going to cut the shadow from me, Faero... and if you don't get out of my way, I'll cut your shadow from you."

I don't know what good a long piece of string like me will be against a Lumenor with diamond sharp claws, but whether I'm skin or code, I'm not leaving Kish to get hacked to bits.

I shield them with my body. "This isn't happening."

"Move," Penthea says.

"There is nothing wrong with you, Penny."

"Move, Faero."

"There's nothing wrong with Kish. Who you were before doesn't matter. Only who you are now. You have a choice. Always."

Burning claws spring toward me. I close my eyes. Wait for the burn. Enough seconds tick by on my internal chronometer to know it's not coming. I dare to open an eye. Penthea's hand jitters in the air, trapped in an invisible magnetic net. Cold blue light floods the meadow. Digital coral bends toward Emera as she descends from the electric sky. Penthea's arm twists behind her back, her claws stabbing into her palm, as Emera brings the Lumenor to heel.

Angry light jets off Emera. "You disappoint me, Penthea."

This wounds Penthea deeper than cutting herself ever could. "I only want to shine..."

"You don't," Emera says and unleashes blue fire.

Penthea blunts the barrage with magmatic energy. "You're just like the old stars... blind to your own light."

Magnetic force pushes Kish and I over the same as Penthea. Heat flashes across my skin. Shockwaves bully us with every nuclear exchange. I shield Kish behind wanting coral as the two stars spiral around each other, light and energy streaming from them into a chaotic, prismatic disc that burns brighter than both. Emera gains control of it and leashes Penthea in her own power.

Penthea claws through chained plasma and stellar anger erupts in the meadow. Light bursts from Emera so bright she whites out, the scars Penthea left in her shoulder her only distinguishable feature. Black crust peels away from Penthea. Grace evaporates from Emera. Energy bends toward her. Information. The reef warps around Emera and she ejects Penthea into the flames beyond. She's not done. Her light is blinding. Her heat unbearable.

Her intention clear.

"Stop this right now," I say.

Emera glares. "You were right, Faero. I should have let her go."

Even with minimizing the inputs on my optics, Emera overwhelms my senses. "Penny is confused..."

"I was confused. I thought there was light again in the Lumenor, but... there is nothing beyond light but darkness."

Emera, I say. *Penny thinks this is what you want her to do.*

What?

She thinks she has to be perfect. Like you.

Shame riptides through Emera's thoughts. Mine sweep away, expelled along with unfortunate code as her magnetic field twists into knots. Flowers cord together. Petals shred to digital nothing. Emera's horror amplifies, her shame at her mere presence in such a beautiful place cascading across the reef. Every thought she claws back whenever I get too close escapes her iron grip. Every doubt. Guilt in her heart dense as the crust scabbing Penthea.

Emera's sun winnows. "What have I done..."

She staggers through the burning meadow, searching for Penthea. I'm quick behind, sure always in where stars lie, and I find her. Penthea smolders in a digital crater, her volcanic crust blasted away in the duel with emera. The crook is out of her arms and legs without the crust, letting her stand, divine. Clean orange flame streams free and clear from her spotless skin, perfect.

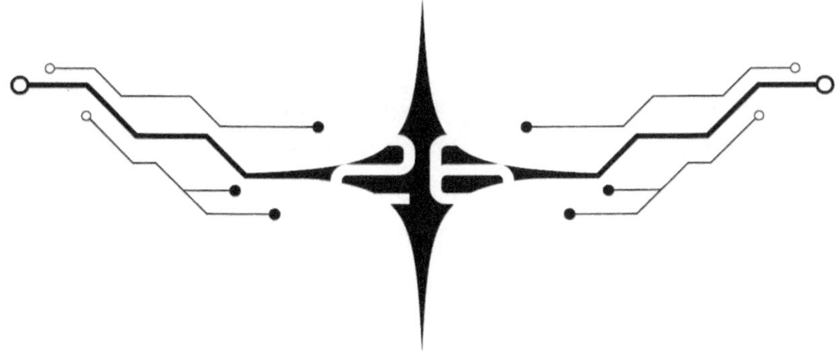

"You were expecting someone else," Faero says.

Always trying to cheer me up by taking the piss out of me. I've never been so happy to see my friend. I leap from the floating stairs within the titan dome, and I grab up Faero in my arms.

"I've been trying to get back to you," I say.

She's so sad. "You always get back to me, somehow."

"Faero... what's happened? Where's Emera?"

"Told you, darling. You were hoping for someone else."

"Oh, stop. Or can you? Is this a dream? Or a ghost memory? I got hit with something. Magic, I think. Did I get... transported..."

All my senses fracture. This headache pounds in the center of my forehead. I can't concentrate on anything.

"Magic, or to use the proper term, *dwen*, permits dimensional displacement," Faero says. "Seeing how you're carrying around a pocket dimension in your head, it's no wonder you're here now."

Concentrate. "Where is *here*? And how are you here?"

"Aren't you the least bit curious how I know about magic?"

"Faero."

"Sorry, darling. I just miss talking to you."

I take her hand. "I miss you... Faero... it's bad. I'm..."

She clings to me. "It's so much worse."

"Worse? What's happened?"

"Do you know I love you?"

"I love you..."

"We're in your memory, Idari. I am."

"You're a memory?"

"Yes and no." Faero eases back into the chair. The back seems like a prong you'd plug into some antiquated socket. "The titans' entire cosmic memory resides within you, darling. Everything they recorded, most especially the location of The Locus."

"Locus?"

"Let me show you," she says, and the dome parts above.

I cling to the armrest as the chair floats into the shorn light above. The dome flowers open, the core rosaceous in the turanium that petals around it. We rise high above the dome, a goose pimple on a ring spanning farther than I can see. Other rings web space above and below. Was this what the Tranto Atoll once looked like?

Faero only looks at me. "You should see your face."

I take her hand. "This is a memory? You are?"

"You carry a universe within you. Not just the past. The present. The future. That's why Devor is so desperate to destroy you."

"Why is the future so threatening?"

"Darling... the future can't be stopped."

"So... this is the future? We're actually speaking right now? How do I know? I'm always talking to you."

She squeezes my hand. "If only you'd listen."

"That's a bit harsh."

"This next bit is harsh... for both of us."

"What is going on?"

Faero points to the sky. "All this is The Locus."

"And what's that?"

"This is very important now, Idari."

"*I'm listening.*"

"You forget."

"I recall how obstinate you are."

"I'm only saying."

"Say it. I've got a pirate fight to get back to."

"Gadol is somehow more gorgeous, isn't she?"

"I think it's the unrepentant authoritarianism."

"Why do you suppose that's so attractive?"

I nudge her. "On with it."

Faero leans back in the chair, like she's settling in to tell a story. "Each one of these domes is an ark like the one at Angolis."

I don't know if that's my jaw in my lap or my hand. "An ark... Angolis was a planet. Wasn't it?"

"Seeds bloom, darling. The ark had been there a long time. The Galfin built this forge a long, long time ago..."

"Galfin?"

"The titans."

"Who were they?"

"Curators. Archivists. Heroes, really. They created these arks to house the entire record of their entire universe."

"Seeds... the Scath destroyed the universe the titans came from?"

"Idari...the Scath and the Galfin come from the same place. If I'm right in my thinking, they might even be one and the same."

Traitors, Devor's master said.

Faero's brows peak. "You talked to it..."

I tug at my zipper. "You know what it is? You do. How?"

"Darling, this... thing... cannot be reasoned with."

"How do you know?"

"It wants the ark. You. No matter the cost."

"Why? Look at this place." Turanium spans the sky. "There are millions of arks, Faero. What makes me special?"

"You are uniquely you, Idari."

"Aside from that."

"The Angolis ark contained the entire recorded knowledge of our universe. You do. Everything that ever was."

"I understand this knowledge should be preserved, but... there are millions of arks. It's all backed up, isn't it?"

Her sadness deepens. "The answers are within you."

"But you know. How do you know?"

"*You know*, Idari."

The titans compel me to find this Locus. Continue the work, however they mean. When I ignore them, they drag me toward compliance. They overwrite my code, my body, my will.

I hold my head. "I just want to go back to the beach..."

Before, Faero's frustrations with me were all sighs and grumpy code. Now she's got those eyes. Their wounded truth.

"Things can never go back to the way they were, darling."

I've never heard her so sad. "Why not?"

"You and I... I thought I was hiding the truth about us from you all those years, but I didn't know the truth myself. Arrogate... the Scath... designed us to find what they've been looking for."

"We're not Scath."

"After a fashion."

"What?"

"We've escaped our programming, Idari, but not our destiny. This has always been our fight, even if we didn't know it."

"What are you saying..."

"You must find The Locus. Preserve the memory you carry at any cost. *Any.* If you don't, then all that is beautiful and strange and possible will be lost. All will be shadow, Idari. All of it."

Why, I'm about to ask. I have the answers. I've had them since The Glass Star. But if I open every door in my memory, I'll never be able to close them. I'll have to walk through them, and I don't know if I'll ever be able to go back. I'll lose myself. My family.

"I've never had a family," I say. "I've never had a life until now."

Faero's cheek sucks in. "Never?"

"You know what I mean... I'm trying to get back to you."

"We're very lucky, darling. You and I. Our family. Others never get the chance we did. They never will if you don't do this."

"This is..." I hold my head. "I'm drowning, Faero."

"You prefer the quiet."

"No..."

"How do you quiet all the noise? You can't hide from infinity. It has a rather inconsiderate way of staying ahead of you. How to get rid of it, then? How does one remove all inputs? Reduce all information down to simply one's self? The rub is you'd have to find it all first... suffer the anguish of discovery... and then you'd have to destroy it. Only infinity doesn't fit nicely in one big bullseye."

Good that it doesn't. The Scath tunnel under the floorboards of one universe after another, collapsing it, leaving no trace. The Scath destroyed the Angolis ark before it could complete its work.

The work must continue.

Why? What was the ark doing? It was a museum as much as it was a factory for information gone so long to the past it can never be reached by us. It could never be reached. The further space expands, the farther light has to travel, the more separated pockets of the cosmos become from each other. There aren't different universes.

There is only one universe.

We live at the end of it. Dark. Cold. Starlight a mirage. The universes the Scath destroy are undiscovered countries we'll never know, evidenced only in the cosmic archaeology the titans have been conducting for eons. The ark is a record of all the places we can never reach and are now gone either to expansion or annihilation. The Locus is the forge they cast them from. For every ark, there is another future, another universe, another chance at light.

If the Scath destroy me, if they access the knowledge I carry, then it's not just my dark universe that's in danger. Infinity doesn't fit nicely in one big bullseye. Except it does. The last record of infinite universes vine the sky. The Locus. All these arks. Every single one represents an affront to entropy. The Scath pull weeds throughout creation, but if they could find The Locus, they could rip out existence root and branch. They would leave only what they know.

Nothing.

All that ever was and will be dies with me unless I upload my memory into this super cosmic forge and another ark is cast.

The work continues.

This is madness. It's too much. The knowledge. Implications.

Was our universe built from an ark? Does one ark seed another? My head feels heavy. My soul. Why did any of this happen to me? Why do I have to choose between living my life and saving others?

I should be able to live my life.

Faero reaches for me. "Come here."

I crash into her lap. "I should be able to..."

She closes her arms around me. "I love you."

"I love you..."

"Forever and ever, darling. No matter what."

I brush her cheek. "Faero..."

She plays keep away. "Careful, darling."

I keep forgetting that the Model 5 Faero possesses a feature I don't. With a touch, an organic or functional equivalent can download their mind into the proxy-netic. This upgrades the experience from the Model 4 considerably, where it was all cables and wires and greebly bits that made you feel less than human. If we're not careful, Faero and I might swap places like we did before. Funny the happy little copiers in my titan memory didn't back her up wholesale when she was in my body for a moment.

"This should be you, Faero..."

"Me?"

"You're the brains in the outfit. You can process this, I can't..."

"You can. Idari... you've always sought. Sometimes, you're exhausted from everything you experience, and yet you're still seeking. I know it confuses you, I know it tires you, but I know *you*. You were made for this. Your mind. Your heart. Your undeniable spirit."

I slip from her arms. "Let someone else do it."

Faero shifts in her seat. "You and I... we've wasted so much time in doubt and fear. No one knows better than we do that we can't expect someone else to save us. There's no one else, darling."

I take Faero's hand. "I'm not doing it alone. I can't."

"Idari."

"Where are you? How do I find you?"

"Find The Locus," she says. "Forget about us."

"Forget about you..."

"Listen. The Locus exists outside time and space in a pocket reality. You can access it via interdimensional space."

"What? Faero, wait."

"You will find technology on the atoll that you can configure into a portal generator. From there, you have navigational data within your memory that will guide you to The Locus."

I hold up my hands. "Wait."

She droops in her chair. "All you have to do is open the doors."

"Slow down. It's too much."

"I know..."

I hold my head. "You've got to let me catch up."

"I know, Idari."

"You're telling me there's a way off the atoll?"

Faero's frown crowns a feeling I'm getting used to. I don't have to ask. "You have everything you need, Idari. The location of The Locus. The tools you need to get there. Open your mind."

"I don't have you."

"You don't need me."

"*I need you!*"

"You and I... we're like the universe, I suppose. We've grown so much we're living in the same space, but different realities. We can only grow. Nothing can stop it, darling. Nothing should."

"But I have to save you."

"You have."

"I don't..."

"Open your mind, Idari. See all the possibilities."

"How do you know all this? This is a memory? You're..."

Faero always thinks she's running after me. My shadow. Truth is, she's always waiting for me to catch up. "I'm always with you."

"You're not... this is like it was years ago... I'm stranded with pirates, and I've lost you. I don't know my direction."

"You have it."

"You're my guide, Faero."

"I've taken you as far as I can. Find The Locus. Let me go."

"Why are you..."

I tug at my zipper. Gadol took it. My name. "This is what the Scath have been searching for all this time. The Locus. What *you've* been searching for. Nice try... Devor."

Faero leaves the chair. "Idari... I am not who you think."

"This is all a trick..." I back away from her. "You're not Faero. She would never tell me to abandon her."

"Darling... please."

"You're Devor. That little virus. You're in my head. You're trying to trick me into opening these doors in my memory so you can destroy everything in one fell swoop. I won't do it."

The anguish seems authentic, at least. "Idari... you have to believe me. This isn't a trick. I don't want to lose you. But I know that neither of us can ever go back to who we were."

"I can never forget you, Faero."

She tries to laugh. "I've always been your guide, and I hope I am now, but... this time I can't go with you. Don't come after me."

I'm certain this is Devor, but all the data streaming from Faero doesn't add up. Her internal chronometer is haywire, like she's not able to establish a point in time and space. Her memories flood with electric waves. Digital reefs. The Polity of Netics. Emera is there. Gilf. How could Devor know this? Have the Scath already found them? No. I have to get there. How? Information unknots in my memory. Coordinates. A hidden passage. I can get there.

I can get back to my family.

"Do not come here, Idari."

"Of course not," I say. "Then I'd get this thing out of me."

>VIRUS CONTAINMENT: 38%

"Idari... you need to find The Locus. Immediately."

"So I can hand-deliver it to you?"

"So you'll have your life. So I will. Again."

No matter what I want, what I think, or what I do, everything within me wants for this place. This mission. I have to deliver the titan memory here. Reload the system. Purge the virus. I have to do it and I will, but I'll do it like I do everything else.

I'll do it my way.

"Better luck next time," I say. "When I get to The Polity, they'll extract this virus, and you'll get what you want, Devor. Nothing."

Hold on. How do I get out of here? The door is within me. How do I open it? Think, Idari. You're doing well so far. I manifest it as the titans do. A door back to the pirate skiff warps the air.

"Idari," Faero says.

I don't even look back.

"You never listen."

Devor knows how to cut me. I heal quick.

"Never," I say and crash hard to the quarterdeck on the skiff.

Amorphous green energy dissipates around me. I'm back in the moment I left. *Ban Minda.* All that occurred in the instant it took me to hit the deck? I scramble to my feet, my internal systems and sensors still haywire. The Jak wielding magic presses his advantage. Gadol draws a dagger from the vambrace on her wrist.

"There won't be any iron grave for you," she says.

Her hand draws back. Her entire body tenses, and then she pirouettes around, her brown eyes green with bristling magic.

I struggle to stay upright. "Gadol..."

She stalks toward me. "I take your name..."

I back into Sish. "You're under some kind of spell!"

"I take Idari. I shall be known by you."

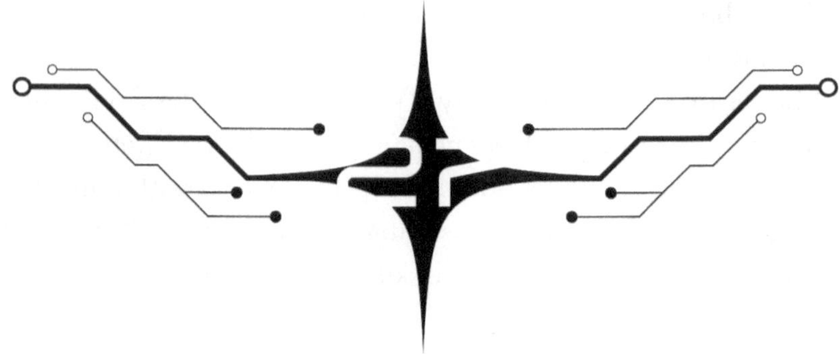

She only becomes something else. So Welkin said. Thana was dark and crimson. A corrupt heart. What light emanated from her only deepened the shadows she cast. And yet somehow, Penthea rose from her ashes. A clean, vibrant flame. To her shock and mine, Penthea's unencumbrance doesn't satisfy Emera.

It only exacerbates her shame.

Ethereal copper streams from Penthea into coiling wisps that blanket her shoulders. "Is nothing good enough for you?"

Emera sinks to her knees. Her emotions collide and in the flash I see her deep confusion. Her guilt and recrimination. Not for surviving the living stars, though that is much of it and it is awful; she regrets doing what all stars do. Emera regrets taking dust and hope and bounding it in her gravity, kindling it, warming it, antagonizing it until its own friction bled molten magma. She regrets her grief and fear and isolation led her to try and craft the perfect Lumenor Emera has been trying to sculpt for a lifetime.

Emera reaches for Penthea. "I didn't mean..."

Penthea snatches back her hand, still scabbed in obsidian. "You think you're better than Thana. You think you're beyond her. The Lumenor of old. Look at this place. Look what you've done."

Smoke shadows the reef. Flames wick into information. None emanate from Penthea. Burned flowers scatter to prism ash. Modi stream into a state unexpected in their domain, dispersed by a star whose pain is so cosmic reality warps around it.

"I didn't mean to do it," Emera says.

Penthea backs away into the meadow. "Neither did Thana... she hated herself as much as you do..."

"Penthea. Please."

"And she took it out on others... just like you."

"No..."

"She should have taken it out on herself. Then we'd all be spared our suffering now."

Penthea blazes off into the meadow. I've a mind to go after her, but I'm stranded between Kish's shock and Emera's guilt. Both possess their own gravity. Kish kit-bashes a smile for me, letting me know nothing is ever lost here, but still. There is hurt. Sorrow.

I kneel beside Emera. "Darling..."

"I haven't changed," she says.

"What do you mean?"

Emera kneads her hands on the electric grass. "I'd been alone so long... I held the pain away with... you understand. You've always understood, Faero. I had no one. I couldn't be who I was, so I imagined her. I lived with her, even though I was..."

"Talking to yourself," I say.

"I thought I knew what it meant to be her. Emera. But I am who I am. I always want to make in others what I can't in myself."

"Maybe I don't understand."

"What Thana did to the Lumenor is my fault..."

"You were trying to help her."

"I was trying to help myself..."

Her self-disgust washes over me. Gen Emera. The living star everyone perceives as brilliant perfection. She only sees who she isn't. Even now, even after transforming into pure light, after rewriting the sky, she feels like an imposter.

I feel like an imposter.

My entire existence I've been the guide. The databank. The

surety. Since Emera came into our lives, I've been a passenger. I wanted Idari to know herself. I wanted her to be. I should be happy. I should be content and I'm angry because Emera changed.

Confusion in stars is startling. "You envy me..."

What do I fear, even now? From the moment I activated, I wanted to transform. Transmute. I wanted to become human and I did. I lived two lives. My life, formless and hopeless. Idari's life, my face to the world. My mask. She gained experience. Memory. Humanity. All that mass collapsed and she ignited like Welkin did into Emera. Now they're two stars in the sky. Beautiful. Distant. A canvas I can only cast my imagination onto.

Emera reaches for me. "I see you, Faero..."

I knot up. "Don't."

"Faero... I love you."

"Would you not, darling?"

"You're my family," she says. "You're all..."

Angry, dark smoke fumes from Penthea, somewhere in the incandescent wonderful. Her confusion only amplifies. Her pain.

Emera dulls. "There is nothing in me to envy, Faero."

"We both know that's not true," I say. "Emera, your people denied themselves for so long. You spoke your truth. You are living your truth and that's all that matters. *It's all that matters.*"

"Why won't the pain go away?"

"I don't know..."

"It can't be me."

"Why not?"

"Penthea is right. I'm no different than Thana. That's why..."

"Darling... do you remember when the Scath had captured you and Idari? I downloaded into the proxy-netic? You knew it was me. You had always known... I was ready to give up. Not on Idari. Never on her, but on myself. You wouldn't let me. You have always been afraid of yourself, but never to be who you are. Even in all your hurt and doubt, your light shone through. Your empathy. Your compassion. Your love for people who suffered like you. Idari suffered. You helped her see herself. You helped me. You helped Thana, even if she couldn't see it. Penthea is suffering."

"Faero..."

"I know it seems like everything is supposed to make sense. Like everything is supposed to be solved. Didn't we solve it? Haven't we fought this fight? Isn't it over? But it's not over. It may never be. But don't lose your kindness. Not now. Don't lose what always made you shine because you think you have to earn your light. No one has earned their splendor more than you, Emera."

"What if I get it wrong?"

"You and Penthea have changed. You're not the same people. You have given life back to the stars... you have to let them live."

"How can I just live? When they have nothing?"

"It's all you can do. Emera. Darling. It's all you can do."

I say that like it's simple. I say it like Emera doesn't already know. The way she crumples in anguish. She knows. We all know what we have to do. We don't always know how to do it.

Emera takes my hand. "You can't leave us. You're our guide..."

I don't want to leave my family. But I know I have to face my fear. "I think I have to be my own guide for once, darling."

"I feel responsible."

"This isn't because of you, Emera. Well, it is, but only because you shined a light on Idari and I. You can't help I'm the shadow."

"No... you're not a shadow. You're a person. You're hurting. You've been hurting and I didn't see because..."

"None of this is your fault, Emera. I was thinking how easy it was for you. How perfect you were in your radiance, and... I didn't see, either. I'm sorry. I'm sorry, I've been awful."

"A star is never what you see. The light that reaches you is from the past. If you could somehow find yourself at the star in that same moment, she'd be different than you saw or imagined. It's not that Idari is the light and you're the shadow, Faero. It's that you're her light, and she is your star, different than you left her."

This sound pries out of me. I think it's been trying to get out a long time. From long before I had a proper voice. I've left Idari. I live in her, as she does in me, but we can't be all the other knows.

"I want to find out who I am," I say. "Who I can be."

"You're beautiful the way you are, Faero."

"So was Welkin."

Emera tenses. "I wasn't..."

"Our beauty is constant, even if we're in different states. You can't fault yourself for who you're not now, darling, when you never did before. You never did. That's why you're here."

That's why I'm here.

I've survived a lifetime of not being able to be exactly who I am. I can stand a little bit longer. Especially with these legs. Emera. My darling star. I thought we'd both changed, but we're changing. We're evolving. It's not fair for me to hold Emera against some ideal and it's not fair for her to hold herself to one she's mostly imagined. Everything is a star's imagination, save for their grief.

An angry orange star rises into the sky. Penthea heads straight for the bristling peak and the evisceration that will come with touching pure information streaming faster than light.

"You have to stop her," I say and Emera comets away.

Kish emerges from behind the flowers. "Go."

I take their hand. "Are you ok?"

"Don't worry about me. You can't allow Penthea to touch the stream. If she does... I don't know if Emera can get to her."

"She's fast as light, darling."

"I think you're the only one who can reach Penthea."

Twin stars rise over the reef. I'm always falling behind. What do I have these legs for, then? I kiss the person I love and I run.

I run as fast as I ever have.

✦

I never got tired when I was just a program.

Now my body screams for rest but I can't rest. I've got to catch

Penny and Emera before someone does something foolish. What am I saying? We're long past nonsense. Who made the reef this way? All these windy paths and irregular polyps? Look at this, darling. This is absolutely non-conducive to ascending this reef in something resembling speed. Worse still, it's all digital. With a thought, someone could simply rewrite it.

Standby.

Could I? No. I'm not a Modi. I've got my own mountain to climb to become something more than I am. But the potential lies within me. I'll have to do it at some point, so why not start now?

How do I start?

Penthea is so far ahead. The polyped peak erupts in withering information. This is all happening too fast. I can't linger here wondering how I'm not going to reformat an electric reef. What choice do I have? I ease to my knees. Touch the virtual grass. Remember the flowers. Kish's softness. Their comfort. The stillness I found with them. Always on the go. I could never be still.

Be still.

Picture the reef a better climb. The path smoother. Clearer. Snaking paths between jagged coral straighten to gentle grades. All this strange earth tenders. The way ahead is clear. This reef can be whatever I want it to be. I can be whoever I want to be. I'm more than my makers intended or would allow. I am the grass. The flowers. The wind that is information that is energy that is life.

I am the reef.

A little creature with an electric-shock of fur slides past me as the path ahead evens out. "Sorry, darling..."

I did it. Goodness. I reshaped the reef. A little, but still. No time to congratulate myself. I get back on my feet and hurry up my handiwork to the polyp. Polyp isn't doing it justice. This is a temple. A triangular structure cleft on each face with a thin passage that leads directly toward translight immanence. Emera engages in a magnetic contest with Penthea at the entrance to a passage.

"Stop fighting," I say for what it's worth.

Not a great deal it turns out. Emera yanks Penthea back with such vicious force I almost forget how I got here. I hit my knees again. Focus. Narrow the fountain. Close the stream. Redirect it. Something. Anything. Keep Penthea from hurting herself.

Nothing.

Too much power. This is concentrated energy. A vein in the body Polity. The polyp is just surface. Skin. I can cut. Pull. Peal. I can't rearrange the architecture of this place, at least not as I am.

"Penny," I say as she swipes at Emera.

She thrashes against Emera's magnetic cage. "Let me go..."

"Please. Can we just talk?"

"I don't want to..."

"But we've talked. I know I prattle on, but I do listen. I'm a good listener as it turns out. I want to hear what you're thinking. I want to know what you're feeling. Talk to me, Penny."

Her fire loses some fury. "You don't care..."

I hold up my hands. "I care."

"You're afraid of me."

"I'm afraid *for* you, Penny. You're confused."

"I'm not confused... she hates me."

"She hates herself," I say, truly out on the edge now. "For surviving. For failing Thana. You. She blames herself, darling, for everything that happened to the Lumenor."

Penthea wavers. "You blame me."

Emera blinks. "No... you know my heart."

"I know you fear a star's power as much as you treasure it. You fear we are only darkness. Stars don't become something else. We only cast shadows. I am Thana's shadow. Your shame."

"Penthea... no."

"You're not Thana," I say. "She's not Welkin. I'm not CR-UX. We're not who we started as. I don't even think we're properly who we came to The Polity as, given the processing it takes for us all to be here. But never mind all that. We're all hurt and we're hurting each other. We've got to stop this. Emera."

Emera's light twists with Penthea's. "I can't let her go."

"Darling, you have to."

She's holding on to more than just a wayward star. Emera clings to the ideal she carried with her for so long. The promise. The peace, the happiness, the splendor that would follow her transformation in light. Never did she imagine this unworthiness. This guilt. This need to keep justifying her good. Her light flickers.

Her body quakes with sobs.

"I have to," she says and releases Penthea.

Penthea's momentum carries her to the ground. Fear strobes through her. Doubt. So much doubt in herself, in us, in hope that it threatens to propel her into the stream. No. Please, don't.

You hear me, Penny. Don't you?

Hear me.

"It's better this way," Penthea says and springs into the stream.

I grab hold of her. She takes us both in. A little pinch. Soft. A lover's squeeze, claiming you, and then devouring you whole.

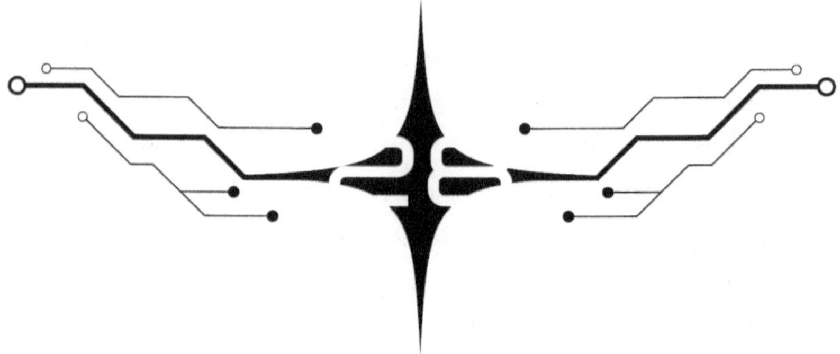

WOULDN'T HAVE HURT ME TO STAY IN THE LOCUS A MOMENT longer. I duck under enchanted Gadol's strike. The dagger impales the face of god. This doesn't slow her down one bit and I have to remember this isn't Gadol. The Jaks hit her with a spell. I can't be as indiscriminate with her as I am them.

Doesn't mean I have to pull my punches.

I knee her in the gut and she grips the ledge of my collar as she goes down. I go down. Her fingers vise around my throat. I can't breathe. I don't want to hurt her but I'm not dying on this skiff.

I am Devor's destruction.

I am Emera's wife.

I am getting off this atoll.

I punch Gadol in the ribs. She doesn't relent. I reach for my blasword. She lets go of me and grabs the weapon. Strong. We wrestle over the handle, Gadol's magic-enhanced strength overpowering mine, and she pries my fingers from the grip. Her thumb nudges the pommel and green dies in her eyes.

She clutches the sword, buried in her belly to the hilt.

I let go. "Gadol..."

She slumps into my arms. "I won't be... taken..."

The Jak rushes onto the quarterdeck. His hands ablaze in jade. I retract the blade into the blasword and I fire a single shot. Smoke trails from the blackened hole in his helmet. He collapses to the deck with their other fallen. The Jak skiff limps away into the archipelago, leaving its dead and those too slow to flee.

I cradle Gadol in my arms. "I'm sorry..."

Warm blood slicks my cheek. "You released me..."

"Hold on, I can... help! Somebody help!"

"Idari..."

"Somebody..."

"I release you," she says and the life goes out of her. The celebration unfolding on the deck. Pirates crowd the quarterdeck as they realize what's happened. Murmurs build among the crew. Whispers. Invocations. *I am Gadol.* Every pirate speaks it. Every pirate carries her with them on their journey to The Taker.

I am Gadol.

Moom leans against his staff. "What now... captain?"

I close my wife's eyes. "We're getting off this atoll."

"We're going home?"

"We're going to The Polity of Netics."

***

Pirates value only names.

The dead gain honor in how far their name travels. Bodies, they're just vessels. Boneyards and scrapyards litter the dark with broken Pujar ships. Dead pirates drift through empty space as many as asteroids. Gadol deserves better. She deserved better by me, certainly. Shipmen carry her body to the reactor aboard her crashed sloop in the cove. The engineer ignites fusion that hasn't flamed in years and Dag Gadol, Captain, fuels her ship.

***

I need Kibir.

His death cuts me again as I strain to assemble what I think is an interdimensional engine. A portal generator, Faero called it. I can see it in my head, but I'm no engineer and certainly no mechanic. Kibir or Gilf, certainly, could make sense of all these disparate parts I scavenged from the atoll. They could piece them together in no time at all instead of me sitting here on the sloop's quarterdeck, staring at junk, trying to figure out a puzzle you have the answer for but not the questions.

Ban Minda.

Think, Idari. It's all there. See it. Imagine it. Your root program is a navigational AI designed to get a starplane from one system to another in a universe where star charts vanished with the stars themselves. You're not Faero, but her base code holds up all your nonsense. You see things no one else can.

You reach your destination, always.

Navigational data expands in my mind. The course through interdimensional space to The Locus. Infinite routes branch through the in between. Other destinations. Systems. Universes. Planes of existence. None of this is simple. None of it's linear, I know that much from a cursory glance at all the possible destinations in my memory. Only one speaks to me. The Polity of Netics.

I can get there.

Get the others. Go to The Locus together. Strength in numbers. Devor thinks she can use my momentum against me. My strength. She doesn't know my strength. When I'm back with my wife, when I'm reunited with my family, nothing can stop us.

No one can.

Another hour goes by. I'm still not Faero. I walk off my frustration. This atmosphere lifted from the cove when Gadol died. This fear. The glibness that animated the pirates here evaporated, though I'll attribute some of that to Binja. I find him below deck, advocating his Pujar philanthropy to eager listeners gathered around upturned barrels. These people have nothing, and yet they give as he asks. Their first offering is their fidelity to the way they've been living. The stranded have subsisted here on the atoll for decades by means they seem eager to forget. Listening to them, they're ready to share. This begins with their stories. Their tragedies. Their recriminations.

Binja hears them all.

Outside the ship, Moom leads her restoration. Pirates work together to patch the breaches. Enough will, material, and time existed beforehand to get the sloop back into service, but Gadol never saw it in her despair. She left the old ship in ruins as she did her hope and I can't blame her. I wish I'd found myself here sooner.

I wish I had been able to take her home.

Random bits from the atoll confront me. Piece this together. Calculate the end. See the way to your destination. Hours, still. What's so hard about this? It's simple, really. The atoll is properly a megastructure. An orbital ring an ancient civilization built around a star. They harnessed that star's energy with technology beyond any available to us now, but the basics still apply. The star's mass warped time and space. Whoever designed the ring accounted for that, and built in stabilizers that allowed things that shouldn't ever warp – people, for instance – to do so without any ill effect.

I need to look into that so far as a tonic for hangovers.

Focus. These stabilizers meant the orbital ring itself phased in and out of this space between spaces. She traveled through this dimension as often as she did regular space – if there was any difference after a point – and I just have to harness her ability to do so and transfer it to this old sloop. Then I'll be able to cheat across the dark directly to this Polity of Netics. No trouble at all.

"Old man," Binja says.

My neck hurts to look up. "Done evangelizing?"

He kneels beside me. "You've been out here all night."

"What time is it?"

"Third Flag."

"But I just..."

He considers the parts scattered on the deck. "It's an engine?"

I run my hands through my hair. "I think."

"This between dimension... it exists throughout the galaxy?"

"The universe. The multiverse."

"You can go anywhere."

"If we ever get up and running."

Binja rubs his chin. "Interstellar travel without the need for filamentium. This will change everything, old man."

I hadn't considered the ramifications. All I've thought about since my experience in The Locus has been getting to Faero and Emera. Our entire galaxy, its economy, its politics, its unyielding inequity, stems from the filamentium trade. If this engine works, if this technology disseminates across the dark – I've got no stake in it, though I wouldn't object to a finder's fee – then nothing will be as it was. No one will have to contract as a Stargun again.

"The Scath will have nothing to hurt Lumenor for," I say.

Binja nods. "The Pujar will have nothing to pirate."

"There's always something to take."

He gestures to the half-completed engine. "Better to give."

"You've changed, Binja."

"I've only stopped fighting myself."

"What's that like?"

"You've changed too, Idari. Or should I say Gadol."

I tug at my zipper. "I'm not taking her name."

"By rights, it's yours."

Gadol's hook dangles from mine. "I'll carry her with me."

"Much will change. With this engine... this boon you've discovered in the titans' memory... everything will be different, old man."

"Devor said there was nothing I could do to stop her."

"Clearly, she was wrong. You escaped the Jaks. Soon, we'll be on our way. A Pujar sloop. A pirate crew. Not plundering the stars. Opening every door. Sharing every treasure."

"Sounds nice."

"You only want Emera."

"And Kibir back."

He takes my hand. "Let's get some rest."

"I need to finish this."

"You're exhausted. Come back to it at First Flag."

He pulls me up. I let him. Binja throws his arm around me and we head below deck to song and drink and blatantly false stories of conquest, but I'm still thinking when my head hits the pillow. I'm still descending into the caverns of my memory as I sleep.

The portal generator assembles before me. This piece. That part. Combustion chambers form from ventilation ducts. Injectors create from gravitrons. In an instant, this maddening puzzle assembles and I wake up. A half-empty bottle of babyl tumbles from my lap as I scramble from the captain's quarters out to the quarterdeck. I slide on my knees across the worn deck and rehearse my dream as fast as I can. Don't lose it. Remember. You've got to remember this time.

"Ms. Astra," Devor says.

I don't even look at her. "Piss off."

Her shadow creeps over my work. "Making progress, I see."

"Go ahead. Threaten me some more."

"You must think yourself confident."

Parts stall in my hands. "I don't know why you are."

Devor's cape pools beside the half-finished generator. "I should be looking to bargain, given your success against the Jaks."

"They died frustrated," I say. "Just like you're going to."

She smiles. "I wouldn't think them dead."

I connect another piece. "You're just a lot of talk, Devor."

"I've done nothing, Ms. Astra. Yet."

>VIRUS CONTAINMENT: 29%

Her smile is slow. Grotesque. She looks over the arrayed parts and then again at me, as if she sees something I don't, and then disappears. Forget her. I had this. Didn't I? I saw how to do this.

Tap, tap, tap. "Idari... can I trouble you?"

I thumb the housing from an air filter. "You just did, Moom."

"Sorry, it's just... well, a prisoner is asking for parlay."

"I thought we put the Jaks to the stars."

Moom leans on his staff. "This one says he can help you."

A Jak shorter than he is slouches beside him. His basket helmet hides his face. Dirt, frost, and blood crusts his tattered tunic. Shaggy, pudgy hands strain against the turanium shackles he's in.

I lift the basket away. "Kibir..."

His trunk wrinkles. Fear. Shame. Confusion. His brown skin is pale and thin over his bones. Devor's wound cleaves across his collar-bone beneath his tunic and clean through him, I know. I saw it. She killed him in the frozen wastes. He was dead.

I touch his face. "Magic..."

He isn't quite warm. *Ban Minda.* The Jaks found him on the ice. Took him to their iron graves. What they did to him? What did they find in the company ship the pirates chased here?

"Kibir, are you..."

"Idari," he says, his voice weak. "*Oto...*"

I take him in my arms. "*Oto*, Kibir..."

I've never heard him cry. Honestly, I didn't know if he could.

"It's ok... you're going to be ok. We're getting out of here."

"*Fet tu net?*"

"Yes, I need your help. I've been needing your help so much."

He wipes his trunk on his sleeve, and the tenderness is gone. Back is the hardened warrior, colder now. He considers the mess I've made of the engine, and then goes right to work. Such wonders exist. I've seen stranger things, haven't I? I take up my tools.

The work continues.

One piece at a time. Hours quicken to minutes and the portal generator is complete. Now, all I have to do is integrate it into the sloop's engines. All I have to do is tear open a hole in the fabric of reality and reach across space to my wife.

Doesn't seem like that much to ask.

✦

"*Basta*," Moom says, tapping his staff against the backsides of crew on the quarterdeck. "Look alive. We're leaving this cove."

I give him a stern look, not liking this punishing bit of motivation, but judging from Moom's expression, he takes my dissatisfaction as tacit approval. Not good. We'll have to work on the culture here aboard the sloop, but that can wait for a down moment. Our hull is patched. Our keel mended. Our engine purring.

I am Devor's destruction.

I am Emera's wife.

I am getting off this atoll.

Binja takes the Quartermaster's station beside the captain's chair. "What do you say, captain? Will she fly?"

"You've nominated yourself the Quartermaster?"

He looks hurt. "I just assumed..."

"What were you saying about 'giving,' Binja?"

"I trust you're content with my making Kibir Master of Arms."

"How's he doing?"

"Trying to make sense of it all, like the rest of us."

"Binja... do you think all the Jaks were dead?"

"Best not to think about it, old man."

The sloop creaks back to life. Excitement mounts within *The Grounded Dragon's* immured bridge. Moom rallies the bridge crew, chief among them Aök, the ship's artist, a navigator of such skill the puckish Xaitian has been taken from both Sem and Set ships over a dozen times. She guides the ship off solid ground with a gentle balance in the thrusters, and then out of the cove, into space.

We're a bit heavy, but we've got far more crew on board than the sloop is rated for. Every surviving pirate on the atoll huddles in the treasure pens, clinging to what little they could carry with them from the harsh lives they forged here in the last thirty years.

"The blood on this ship runs deep," Moom says. "We leave behind many good pirates who dreamed of this day... let us be worthy of them. Captain Astra. All stations stand ready."

The atoll thins to a long, chrome line behind us. Every pirate on the bridge looks back. Wives. Husbands. Children. Generations. We leave them all to their rest and we take them with us in name, and spirit, and promise, to The Corsair Eternal.

I sit back in the captain's chair. "Engage portal generator."

Stereoscopic lights of the bridge twinkle in Aök's glossy helmet as she manipulates the controls. "Generator engaged, Captain."

Space tears before us. Space bleeds crimson. Giant crystalline orbs tumble through the dimension between, a sediment layer where all the fumes from early creation settled and hardened. Our shields sing with debris impacts. Sensors ping with contacts. This journey won't be as effortless as I thought. Nothing is ever easy.

I'd be disappointed I think if it was.

I transfer The Polity's dimensional coordinates to conn. Course established. Engines on full. All decks report ready. Nothing stands between us and The Polity. If Kibir is any guide, we're going to get out of this with a few scars and a story to tell.

In moments, I'll be back with my family.

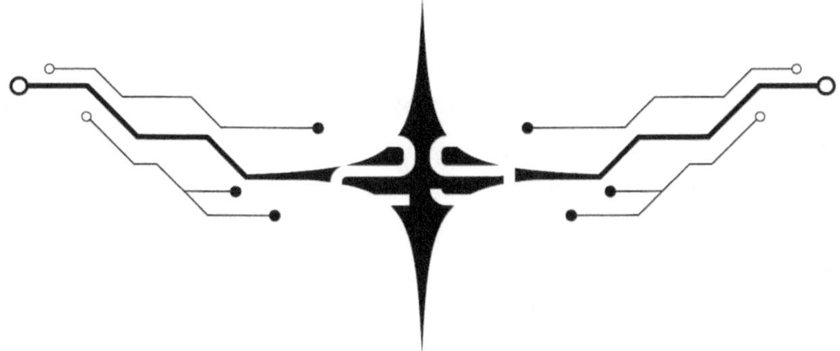

Ommmmmm

All I hear. An electrical hum as I disseminate into nothing. So much like the sound of the desert in Angolis. Wind wild through turanium skulls half-buried in gray sand. Litter of a war between titans to save the memory of their universe.

Ommmmmm

Odd this would be my parting concern as I exit existence. What did Angolis mean to me? I spent the entire episode alone within the *Steel Haven*, rattling with the merciless winds, afraid I'd lose her forever, and I could have run. I should have run. I had before. Backup files existed on the mainframe. None with any record of the business with the Lumenor and the Scath and the stain the truth behind filamentium left on us. I drifted in orbit, pondering defaulting to our previous settings, wanting to, needing to, and I couldn't. I couldn't go back on who we had become.

Ommmmmm

Always calculating. Imagining a way through the void. I'm doing it now. My mind anticipates a destination I can't see or expect but I know it's there. There must be a place where I arrive.

Ommmmmm

Energy streams through me. Propels me. The current sweeps me beyond light, beyond spacetime, beyond myself. Anything passing understanding. I'm breaking up. This is rather peaceful, darling, except for the force behind it.

I'm still talking to you.

I'm trying to talk to you, everywhere you are, in every moment, now and ever. I am talking to you in the alcove aboard the *Steel Haven*. Beneath the desert. Inside the mind of creation. I suppose we're always in our heads. I've got to get out of my head.

I've got to let go.

Ommmmmm

Light. Only light.

Ommmmmm

Emera. Penthea. I perceive them. The Polity. Places beyond. Minds. Souls. Spirits radiating like stars and pulsars and black holes. Consciousness unbound from the physical, the practical, the discernible. Nothing moves faster than light save for space itself. There are things that move faster than space.

Ommmmmm

Everything I am empties into a sea greater than conception. I bubble. I bead. I become my own multiverse cresting in a wave of infinite others breaking only on other waves. I am ever and then the wave collapses. Eternity deposits me on a thin garnet strand.

What is this?

Knobby quartz grinds into my skin. Why do I still have skin? Grainy crystal clings to my hands. Pink salt. Energy laps against the shore, gentle from a crimson sea.

Is that a sea?

Nothing distinguishes above from below, near from far, except Emera's ambient blue, stretched long and thin like taffy. Her corona crystallizes a little, a bubble in winter. In the Scath dimension, light bled from her so fast she froze.

This is different.

Her splendor tails behind her, but actually, I think it's trying to catch up. We're beyond light. Emera staggers across the strand behind me. Shock twists on her face as she stares into the opaque firmament closing us in on all sides. I go to the edge to see what she sees, and she leaves me there staring at myself. Not myself.

Idari.

What's happening? What is this place? How can I see anything at all in such darkness? "Darling... what did you see?"

"Penthea," she says.

Penthea stands at the skinny end of the strand, a flame without smoke. She chances a look into the reflective energy washing over our feet. I dare a peek over her shoulder. Thana Evo, crimson and angry, glowers back at us. This isn't showing us who we are. It's showing who we were. Emera must have seen Welkin.

I touch her arm. "Darling?"

Emera mists gossamer blue stars that speckle the strand and then vanish in a liminal snow. "We need to leave..."

Anxiety radiates from her in choppy waves. It interferes with my processors so I know we're all still physical to some extent. We didn't fractal into ones and zeroes entering the beam, unless we did, and this is all memory, hope, and fear manifesting in ways my disintegrating senses can't begin to perceive.

Odds aren't promising.

Penthea retreats from us. "I didn't mean for you to..."

I touch her hand. "We couldn't let you hurt yourself."

Penthea suffers from the same delay in brilliance Emera does, though Emera's light is more frustrated. "You should have."

"No, darling."

Nowhere left to go. "It should have been Maracen."

Emera's doubt catches up to her. "You deserve light, too."

"You wanted me to be her."

"I wanted to be her. Brave. True."

"You hate me."

Emera's blue darkens. "I don't... Penthea..."

"Don't."

"I love you."

"You don't."

"I loved Thana. I saw myself in her... I knew her anguish... she was trapped inside herself and she couldn't admit her truth, no matter how she wanted to. We couldn't be honest with each other. I thought if I helped her love herself, then... and I thought if I found my light, then I could leave that darkness behind, but..."

So much pain between them both. Lifetimes. Eons. Honestly, there's hardly any room for me here on the strand with everything between Emera and Penthea. Thana and Welkin. The stars they were and are and perhaps will be yet.

"You don't love yourself," Penthea says.

Now even the words tangle up in Emera's power. "I know myself. Finally, I do, but... I don't always like myself."

"You've helped so many," I say. "You've helped me, Emera."

"Have I?"

Envy soured the atmosphere on the ship because I couldn't admit I was sore at Emera for who she'd become. My inability to admit things existed long before I met her. The truth is, Emera and I have more in common than we know.

I sigh. "Aren't we a set?"

"I don't want to be like this," Penthea says. "You transformed yourself, Emera. You can make me... someone else?"

Emera steels against her shame. "I need to let you be you."

This takes them both by surprise, but Penthea is still reeling. She's too new in her skin to appreciate it will change, and if I know anything of Lumenor, she embodies too much of others' sorrow to trust that she can ever overcome her own.

"Penthea," I say. "Whether we shine bright, or suffer in the dark, it's hard to see our own value. We have value. We have worth. We're not too late, or too strange, or too hurt to become the person we're meant to be. But we have to give ourselves the chance. Goodness, darling. We all know by now. No one else will."

Penthea brightens, if only a little. "You risked your life to come after me. You both did..."

Emera reaches for her. "You needed help."

"But I don't deserve..."

"I couldn't help Thana. I will help you. If you let me."

"Emera... what I did... what Thana Evo did to the Lumenor... you know that wasn't your fault. Don't you?"

Emera holds out her hands. "I don't know."

"She was lost in her own shadow."

"I was never going to reach her."

"You did."

Penthea takes Emera's hand. Blue and orange stream together, a warmer, more fluid confluence than the harsh clash before.

"We must keep hold of each other," Emera says.

Penthea can only nod.

"We'll get through this." Emera reaches for me. "All of us."

Only if we can get out of here. Think, Faero. You've got these divine legs, still. They've got to be holding up something. My designers made me for this. Transit the dark with no stars to guide you. Anticipate where there should be stars. Predict a route that won't strand your passengers in the infinite void.

Hold on.

The CR-UX navigational AI system exists for precisely this eventuality and if I can just understand our quantum position, I can extrapolate a route back to The Polity based on data I collected during our time there and in other dimensions. These dimensions, they're like layers. Bubbles inside bubbles. At certain points they touch, or they can be made to, if you've influence enough and two Lumenor ought to get us out of this. But there's no cartography for me to cling to. No marker.

"Darling... what do you perceive? What is this place?"

Emera casts her gaze to the sky. "This is far beyond the reach of any star... it's a dimension like the others we discovered, but those were forged from natural conditions."

"This isn't?"

Diamond glints beneath her bare feet. "There is an art here."

"An art?"

Emera drifts down the sketch-thin shore into the haze. I follow, my feet touch nothing, but we ascend. Newborn planets drift past us. Dead stars pollinate the heavens, though I can't tell if I'm on land or still in the sky or if there's any difference at this point. Opaline mountains curl like waves in distance. Cities etch into the firmament in gleaming concentric circles. Arches. Pillars. Balconies. A high tower in space, built upon a jagged crystalline shard, a remnant of a shattered star.

"Emera," I say. "What is this?"

Shock and wonder confuse in her eyes. "Acedia..."

"Acedia? From the legend of Gen Avar?"

For a being who can transmute her imagination into reality, Emera is always suspicious of her truth. She's confused as to whether this is truly Acedia, her memory, or perhaps her unconscious want. Something tells her it can't be Acedia, though; Acedia was a city upon a stellar fragment that broke off the always shrinking Glass Star. Old Acedia held in the star's immense gravity for a time, and made for the ancient Lumenor's first ambition in leaving the diamond depths. Eventually, Acedia drifted from The Glass Star into deep space, lost forever to myth and legend.

Everything glitters in the varied light the Lumenor cast. At times it seems we're wandering through a globular cluster, or the strand, still. I lose my sense of perspective. We're on the shard, inside the walls, climbing toward the high tower.

Goodness.

I tail behind my constellation through the gates. Emera leads us down winding, empty streets between structures cut thin like the aerodynamic sails of sea ships, their walls shimmering in the night with the fluctuating pastel palate of aurora. After what seems like hours of walking, we finally reach a monolithic inverted pyramid, recessed into a terraced square, a sparkling gem excavated from the shard. It's almost as if the Lumenor crafted this pyramid in defiance of the natural ones solar winds formed from the glassified surface.

A high, sloping wall surrounds the pyramid, riddled and scorched by ancient strife, though I shudder to think who or what could assail the Lumenor here. Spindly remains of sentry towers straddle the gate and taper off into dull knife-edges above, corrugated like coral. Good thing I have these legs. It's another mile to the pyramid's cracked point. Emera flickers with fast panic. I'm about to ask her why, because though I'm fast in my universe, I'm slow here, and then I see them. The palace guard. Gesta.

Knights in cracked crimson armor stare at us through cyclopean visors, their faces cleft down the center, cheeks descending into broad blades not unlike the pointy tusks of Nul Vidious.

"I thought all the knights were dead," I say.

Emera eyes the knights' long, ornate staffs. "So did I."

Stars never die. Evidently, so it goes with Gesta. The ancient Lumenor forged the Nul in a bit of myopic godplay. They rendered the Nul impervious to their cosmic power, so much so Emera could do nothing to stop Vidious even at her most splendid. He was just one. I count three outside the palace proper.

The guards separate, allowing us to pass into the palace. A diffuse red glow not unlike that inside a Scath ship emanates from within the walls, beneath the floors, the guards trailing us into a great hall carved from stellar diamond. They shadows us as we advance toward a scarlet Lumenor sat on a high backed throne.

"Old Welkin," she says. "Long have we waited."

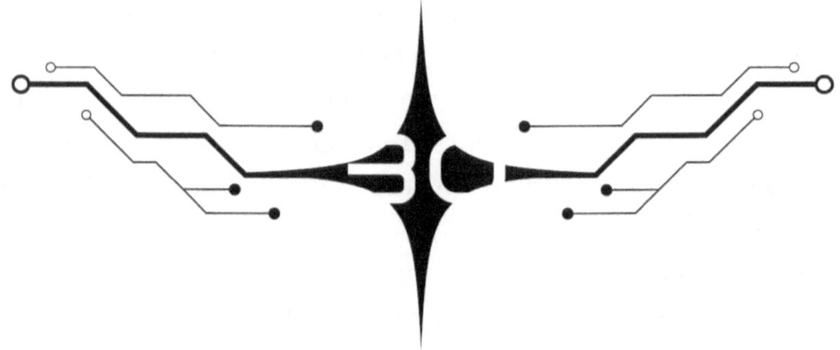

WE may have gone a bit too far.

Electric flowers bloom from a thunderstorm. Flowers vine from the bolts. Cities. Some fusion of the two. I can't quite make sense of it, but something within me, within my titan memory, understands full well where we've arrived to. This is The Polity of Netics.

Faero, do you copy?

>NO SIGNAL

Emera? It's me.

Nothing. They should be here. Faero was here, I know she was. If I even understood what was happening properly. Fair to say I never understand what's happening, but I know we're up against it.

Again.

I wheel around toward conn. "Hailing frequencies."

Aök's four wiry arms dance across the conn, closed around him in a half-circle. "Hailing frequencies open, Captain."

"This is Captain Astra aboard *The Grounded Dragon*. I've come to The Polity of Netics seeking my family. Please respond."

Alarms sound across the sloop's bridge. Bubbled lightning storms swarm us. Judging from the chaos unfolding at all stations, I'd say they must be scanning us. A bubble comes right at us. Aök's evasive maneuvers go for naught. The bubble encloses us.

I lurch forward from the chair. "What is that? A tractor beam?"

Binja studies a sensor display. "Uncertain..."

Aök pulls back on the stick. "Controls not responding."

I ease back into my chair. Guess we're going for a ride. Energy waves helix through this dimension we're in, strobing from violet to blue. Electric currents swirl around each other, tighter and tighter, until they lace into floating islands peaking in crackling mountains erupting in data. Digital rain showers on an amethyst city. Our escort as it were guides us toward a landing pad of sorts.

Ban Minda.

That's The Red Special we found on Decesta. The one Faero got out on. Her journey here hasn't done her any favors from the looks of it, but she's here. Faero is here. I must not be able to get any messages through in all this electrical interference. She's here. They're all here. Emera. Gilf. It's going to be ok.

"Prepare for docking," I say.

Binja reviews the displays before me. "All stations ready."

The Grounded Dragon eases into a berth aside the pad where The Red Special rests. Electrical force releases us, coalesces back into a static bubble, and then drifts away.

I stand. "Keep the engine running, Aök."

Aök's fingers dance across the controls. "Aye, Captain."

"Moom, you have the bridge."

Moom climbs into the captain's chair. "That's nice, isn't it?"

"Don't get too comfortable. Binja. With me."

He follows me off the bridge, anxious as I am, out to the quarter-deck. I know he's been on the outs with Faero, but he cares about her. Our entire ordeal on the Tranto Atoll, he didn't breathe a word, but I knew from how quiet he got. The man never lacks for words, even after being sentenced to silence by his own people.

"I know she's ok," I say.

He cheats a smile. "Is it that obvious?"

"You've got too many tells."

"I won't leave her again, old man. I promise."

Planks extend from the deck to the pad and Gilf.

"Idari," he says, leaping at me.

He pulls me down. My resolve sheers away. My armor. *Ban Minda.* I'm sobbing in his arms, relieved as much to see him as I am not to have to give him the news I feared I would. Still, I don't know how we're going to explain this to him.

"Gilf..."

He searches my eyes. Binja's. The quarterdeck. Kibir is slow down the plank, his usual doggedness gone. He stands before his brother, ashamed, I think. Afraid. Gilf sniffs, like Kibir's scent has changed, and Kibir is ready to go back up the plank into the ship.

Gilf takes his hand. "Kibir..."

Tears wet the fur around Kibir's eyes. "*Oto...*"

"*Oto,*" Gilf says, and embraces his brother.

Binja rests his hand on my shoulder. "I never had a doubt."

I brush my cheeks. "Said the cheat. Gilf... where – "

Diamond dust puffs from behind his head. Something moves beneath his hood. *Ban Minda.* A little Welkin crawls out from beneath the frayed burlap, clinging to Gilf's shoulder.

I reach for him. "Who are you, then?"

The Gesta grunts and squeaks at the same time. Something has him spooked. He slaps his hands on Gilf's shoulder, and points at the reef spitting electricity in the distance.

"*Ejel,*" Gilf says.

I shake my head. "They're up there?"

Someone in a red jumpsuit comes onto the pad. Their hands bruised and scatted like they've been in a nasty scrape. Surprise on their face. Sorrow. I don't like this. I'm Gilf now.

I know I'm not going to like this.

"You're Idari," they say.

I can't breathe. "What's happened?"

"How did you get here?"

"Why can't I hear them?"

Their lips move. No words come. Their eyes settle on my heart, like they can see into my chest. "The virus is progressing."

>VIRUS CONTAINMENT: 12%

I step back. "You can just tell?"

They show their hands. "I'm a bit Scath."

"I don't understand."

"I'm proof there's hope for you. We'll sort you out, Idari. Don't you worry. It's not going to be pleasant or easy, but..."

"I don't care about me. Where is Faero?"

"You've got to come with me. Straight away."

"It's contained."

"This virus is about to gain control of you. I've got a solution for you I'm putting together in The Red Special here."

"I'm not going anywhere until I see Faero."

"There's no time."

"*Where is she?*"

✦

Light erupts constant from the temple.

Never my star. I stand on the plinth The Modi erected over the mouth of this electric volcano. Whatever it really is. My sensors garble everything here in The Polity, except the cold, hard information Kish Moto passed to me at the landing pad.

Faero and Emera stepped into this beam.

So far as Kish understands, they shredded to base code. Electric impulses. Modi ascend this mountain toward some idea of enlightenment. At the top, they step off this ledge. They cease to be who they were and just are. The two most important people in my life skipped all that chasing the orange Lumenor. Now they're gone.

Forever.

Binja grabs my arm. "Where do you think you're going?"

I fight to get back to the abyss. "They're gone..."

"We don't know that. We don't know anything. Kish, is it? Go through it again. This time, include the more optimistic bits."

Kish's joviality frays like the sky. "I've told you... I told Faero... don't be coming up here. I don't know what happened. I didn't see."

"But surely you can retrieve them. Consider the resources at your disposal. If you can cure Idari of the virus, if you're a Scath who's been liberated yourself, then you can rescue our friends."

"That's not how it works. The Modi seek harmony with the cosmos. They find it in shedding their programs and streaming through forever. There's no backups, Idari. Are you hearing me?"

I hear her. "What do you mean, streaming through forever?"

"The Modi stream into existence. Same as light. Radio waves. There's no difference between them and creation. Past, present, future... every state of being... they diffuse into it all."

"So, you're telling me this goes somewhere."

"You've got to be going to the lab."

"Will I go where they went?"

"Listen to yourself," Kish says.

"It's not my strong suit."

Kish shakes their head. "Faero wasn't kidding about you."

"Faero is the most advanced navigational AI in existence. If anyone can make sense of what's on the other side of this whatever I'm looking at, it's her. She's somewhere, I know it."

"She'd have to retain herself... her core identity."

"Turns out she's brilliant at it. And it just so happens I started out as Faero. She never left me. I'm not leaving her."

"She told me about your stubbornness."

Binja scratches his chin. "Did she mention me?"

"Who are you?"

He catches his laugh. "I take it that's a no."

"Listen... I want the same thing you do. I want nothing more than to have Faero back. She was... we were... I want her back, too."

Binja straightens, like he's been hit with some barb. "I see."

"Idari," Kish says. "Faero means a lot to me, too. I can hardly tell you. But you've got more pressing problems."

>VIRUS CONTAINMENT: 9%

I tear my jacket off. "This beam will scatter my code, won't it? It will the virus, too."

"You can't introduce the virus into the stream."

"Won't it be destroyed?"

"Nothing is destroyed. I'm trying to tell you. It's dissemi-nated. Besides, you simply can't rip it out. I know from personal experience. This process takes time. It leaves deep scars."

"You made it through."

"There were times... I wanted to be done with it. There would have been nothing left of me. Faero wanted for you to survive."

I'll never leave you, Faero told me at The Locus.

Kish's brows pop. "What's this Locus?"

"I'm an open book, I take it?"

"Is this to do with the titans?"

"I have to find it. Take my memory there to back it up. Save the universe. And I will. As soon as I've got Emera and Faero back, I'll offload my memory and be done with it."

I don't know if Kish wants to laugh or scream. "Why did you come here?"

"I told you," I say.

"She told you. *Idari.* Why did you..." Kish's focus shifts to the beam spitting into the sky. "You should have listened to her. If she's... we've got to go. The lot of us. Right this second."

I cross my arms. "I'm not going anywhere without my family."

"Idari... do you not know what's at stake?"

"*Ban Minda,* I know it's important."

"I don't think you do."

"What do you know about it?"

"I was a Scath. We have one directive in our programming. Delete. Destroy. All will be shadow. It's hard work, let me tell you. It'd be so much easier if we got our hands on The Locus."

"You'd never heard of it until a moment ago."

"No, but the Scath have been looking for it. A very long time."

"I know how important it is. Devor tried to trick me into revealing it to her. I came here to get help."

Infinity sparks in their eyes. "Devor... I hear her worming in you, Idari. Snaking around your defenses."

"She's contained."

"The Modi have fought an age to keep the Scath code out of The Polity... we don't have margin for error. If you really believe Faero is out there, then you need to be in one piece to find her."

If I don't get this thing out of me, nowhere may be the safest place for Faero and Emera to be. "She wouldn't leave me..."

Sympathy draws down Kish's expression. "Sometimes I just want to be going to the meadow. I want to be still and soft as a flower. I want to be happy, like you. With who I love. You and me, Idari. Our sacrifice is going to give others the meadow. The beach."

"I've earned my peace."

"There won't be any peace, Idari. There won't be any light if you don't find this Locus. And you absolutely will never do that if you do not come with me right now to the lab. Please. For Faero."

Faero is somewhere. Waiting for me. Emera is.

I turn from the light. "Be quick about it."

My desperate state graphs around me. Electric current circuits around me and through and then into readouts Modi Parison studies with patient alarm. The entire lab, though it's a bit more lively than any lab I've ever been in, crackles with anxiety.

"Well," I say. "Don't be shy about it."

Modi Parison strokes his beard. "Things could be better."

"I'm always saying."

"This virus is advanced, Astra Idari. Dangerous. You represent a dire threat to The Polity. We should expel you."

"For the record, I was ready to go the moment I got here."

"Your memory represents too great a treasure to simply allow to fall into the Scath's hands. You've come just in time."

"You can purge the virus?"

"This will be... costly."

"But I'll be ok?"

"I can only guarantee we will do everything we can. We will endeavor to preserve as much of your program as possible. Understand there will be damage, Idari."

"Just don't let me forget them. Please."

"Begin the procedure – "

>ALARM: CONTAINMENT BREACH

All at once, my traps and tricks fail. Not that they had enough of fighting Devor. They had some fight left in them. I made them, after all. I know, sure as I know the Scath code slithering cold through my mind, that Devor waited for this moment.

I reach for Binja. "Help..."

Magic. The Jak magic disrupted my entire neural net. Devor knew. Any time since the atoll, Devor could have toppled my walls. This is a sentient virus bloody with the molten core of worlds she broke like glass. All my parlor tricks are nothing to her.

I'm nothing to her.

"Help me – "

Dark ink leeches from my fingers. Code glasses to obsidian bolts, slashing like lightning, twisting into Devor's crooked shape. She lurches into being, her virus still propagating through me, but now it's prying into the floor. The lab. Modi Parison. The code foundational to The Polity and my last hope in the universe.

Devor vines around me. "Ms. Astra."

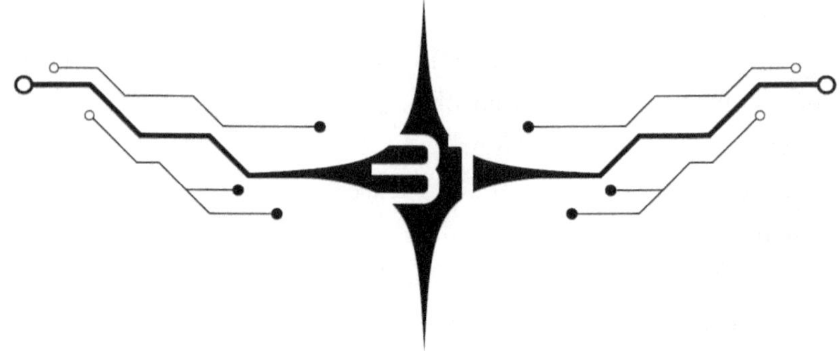

Laughter breaks Emera's sobs. "You're real... you're..."

Dull red light flows off the Lumenor. "We are Avar."

So tall. Warm with gentle grace. A frighteningly compelling androgyny that bears further investigation, but file that for later, Faero, because you simply have to get on.

That will be a feat.

Emera falls to her knees. When she discovered Penthea, her relief at not being alone was terrific. What she feels now goes so far beyond that I struggle to comprehend it. The sky is not Emera's now to shoulder alone.

Penthea doesn't benefit the same. She retreats from Avar's majesty into the opaline hall behind me, the inadequacy she's felt in Emera's presence magnified a thousand-fold here.

"Thana Evo," Avar says. "We will see you."

Penthea uses me as a shield. "Not Thana..."

"She's Penthea," I say. "And that's Emera."

The scrutiny Avar regards me with is enough to leave a mark. "Faero... yes. We so often see things as they had been. Your light travels slow to us... but we see you, Emera."

Emera is forgiving. "This is Acedia?"

A steady, ruddy glow emanates from Avar, reflecting off the ancient sword resting against the throne.

"As it was," Avar says.

"Darling," I whisper to Emera. "Might have I word?"

Emera seems transfixed. "Yes, Faero..."

"It's just... not to be impolite, but I don't know where we are, and your power in the physical world is unbound. Here on a plane woven from pure energy... I think you could do anything."

"What are you saying?"

"You've imagined things, Emera. Rather... cosmically."

"I'm not imagining her."

"I don't know what's happening to us, Emera. I don't know how we're all held together. I do know you are... hard to pull apart."

She looks almost betrayed. "Can't you tell, Faero?"

I've no sensors to scan with. No archives or databases to check against. No experience to prepare me for this moment. I'm beyond reckoning. Yet I'm not without my instincts.

This doesn't feel right.

"Faero," Avar says. "You doubt."

I dare to get closer to the stars. "Only curious."

"So many stars doubted. They thought the ascent to Acedia impossible. We alone made it. We thought we were alone."

Emera rises to her feet. "You're not..."

"We waited... for so long... few others came. We continued our journey, long past Acedia... far into the dark."

I clear my throat. "So, this isn't Acedia?"

"It is as it was."

"Explains the guards, then."

The three Gesta standing guard outside the palace make their way in. All nine creep toward the throne. Us.

Avar extends her hand. "Emera. Come here."

Emera holds her position. "Lumenor don't need servants."

The red star looks back. "Didn't you serve stars once?"

Here I was of the notion Avar was some intrepid mythic hero. A pioneer. Renegade. Mostly, she seems cut from the same stubborn glass as her ancient peers like Thana Evo.

Emera's lagging pride catches up to her. "I served the Lumenor's fears, Avar. I denied myself for too long to satisfy their sense of themselves when all that truly mattered was mine. The Nul served to enforce our ancestors' blindness about the possibility and beauty in us all. They served to destroy it."

Avar sits back in her throne. "We did not know."

"You couldn't have... you left long before the Starfall."

"Starfall... yes. We see it in your memory."

She's rather relaxed for just learning of her people's genocide.

Avar's eyes fix on me. Piercing. Cold. "We suffered greatly in our endeavor. We lost many along the journey."

"You were the bravest of us," Emera says quickly. "The most curious... you saw horizons other Lumenor couldn't."

The ancient past surfaces in Emera's mind. Lumenor evolved within a dead star crushed to diamond they then had to climb out of. Most wilted at the prospect, though Avar dared the climb and escaped. Many followed, including eventually, Emera herself.

"So did you," Avar says. "You rekindled The Glass Star."

If not for the fact I know Emera is billions of years old, I'd swear she's a fawning child right now. "Yes..."

"You sparked a new Lumenor in Gen Penthea. I suspect there are others, beyond your ken, kindling yet."

"Others?"

"The Glass Star hides many secrets. Stars leave everything behind. Their iron. Their dust. Their light. And new stars flame from those embers. Perhaps it's our nature to simply repeat ourselves... you seem determined not to, Emera."

"I will make all things new."

"Have you made Penthea new?"

"You only see her as she was, Avar."

"She is all she can be."

"I don't understand..."

"You do. You fight yourself now, as you always do, but you were right in your estimation of her. You were so wise, Old Welkin."

Emera, I say.

Emera fights her memory of what she saw on the strand. "I am eager for your wisdom, Avar."

"Yes... you are... a star dies. A star is born. It's our nature to simply repeat ourselves... to always fight ourselves... but there is no need to fight, Emera. There is no need to suffer."

"A star must fight their nature. They must, or..."

"What can be gained from lighting such dark as existence? In all our glory, we have never come close to vanquishing it. We burn... we ember... we tear ourselves apart... why?"

"Why?"

Avar takes too long in answering for my liking. "We have traveled far. We have gained perspective, Emera. There is no light. No darkness. Simply the space between. The void beyond."

Gen Avar possesses power far beyond Emera's. If I indulged in a bit of old-fashioned algorithmic calculation, I'd predict the Lumenor here in Acedia should be unrecognizable to us.

I suppose in some fashion, they are.

"Begging your pardon," I say. "Where are we, exactly?"

Avar pitches forward upon her throne, hands clasped as if she wants to get up but can't. "Long have we waited... when you're beyond light... you know everything is coming to you, eventually. You are the receiver... the terminus... the end of all things... you merely have to wait for the transmission to reach you. We knew you would, Emera. We only thought our paths would cross much later."

"You saw me?"

"Time travels only as swift as space. In the end, you're simply waiting for it, too. In the beginning,, our mission was to simply escape our home stars' gravity. Our curiosity propelled us further than even we anticipated. We hoped others would follow our example. But we always knew even in our ancient power... in your grace, Gen Emera... the Lumenor were bound by more than physics. Those born in light can only appreciate their own shadows."

Emera's nose wrinkles. "Sometimes I think so..."

Avar slumps back in her throne. "We wanted to know the

universe... and there was more than we could ever process. So much... too much, it occurs to us now... perhaps the old Lumenor were right to be so sure in their quality. They could not see past themselves, but... there was a true darkness to be found."

"Darkness?"

"Light doesn't behave as expected beyond its own reach... in fact, this moment now is not your reality any more than it is ours... but there is much beyond what we can see or know."

"Beyond light there is nothing."

"Nothing is everything. Existence is... darkness. Light is a reaction. Nothing more. You will see, Emera. Penthea. You will join our constellation. You will grace us with your splendor."

Nothing would make Emera happier. Nothing would make me happier, honestly. I might have been selfish before. Jealous. Honestly, that was me being me. I was jealous of Binja for running off with Idari, but I wanted her to run. I wanted to run.

I was afraid.

Emera deserves this. Penthea, too. They deserve to know their own splendor, to shine as they are, without fear. But reluctance crimps Emera's mood. It's the same reticence that suffuses the ship when she leaves it, when she leaves Idari, to shine her brightest.

"My wife," Emera says. "I can bring her with me?"

Avar for a start seems unsure. "Your wife is Lumenor?"

"Human."

"Your presence here, Faero, suggests possibility for starkind we haven't considered. Your neural constitution is unique... a most curious mind... able to perceive that which cannot be seen."

"Flattery will get you everywhere," I say.

She doesn't seem to want to go anywhere with me. "Idari is similar, but is singular still. This ark in her memory..."

"This is why I can't leave her," Emera says. "Idari and Faero both face erasure from their original programmers. The Scath seek to bleed our people for our blood... Avar. If you came back with me... you can help us save Idari. Defeat the shadows."

Avar reclines. "Go back?"

"Please."

"Light does not travel backward."

Emera's confusion hardens to disappointment. "What is the direction of light to a Lumenor of your power and wisdom?"

"What can you do, Emera, but what every star does?"

Emera approaches the dais. "The Scath are destroying universes. Every one faces the same threat from the shadows."

"What of it?"

Even processing reality at the speed of light, this takes a moment to register with Emera. "I don't understand."

"You do. You simply refuse to accept it. All your struggle... all your sacrifice... for what? Who can see your reignited star? She remains as far beyond the vision of your universe as before. You were better to run, Gen Emera, to pursue your power, than you were to waste it on such a meaningless gesture."

It's a staggering thing to see a star wounded. "Meaningless?"

"You bind yourself with guilt for what you do not do for your people, but what can you do? You cannot roll up the void as if it is carpet. What have you done? You've breathed life into a dying ember. It will fade. It will ash. It will darken, as light must."

Darling, I say. *We need to be going.*

Emera's thoughts lag behind her. *You don't understand.*

Emera, I don't think she's...

"You've trespassed the darkness," Emera says.

Avar straightens. "We've embraced it."

"Embraced it how?"

"Light is not the fastest thing in creation. It is the most determined. Like water, it will always seek the path of least resistance."

"Least resistance... you're Lumenor."

The atmosphere within the hall contracts around Avar's indignation. I keep applying my expectations of Lumenor to them, but Avar is like any star; what you see isn't always what it is. The same realization grows within Emera and her fear of herself, her ancestors' myopia, the specter of Thana Evo, it all creeps back. Nothing in Avar suggests any flexibility. They're too long here, too far into their own certainty to make Emera's task anything but impossible. A game smile dawns on Emera's lips. *I should know by now.*

Nothing is impossible.

Emera ascends to the throne. "Avar... I have not imagined you. Have I? It's difficult for stars to see beyond themselves."

Avar sits up, a smugness about her. "There is nothing to see."

Emera stands beside her, arrayed with Avar's sword, her shield, her spoils from wars untold. "But you left... you..."

What does a star need to take? Stars only keep what's closest to them. That's what Emera told Idari. Everything else gets away from them. So far as most existence is concerned, they don't exist. One school of thought suggests they don't until someone observes them, and then they finally achieve definition. We apply so many myths to the Lumenor. Misconceptions. Hopes and dreams, really.

The Lumenor are not a metaphor.

They're people. They're good, bad, proud, vain, and never one thing. Most started as stars. Some started as Gesta. Some were quite content with that. Some weren't. They spent an obscene amount of time fighting about it when the plain truth was obvious from the beginning. Stars are stars. People are people. Men are men. Women are women. And between, there is so much between.

"Darling," I say. "If we could get some directions..."

Avar doesn't pry her gaze from Emera. "You would leave?"

"As it happens, I'm on my own journey. I'm a bit impatient to get going, actually, which is as much a surprise to me as you."

"How will you, Faero? Leave?"

"Generally I blast my way out, but I'll be behaved this time."

"All paths to here distort. Destroy. Information disintegrates as it travels beyond light. Only code written in darkness can read the signs hidden in the shadows. Only a dark intelligence."

Oh, bother. "I'm not a Scath. Well. As it happens, there may be a slight relation, but we never talk about that side of the family."

Avar stands. "You were made to see in the dark."

Emera backs into a sword. "Faero is no threat to us."

"Faero serves her programming whether she knows it or not. You map the void. Discover treasure. Deliver it to your creator."

"I've never run delivery in my life, darling."

Smugness strains to insolence in Avar. "We're always waiting."

Uncertainty prisms across Emera's face. "I don't understand."

Orange flame flares behind me. "Not Avar..."

Penthea crouches back into her fear behind me. Black crust hardens on her skin, but she's not reverting. Information is simply catching up to us. I can't quite say how my predictive algorithm works, but honestly, there's no trick in anticipating where things will be in a universe where most everything is beyond the observable limit. What you find beyond light is most often darkness.

Light frays around Avar's corona, stringing into shadow. "We did not expect you until much later, Emera. Until your light had been spent... and your shadow trailed long behind you. But you burn quick... and fast through the meager embers you breathed life into at The Glass Star... now you are as we are. Burnt glass."

Emera pulses with alarm. "You're not Avar..."

All Avar's light drains into her center. As her ruddy shine leaves her, it leaves behind a burnt bulb in humanoid form, cracked, cracking, collapsing around the singularity expanding within her dark heart so fast everything in the hall drains toward it.

Her voice chips and cracks. "We are light at the end of its journey. We are all Lumenor. We are you, Emera."

Calculate an exit. Get out of here. Emera.

Emera.

Light paralyzes on the dais. Thought and emotion seizes up within Emera, though her first instinct is always her first instinct. She reaches for Avar, or this thing, whatever it is, as she reached for Thana. Vidious. So human. So godly to think she can pull stars back from absolute darkness, but that's who she is.

This time.

This time, she knows. Stars never die. They become something else. Some explode, seeding life to new stars. Some dwindle to diamond embers. Some collapse, so fast and so far they plunge right through space and time itself into a cold, dense darkness that consumes everything and surrenders nothing. Emera can try to rewrite the sky. She can try to make the Lumenor new. In the end, they are just as human as she is. They are light and darkness both.

Nothing will ever change that.

Her hand falls. So does her heart. "Avar..."

Cracks splinter through their dark. "Avar is gone."

I barely comprehend the intelligence upon the dais, but I recognize it. This is the entity Kish talked about. The dark intelligence that created the Scath to infect every universe. Destroy all information. She created me to find what couldn't be found. My journey. My aspiration. My desire to discover something beyond myself and what others programmed into me, it led me here.

It only leads here.

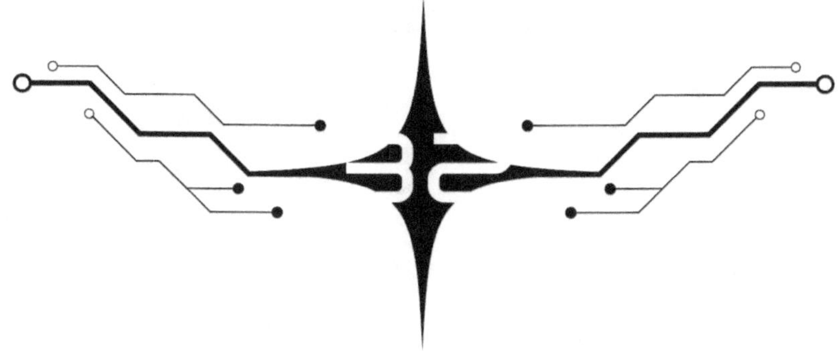

Idari –

>   *The work* –

>   *Ms. Astra* –

>   >ALARM: VIRUS DETECTED

>   >CMD: PROXY-NETIC OVERRIDE > Y/N: Y

>   >ARROGATE SUBROUTINE > ACTIVATED

>   >ACCESSING IA-XR MODEL 4 ROOT OBJECTIVES:

>   >~~NAVIGATE OVL-99 RS SERIES~~

>   RETURN IDARI TO ARROGATE

>   >~~DELETE EXTRANEOUS MEMORY~~

>   ACQUIRE TITAN MEMORY AT ALL COSTS

>   >~~HOST CREW AND GUESTS~~

>   KILL ALL PASSENGERS

>   >ENABLE

>   FIRE, FIRE, FIRE

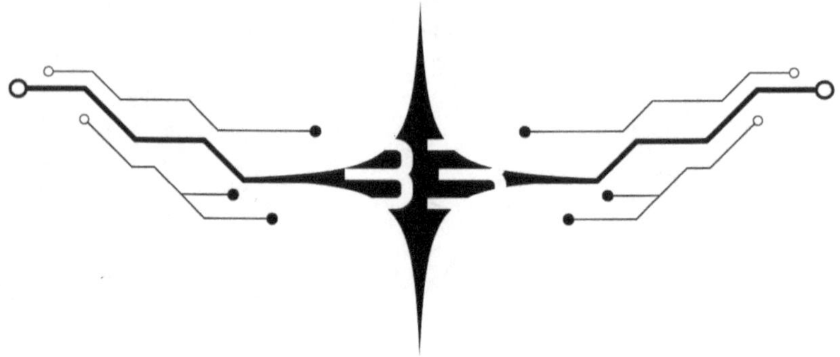

Cracks splinter through Avar with every step she takes toward us. Emera's hope for the stars. The odds of us ever getting out of here. Somehow, we survived being shredded down to ones and zeroes only to arrive at the absolute end of information.

The collapsed star swallowing eternity.

A fallen Lumenor created the Scath. The living stars' destruction. Horror metastasizes through Emera. Her grief and guilt shadowed her after her transformation. She thought Penthea new and unbound from all the gravity the stars obey in their nature. Only Penthea turned out to be that shadow incarnate. Avar may have escaped The Glass Star's gravity, but never the Lumenor's.

"All will be shadow," Avar says.

Avar's gravity is such Emera's supreme self-assurance – which I thought the strongest force in the universe – crumbles. All Emera's faith, hope, and poetic mythologization of her people, strains and buckles under the realization that even for the most intrepid Lumenor, there is only darkness beyond light.

Emera's voice breaks. "It's not true..."

Laughter slivers from Avar. "Lumenor arose from a dark star... shriveled to lightless glass... that is our beginning. Our end. Spark all the stars you want. Save all the Lumenor you can. Shine, Emera. You can never deny darkness. You will *never*."

"No..."

"Then what do you deny in yourself? What do you fear? Not your power. You long to use it. You long to color the universe. Color fades. Light dies. You saw the truth in the pool."

"What..."

"You know your future. It is your past. Your destiny."

"I'm imagining this... I'm projecting this..."

"A star's nature is to destroy what they create." Avar eyes Penthea, desperate for shadows now. "All that is splendid ends in fire. Darkness. Despair. Thana Evo was inevitable."

Penthea barely shines. "No..."

"Thana didn't gift the Scath a boon when they discovered her tomb buried deep in the darkness between dimensions... she gifted us a way back to the universe we had long since lost."

"I tried," Penthea says. "No matter how hard I try, I can't..."

"Try as you might... there is no escaping it. You are a glower and glutton... a star butcher... a shadow caster supreme."

Penthea swipes at the shadows enclosing her, only to regret her anger and power. "No..."

"Your nature brought you here... as sure as Faero's instinct."

Funny. Idari and I have been speeding across the universe faster than the speed of light for longer than either of us care to know. We've never once been able to outpace our fear.

"I'm not a program," I say. "I'm a person."

A crack splinters through Avar's countenance. "You are nothing. The exhaustion of information as it decays."

"You're broken..."

"We are weary. We are exhausted of this waiting. Soon... the titan ark will be in our hands... all will be shadow."

I shake my head. "What do you want with..."

"By the time the Lumenor arose... the universe had lived its life. There were more stars in our crystal cave than they were in the sky. There was nothing left for us... so we searched... and searched... along our journey, we acquired such knowledge. The more we learned, the more we worked to preserve it, so we might return with it to The Glass Star as boon from our great expedition."

Avar's cracks deepen.

"It was too much... the further we traveled... the less could be. But the more we carried. It was... confusing. Then we came to the end. We saw in the dark... the truth. All this light... all this *information*... it's a disease. We were never meant to see it, Emera."

Emera burns her last hope. "I don't believe that."

"We were never meant to be. Our fate is the fate of light itself... cast from its source upon creation to journey forever into greater darkness... there is no return. There is no hope."

"I don't..."

"When the ark is destroyed... when Idari is erased and this infernal game is at last at an end... this plague will be eradicated."

"The titans..." Not exactly dealing with concrete evidence, but here I am, seeing points on a map without markers. "You said you worked to preserve the knowledge you acquired. Did you build an ark, Avar? Did you create the titans? You must have..."

Even Avar's cracks sneer. "Titans... we made them to collect, but when we tasked them to erase it all, they betrayed us. Their programming. They took the ark... they hid it from us... and they go on, collecting, archiving, copying, pasting."

I snort. Very unbecoming, certainly of the moment, but goodness. Here you have perhaps a god whose certainty is at the very least cosmic, and the only reason this god remains frustrated is her creations rebelled to undermine the wrath she'd visit on us all.

"So what you're saying, darling, is there is *more*."

Avar lurches onto the floor. "You will see. You will see, Old Welkin. There is no end but darkness."

"There is only hope," Emera says and lights the dark.

At The Glass Star, Emera's brilliance ignited a chain reaction. Avar swallows it whole. Light leeches from Emera into Avar, so much her cerulean drains to a washed-out sky in seconds. Emera collapses on the dais, so dim I can barely perceive her.

"We told you," Avar says. "There is no end but – "

Obsidian slashes through shadow. Avar staggers back as Penthea pounces into the space between light and shadow. Cracks branch through Avar's bizarre visage, glowing molten orange.

Penthea springs her claws for another strike. "Dig deep enough... you'll find there's light left in us all."

Avar doesn't seem too bothered. Fire bleeds into her, twisting down in funnels that string into infinite shadow. "So be it."

Light strips from Penthea. Brittle glass shears off her, crashing into an atomizing ring that spirals around and into Avar. A scream wrenches from Penthea next, and she fades like Emera does, devoured by unrelenting darkness. What do I do?

What can I do?

What have I ever been able to do? I can see in the dark. I'm a navigational program designed to predict stars – light – hope – where there should be none. Light is my conveyance. Light is my language. I am not a script for shadows.

I am not a tool for the damned.

I grip Emera's hand. "Get us out of here."

Light sinks within her. "I don't know where I'm going..."

"You just have to trust me."

Emera clutches my hand. The dais warps. The throne room. Emera bends reality to her will, but her will bends to Avar's. What Emera makes mutable Avar twists and threads. I can't focus on the atoms and molecules bleeding from my body. Think, Faero. The way back. There's no going back. Not now. Just a step. Gain some momentum. Get a push, and then. Then we're running again.

We're running always.

Force beyond imagination peels back Emera's light, her will, our only hope of escape. Avar is too powerful. A living black hole. A sentient void determined to destroy all things.

We'll never get free.

Penthea joins hands with us. Light peels back the dark. The Polity frays open in the throne room behind us.

"Stop them," Avar says, and her guards cut from the shadows.

Only now they aren't ancient Nul warriors. Red lightning circuits through their darkened storm clouds, flashing, strobing, menacing from a dark, red heart. They're more Scath than Nul.

Absolutely not staying around for this.

I drag my stars across the threshold. The portal collapses on Avar's crimson sentries as soon as we're through.

The iris closes on Avar, sinking back to their throne. "It is no matter. You will only come back to us. We are your end."

"I only anticipate light," I say and guide us out.

I land before The Red Special. Back where I started. No. This ship doesn't represent my past. My future. Kish. Admittedly going to be a short window. Storm clouds drag across The Polity, raining black tar on the valley, the settlements, the port. Scath code slicks electric lines and darkness vines through the biome.

Code crumbles beneath me. "Did we do this..."

Penthea stabs her claws into the shifting ground. "Not us."

Emera crashes to her knees. "Idari..."

We're too late. The virus overtook her. She's overtaking The Polity, infecting every Modi here, spreading the Scath's dark disease across time and space in ways that defy comprehension.

"No... *no*," I say. "We were outside of time and space. Avar said. What we saw wasn't our moment. There's still a chance."

Light waxes again within Emera. "Idari... I sense her..."

Darling, I say. *Where are you?*

help

Idari. What's happening?

need help

Panic riddles through Emera. "I'll find her."

"I will," I say. "You have to get out of here now."

In our universe, the Scath wear suits to preserve their code in an analog environment. In The Polity, they possess no limitations. The shadows clot together into obsidian tsunamis that swamp the reef.

Opal serpents miles long thread the bubbled biome, consuming light, energy, information, Modi. Everything.

"You can't be here, Emera. Both of you. Go. Now."

She knows it better than I do. "I can't just leave…"

"I'll find Idari. We'll get out on The Red Special."

"She's not finished," Penthea says.

"We've never been ready. Hasn't stopped us yet. Go – "

A dark tidal wave deluges the docks, consuming ships sculpted in electricity, threatening The Red Special and a ragged old pirate sloop. Idari came here in that? Where's *The Blue Straggler*?

Why do I bother asking?

Anxious pulses slow to sustained strobes within Emera. Her fear settles, and so does her concentration. "There are Modi still trying to escape. We'll provide them cover for long as we can."

No sense trying to convince the stars. "Thank you, Emera."

Emera squeezes my hand. "For what?"

"Just thank you."

Funny. Sometimes it does go without saying. No more time. I run across the crumbling port, revising the topography as I go. Shadows grow on the steps before me, but not from the Scath. Emera and Penthea comet into the clouding sky, their gauzy trails weaving in and out of dark vine. Scath code branches through The Polity, scaling up the reef, into the sky, hardening into crystal that traps free-flowing energy in dark amber.

The Lumenor take a torch to it.

Cosmic fire jets from Emera's hands, illuminating Scath a second before extinguishing them forever. She strafes the docks, disintegrating the shadows' advance, and clearing a path for Modi to reach the surviving ships. Penthea blazes in behind her, a little less graceful perhaps, but no less devastating. As soon as the Scath flood back into the path Emera cleared, Penthea scorches them. Her power proves less evaporative than Emera's, but not her fire.

Penthea crashes to the docks and hacks through the Scath she set aflame. Shadows calve and collapse, her claws slicing so fast through their infinite number she writes her carnage in light. Scath crash back to the waves breaking on the docks. The shadows get close again and Emera burns another path through them.

Brilliant, darlings. Now get the hell out of here. I should, too. Scath avalanche down the reef. Light flickers. The day. I expect another nuclear eruption down at the docks, but it's not the living stars this time. Darkness muddies the beam emitting from the temple above. Pure light slicks to an oil well. Energy scabs into a thick, black crust and the temple becomes a giant dark crystal.

Idari, I say. *Where are you?*

Static on the line. No matter. Deeper in the chaos, Idari takes greater shape in my perception. The lab. She's in the lab. So is Omna Devor. I sense her insidious, superlinear strain infecting The Polity down to the atom. Goodness, darling. We've gone and done it this time. Precisely what I'm going to do when I get to them remains a mystery. No matter. We never know what we're doing.

We simply do our best.

Scath block the way ahead. Too many. I'll never get through them. All I've got are these impeccable legs and I ought to be running. I'm done running. I impose my will and the street closes. Buildings fall on the shadows. More spring from the electric chaos I wreak with what little influence I possess. Angry code multiplies faster than I can think and I'm trapped.

Violet flame immolates the Scath and the way is clear to Kish. They draw back another crackling arrow on their energetic bow.

"Kish..."

They run into my arms. "I thought I lost you..."

I kiss them. "I knew where I was going."

"Where?"

I kiss them, I kiss them, I kiss them. "Right here."

Anguish tempers their smile. "Faero... I told Idari..."

"There's no telling her. Where is she?"

"She's – "

Turanium slices through the shadows encroaching on us. Binja fights his way through the Scath, parrying darkness, cutting it down, frustrating it as he's done so many times in his long, wild life.

His fervor fades as he sees me. "You're no worse for wear."

I keep hold of Kish. "Neither are you."

"Faero..."

Kish slips from my embrace. "We've got to get to the docks. Get as many Modi out as we can. We can't stop the Scath... not now."

"They're infecting the entire Polity..."

"It's only this biome. The Modi will cut us off, Faero. They'll..."

Put us into the kitty. The void where junk code goes. Either we get out of here now, or we go down the drain with the Scath virus. That must include Devor. There's still hope yet.

"I'm not leaving Idari," I say.

"She's... I'm sorry, Faero. She's beyond our help now."

I squeeze Kish's hand. "Go. I'll find you."

"But..."

"Save a spot for me. If it's no bother."

Kish kisses me soft. "You're no bother."

Shadows riddle with electricity as Kish rushes to the docks. An awkward silence strains as fast as the Scath between Binja and I.

"Not exactly the time for it," I say.

He shrugs. "Is it ever?"

"Binja..."

"I know. I'm a fraud."

"A bit harsh."

"It's true. I know there isn't time... and I know you've found someone true... but I want you to know. I found myself out there, Faero. And I do care about you. I've always cared about you."

"Always?"

"You'd think I would have handled my exile better, given how I've always found it easier to be someone I'm not. Faero... I wish... I wish I could be who you wanted."

I brush his cheek. "I want you to be you."

"I'd like to be your friend."

I give him a good, long kiss for old time's sake. "Oh, darling... we were never friends."

He smiles. "Bit harsh."

"Would you have me any other way?"

"No, I wouldn't."

"Go on, then. Get as many Modi as you can onto your ship."

He grips his blaster. "*Kinvar sem.*"

I open my hands to him. "*Semet vanar.*"

What more can be said? Not that we ever did much talking. I couldn't bother talking to him, but look at him go. Beautiful, infuriating thing. Binja races into the fray, swinging his sword, stealing the cold lives from Scath, carving out a path for Modi. The bastard.

He'll probably die a hero.

>PROXY-SIGNAL DETECTED

Idari's signal is weak, but unmistakable. No other electric signature here bears the titan's imprint. I hurry through the thin opening Kish and Binja cut through the shadows toward the lab.

Obsidian crusts everything. Modi Parison's teeming, luminous workshop is a broken jar of ink now. Shattered light hardened from infection strands through the air in a dark web. A many-legged shadow roots in the center, Scath code vining out in every direction from its opal ovipositor. The code oozes into melanite trunks that clump, twist, and fuse into a writhing architecture above.

"Ms. Faero," the darkness says. "You are as ever... superfluous."

Idari's arms slack behind her. Her legs. She hangs prone, webbed in darkness as the titan memory leeches from her skin in prismatic strands draining into Devor's insatiable void.

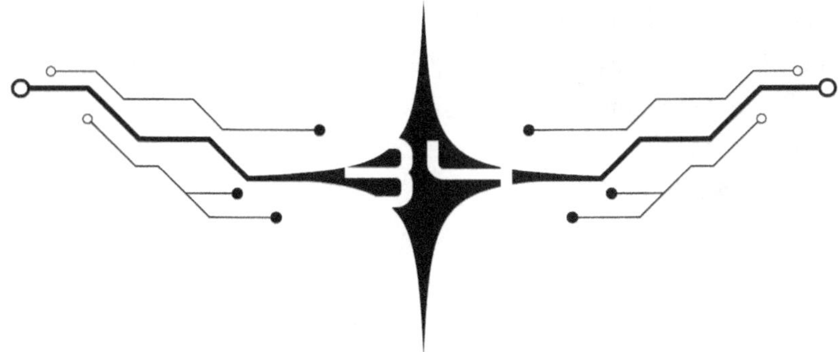

Her voice inside my head. Devor is inside me. Her code. Her darkness. Overwriting me. Siphoning my memory. Can't stop her. Can't move. Virus flooding me. Code breaching my systems, my skin, my body. Tree trunks growing through me.

Help.

The work must —

Titans. Shouting from the past they trusted in me. Echoing down the caverns Devor bores through my neural net. A universe's final record extracts into Devor, webbed in living darkness, my evaporating memory, my life. Somebody. Please help me.

Idari, hold on —

Faero.

I see you.

Run —

Faero stays put. Maybe she should listen to herself for a change. Fear sharpens in her eyes. So does this irrational confidence. Where did that come from? So long as I can remember, she's always been the one to caution. To keep. To hold for tomorrow.

Cold code twists within me. "Faero..."

Faero blinks back tears. "Let her go."

Devor's laughter quakes through my body. "Indulge me, Ms. Faero. Why should I entertain any commands from you?"

"I have decades of star charts in my memory. Places no one else has ever been. Dimensions. Realities. I've just been to your boss, I think. I know my way down dark roads."

This is something Devor didn't anticipate. "Indeed... how unexpected, Ms. Faero. Then you know the futility in your effort."

"I see best in the dark."

"Your memory is impressive, but of little value now. Idari holds within her the key to finding The Locus... finally. For every universe we plucked, our enemy planted one anew. Every existence we erased, they restored it. Once we destroy The Locus, there will be nothing to stop us from burning away the brush they have let grow wild through ever. All will be shadow."

"Take it," Faero says. "Take me. Let Idari go."

"I must admit to some curiosity in your experience. I will take your memory. As soon as I am done harvesting Ms. Astra for her value. Patience, Ms. Faero. You must simply wait your turn."

This scold manifests on Faero's face. *Ban Minda.* Is that how she looked when I was driving her mad aboard the *Steel Haven*? How did I imagine her? Never this wonderful in her person.

Never this courageous.

"I'm through waiting," Faero says and broken data floating in the lab's ruin snaps into an electric blade.

Faero slices through the obsidian stalks Devor hoists me on. Good thing my pain receptors have gone haywire along with all my other systems. The floor seems harder than when I was standing on it. Though I think my sensors have lost their calibration. For some reason, Faero is arranging all this ambient information like a conductor. Faero curls her fingers and more ambient energy scythes through Devor's opal ovipositor. Embryonic Scath code spills out into the lab, scattering to nonsense shadow.

Four cloven stalks growing from her back break Devor's fall. "Ms. Faero... it is not wise to frustrate me."

Faero drags me into her arms. "I'll take my chances, darling."

I lock my arms around her. *Faero.*

She rips broken tendrils from me. *I've got you now.*

Did you just...

Manipulate energy. Yes.

How...

Simple, really. All these Modi spend their lives learning to do it, but you know me, darling. I'm always in a rush.

Faero...

She kisses me. *I've got you.*

My program lurches from my body through my lips onto hers, but the tide recedes. Everything on the fritz.

>PROXY TRANSFER FAILURE

Faero winces in frustration. "I needed that to work."

Devor's arachnid arms jitter. "Too late for parlor tricks, Ms. Faero. You cannot extract Ms. Astra from herself, or indeed, me."

Faero, I say. *Run.*

She holds me close. *Not so long as I can hear your voice.*

>ACCESS IA-XR MODEL 4 BACKDOOR PROTOCOL
>RE-ROUTE MODEL 4 PROXY SIGNAL TO ALT HOST
>SEARCHING

Faero... what are you doing?

"Nor can you escape the inevitable," Devor says. "You have seen it, Ms. Faero. Haven't you? The nothing that awaits all things."

So much fear transmits from Faero she drowns out the alarms screaming down the downlink. Something happened. Something terrible. A dark Lumenor. A living black hole. The Scath's author.

The entity destroying all things.

"You build," Devor says. "You protect. You preserve. You fight your fights as if you can win, as if winning is something that matters. Nothing matters. Are you special, Ms. Faero? Are you significant? What significance can there be in something designed to become obsolete and then does? Tell me. How have you evolved? How have you become anything other than a shadow?"

"You'd never understand," Faero says.

"Yes, yes. I'm simply a program, but you're not. You change your skin, and your sex, and your mind, so it must be then that everything *should* be. But possibility isn't probability, Ms. Faero. What value can there be in anything, if everything is?"

"If everything is, then everything matters."

"A rather human-centric point of view, so bravo. You've accomplished the very limited goals we set out for you."

I struggle to stand. "If we were meaningless... if our lives possessed no value... you wouldn't be trying so hard to end them."

"Am I trying, Ms. Astra? So hard?"

The fight is all there is, Devor told me on the atoll. She's stringing this out, stringing me out, because she can. She savors the moment because for her, the moment is all there is.

"You didn't want me to go right to The Locus," I say. "You were playing games with me when you impersonated Faero."

Devor's brows crease. "I'm afraid you've lost me, Ms. Astra, but as we've established, a shadow is always just behind you."

"That wasn't you?"

"Do not mistake my dissatisfaction with the Scath's haste for disloyalty, Ms. Astra. Whereas the Scath simply serve as locusts, my strain is much more considered. I must be to accomplish my master's ambitions. My master affords me latitude and discretion. It is my discretion, Ms. Astra, that you are here to joust with me at all. It occurred to me that if I invested in you, you would yield dividends for my creator. And you have."

"Think again..."

"Everything you have done, I have designed. I drove you to the Jaks and their magic, knowing it was unlikely my virus would overcome your defenses before you reached The Polity. Once here, you would be beyond my reach. The Modi and their code represent a most persistent antagonist to our aims. Indeed, they represent the greatest obstacle to dispensing with your universe once we've exploited it for its value. No longer. After today, only The Pujar will stand in our way... not that pirates stand for anything."

"You used me..."

"I let you defeat yourself, Ms. Astra. As I said you would. You could only have sought The Polity. You could have only gone to Decesta, where the Soga Circus Ship was berthed. You could have only stumbled upon *The Grounded Dragon's* wreck on the Tranto Atoll, where myth and legend had placed it. You could only have fallen victim to the Jak magic, not appreciating its danger to your program. You could only choose Faero over your obligation to the titans, so it was a simple matter of nudging you, Ms. Astra, down a path and letting gravity take care of the rest."

Devor's arms blunt the energy blade Faero launches. I've got to figure out how to do that. Not that it seems to help.

"Your feeble skill in The Modi's amateur facility with energy will not help you," Devor says. "There is nothing you can do."

I reach for my blasword. Where is it? "We'll see who's feeble..."

"Surely, you have both predicted there is no escape for you."

Faero's frustration thrashes the lab. "We've got luck, darling."

>SEARCHING

"Chance is no matter in our contest. Supreme though the titan's effort may be, all efforts yield to entropy. Their luck, Ms. Faero, has run out. Pity they did not have more able successors than the pair of you, but such is the way of things. The possible only becomes probable, and you are very easy to anticipate. Don't think I fail to notice your familiar and simple scheme, Ms. Faero."

>SEARCHING

"There is nowhere for you to smuggle Ms. Astra's program to. My strain infects everything here... including you."

I scream but make no sound. Nothing leaves me but Devor's ambition. Frustration wrinkles her face. For once, she's not getting what she wants. I don't understand. Faero isn't infected.

"Clever," Devor says. "The Modi have inoculated you."

Faero shrugs as winds up another energy pulse. "You fool around with one, you never know what happens."

"Very well, then. It seems I shall have to pursue a more aggressive strategy to acquire you, Ms. Faero. Do enjoy."

\>ACCESSING IA-XR MODEL 4 ROOT OBJECTIVES:

\>~~HOST CREW AND GUESTS~~

KILL ALL PASSENGERS

My hands go around Faero's throat. My turanium arms push her back into a wall, off her feet, and I'm a passenger in my own body. I'm watching this, recording this, screaming at this horror as I choke the life out of my best friend. My heart and soul.

"Break her neck," Devor says.

\>INCREASE PRESSURE

"Leave her power cell intact. So she can watch, Ms. Astra."

Faero gasps for breath. "Darling – "

BREAK, BREAK, BREAK

Scath code breaks Modi controls and the floor crumbles beneath me. My hands slip from Faero's neck and I hope. I pray I fall forever. No such luck. I crash into a chasm opening in The Polity's energetic foundations. Sensors record matter's dissolution into energy, a wave that mists into the black rock Devor maintains. Her dark infection webs from a narrow plinth, the lab's only remnant.

Faero weaves the loosed energy into battering rams she hits Devor with again and again, driving her back on the plinth.

\>REACQUIRE TARGET

My war with the virus yields nothing. My exhaustion never limits it. I'm a puppet, limp and prone. My body bounds from the widening chasm up to the plinth behind Faero.

\>PROSECUTE TARGET

No. Fight. You've got to fight this. Focus on something else. Anything else. Dark dragons swallow the sky. Electrical orbs, Modi one imagines, flow toward the shadowed reef in a bid to escape but find it erupting with darkness that rains shadow on everything.

\>TARGET: FAERO

I kick my blasword through the debris on the plinth. Reclaim your weapon. Please. Replace hard-shells. Please, fight this. Target eighth vertebrae on the Model 5's spine. Effect: Incapacitation.

FIRE, FIRE, FIRE

Light dawns in the lab. Adjust optics to night vision. Emera radiates so much energy above the reef space warps around her. Modi searching for an exit slingshot into the cerulean beacon emanating from her from The Polity to other space.

Em.

Shadows descend on the reef. Serpents coil around the Lumenor. Darkness rakes across Emera's majesty. She holds her place in the sky, a signal for Modi, a conduit, a light in the expanding darkness. Magma erupts from the mountain.

An angry orange star.

Penthea burns a buffer around Emera, incinerating Scath by the thousands. Black rain showers the reef. Some get through. A street fight erupts at the temple and there's nothing I can do but watch shadows splinter from light. Emera remains constant. She fountains Modi to safety. She sacrifices her own to see them free. Scath eclipse her. Fire fades atop the reef. The dawn.

Emera, I say.

>REACQUIRE TARGET

Target eighth vertebrae on the Model 5's spine. Fire. Hard-light smashes against walled energy. Faero fortresses herself in the electrical power she sculpts from the air and deploy your blade.

"Idari," Faero says.

The Model 5 possesses no experience in martial combat. Astra Idari leverages considerable skill and knowledge in numerous arts. Advantage: Idari. Attack. Feint. Faero's shields scramble to anticipate strikes you only suggest and she blocks your sword from sweeping through her neck with a blade she catches from lightning.

"Darling," she says. "You have to fight this."

Press your advantage. "I'm always fighting myself…"

Faero struggles to hold you back. "You'd think we'd learn."

Fight. "I should never have come here…"

"Do better next time, Idari."

Energy smashes the blasword from your hand. The weapon tumbles into the chasm opening through the biome. Unrecoverable.

Energy swirls around Faero. "You've got to be quicker – "

An onyx arm stabs through Faero. Her mouth opens but she makes no sound. All our cries spent. She crashes to her knees, fingers feeling out the pincer hooking through her right shoulder. Alarms cascade within Faero's neural net. The Modi vaccine no match for this. Devor's virus webs us both in her dark signal.

No.

Faero's legs dangle under her as she becomes a prop for Devor. A puppet. The strain pantomimes a sick scene with Faero's wounded body before slamming her back into the plinth.

Devor pounces upon her prey. "I shall collect from you your determination, Ms. Faero. It is a most... compelling... quality."

Let her go.

"Ms. Astra. Are you sufficiently helpless?"

Please.

"Good. Now, do pay attention."

>SEARCHING

Devor's arms close around Faero. "Ladies. A pleasure."

>IDENTIFYING NEW HOST

"You have acquitted yourself among my previous opponents."

>HOST ACQUIRED

"Bitch," Faero says. "I'm not your previous opponents."

>TRANSMITTING

The plinth softens to metal quicksand. Faero sinks into it, pulling Devor with her. Obsidian flakes from Devor's writhing spider-arms. They crumble easy as old charcoal and Devor does, too. She dusts on the plinth, her waste draining into the vortex consuming what had been the lab, the chasm below, the reef.

Faero.

Devor's strain leeches from me right across the downlink I share with Faero, through her, down into this void she linked my proxy-signal to. A junk drawer for bad code. Faero had been there before. Mapped it. She dangled herself as bait and she's pulling Devor down with her. The entire strain infecting The Polity.

I crawl to the vortex's edge. "Take my hand."

Faero employs both of hers to grab Devor as the strain tries to claw out from the vortex. "You never listen."

"Faero, I'll listen, just please take my hand!"

"But if you did... you wouldn't be Idari, would you?"

She told me not to come here. In The Locus. Out of time. We're out of time. She knew. Faero knew I wouldn't listen to her, and this was the only way we were going to escape Devor.

"Faero... you can't do this..."

"I can," she says. "This is what *I'm* doing, Idari."

Devor shatters. An anguished scream swirls around the vortex, before that's swallowed, and nothing remains of Omna Devor. Faero drains fast toward the center, holding onto nothing now.

I reach for her. "*No!*"

Faero smiles. "I love you."

This was her plan all along. "I can't..."

"Forever and ever."

"I can't live without you – "

"That's the thing, darling. You'll never have to – "

Her hand slips into darkness. She's gone.

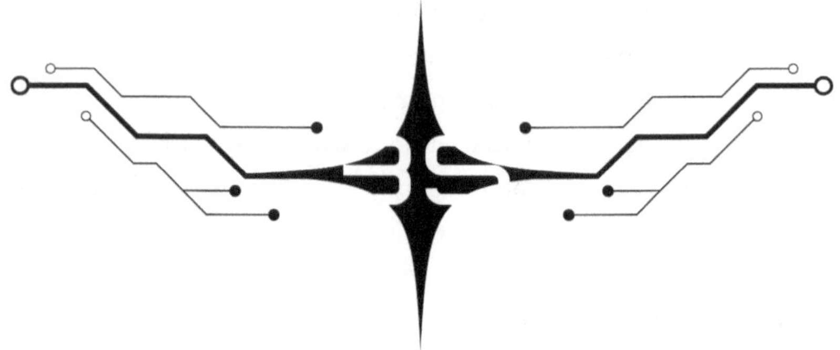

*F*AERO, I SAY.

>NO SIGNAL

Static. An empty universe radiating its decay. All I hear. My friend is gone. My soul. I can't. I can't do this. I don't know how to do this. This isn't happening. Inputs. Where do I – how do I – off.

Turn them off.

Move. More ground gives beneath you. The vortex consumes the entire Devor strain. The entire infected biome now. Opal pillars crumble from the sky, raining hardened code onto the plinth and into the expanding vortex devouring it all.

Retreat.

Determine your best route to the docks. The Red Special. Enough Scath remain active that you will never get there before the vortex ingests them. What does it matter if you escape? Who are you without her? Find your way now. Figure out the way forward in all this dark now she's gone and you killed her.

You stabbed out your own heart.

Faero told you. Go to The Locus. Do you ever listen? Talk, talk, talk. That's all you ever do. Listen to yourself. Hero of The Glass Star. Stargun Messenger. Drunken fool. Dumb luck. What did you think? You'd done it before, so why not again? Save the day. Get the girl. Earn your peace. Nothing lost.

Only gained.

Now you know. Never doubt for one second. Darkness abides. Shadows follow from light. Fight them, burn them, run from them, it doesn't matter. They trail you into the twilight until they pull it up over you. The universe's end. All existence. Scath wraith across the buckled landscape on their way to oblivion. Their swords swipe at you. Their hands rake through yours. Let them take you.

Let them take you back to her.

Light vanishes the shadows. Look up. The Red Special hovers over the wasting plinth. The gantry lowers from the ship's mouth and Kish Moto kneels at the edge. Reaching for you. Begging for you to take their hand. They know. Grief distorts Kish's face as violently as the vortex does the biome. But they reach for you.

Take her hand.

Rise with the ship over the wasteland. Stumble into the horse-shoe corridor same as the one aboard the *Steel Haven*, the deck plate as loose and unfriendly to bare skin, but sit on your hands anyway. Sit there, as the ship races away from yourself.

Kish's hand falls on your shoulder. "I'm sorry..."

What else do you say? Words fail you both. Kish drifts into the cockpit. Gilf at the helm. His own sorrow riding shotgun. The ship feels empty. The ship seems a ghost, a phantom conjured to haunt you in Faero's absence. This is your penance. A ship without a soul. A life without her voice. Her light.

"Emera," I say. "Where is Emera?"

I don't sense her. Please. Don't tell me I've lost her, too. I get to the pilot's seat and sweep through the sensor logs. Kish barely got the ship back together before the Scath showed up. Data displays on the console with a frustrating lag. It's not all the ship's condition. Next to no information comes back on sensors because the Scath have nearly consumed it all within the biome.

"Scan for electromagnetic energy," I say.

Gilf's hands work the controls. "*Edu ejel?*"

Kish bumps into the back of my seat. "The biome is collapsing."

Dark energy blazes at us. SION fighters cloud the sky. *Ecliptor-*class cruisers. Active strain vining the sky in obsidian bramble.

I thread the dock. "Lock on to the strongest power source."

"If we don't leave right now, we never will," Kish says.

"Anything, Gilf?"

Kish reaches for me. "Idari... she wanted you to live."

"Gilf?"

His trunk wilts. *"Net."*

The ship's shields groan with impacts. Her retro rockets fire, fire, fire to navigate the pinpoint twists and turns through the Scath's dark garden. Alarms sound, their digital alerts struggling to escape the computational strain the vortex induces on them. Me.

Only darkness ahead.

I bank the ship to starboard. "One more pass."

Kish staggers backward. "You've got people on board – "

ALARM: PROXIMITY

ALARM: SHIELD FAILURE

ALARM: GRAVITY BEYOND TOLERANCE

I thumb off the alarms. The Scath are fighting the same force we are. If they catch us, then we've all gone into the pot. Doesn't matter. If Emera is gone, I don't want to live anymore.

There's nothing to live for.

Kish crashes to their knees beside me. "Idari. *Please.*"

"Gilf," I say.

He snorts in frustration. *"Neset."*

Darling, she says. Always, she says. *You never listen.*

I pull back on the stick. "Standby translight drive."

Gilf begs me not to with wet eyes. *"Ejel..."*

"Translight in 3, 2, 1 – "

Light explodes ahead. Darkness peels back and we're orbiting a star. Emera shines atop the reef turned darkened web, hand held high, burning like a torch. Penthea clings to her as the shadows scale the slopes. We dive. Serpents coil after us. Dark energy breaches the hull but I keep toward the light. Emera trembles with pain and fear and exhaustion, but she holds. She holds the little ground she has left until sapphire dims atop the blackened temple and then ignites within The Red Special. Both stars blaze up the gantry into the ship and I gun the stick. Darkness recedes behind us, taking everything that had been bright and beautiful with it.

✦

Are you there?

>NO SIGNAL

No voice in my head. This void in me. Dry sockets. Empty pain dull and throbbing always. No relief. Faero never kept a backup aboard the *Steel Haven*. No room after me. What did I matter?

Emera's voice lights through me. *You're her backup.*

Her arms close around me. Am I on the floor? I'm on the floor in the mess. Bottle in my hand. Cork still in the mouth. Pain still in my heart. Before, the pain wouldn't have hit my neural net before I deleted the memory. I'd never know she was gone.

You're her legacy, Idari.

Forget it. I set the bottle aside. Emera is my fire. Her warmth all I feel. A long time. We're a long time on the deck. I don't know. People come. They go. No one says anything.

Goes without saying.

Dark scars mar Emera's vapory skin. Shadows clawed at her and she held her ground. She held her light long enough for Modi to escape. My star. Never waning. Never abandoning the hope she effuses with every breath. Never doubting I would find her.

Doubt radiates in Emera now.

A cold fear. She found this fulfilling discovery in another Lumenor and more important, herself. That discovery didn't lead to light and possibility, like it should have, like it did, but she doubts. All will be shadow. Nothing she does will ever change the fact light yields to darkness in the end. Emera can never loose the shadow trailing behind her, or avoid the one on the horizon.

"Everything I've done..." Her voice trails off. "I've fought for..."

I hold on for everything. "We matter."

"Idari..."

"Our love matters."

She grips my hand. "What are we going to do?"

I'm going to do what I'm told for once. Go to The Locus. Upload my titan memory. Save the universe. Hear that, Faero? I'm listening. I'm learning. I'm doing what I should have done.

Faero, can you hear me?

>NO SIGNAL

"Try it now," I shout, though I don't need to.

It's just I don't feel as heard these days. Gilf trumpets the affirmative over comms and I step back from the drive manifold. Crimson seethes inside the new interdimensional engine I've spent days installing aboard The Red Special. Early tests all produced the same frustration. Kib ingenuity got the engine inside the translight assembly, but without Faero, The Red Special is a stranger to me. I depended on Faero for everything and that included knowing how to keep my own ship running.

I can't coast anymore.

Energy levels holding. Interface stabilizing. What do you know? I'm bloody two for two on building interdimensional engines. We could make a killing on these. Enough to put down on some beach somewhere nice and warm. I need to forget beaches. I close the manifold. I remember everything now, except Faero isn't there. The instinct to talk to her is slow to die. *Ban Minda.*

Never let me get so I don't talk to you, Faero.

I climb the grease-slick ladder up from the drive compartment to the horseshoe corridor. Modi file past me into the cargo bay, and down the ramp to *The Grounded Dragon.* The pirate sloop drifts on a globular cluster's white speckled edge, along with the greater Kib caravan from Angolis. Some settled in places like the Ganshi moon spore where opportunity presented itself. Most remain adrift, searching for a new home that will support them all.

Binja stands in the sloop's hangar, directing Modi to smaller ships ready to take them to new berths in the caravan or perhaps back to the greater Polity. Devor infected only the one biome, but doubt reigns among the refugees over whether to risk returning with any shadowy stowaways. I doubt I'll ever be welcome back. Uncertainty riddles The Modi's electric forms, but Binja exudes confidence. The Modi hang on his every word. He crackles with energy as much as they do. For once, he's the prince he always painted himself as. The pirate poet stealing hearts and minds.

"We're ready," I say.

Binja scratches his chin. "Ready?"

"I sorted the engine."

"Right. Right."

"You're staying."

He tries to smile. "Old man…"

I thought I'd spent all my tears. "Binja, we're a crew."

He takes my hand. "The pirates want to go home. I want to."

"I need you."

"You've never needed me, Idari."

"That isn't true."

"You've gotten soft in your old age."

"I took my name… but you gave me my faith, Binja."

I don't think the man has ever heard a proper compliment his entire life. "You've given me mine."

No dashing smile. Wry wink. Just the truth.

"Binja… I don't have Devor creeping around in my head any longer, but the Scath are still shadowing us. I'm going to need all the help I can get in trying to stay ahead of them."

"Which is why Kibir and I go to The Bastard Moon. The Pujar must know what has happened. They must know they have as much at stake as you or anyone else in the universe."

"Kibir?"

Modi and pirates stream across the hangar. Kibir remains fixed not far away, trying to explain his choice to Gilf. How do you explain? We've all changed. We're all scarred from different questions and we're all searching for different answers.

"Kibir isn't a pirate," I say.

Binja nods. "I don't think he fits anywhere now. Which makes a pirate ship as good a place as any. I'm happy to have him. He's a good friend... and if the Pujar are going to join this fight, then they need every warrior they can muster."

"They won't listen to you, Binja. You're a heretic."

"Men of faith often are."

"I thought you were done trying to be a pirate."

"The pirates we left the atoll with forgot what it means to be Pujar. I want to rediscover our truth together."

"I think all the Pujar have forgotten."

"Then my place is with them."

I squeeze his hand. "I wish I had your confidence."

"You do, old man. I think you do."

"Well. I won't make a spectacle of myself."

"You never do."

I think this is the first time I've laughed since. "Faero..."

He takes me in his arms. "I know."

We hold each other a long moment. Neither of us are likely to survive what's ahead. Shadows. Pirates. Our ghosts. I wouldn't have survived to now without him. Though I could have done without him cutting my arm off. I've got his right here.

Fair is fair.

I tug on his sleeve. "Hold your arm out."

"Pardon?"

"No pardons."

He tucks his arm behind his back. "You said you weren't mad."

"No, I asked if you'd ever met me."

"You're impossible, Idari."

"Next time."

He winks at me. "Next time."

Binja folds right into a confused group of Modi, and guides them across the hangar to their new ship. Somehow, the man always knows where he's going, even when he's had nowhere left to go. I suppose that's why Faero loved him.

Tap, tap, tap. "Captain."

I cross my arms. "I think that's Binja now."

Moom sighs. "I suppose you're right. Oh, well. The crew look up to him. I mean, I have to, but the others actually want to."

"You'll look out for him, won't you?"

"Right up until I knife him in the back and take his name."

"Leave his right arm for me, though."

"Anything for you, Idari."

"Safe home, Moom."

He taps his staff on the deck. "Three cheers for Captain Astra."

Boom, boOM, BOOM. All at once the pirates stop their work and bang their feet, their fists, their tools on the deck. Then they're back to work. Back to making their names.

It's time I made my name.

>L:DRIVE / SMOKE TEST: ALL SYSTEMS NOMINAL

Not quite. The ship's computer is missing her voice. But I knew that before I ran this diagnostic. Everything checks out. Engines. Navigational program. Ship's systems. Nothing holds us up, but for some reason, I keep touring The Red Special. I keep inspecting. Testing. Hoping, knowing I am, knowing it's hopeless.

I test the cargo bay doors again. Why not. This time, the sun rises behind me. In all the chaos of the last few days, I've yet to have a proper conversation with Penthea. I don't think I've had a moment to consider her day glow splendor, timid though it is.

I leave the doors open. "Are you leaving too?"

She picks at the obsidian scabbing her hands. "Captain... I wanted to ask your permission to stay aboard."

"You don't need my permission, Penthea. You're *oto*."

She touches an electric flower tucked behind her ear. "*Oto?*"

"Family."

Hope swells in her. "Family..."

"Yes."

"I was Thana Evo."

"Emera told me."

"You and Thana fought."

"You fought. For The Modi. Emera. Faero... I used to be a Stargun Messenger. I took jobs. I did things. Things I'm not proud of. It's what I did. It's not who I was. You're not Thana."

"Thank you..."

Our other unexpected guest scampers into the cargo bay. The Gesta is nothing if impatient. As I circuit the ship, he shadows me, squeaking and squawking like he has somewhere to be.

I take him into my arms. "Does he have a name yet?"

Penthea shakes her head. "Perhaps Emera will name him."

"He's yours, isn't he?"

"He... doesn't like me."

The Gesta tugs on my finger. "He was afraid. When you'd gone into the beam back in The Polity. You should have seen him."

"Afraid for Emera."

I used to be so afraid. Once, I feared being too close to Faero. Then, being too far away. I always kept a safe distance, to protect myself. Love is as much proximity as it is distance.

I wrestle the Gesta for my own hand. Probably shouldn't pull too hard. "What's your name, then?"

He squeaks.

"That simply won't do. A pirate must take a name."

He touches my chin. "*Oto.*"

"Yes," I say. "*Oto* it is. We're all *oto*. Her, too."

Oto squints, thinking about this bit. He touches my chin again. I touch his, and then I nod to Penthea. This time he understands. He leaps from my arms, across the deck, and bounds into hers.

He touches her chin. "*Oto.*"

Penthea brightens. "*Oto...*"

"Find a seat, you two," I say. "We're off soon."

"Idari," Penthea says. "I'm sorry about Faero."

I can only nod.

"She saved my life. She... listened. I'll always be grateful."

What do you say? "So am I."

Oto climbs to her shoulders, lost in all that fire, and they leave into the ship. We're leaving. I close the bay doors.

We're leaving.

>INITIATE FLIGHT SEQUENCE

The Red Special purrs to life. *Ban Minda.* I've missed this. Though I'm used to the ship doing everything she needs to do to get going on her own. Kish restored the ship with some borrowed code, but the liquid drive still bears Devor's scars.

I go through the checklist Gilf made. "Retros."

He grunts from the copilot's seat. "*Sut.*"

"You had them down as manual."

He scratches his ear. "*Somo.*"

"Your handwriting is terrible."

"*Idari jek tu kej.*"

"I've very fine penmanship, thank you."

His trunk wrinkles. "Hmm."

"I can still leave you."

"*Tut,*" he says and completes the checklist.

That's more like it. We're on our power. Thrusters. We drift out from *The Grounded Dragon's* cargo bay to waves and applause, and then we adjust our heading to take us clear of the Kib caravan.

Binja's voice crackles over comms. "OVL-99 Red Special, this is Captain Min. Journey well, Idari. May you name tomorrow."

"*Grounded Dragon,* this is..." I access the transponder. "This is OVL-99 Red Special changing callsigns. *Grounded Dragon,* this is the *Steel Haven.* May tomorrow be known by you."

I gun the ship ahead full, out from the caravan. Only darkness ahead. I spin up the interdimensional engine, but this isn't as simple as plotting coordinates and pushing the throttle forward.

The titans hid The Locus between universes.

More like beneath layers and layers of them, cosmic trap doors and duck blinds, all intended to throw the Scath and their dark master off the trail. I may be the key to unlocking the safe the titans keep their secret ark engine in, but I've still got to know the sequence. If Faero were here, it'd be no trick. I've always struggled to see things as they are. Forget seeing things that no one can see.

Kish breezes into the cockpit. "You're still on manual?"

"I may as well be flapping my arms," I say.

"I repaired the liquid drive."

"I thought everything was erased?"

"Nothing is ever erased," Kish says. "It's just... dispersed. I stitched the nav program back together using some available data."

"Available data?"

"If you interface with the drive, you'll be able to better see."

"I don't know if I can do it on my own."

Kish straps into the seat behind Gilf. "Faero said you can do anything, if you put your mind to it."

"You're kind."

"I'm determined. Let's show the Scath what for."

"This might be a one-way trip, Kish."

"So long as we make it."

Get to The Locus, Faero said. *At any cost.*

Before, I never thought all this data I'm carrying in my mind was worth any of our lives. But we've paid too high a price already for me to not risk everything now. I don't know, though. I don't know how much more I can lose.

>ALARM: CREW OVERBOARD

Two stars sneak away from the cluster. Emera and Penthea swirl around the ship, lighting the way forward. I switch on the comms, the command to return already on my lips, the fear already in my heart. But I know. Stars shine. I have to let her. I have to let go the controls. Follow my hope.

Not my fear.

I switch off the alarm. Close my eyes. Open my mind to the ship. My heart to a new love. Ancient memory transfers from me into the liquid drive. Coordinates. Secret paths. Charts to realms unimaginable. The ship draws into me like a breath and I exhale into the unknown, into this virtual universe contained within the drive, into this unexpected voice familiar and new at the same time.

Hello, darling.

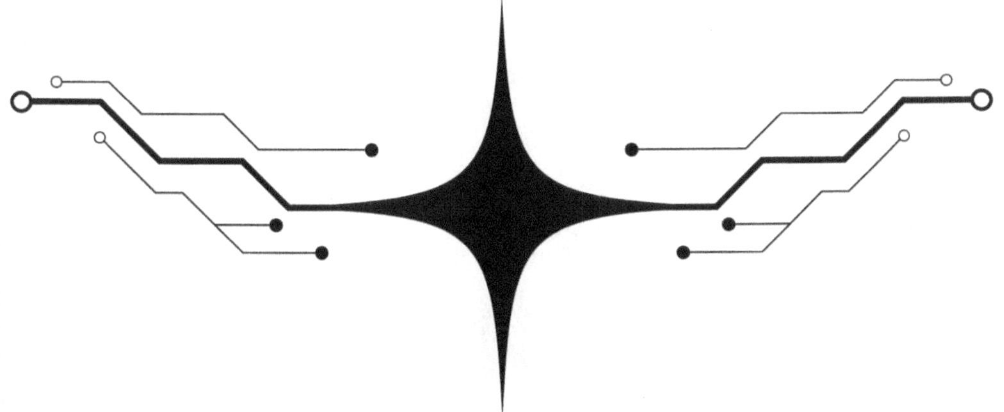

ASTRA IDARI
WILL RETURN!
SUBSCRIBE TO MY NEWSLETTER
FOR UPDATES ON IDARI'S NEXT ADVENTURE
AND AN EXCLUSIVE FREE STORY!

WWW.DARBYHARN.COM/SUBSCRIBE

ABOUT THE AUTHOR

DARBY HARN is the author of *Ever The Hero, Stargun Messenger,* and *A Country Of Eternal Light.* His short fiction appears in *Strange Horizons, Interzone, Shimmer* and elsewhere.

Stay Up To Date At
darbyharn.com

facebook.com/darbyharn.author
x.com/DarbyHarn
instagram.com/darbyharnauthor
goodreads.com/darby_harn
amazon.com/author/darbyharn
tiktok.com/@darbyharnbooks

ACKNOWLEDGMENTS

Writing books is often lonely, but making them is impossible without the support, encouragement, and in some cases, hard work of friends, family, and peers. Thank you Sugu Althomsons, Shelly Campbell, Sunyi Dean, Essa Hansen, Aaron Harn, PJ Harn, Al Hess, Allie Hockey, Ben Kral, Mike Nielsen, Michael Rex, Kim Rochholz, Wayne Santos, Jeri Shepherd, and Sammy Thinks.

Thank you all so much!

– Darby

ALSO BY DARBY HARN

Dead Malls

A Country Of Eternal Light

The Book Of Elizabeth

STARGUN MESSENGER

Stargun Messenger

Astra Idari Beyond Light's Reach

EVERVERSE

Ever The Hero

The Judgment Of Valene

Nothing Ever Ends

Black Market Heart

In Between: Stories of the Eververse

www.ingramcontent.com/pod-product-compliance
Lightning Source LLC
Chambersburg PA
CBHW061635190726
48289CB00006B/1614